TAKING TOMORROW

BOOK 5 OUTLASTING SERIES

LK MAGILL

FIRST HALE PRESS

Copyright © 2020 by Lindsay Magill

All rights reserved. Published by First Hale Press. No part of this publication may be reproduced, distributed or transmitted in any form or by any means, without prior written permission.

This book is a work of fiction. Any references to historical events, real people, or real places are used fictitiously. Other names, characters, places and events are products of the author's imagination, and any resemblance to actual events or persons, living or dead, is entirely coincidental.

Taking Tomorrow/ LK Magill – 1st ed.

Ebook ISBN 978-1-950928-14-9

Paperback ISBN 978-1-950928-15-6

Hardcover ISBN 978-1-950928-16-3

DEDICATION_

To God, thank you for allowing me to write another.

Also to Sara Mae and Emily, for your Beta reading skills. I thank you.

PROLOGUE_

THIS IS BOOK 5 IN A CONNECTED SERIES...

If you haven't already, please make sure to start with Book 1, OUTLASTING AFTER.

CHAPTER ONE_
DAVEY

He could hear her screaming. It was distant, but there. She was calling out for him.

Sucking in a breath, Davey tasted dirt on his tongue... and blood. His mind was muddled, his eyes closed.

Then she screamed again. Louder. Closer. Right in his face.

Davey's eyes fluttered open and they locked onto Mia. She was flat on her back, her face twisted to the side, her chocolate-brown eyes staring straight at him.

Terror transformed her pretty face. Because there was some guy on top of her, holding her down, ripping at her clothes.

Davey's heart rocketed through his chest, pounding like thunder inside his ribcage. He'd been shot in the back, hadn't he? It had knocked him clean out. He was dead... right?

But none of that seemed to matter as Mia's hand reached out to slap at the ground just inches from his face. The dirt puffed up in the air and he inhaled it into his nose. Blinking slowly, he frowned.

Dead or not... Davey was about to kill someone.

An animal-like rage took him over.

That was it.

Davey was up off the ground in the next instant, launching himself at that fucker on top of Mia. Their bodies impacted. Hard. Chest to chest. The guy was knocked flat onto his back, and Davey kept coming, kept scrambling until he was the one on top.

Then Davey was seeing red. Literally. A curtain fell, clouding his vision.

His fist slammed down on the guy's face. He felt a crunch, then a familiar zing vibrate right up into his wrist. Cocking his arm back again, Davey hit harder, faster. Then again. Then again.

This guy had his hands on Mia? Taking what wasn't being given to him? What didn't belong to him?

Holding his breath, Davey's jaw cinched down tighter with each hit.

Again and again, he swung down. Harder. Faster. More. He couldn't stop if he tried, and the thing was... he didn't want to. The guy's head was flopping side to side now, blood was everywhere. It was slick, making his fist slide against flesh.

In the distance, he could hear Mia screaming. She was still fucking screaming.

Davey's lungs were burning now as he continued to hold his breath. His brain began to swim. Floaters clouded his vision, demanding that he take in air.

Breathe. Slam.

Inhale. Slam.

Just take...

One breath...

Sitting up in bed, Davey gasped for air. It was like his whole body was starving for it. His chest was heaving and his limbs were bursting with angry prickles. Fisting one hand, he pounded the center of his chest until he started coughing. His other hand shook like a leaf.

Shit.

It was that dream again.

He was haunted by the memory. He was haunted by *her*.

Rubbing his hands over his face, Davey groaned. He was hundreds of miles away from her now, away from what had happened. Mia was safe inside the Wall and Davey was safe here in the compound. And that was exactly how things should be.

Shoving out of his blankets, Davey swung his legs over the side of his bed and planted his bare feet on the ground. His hands were still trembling, so he braced them on his thighs and bowed his head. It was dim in his small cabin but not dark, which meant dawn was approaching.

Would he ever get a solid night's sleep again? He thought not.

Lifting his eyes to a solitary window, Davey studied the gentle sway of branches drifting outside. There was a slight breeze in the air, but it was already warm. Dead middle of summer. Today would be another hot one.

Pushing up to standing, Davey rolled his shoulders in an effort to dismiss his nerves. He huffed a frustrated breath, jumped up and down a little. Dreaming about how you killed someone was one thing, he'd done that before, and it was no big deal. Eventually, the dreams would fade.

But this particular kill, *this* dream, it was different. It was like he was living it all over again. His body truly thought it was happening. The whole thing was just so damn vivid. Too vivid. He didn't like it.

Stalking over to his long wooden dresser, Davey eyed the

messy pile of clothes strewn over its surface. It was wide, with three wooden drawers that had once been filled with perfectly folded clothes. His clothes and Ryder's clothes. They'd shared the dresser, like they'd shared the cabin.

Grinding his teeth slowly, Davey did his best not to look at his brother's empty bed. It was pushed up against the adjacent wall. Ryder's pillow was still a bit crooked at the end of the mattress, but his faded gray blankets were smooth and square.

Swallowing thickly, Davey closed his eyes. His stomach kept coiling and uncoiling so he splayed his hands out in his heap of clothes and forced his breathing to remain even. He couldn't bring himself to open a drawer, let alone keep his own stuff inside. Not with all of Ryder's things still there.

Blowing out a slow breath, Davey blinked his eyes open. His fists had clenched themselves around a wrinkled blue shirt. It should work just fine, he figured, it was as good as anything else he had lying around. Stepping back, Davey yanked it on over his head.

On the floor were a pair of stained jeans that he'd worn the day before. With a grunt, he stepped into them and then fumbled around for some socks. They were still on the floor too, right where he'd left them in two crumpled balls.

Crossing the space quickly now, Davey slipped into his boots before shoving the front door wide. For a moment, he stood still on the threshold and listened.

It was quiet.

The sky was the softest shade of light-blue with not a cloud in sight. In the branches overhead, a pair of red-chested birds were already stirring, making Davey's heart fold in on itself. This day would go forward like every other day he'd spent walking the earth since Ryder's death.

It was painful how normal everything was, how typical and thoughtless and bright. Didn't they know? Didn't they care how empty life was without Ryder in it?

But the world refused to stop turning. People didn't stop living, they didn't stop changing. And yet even the compound itself had changed, had grown. In another hour or so, the whole place would be bustling with activity. Seven women lived here now, along with twenty or so men from behind the Wall, and of course Cookie, Ace and himself.

Frowning, Davey stared down at Cole's cabin. It was larger than it had been when their team first found Hannah, but that was almost two years ago now. Its front windows were all dark and dusty. The door was locked. The space inside, with all of its handmade furniture, stood silent and empty.

Cole, Hannah and Liam were all still back at the Wall. Hannah was pregnant, and that changed things.

Reaching for his rifle propped up inside the door Davey slung the strap over his shoulder. He never went anywhere without it. Ever. Stepping out onto the dirt, Davey shut the wooden door behind him and began to pick his way carefully down the hillside.

He liked to get out of the center of things before everyone else woke up. He didn't like too much activity or too many voices.

If he'd of had any balls at all, he'd of moved to the outskirts of the compound a long time ago, but that would mean leaving his cabin empty. That would mean leaving the last place he'd seen his brother alive.

Placing his boots deliberately, Davey headed for the far pasture. He practiced being absolutely silent. He practiced his stalking.

Controlling his breathing, he let his eyes dart all around, taking in each tiny detail and scanning for changes. There were none. As usual.

Finally, a long stretch of makeshift fencing came into view. On the other side of it stood two tall horses and an old mule. The later made an awful braying sound at his approach, causing Davey to snort in response. So much for staying quiet.

When he reached the gate, Davey didn't bother to open it. He barely even broke stride, as he reached out and climbed up the side of the gate like it was a ladder before hopping over. His boots landed without a sound in the soft grass.

"We should really set you up by the front," Davey murmured to the mule as he passed. "You're the best alarm around here."

At his words, the mule stamped a hind foot, his long brownish tail swishing angrily at a fly. There were a bunch of them buzzing around already, Davey noted, and kept walking.

At the top of the property there was a plateau of sorts. The ground flattened out into a meadow and that's where the group did most of their farming. On the far side of *that* area was the graveyard. It was a pretty spot, with a bunch of wildflowers crawling all over the place. Davey preferred it that way. At least his brother would have the beauty in death that he'd been robbed of in life.

But as Davey drew closer to his destination, he stopped short. Setting his hands on his hips, he frowned. Cookie was already there, waiting for him.

Damn.

"Let's not pretend like you don't see me and I don't see

you!" The older man called. "I just came to pay my respects, same as you."

Letting loose a low groan, Davey's arms fell back to his sides.

"Yeah right," he murmured to himself, but started walking forward anyway.

He wanted to see Ryder, and if Cookie was the price he had to pay, then he better get his proverbial wallet out and pay the piper. The old man had taken to lecturing him lately, and with Cookie things didn't ease up and go away, they usually only intensified.

What's the matter with you? Do you ever bathe? Eat this, I made it for your ungrateful ass.

Cookie was worse than a mother hen. Pecking. Always relentlessly pecking.

Avoiding eye contact, Davey opened the small gate that led into the graveyard and crossed to his brother's marker, a wooden cross with Ryder's name etched deep. It was still kind of hard to believe, actually. His brother's body was buried right here. Davey hated to visualize it, but it was practically impossible not to do so. After all, he'd laid Ryder in the ground himself.

"Got flowers for each of 'em." Cookie shoved both of his hands into the front pockets of his pants as he spoke. "More of those yellow ones for Flynn. She'd of liked that."

Firming his lips, Davey surveyed the small collection of wild flowers. There were yellows and oranges and purples even. It was nice this time of year, with all the colors.

"Looks good," Davey admitted and crouched down to trace his finger along the etching of his brother's name. He'd carved that too, with a knife he'd eventually had to throw away.

"You look like shit, you know that?" Cookie commented. "When's the last time you shaved?"

Rolling his eyes, Davey dropped to his knees and began tugging at a collection of green weeds. He tried to keep each of the graves as reasonably clear as possible, but the damn things grew faster than you could pick them this time of year.

At least during winter he didn't have to shovel snow off of the graves anymore. Cole and Liam had erected a cover, and that helped a lot.

"You could cut your hair at least," Cookie went on. "You're scaring some of the women. You look like a damn hobo."

"I am a damn hobo," Davey exhaled the words and kept working. His fingers scratched in the cool dirt.

"What the hell happened to you at the Wall?" Cookie demanded. "You were getting better before you left. Now it's like you're back to square one."

"Square one," Davey repeated the words, but kept his head down. "You mean like when I first found my dead brother? Or maybe you mean when I dug his grave? You'll have to be more specific."

"Oh for shit's sake." Cookie threw up his hands. "You know what I mean. You were functioning. You showered. You let Ace cut your hair. You ate food. Now you look like a drug addict digging for trash in a dumpster."

"Wow." Davey huffed a breath and finally looked up. "Alright Cook, you've got my attention. No need to go saying nice things. I'm immune to flattery."

"I've been on the radio with Liam," Cookie began, ignoring him. "And he mentioned how maybe you almost shot Jameson but then backed off on it and then there was some blonde girl you saved... Mandy or Maddy or something like that."

Shoving up to standing, Davey brushed his hands together and glanced away. *Mia.* The correct name pounded around inside his head, but he didn't let it out. He fought the immediate twist in his chest and instead focused all of his attention on the tree line.

The pines and oaks were filled with birds and their morning songs rippled amongst the branches. It had him flashing back to that abandoned farmhouse where Mia and Cass had insisted on showering.

Closing his eyes, Davey exhaled. So many mistakes. He'd made so many fucking mistakes and ultimately it was the girls that had paid the price. Mia and Cass both.

"What's your point?" Davey gritted out the words finally as his eyes popped back open and locked on Cookie. "The radio is supposed to be official business only. It's not a gossip line."

"We're worried about you," Cookie admitted and ran a hand along the back of his neck. "Me and Ace, Liam and Cole. Hannah, too. We're your family and..."

Huffing a laugh, Davey took a step away and gave his head a little shake. Family? Cookie was playing that card?

"That's a low blow Cook," Davey remarked. "Even for you."

Davey had no blood family left. His mom had died of cancer when he was ten. His father died in a chemical weapons attack during the first six months of the war. And then of course Ryder was next. So his team, his brothers in arms, were all he had left in the world. He would lay down his life for any of them, for all of them. He would do almost anything they asked of him. Keyword there being *almost*.

"You're worse than you were before you left," Cookie insisted. "It's either the beef with Jameson or the girl. So which is it?"

"Does it matter?" Davey frowned.

He was still twisted up about Jameson, that was true. But it was more disappointment than anything else. He would never have the vengeance he wanted. He would never get to kill his brother's killers. Those men were already dead.

Pacing away, Cookie's mouth snapped shut and his jaw ticked a moment.

"Can you keep your shit together?" He asked finally, his gaze swinging back to lock on Davey. "That's all I wanna know."

"Again." Davey studied him, eyes narrowed, head cocked to one side. "Why?"

"Liam intercepted a radio transmission," Cookie offered. "Another distress signal calling for help for women and children."

Another transmission... like the one from Hermiston?

Davey's mouth dropped slightly as his heart picked up the pace. More men with tattoos? More men like the one that hurt Mia?

"Good ole' Uriah Linfield wants to reassemble our team," Cookie went on. "Now *I* told him to shove it where the sun don't shine, and you know Ace ain't leaving his new girlfriend here, but they did ask about you. They wanted to know if you were fit for a mission."

Davey's pulse was skittering now and his throat was bobbing. A million things flashed through his mind, and in that moment he actually felt... *normal.*

When he was running a mission, Davey realized, he felt okay. In fact, when he'd been on the hunt a few months back with Liam in Hermiston, it was the closest to good he'd been since Ryder's death.

Suddenly, he wanted that again. He wanted it desperately.

"And what did you tell them Cook?" Davey asked, trying to keep the pant from his voice.

"I lied," Cookie answered finally. "I told them you were good to go."

CHAPTER TWO_
MIA

TUCKING A STRAND OF STRAY HAIR BEHIND ONE EAR, MIA perched on a plastic chair in the narrow hallway. It was barren. The white walls surrounding her held no decoration. There were no pictures hanging, no color, no art. There were no windows either.

Across from her, a lone receptionist sat behind a wide wooden desk. The woman had a big black telephone, a jar of pens and a thick stack of paperwork spread out in front of her.

There was no one else waiting. It was just Mia, and about a half a dozen empty seats.

"He'll be with you in a minute," the receptionist assured her, causing her sweep of brown hair to bob with her movement. The woman's hazel eyes were warm as they drifted back down to her work.

Forcing a small smile, Mia nodded her head and swallowed her bundle of nerves. She'd never been called into Uriah Linfield's office before, and for the life of her she couldn't figure out why she was being summoned now.

Bringing a delicate fist up to her mouth, Mia cleared her throat and glanced around. It had been two months since her attack outside the Wall, but she still felt wary. She knew logically that she was safe. There were no scary men coming for her, with their stomping boots and their dirty hands and their stinking breath. Everything was fine.

In fact, this spot right here, outside of the Commander's office, was probably the safest place on the planet. Nevertheless, her tummy took a slow roll inside of her. This feeling of unease, this feeling of fear, it defied logic.

Closing her eyes briefly, Mia exhaled through her nostrils. On the outskirts of her mind she could sense a flashback coming.

Mia swallowed thickly. Why now of all places? Could she fight this one off?

Her memories had been returning to her, like little snippets of a film reel flickering inside her mind. She'd started having them right after the attack. Something about the violence of what had happened… of the man hurting her… had triggered them.

Lowering her hands to her sides, Mia gripped the arms of her plastic chair and leaned against the seat-back. The memory was blurry but it was coming closer. She wouldn't be able to stop this one.

There were voices already beside her and the bodies of people shifting. It was as if they were standing all around her now, and although she couldn't see them clearly, she would soon.

Exhaling, Mia gave in to the inevitable. If she was lucky, and this was a short one, then she could probably keep herself from passing out.

Sucking in a final quick breath, she felt her mind swirl and then drag her under.

"Are you nervous?" Aunt Jean asked. "If you just give them the answers like we discussed, then everything should be okay."

"Um..." Mia tipped her head back to look into her aunt's face.

Aunt Jean's hands were twisting in front of her body, she was trying not to pace. Mia's heart was pounding inside her chest and her hands gripped the arms of her wooden chair tightly. They'd been called in to meet with Child Protective Services. Someone had said something.

Uncle Everett stalked like a lion just behind her aunt. Both of their faces were serious, taut with tension. Mia had only been living with them for a few weeks and everything was still so new. She'd never had siblings before or done homeschool or worn such awful constricting dresses.

"Let's go over it again." Uncle Everett's bright-blue eyes bored into Mia as he nodded his head. His thick brows furrowed as he stared.

"What are you going to say?" Aunt Jean asked.

Her dark hair was fastened in a tight braid that coiled over her shoulder and fell all the way to her hip. Uncle Everett placed a steadying hand on his wife's shoulder and squeezed.

"What's your name girl?" He asked gently, testing.

Swallowing, Mia blinked away the answer that she'd been giving for the last nine years of her life. She forced the truth down her throat and into her belly.

"Mia Analiese Jones," she answered quickly. A lie.

"How old are you, girl?" Uncle Everett again, nodding.

"Ten." Another lie.

"What happened to your parents?" His mouth twitched slightly on the question.

This part even made her uncle nervous. Mia's stomach folded in on itself.

"They died," she said. "In a car accident."

"Good." Her uncle blew out a breath as his hand dropped away from his wife. "Now if they ask you anything more than that, then just pretend like you're gonna sneeze. I'll supply the answer for you. Understand? We've got all the paperwork in place, this should work."

"Okay." Mia bobbed her head. She was going to throw up.

"Remember..." Uncle Everett lowered his voice even though they were all alone in the small room. "If you slip up when we go in there... then we're all dead."

Opening her eyes, Mia held back the gasp that wanted to escape her throat. Her stomach pitched momentarily and she didn't know where she was.

But then reality came roaring back. She was still sitting upright in the plastic chair in front of Uriah Linfield's office. Her short red dress was unruffled, her feet were crossed at the ankle, her knuckles were white as she continued to grip the arms of her chair.

She hadn't fallen face first on the floor. That was good.

Across from her, the phone on the receptionist's desk began to ring… or maybe it had already been ringing and that's what had brought her back to the present.

Mia's eyes flew to it just as the receptionist picked it up.

"Yes Sir," the woman said and looked to Mia before nodding. "I'll send her right in."

CHAPTER THREE_
DAVEY

STANDING OUTSIDE OF BUILDING SIX, DAVEY SMOOTHED AT THE front of his uniform. He was clean-shaven, his blonde hair had been cut short and combed. The boots on his feet had been shined. His socks were fresh, his rifle was oiled, hell… even his underwear was new.

Clearing his throat, Davey stared at the glass double doors leading to the Command Center inside the Wall. Uriah Linfield was somewhere in there, making decisions that would affect Davey's life. And for the the first time in a really, really long time, Davey actually gave a shit about what that entailed. Uriah Linfield had him by the balls, so to speak.

Davey's jaw clenched and his fists curled as his heart gave an involuntary thud against his ribcage.

He wanted something.

He wanted to be a part of a strike team again. He wanted a purpose. Goals to accomplish, enemies to capture, subdue, maybe even kill. It's what he excelled at, after all.

And if he died in the process? So much the better.

Stepping forward, Davey pulled open one of the doors and

crossed the threshold inside. The mid-summer heat that had settled all around him was quickly replaced with a cool, dim interior. Everything was sparse, no frills. Blank white walls, minimal noise, cold tile flooring.

Spotting a lone bulletin board fastened to one wall, Davey walked over to it and frowned. There were suite numbers with names and arrows, just like any office building before the war, directing you where to go.

Commander Linfield was the only name listed on the third floor so Davey headed down the hall to his right and entered a stairwell at the end. His boots echoed on his way up the short flights of stairs and his pulse seemed to match their rhythm.

Two weeks ago, Cookie had vouched for him over the radio. *Against his better judgment, blah, blah, blah.* And recommended him for the job. Ace had then spent another half a day cleaning Davey up so he didn't look like such a drug addict bum. *Cookie's words, thank you very much.*

After that, Davey had started walking back to the Wall.

He was all alone for the thirteen day journey, but that didn't bother him. Not in the least. When thoughts of a certain blonde had popped up in Davey's mind, he'd shoved them away. She didn't belong there, consuming his daydreams.

And he certainly didn't feel the impulse to check up on her now, especially when she was somewhere close by. Nope, he absolutely did not.

Blowing out a long breath, Davey arrived at the door to the third floor hallway and pushed through. The place was just as sparse and utilitarian as the entrance to the building, save for a receptionist desk and some chairs about halfway down the narrow corridor.

Straightening his spine, Davey adjusted the rifle strap on his shoulder and approached the desk. The chubby brunette sitting behind it glanced up from whatever she was doing and offered him a smile.

"Can I help you?" She asked, when he came to a stop in front of her.

"I have an appointment," Davey answered. He was early, he was always at least half an hour early to everything. "My name is David Wells."

"Oh yes." The plucky woman glanced down to her paperwork as her brow furrowed. "Soldier Wells, I see you right here. You're early."

"Yes, Ma'am," he intoned and bobbed his head.

"Well, have a seat and Commander Linfield will be with you soon," she answered, gesturing to one of the empty plastic chairs lining the hall.

In silence, Davey chose the one furthest from the receptionist desk, removed his rifle and sat down.

Balancing his weapon across his lap, Davey leaned back and let his eyes take inventory of his surroundings. He noted the exits, the number of closed doors along the hall, the lights overhead, the venting ducts, the lack of windows.

Without meaning to, his mind began to run scenarios. He imagined how he could use the chairs and desk to his advantage if the hall were to come under attack. He calculated time and distance. How many shots he could get off before having to reload, how much ammo he currently had on him, how long it would take to reach the exit doors leading to the stairwells.

Exhaling through his nostrils, Davey's eyes swiveled to lock on the door to Uriah Linfield's office. Behind that door sat former Command Officer Twelve. Unbeknownst to Davey, Uriah Fucking Linfield had been directing his steps for years.

Since the very inception of Strike Team Three, Linfield had been calling the shots from behind the scenes. Every mission. Every accomplishment. Every failure.

Shit, even the mission that had cost Ryder his life, could be traced back to this one person. Linfield hadn't meant for that particular death to happen of course, but that was part of war. Friendly fire, innocents dying, the guilty surviving, it was all part of it.

And as much as he'd wanted to, Davey couldn't *quite* justify killing Linfield or even Jameson over a mission that had gone sideways. Sure, it had been a crap mission, poorly researched and even more poorly executed, but neither Linfield nor Jameson had pulled the trigger on Ryder. And what's more… neither of them had meant for it to happen.

So here Davey sat with twisting, unclear feelings and no fucking purpose.

He needed a damn purpose.

He needed a new mission now that avenging his brother's death was an empty promise never to be fulfilled. That particular task was done before it started. The ones responsible were already dead.

So now what?

CHAPTER FOUR_
MIA

STANDING SLOWLY, MIA SMOOTHED HER PALMS DOWN THE front of her dress and straightened her shoulders.

She didn't want anyone to suspect that she was having memory recurrence. Not this receptionist, not the man on the other side of that door, not even Cass. She couldn't tell anyone the things she was remembering, at least not until she had the full picture.

Her heart was pounding wildly in her chest still, so she worked hard to control her breathing.

Whatever was waiting for her on the other side of that door, she'd have to face it with her head held high and a fake smile plastered across her face. After all, she'd been taught how to wear a mask at the tender age of nine. If she could lie so easily back then, she could do it even better now.

The snap of her high heels crossing to the Commander's door sounded powerful. Her body took up the feeling and blasted it through her blood stream, making her hips sway confidently.

Curling her lips into a deliberate smile, Mia could hear a distant voice echoing in her mind. *Fake it. Fake it or we all die.*

With a quick exhale, Mia's fingers wrapped around the brass handle of the heavy door and she pulled it open. Stepping into the large office, she didn't stop until she was standing in the center of the room with the door swinging shut behind her.

Two sets of eyes regarded her. One set was more familiar than the other.

Uriah Linfield stood from behind his desk and extended his right hand. Somehow he appeared larger than life, and yet he wasn't all that tall in reality. His chest was broad and his shoulders were strong but it was his personality that took up the entire room.

He owned the space he stood in and he gave you the impression that he owned your space too. Because maybe he did.

Mia maintained her brilliant smile and let her eyes travel briefly to the other man in the room, the familiar one standing off to the side.

Garrett Jameson gave her a small nod from his position leaning up against the wall. His presence at this meeting came as a relief. Mia could trust Jameson. He would take care of her.

"Miss Mia Jones," Uriah intoned as she came forward to squeeze his wide palm. "Please have a seat."

"Thank you." Mia ducked her head before sitting across from Uriah's desk.

"You're probably wondering why you're here," Uriah offered as he eased back into his leather office chair.

Nodding her agreement, Mia glanced around. The space

was utilitarian. It had one wide window, no artwork, a desk, chairs, and bookshelves. Lots and lots of bookshelves filled to capacity, filled to overflowing.

"I've had a report from the agricultural manager, Leonard Vasquez." Uriah's brow furrowed as he plucked a sheet of paper off his desk and began to scan it. "It seems your jurisdiction is flourishing. You have a surplus of oranges, asparagus and wheat. You're successfully growing crops in places they shouldn't be growing during a time when we shouldn't be growing them. It's impressive."

"Thank you." Mia's fake smile turned genuine.

What she did on the farm, it was her favorite thing in the entire world. When her hands were in the soil, she felt the most like herself, the most centered and at peace.

"We have a special project taking place and I think you'd be very interested in it." Uriah set the sheet of paper back on his desk and leveled her with his intense brown eyes. "Have you heard any rumors?"

"Um…" Mia's brow furrowed. "No."

Glancing at Jameson over his shoulder, Uriah gave a quick nod before returning his focus to Mia.

"It's still in the beginning stages," Uriah continued. "Tell me. How do you feel about growing crops beyond the Wall? Do you think it's possible?"

"Well, of course it's possible." Mia snuck a peek at Jameson who remained standing against the far wall. He met her gaze with steady blue eyes. "Without greenhouses it would be more challenging, but that's how crops were meant to grow originally. You can control less variables so you'll have less yield, but you could make up for that by planting more volume."

"Ah." Uriah looked down at his desk and began shuffling

papers once more. “It says here that you're one of the most talented agriculturalists we have.”

Mia's brows raised as a faint flush heated her cheeks. “Well… I…”

“And Officer Jameson tells me that you can be discreet,” Uriah continued. “He's says you're loyal to a fault.”

Frowning now, Mia tried to dismiss the tickle of worry forming in her belly. *Where is this going? Why am I here?*

“Some of our more vocal community members have expressed concerns about me… about my leadership here.” Uriah quirked a small smile.

That little sentence, Mia knew, was an understatement.

“Yes, I've heard the rumors,” Mia acknowledged, tentative. They wanted to overthrow him. They wanted an election.

“My style might be less than appealing,” Uriah admitted with a shrug. “But no one can do this job better than me. No one can protect our people the way I can. I'm just not good at playing the bureaucratic part of the game. I don't do the politics thing well.”

Liar. Mia nibbled on her lower lip and fought the impulse to twist her fingers together in her lap.

“I don't…” Mia's eyes flitted between the two men finally. “I'm not sure I understand.”

“Of course, let me be plain.” Uriah sat up straight and splayed his hands flat on the desk. “Before coming to the Wall my army occupied a large city located about eight hundred miles to the south of us. We had some farming set up, fresh water and housing.

I'm looking to expand our current living capabilities back down to that city. We need to divert some of the assets that we currently have here, down there. The thing is, any large shift in supplies and personnel might panic some of our residents, especially certain community members."

Swallowing, Mia felt her tummy flip.

"You want me to leave the Wall," she stated quietly. "And go down to this city... and not tell anyone."

"Just for a few months," Uriah assured her. "I need you to evaluate the farm there. I want a full report on what's currently growing, what you think needs to be changed, what possibilities there are for the future.

I value your opinion Miss Jones, and this is important to the survival of our people, for you and for Cass, for all of the children currently depending on us for food."

Nodding, Mia squeezed her eyes shut as a ripple of panic washed over her. She was reasonably safe inside the Wall, but she was definitely not safe outside of it.

Look what had happened the last time she left. She could still feel that man's hands bruising her thighs, scratching at her, almost clawing inside of her. If Davey hadn't woken up when he did...

A shudder ran up her spine as her lungs tried to close up on her.

No. I'm not leaving the Wall. I can't.

"Mia," Jameson's voice cut through her thoughts, causing her eyes to open. "I know you're probably afraid to travel, but I promise you, we will not let anything bad happen to you this time, okay? You have my word. I'll be going with you, along with an entire company of soldiers, about two hundred men."

"Will I be the only woman?" She asked, her eyes lifting to lock on Jameson.

Jameson pursed his lips before answering, "Yes."

"What about Cass?" Mia's heart began to race.

"The doctor won't clear her for travel." Jameson dropped his gaze to the floor.

He didn't want to go without her, Mia realized. But he'd just said he was leaving. Jameson was going down south with this company of soldiers and he was leaving Cass here... where she was safe.

"How long?" Mia asked suddenly.

Was there a way to get out of this? She'd be vulnerable, the only woman. She didn't want to get hurt again and that was nothing compared to what had happened to Cass. She'd been shot, she'd almost bled to death in the back of that Jeep, she'd almost lost her leg. It was hell out there, and now they wanted her to go back?

"Three months max," Uriah cut in. "We have a bunker to house you in. I kept my sister and Lena there safely for months."

"And when I'm not in the bunker?" Mia's eyes flitted from Jameson back to Uriah. "If you want me to evaluate the farming, then I'll have to go outside... daily."

"You'll have a personal bodyguard," Uriah offered, lifting his hands, showing her his palms, placating. "One of our top soldiers will be with you twenty-four seven, everywhere you go. His sole purpose will be to keep you safe so that you can focus on your job."

Leaning back in her seat, Mia gripped the arms of her chair and let loose a long sigh.

This scared her.

She felt the fear like a big heavy ball sitting dead center in her chest. It was crushing.

But Commander Linfield was "asking" for her help. He was assigning her a very important task and he was giving her

Jameson to guard her. She could trust Jameson with her life. He was honorable and efficient and head over hells in love with her best friend.

There was no way he'd let anything happen to her, and it would only be for three months. Mia could go there, do her job, and then return. Plus… could she really say no? Did *anyone* actually say no to Uriah Linfield? She didn't think so.

"Okay," Mia relented, still a bit shaky. "I'll do it."

"Fantastic." Uriah bobbed his head, his dark eyes twinkling.

"But you've got to promise nothing will happen to me." Mia's eyes darted up to Jameson. "You'll stay with me the entire time?"

"Um…" Jameson blinked at her.

"Officer Jameson has to run the entire operation," Uriah cut in. "He can't be your personal bodyguard, he won't have the time or the focus to do so effectively."

"But…" Mia huffed a nervous laugh and gave her head a shake. "Then who will be?"

"Soldier David Wells," Uriah offered and shuffled some more papers on his desk, frowning down at one in particular. "He's one of the surviving members of Strike Team Three and you're already familiar with him. Officer Jameson said we can trust him to watch you and not cross any lines."

Mia's mouth dropped as her heart took a tumble in her chest. Davey? She hadn't seen him in two months. He'd come roaring into her life like a hurricane, turning everything she thought she knew about men upside down before disappearing as quickly as he'd come.

"Mia." Jameson this time. "You're comfortable with him, right? He'd give his life to protect you. We've seen that before."

"Yeah." Mia's mouth snapped shut and she ducked her head.

Was she comfortable with him? With those pale-blue eyes that that made her belly do that flip thing? No. No she was not.

But would he die for her? Kill for her? The answer was absolutely yes. She knew that to be true. She'd seen it in person, hadn't she? The killing part.

"Davey," Mia said the name quietly, and bit at her bottom lip. "And you and me, traveling outside the Wall… again."

"It's not going to end like it did the last time," Jameson assured her. "I swear it."

"Fine." Mia sucked in a breath. What more could she do? "Then I guess I accept your assignment. When do we leave?"

"Three days." Uriah bobbed his head and reached out to shake her hand across his desk. "Be ready in three days."

CHAPTER FIVE_

DAVEY

Across from Davey, the door to Uriah Linfield's office popped open, and a five-foot nine-inch blonde angel walked out. Davey's mouth went dry and his pulse dipped on him. Mia.

Damn. It.

"Hey." Mia's already beautiful face lit when she spotted him. "Davey, how are you?"

Standing quickly, Davey looped his rifle over his shoulder and brushed his slick palms down his thighs. The door was swinging shut behind her and Mia was walking towards him. Her bright red high heels clicked across the floor, drawing his eyes downward.

He'd forgotten about the legs... the impossibly long, impossibly smooth legs. And of course she'd be wearing the shortest dress imaginable.

"Good," he managed, before forcing his eyes back up to her face. "What about you?"

"Well..." Tucking a blonde hair behind one ear, Mia tilted

her head to one side and regarded him. "Up for another adventure I guess."

"Adventure?" Davey frowned.

"Yeah, beyond the Wall." Mia nibbled on her lip and sighed. "To be honest I'm still feeling a bit nervous about it, but what the Commander wants, he gets. And anyway working with you again makes it seem reasonable, so there's that."

"Um…" Davey's frown deepened. "I'm not following."

"My bodyguard." Mia pointed a perfectly manicured finger at his chest and tipped her head up slightly to observe him. She might be tall, but he still had a good four inches on her. "You're going to keep me safe. Hopefully it won't be like last time."

"Bodyguard… What?" Davey backed a step and gave his head a quick shake. "I think there's been a misunderstanding. I don't do babysitting work. I'm here to join a strike team."

"Oh." Mia's brows raised and her mouth dropped a fraction. "Well I guess I…"

"Wait." Davey's chest cinched tight on him as her words sunk into his brain. Reaching out, he gripped her upper arm with one hand. "You need a bodyguard? Why?"

Sucking in a short breath, Mia stared down at the point where Davey's right hand connected with her body. It was obvious to him that she didn't like to be touched, probably because of what had happened to her… what had happened on *his* watch.

Davey's stomach sank and his body tensed. Just as quickly as he'd grabbed her, Davey forced himself to let go.

It made him want to go back to Hermiston and kill that bastard all over again.

"Soldier Wells," the receptionist's voice rang out, drawing

his attention over to the desk. "Commander Linfield will see you now."

Nodding, Davey noted that the brunette held a black telephone up to one ear as she gestured behind her and to her right. The thing must have rung and he didn't even notice. That wasn't like him. He noticed everything.

Returning his attention to the leggy blonde, Davey cleared his throat. It was Mia. She'd distracted him all those months ago and now she was distracting him again. He'd make a terrible bodyguard for her.

"I'm sorry," he managed, before brushing by her and entering Commander Linfield's office.

He didn't wait for her response and he didn't look back.

Deliberately he turned his focus to where it should be at all times… on the man who controlled his destiny. And it was a good thing he was paying attention again because what he encountered inside had his already erratic pulse escalating.

Officer Jameson stood calmly against the far wall, a gun on his hip and an unreadable expression on his face.

Commander Linfield, with his golden curls and dark eyes, remained seated at a wide mahogany desk. His hands were folded, his brows drawn together.

"You're going to need to leave the rifle at the door," Linfield instructed. "You understand."

Swallowing his nerves, Davey dipped his head and did as he was told. He never went anywhere without his weapon, but given the history between Jameson and himself, he could understand the request. Plus, he still had his handgun tucked in the holster at his back and three knives concealed on his body.

Not that this was going to get confrontational.

Because it wasn't.

Right?

"Go ahead and take a seat." Linfield gestured to one of the two chairs positioned across the desk from him.

Again, Davey did as he was told. This was all about establishing respect in order to get what he wanted, especially now that he'd made the decision to reenlist so to speak. He wanted back on a strike team and only Linfield could give him that, so he had to play nice.

For a solid minute, silence prevailed.

Linfield shuffled through some papers on his desk, his face serious, his frown deep. Seeming to select one, his eyes darted back and forth over the lined page, reading, scanning, absorbing whatever was written there.

Keeping perfectly still, Davey let his own eyes bounce up to Jameson and then back down to Linfield. Jameson was like stone, watchful, quiet, unmoving.

"You have an exemplary service record," Linfield spoke finally. Leaning back in his leather office chair, the guy exhaled. "From what Officer Tanner and Officer Byrne have included in their report, you were a pivotal member of Strike Team Three."

"Yes Sir." Davey's jaw firmed.

"Calm in chaos, steady under fire, makes sound judgments, executes orders without hesitation." Commander Linfield recited the words without reading them as his brown eyes flipped up to settle on Davey.

"Well-liked by his peers, a natural leader when given the opportunity, unparalleled sniper skills… with the one exception being Soldier Lawrence Smelt aka Cookie who can (and I quote) *shoot the mustache off a bearded lady at 500 yards*."

Pursing his lips, Davey forced his hands to remain loose in his lap. Cole was definitely to blame for that last little comment, no doubt about it.

"Things took a turn, however," Linfield began again. "When your brother was killed. Ryder Arthur Wells, also a member of Strike Team Three, also an exemplary soldier."

Swallowing down the lump in his throat, Davey did his best not to react.

It was still so damn hard. Hearing his brother's name in the past tense, knowing that his brother was dead, was still too fucking hard. Would it ever ease up? Would he ever get a moment to just breathe and forget?

The rims of his eyes were burning. Tears were forming and his throat was clogging and his chest was constricting. He. Would. Not. Cry.

Blinking forcefully a few times, Davey inhaled slowly and suppressed himself. He took hold of his emotions, like so many other times in the past year, and he forced them down, down, down into the pit of his belly. Until they were gone. Until everything he felt was numb.

"I am truly sorry about that," Linfield went on. "I may never have met your brother in person, but when I was running Strike Team Three, I swear to you, I loved each one of you like you were my own. There were nights that I didn't sleep, knowing I'd sent you all somewhere most men would not return from. Ryder's name was familiar to me, as was yours. I'm sorry that I was the cause of his death, even indirectly."

Closing his eyes, all Davey was able to manage in response was a short nod. His heart was squeezing in on itself and his belly was sinking. After a second though, his eyes popped back open and he leveled his gaze at his commander.

Apology. No apology. His brother was still dead, and as far as Davey was concerned this world was still at war.

He just wanted back in the thick of it now. He just wanted back in the fight.

"If you have a problem with me..." Linfield tilted his head to one side. "Or Officer Jameson, now is the time to address it. I heard you had my man on his knees for a few good minutes, wondering if you were going to take your shot. Is that going to be an issue going forward?"

"No issue." Davey shook his head firmly. "No problem. We sorted it out. I'm good."

Raising his eyebrows, Uriah leaned his forearms on his desk and folded his hands together.

Silence crept through the space again, settling in like a blanket being draped over his shoulders. Davey's eyes darted up to Jameson. The guy was watching him calmly, blinking, arms folded casually over his broad chest. *Fucking oversized bear.*

"The assignment we have for you involves a lot of trust," Uriah continued finally. "It's one of the most important missions I'm executing currently, and you'll be working closely with Officer Jameson for several months. Can you do that without putting a bullet in him?"

"Absolutely Sir." Davey felt a weight being lifted off his chest. He would be assigned to another strike team. He would be going back to war, back into the shit. He couldn't wait. "I've had a lot of opportunities to drop him, but I didn't. I could've finished him today before you even stood up from your desk... Sir."

"I'm not sure that's what I wanted to hear Soldier." Uriah huffed an incredulous breath and glanced over his shoulder at Jameson. "What do you think?"

"He's the only one I trust with her and *she's* the critical piece in this mission," Jameson offered with a shrug. "I don't think he's an on-going threat to me, but only time will tell."

Commander Linfield nodded to himself and let his eyes drift down to his desk. Picking up a nearby pen, he began to jot down a few notes. The scratching of his writing against the paper was the only sound in the room for another minute as Davey's heart thumped and Jameson's words sunk into his thick skull.

She's the critical piece. He's the only one I trust with her.

What the hell?

"Who's she?" Davey blurted suddenly.

His eyes danced between the two men. The Commander's hand paused in his writing and he looked up.

"Mia Jones," Linfield offered. "You'll be her personal bodyguard for the next several months. Twenty-four hours a day, seven days a week. She doesn't take a shit without you listening outside the door. Understood?"

"I... but..." Davey's head snapped back as if he'd been slapped. "No. Absolutely not. I'm not a babysitter. I'm here to join a strike team. I'm here because of the new recording, the one like the call from Hermiston. With all due respect, I'm a *hunter,* not a guard dog. Let me hunt... Sir."

"No." Commander Linfield's brown eyes flashed as he regarded Davey.

"Sir?"

"I said: *No,*" Linfield repeated himself. "You're a loose

cannon. I couldn't in good conscience put you on a strike team. Not yet, anyway."

"But…"

"Two months ago you had my second in command on his knees waiting for his execution," Linfield cut him off. "You were a loyal Nor Side Soldier, but that was before your brother's death which can be directly linked to *me*.

This is the *Linfield* Army now. I can't use you until I can trust you, and if you want to start earning some trust… then take this assignment and see it through to successful completion. Then we can come back to this table and discuss your advancement."

Clenching his jaw tight, Davey ground his teeth together as he worked through what was happening. No strike team. No war games. No chance at Valhalla and reuniting with his brother on the other side. Instead… bodyguard work with Mia.

Frowning, Davey's self-centered brain clicked to the next step.

"Why does Mia need a guard?" Davey's pale-blue eyes zeroed in on Uriah.

His body was already priming for a fight without him meaning to. She was in danger? The very idea had his blood heating.

"She has an assignment," Linfield offered. "I'm sending her down to what used to be Utah. I need her expertise there, and while she's doing her work, you'll be tasked with keeping her safe."

"You're sending Mia outside of the Wall." Davey's hands curled into fists. "Even after what happened last time? You're putting her at risk… unnecessarily."

Lifting a hand, Commander Linfield pointed a steady finger directly at Davey's face.

"You see that right there?" He asked. "That's exactly what I'm talking about. You better work a little harder to hide that anger Soldier, because I can see right through you.

Now… will you take this assignment or not? I could probably find some other guy to breathe on her for three months and you can march your ass back home."

Swallowing the lump in his throat, Davey exhaled through his nostrils and bobbed his head. He couldn't believe this was happening. He couldn't believe any of it.

"I want the assignment Sir," Davey replied finally and lifted his now clear eyes to his Commander. "Thank you."

CHAPTER SIX_

MIA

HE WASN'T HOLDING ONTO HER ARM ANYMORE. LOGICALLY, SHE knew that. But even so, hours later, the area on her upper arm was still humming.

Reaching an arm across herself, Mia ran her fingers over her the spot. There was something about his touch, something she couldn't shake. The sensation wasn't bad exactly. It was just… different, achy, lingering.

Grumbling under her breath, Mia forced herself to let go. Damn Davey and his sexy blue eyes that flashed with concern one second and complete dismissal the next. He was like that, she reminded herself. Hot and cold. Here then gone.

He'd kill for you. Hold you while you cried, kiss you on the head even. Then he'd leave.

He was a ghost, flickering in and out of the present, and if she let him get to her again, then it would drive her out of her mind.

"Just do what you came here to do," Mia mumbled. "And get out."

Narrowing her eyes, Mia scanned one long section of

metal shelving. She was in one of the storage warehouses that sat adjacent to the farming section. Light filtered in from windows placed high on the walls, but even so, the place was dim. There were overhead lights, but she didn't dare turn them on.

For the first time that she could recall, Mia was sneaking. She didn't want to be caught. She didn't want any of her coworkers to see what she was doing.

The very idea made her belly roll, and some old lost memories began to flicker and stir. She was tempting fate here, she knew, but if she was going to travel down south to farm, then this just had to be done.

Giving her head a quick shake, Mia dismissed her nerves and shifted the canvas bag on her shoulder. With her head tipped up, she continued to scan the contents of the shelves. Seed canisters, large and neat and orderly, were positioned before her.

Commander Linfield wanted to know the possibility for crop growth in this new area of his. He said they needed to find out if the soil and the weather could sustain a large population of people. Mia *knew* (common sense, intuition, a repressed memory?) that the best way for her to figure all that out was to plant a small sample garden.

She needed to take a variety of seeds from these shelves and test them out. Normally, she would just take what she needed in broad daylight while everyone else who worked at the farm was busy walking in and out.

The catch here was that Commander Linfield wanted her to use "discretion". He didn't want the community to know what he was sending her down there to do. Although after she left, she knew a few people were bound to figure it out.

"Not your problem," she whispered to herself and continued walking.

Beets, carrots, broccoli, spinach. Those were all good fall harvest crops and they actually tasted better after a mild frost. *How do you know that self? I dunno self, but it's the truth.*

Reaching up, Mia selected a few sealed canisters from behind the already open ones at the front. They were heavy and clunky, causing her to scrape and slide them along the metal shelves to get them down.

Biting at her lip, Mia carefully placed the canisters in the cloth bag at her side. These seeds would make for good, nutritious vegetables, but she needed something heartier, too. She needed a grain, something that can be made into bread or used as a filler.

Stepping away, Mia walked the other aisles quietly until she found the section she was after. Her brown boots seemed to echo through the space, causing her to cringe internally. Tap. Tap. Tap. Tap.

She wished there was a way to be absolutely silent in here, but it seemed impossible, what with the metal walls and the concrete flooring.

Coming to a stop, Mia brushed her now sweaty palms down the sides of her blue jeans and sighed. Her eyes flew over the array of canisters until her heart gave up an involuntary thud.

Sweet corn. That should do the trick.

Mia smiled.

Lifting up to her tiptoes, she braced one hand on the cold metal shelf and reached for a canister.

"Hey!" A familiar voice exploded from the far end of the aisle.

Mia's heart leapt in her chest and she stumbled back with a squeak. The voice belonged to Sebastian, a coworker and friend. He ran the jurisdiction of land adjacent to hers and he did pretty well growing feed for the livestock.

"Whoa! Mia, you okay?" He asked, closing the distance between them.

Nodding, Mia felt her heart hammering as Sebastian's dark eyes narrowed. Coming to a stop beside her, he brushed a few strands of chestnut hair off his own forehead before reaching to steady her arm.

No tingles, Mia noted. Warm, not unpleasant, but still... no tingles like with Davey.

"I'm fine." Mia cleared her throat and forced a confident smile.

Sebastian smiled in return, his eyes cruising down the length of her body and then back up. Did he notice her bag? Would he ask what she was doing? What was inside it? Mia's heart wanted to leap out of her body.

You're not doing anything wrong. Sort of.

Sucking in a quick breath, Mia willed her pulse to settle. It refused.

As Sebastian opened his mouth to speak, her ears stopped listening. A memory was coming. A strong one. Mia blinked rapidly, trying to keep her eyes open, trying to stay here in the now.

But she wasn't going to be able to stop this one, she realized. It was like a tornado dropping down to touch earth, tricking her senses and blurring her surroundings. She felt light-headed as her lungs emptied in a whoosh.

Reaching out to brace a hand against Sebastian's chest... Mia's teeth ground together and she fought to stay upright.

But it was too much. The memory came forward and sucked her under.

She was in the barn, where she shouldn't be.

Brushing a delicate hand down the front of her conservative dress, Mia sighed. Women didn't do farm work. Her five boy cousins, yes. Her imposing uncle, absolutely. But her dark-haired aunt?

No. Way.

Her place was in the kitchen, or tidying up the house, or doing the laundry. There were no maids, no nanny, no playdates in the park, no afternoons spent shopping before dinner at the club.

Inhaling, Mia took in the scent of dust, cans of gasoline, and bales of stale hay. Uncle Everett had milk goats and they needed the feed. The older boys saw to that though, not her and not her aunt.

As Mia walked past the twisted metal of farm equipment, she let her fingertips glide over the worn, slightly rusted pieces. In the far corner, there was a massive shelving unit with closed wooden doors. One of which was crooked, hanging a bit askew on its copper-colored hinges. What was inside there?

With a quick glance over her shoulder, Mia hurried her steps. Her heart beat at her and her lungs squeezed. She shouldn't be doing this. She might get in trouble.

But the soles of her modest shoes shuffled over bits of old hay covering the concrete floor, making her steps sound like whispers in the dark.

When she got to the cabinet, her hand hesitated a moment on the handle. She should ask first. If her father were here and he was the one to catch her... Mia's stomach twisted.

No. Her father wasn't here. He didn't know where she was. She'd be safe so long as she stayed on this farm, just like her aunt and uncle said.

Rolling her shoulders, Mia steeled herself and pulled the cabinet door wide. Her mouth fell open at the contents. The shelves were neat and orderly and completely filled with jars. Each jar was labeled. Corn. Peas. Asparagus. Spinach.

"Seeds," Mia spoke to herself, frowning.

Reaching out a hand, she ran a finger over several of the labels. She'd never actually seen seeds before. Was that strange?

"Hey!" A familiar voice exploded from the entrance to the barn.

It was Uncle Everett. He was back from the fields.

With a gasp, Mia stumbled back from the cabinet, her heart doing summersaults in her chest. She'd been caught. She was going to be punished.

Uncle Everett's boots stomped their way towards her. They were so loud against the concrete.

Eyes wide, lips parted, Mia looked frantically around for a way to escape. Her hands fluttered in the air, she slapped at her dress. She was in the back of the barn with no way out. There was nowhere to run. There was nowhere to hide.

Dropping to her knees right there on the ground, Mia buried her face in her arms and squeezed her eyes shut. Her entire body was shaking. She was waiting for the hit, waiting for her punishment. Why couldn't she just do what she was told?

"I'm sorry," she stammered. "I'm so sorry."

Her words sounded muffled as she spoke them into the ground. Tears poured from her cheeks as her body began to rock back and forth. She kept her face buried in an effort to protect it from what came next. She didn't want another black eye that her mother would have to cover with makeup, or a chipped tooth that the dentist would tisk over.

Uncle Everett's heavy black boots came to a stop beside her.

Mia's mouth opened like a fish. She couldn't make a sound. She might pee herself, she knew. Sometimes, if it went on for too long, then she couldn't hold it.

But the attack that she was waiting for... it never came.

The barn was just quiet. Eerily quiet.

"We don't hurt children here," Uncle Everett spoke finally, then dropped to a crouch beside her. "Or women either. It's against God's will."

Holding her breath, Mia peeked up from between her trembling arms. Her uncle was frowning down at her, but not in an angry way. His held tilted to one side and he let out a breath of his own.

"Your father is an evil man ruled by sin," he offered. "Your auntie and I... we tried to warn your mama off of him, but she wouldn't listen. He lured her in with all of his fancy money and his power. I'm sorry he laid his hands on you."

"But..." Mia lifted her head and dropped her arms completely, such was the shock she was experiencing. "You're not mad?"

Huffing a dismissive breath, her uncle glanced around. "Mad about what?"

"I'm in the barn where women aren't allowed," Mia offered.

Her heart was hammering at her not to confess this obvious fact, not to bait him. What if this was a trap?

Uncle Everett lifted his heavy brows then, and looked her dead in the face.

"Why wouldn't a woman be allowed in a barn?" He asked.

"Because it's for men," she supplied.

"Child..." Uncle Everett gave his head a little shake. "Growing God's food is for anyone willing to take up the task. Your Auntie just doesn't like that sort of work and I figured being from the city, you wouldn't either."

"Oh." It was Mia's turn to frown. Sniffing, she ran her sleeve beneath her nose and along her cheeks.

"Would you like to try farming?" Her uncle asked, his face softening. "It's hard and it's dirty."

"Do I still have to wear a dress?" She asked.

"Yes," he answered seriously. "You can still be modest when covered in dirt. Any other questions?"

"Um..." Mia sat up straight and pressed her hands to her cheeks... her cheeks that hadn't been slapped because of her sneaking.

"No Sir," she replied. "No questions."

CHAPTER SEVEN_

DAVEY

As soon as he opened the door, Davey heard them. There was a male voice followed by a female one. His ears pricked at the sound and he sucked in an involuntary breath. He knew with certainty that it was *her*... even though he couldn't quite make out what was being said.

Behind him, he eased the heavy door shut and frowned.

The inside of the large warehouse was dim, but not dark. Briefly, he wondered why the overhead lights weren't switched on. An immediate anger bubbled in his throat at the most likely answer to that question, but the feeling itself was background noise to him.

Davey's mind only allowed one question to zip through his thick skull... What would a man and a woman be doing together, all alone, without the benefit of light?

His frown deepened as his body surged forward. *Not on my watch Blondie.*

Fists curling, jaw tightening, Davey's boots ate up the ground. He didn't want this assignment. In his humble opinion, a bodyguard gig was akin to babysitting and he'd already proven he wasn't that great of a babysitter.

After five long years stuck neck deep in the shit outside of the Wall, Davey was pretty damn certain he was better suited to more proactive work.

Surveil. Stalk. Kill. Burn. Explode. Capture. Whatever.

Something… *anything* that wasn't watching a pretty blonde until his eyes crossed and he stopped thinking like a warrior and started thinking with his… well… she distracted him.

But his Commander had made the game perfectly clear. If Davey wanted back on a strike team, then he had to prove his loyalty. He had to build trust with Jameson first, and to do that he had show him that he could once again excel under orders.

So, Mia or no Mia, Davey planned to do just that. Focus. Excel.

The fact that the leggy blonde made his fingers itch and his body uncomfortable had no bearing. He was a professional. He would keep her safe for the next several months, dump her back at Uriah's front door with a damn bow on her head, and then demand his next assignment.

In fact, screw being assigned to a strike team, he wanted to *run* a strike team. Yeah. It was Davey's turn to call the shots.

So, guarding Mia was a means to an end and he would do his job exceptionally well… starting right fucking now.

Adjusting the rifle strap looped over his shoulder, Davey soaked up his surroundings. The aisles were made up of huge metal shelves stacked to the brim with boxes and bags and canisters.

Voices continued to echo in the large space. Davey

couldn't see the man who was currently talking to Mia, but that wouldn't last much longer, one more row and he'd be on them.

Davey's jaw ticked and his muscles tightened, but he kept his footfalls soft.

At this point, a normal person might call out a warning, but that sort of politeness wasn't in Davey's wheelhouse any longer. He'd spent way too many years sneaking around as a means of survival. The best way to get shot was to warn people that you were coming.

It was always better to appear and disappear like a mist. In that way, he could observe the scene for several moments before deciding whether or not to interrupt it. Was Mia a willing participant here? Or was this guy about to get his ass beat into the floor? Who knew? And honestly, the uncertainty of it was kinda intoxicating.

Davey's knuckles ached to make contact with this guy's face. His body was priming for a fight. Suddenly, he couldn't wait.

"Hey Mia... you good?" The male voice became clear.

Mia's response, though, was unintelligible. Her whispered words were far too low for Davey to hear over the sudden thrumming of his own blood in his ears.

When he rounded the corner, the pair came into view. About halfway down the aisle the man (tallish, brown hair, olive skin) had his arms around Mia. He was looking down into her face and she was looking up, like they'd just kissed maybe. Her delicate hands were splayed on the guy's chest, but it didn't look like she was trying to shove him away.

Boyfriend? Lover?

She was hot as hell so she probably had more than one, Davey realized. *Great. Well, that lifestyle is going to end right about now.*

"Miss Jones," Davey's voice boomed in the space and caused the happy couple to spring apart. "I've been looking all over for you. We've got some work to take care of."

Blinking in shock, Mia pressed a hand to her forehead. Whether she was just surprised to see him or the use of her last name threw her, Davey didn't know. But either way, she was backing away from the guy who'd been pawing at her just moments before and it had Davey's pulse evening out slightly.

The guy, for his part, took one look at Davey and scowled.

That's right lover boy, that's the last taste of Mia you're going to get for quite awhile.

"Who are you?" The dark-haired guy gave him a once over as Davey came to a stop in front of them.

"I'm none of your business," Davey supplied dryly, before giving his full attention to Mia. "I've been looking for you for over two hours. We need to talk."

"Davey." Mia's pouty pink lips firmed as she appraised him. "This is Sebastian Reed, he works with me here."

"Fantastic," Davey responded. *I don't fucking care*. "Can we walk and talk? Because we've got a lot to discuss and only a little time to do it."

Mia's mouth dropped a moment as she took in his request.

Beside her, the Sebastian guy began to protest. Of course he did. The boyfriend didn't want Davey to scoop up his prize and take her away before he had a chance to finish what they'd apparently started.

Davey suppressed a small smirk at the thought, but made sure to keep his features bland as he stared down at Mia.

The blonde, for her part, huffed an indignant breath and shifted the cloth bag that was hanging from a leather strap over her shoulder. The contents of said bag then banged together obnoxiously. Clunks of tin against tin. It had Mia cringing.

Davey frowned.

Quickly, Mia's eyes flew to the boyfriend's face. She looked worried, nervous. But of course the idiot didn't seem to notice anything.

Sebastian's mouth just kept right on running as he zeroed in on Davey.

"Who the hell are you? Do you mind? What do you want? Can I help you find your way out of here?" The questions rolled on top of each other, namely because Davey refused to answer.

Continuing to ignore the guy, Davey lifted a questioning eyebrow at Mia. She was trying to sneak stuff out of here, he realized and she didn't want the little boyfriend to know about it. Interesting.

"Well?" Davey cocked his head, feigning impatience. "I don't have all day." *A complete lie, you've got me for the next ninety days at least.*

"Fine," Mia snapped, seeming to gather herself.

At once her shoulders squared and her spine straightened. Before Davey could blink, the blonde had transformed from freshly kissed and out of sorts to full speed ahead. Turning on her heel, she began to march away.

Sebastian's mouth dropped then, and his babbling ceased. For the first time since catching the couple together, Davey glanced the guy's way. When their eyes met, Davey let that smirk that he'd held back before come out and transform his whole face. You're out, he thought, before turning to stride after her.

The sound of Mia's thudding boots filled the warehouse, making her easy to track. She was moving fast. Her steps echoed and popped, while Davey's were barely more than an exhale of air. At the end of the aisle, he caught a flash of her before she darted around another packed shelf and disappeared from view.

Firming his lips, Davey quickened his pace.

She wasn't wearing that tiny red dress from earlier, but the white tank top and skin tight jeans that she'd changed into were almost as mouth watering. Not that he cared about that sort of thing, because he didn't. It was just information that passed through his mind.

By the time Davey rounded the end of the aisle and Mia came into view again, she was halfway to the exit. Was it his imagination or had she been jogging? Her blonde hair bounced and brushed at her shoulders as her legs ate up the ground. Without meaning to, Davey's eyes dropped to that ass of hers and noted how it swayed with her movement.

Gritting his teeth, Davey forced his eyes back up where they belonged and picked up to a jog. Damn those long legs of hers and his need to cruise along the aisle and play it cool.

Thankfully a light jog from him was all it took to close the distance. By the time Mia slammed out into the evening air, Davey was right behind her.

"Whoa, Mia." Davey tugged on her arm and brought her swinging around. "You can't run off on me like that."

"What are you doing here Davey?" The blonde wrenched her arm from his grip and kept right on walking. "I thought you didn't do babysitting work."

Shaking the tingle from his hand, Davey decided to ignore that last little jab, as it was maybe somewhat deserved. Coming up alongside her, he sucked in a breath and tried to steady himself. He had to remember not to touch her, she obviously didn't like it.

"Let me carry that for you," he deflected and nodded towards her bag. It looked pretty heavy with all the stuff inside clunking together.

"I don't need your help," Mia countered as her chocolate-brown eyes slid over to lock with his. "What I'm doing is none of your business."

"Actually it's completely my business," Davey corrected. "I'm your bodyguard now."

Mia's head jerked, and for a moment she stopped walking altogether.

Davey came to a stop too and rubbed a rough hand over the back of his neck. His mind was busily reaching for something else to say, but as usual he was drawing a blank. Was she pissed? Would she refuse him? At this rate, he'd never get a chance at that strike team.

Giving her head a shake suddenly, Mia tipped her chin up and started walking again.

Like a dog, Davey followed.

"I thought you didn't do bodyguard work," Mia stated flatly, refusing to look over at him.

"I misinterpreted my assignment," Davey offered. *Sort of.*

"Misinterpreted?" Mia scoffed. "I don't want to be protected by someone who doesn't want the job."

"I want the job," he said. *Did he?*

Coming to a stop once more, Mia let loose a long sigh. Her pretty face tipped up towards the darkening sky and for a moment she closed her eyes. Davey came to a stand still in front of her this time and let his eyes cruise her face. His heart skipped in his chest and his tongue snuck out to wet his lips.

"Mia." Davey cleared his throat and took a purposeful step back. Absently he rubbed the heel of his hand over his chest.

"I don't know if I can trust you to do a good job," Mia said finally.

Her head tipped forward again and she opened her eyes. Instead of looking at him though, she stared off in the distance.

They were surrounded by green trees and tall buildings. There were a few people walking along one of the sidewalks about a hundred yards away. It was the middle of summer, so the air still held heat even as the sun gave up its last rays in the west.

Davey took stock of all these details before settling his gaze back on Mia. Nobody was close enough to be a threat to them.

"I can do the job," he insisted. "It won't be like last time."

"Davey, you ditch without warning," she countered. "I need someone who will take this seriously. Believe it or not, I don't want to go back out there. I *have* to."

Composing his features, Davey took a step closer to her and stared down into her questioning eyes. She was worried about his ability to do the job and she had every right. He'd screwed up last time. He let the girls go to the farmhouse and shower when he should've had them locked down in the Jeep, waiting in case the op went south.

It was Davey's fault that asshole had a chance at Mia. It was Davey's fault that Cass got shot. It didn't matter that he'd been knocked out with a hit from behind at the time. It didn't matter that Cass had run from the Jeep and caused him to follow. All that mess was on him.

Admittedly, his head hadn't been in the game all those months ago. He'd been torn up about his brother first, and then torn up further about Jameson and his lack of involvement in Ryder's death. He'd been too soft with Mia, letting her pretty face and pouty lips dictate what the girls did and where they went.

But things would be different this time. *He* was different, changed, ready to be a soldier again.

"I swear to you, I am the best man for this job," Davey assured her, despite his own misgivings. "No one will lay a hand on you. Hell, they won't get within six feet… starting now. I'll be your shadow every second, day and night, you'll see."

"Starting… what?" Mia's face screwed up. "You're going to follow me around… now? No, I don't think so. We don't leave for another few days."

"Consider it a trial," Davey offered, his heartbeat accelerating. Would she refuse? Demand another guard?

"Look, I know you can do a good job guarding me." Mia's gaze bounced from his eyes to the rifle on his back and then to the fists at his sides. "What happened before with Cass and… and that… man."

Sucking in a ragged breath, Mia swallowed before continuing. "It wasn't your fault. If Cass hadn't jumped out, then we would've been out of there in time. Your skills are not the issue."

Puzzled, Davey held back about a dozen retorts and

blinked at her. Mia's cheeks tinged pink. For a moment, she glanced away and nibbled at her lip.

"After everything happened, you just... left. You didn't even say goodbye. You ditched." Mia shifted the strap on her shoulder and let her eyes dart to his face briefly, then away.

"The op was over," Davey supplied. *I failed*. "I barely got you back to the Wall. That was it, my job was done."

Huffing a breath, Mia's brow furrowed. "It was all work for you, that's what you're saying?"

"Ummm..." Davey was at a loss. His mouth parted slightly as confusion fogged his brain.

"You know what?" Mia rolled her shoulders and straightened her spine before looking him dead in the eye. "That's great. That's exactly what I need. You keep me safe and I'll do my job for Commander Linfield and that will be it."

Relief flooded him. Davey's chest eased and the first genuine smile he'd had in a very long time took over his face. He was in.

Phase 1 of his master plan was under way, which brought him that much closer to his end goal. Running a team, risking his life, the path to Valhalla lay before him once more.

A warrior's death. It was what his brother had and it's what Davey craved. The only thing he craved.

His eyes drifted over Mia now as disappointment rippled her features. At least, he could've sworn that's what it was, but the emotion was there and gone before he knew it. Taking its place was her signature megawatt smile, the one that melted every man within a three block radius.

Sticking her hand out between them, Mia offered him a shake. After a moment's hesitation, he took her slender palm in his rough one. The squeeze she gave him was surprisingly strong and he even noted a callus or two. Farm work. Right, he'd forgot about that part.

"See you in three days," she said.

Retracting her hand, Mia ran it through her tussle of silky blonde locks before turning away from him.

"Wait… what?" Davey stammered, a little taken aback at her dismissal.

He intended to start shadowing her now. That meant no more boyfriend visits, or sneaking supplies in secret, or basically anything where Davey didn't have a say.

Controlling? Maybe.

Necessary? In his mind… absolutely.

She needed protection and he wanted practice.

"I don't need you until we leave the Wall," Mia threw the words over her shoulder as she continued to stride away. "This is just business remember? I still have a few days of personal life ahead of me, and I intend to use them."

Stomach sinking, Davey watched her long legs depart. He couldn't really argue with what she'd said, even though his instinct was to chase after her and do just that. She was right, after all, she didn't technically need protection here. She was safe, and so he was unnecessary to her.

Unnecessary.

The word had his jaw snapping shut and his cheeks heating, though he didn't know why.

Sucking in a breath he dismissed his flash reaction. Oh well, he told himself. She could spend the next seventy-two hours running around with her harem of boyfriends. Davey didn't care. Nope. It didn't bother him in the least.

Running both hands through his freshly cut hair, Davey

held back a growl of frustration. He'd be the one calling the shots soon enough, he reminded himself.

But even so, he stayed standing exactly where he was, staring after the leggy blonde until she disappeared around the far corner of a building.

CHAPTER EIGHT_
MIA

"Does he make you uncomfortable?" Jameson lifted a heavy brow as he appraised Mia.

They were positioned directly across from each other. He was chopping red and yellow bell peppers on the kitchen counter while Mia perched on a tall stool just opposite him.

They were in his and Cass's new apartment, having one of the last "family" dinners that they'd share for awhile.

Behind her, Mia's best friend was propped up among half a dozen pillows on the living room sofa. Cass had been reading quietly for the past twenty minutes while Mia complained to Jameson about her recent adventure in the warehouse.

Seed canisters. Sebastian. Davey.

Of course she left out the part about her fainting in Sebastian's arms and having a memory. Whoops. Was that important?

A twinge of guilt curled itself in Mia's belly at the thought of keeping things from her best friend, but she just wasn't ready to confess. Everything she was remembering was just too awful.

Waving a dismissive hand, Mia finally answered Jameson's question.

"No, not like that," she said.

There was bad uncomfortable and good uncomfortable and she knew Jameson meant the former.

Although Jameson appeared to miss the distinction, Cass latched onto it the way only a best friend could. Shifting in her position on the couch Cass grumbled something about Davey being the new Mr. Hot Stuff.

Refusing to turn around, Mia rolled her eyes.

"What was that?" Jameson's eyes narrowed at Cass and he paused in his chopping.

"Oh nothing," Cass purred.

Mia could feel her best friend's eyes boring into the back of her skull and it was an effort to hide her own smile. Just because she'd teased Cass mercilessly about her own Mr. Hot Stuff (Jameson) for *months* didn't mean Cass got a free pass to return the favor. Mia was absolutely not going to react.

Besides, there was nothing going on between her and Davey. *Nothing.*

"Do you want me to get someone else to be your guard?" Jameson returned his attention to Mia. "I just thought we could trust him. You know… after everything that happened before, I figured he could be left alone with you and not try anything."

Huffing an indignant breath, Mia brushed aside a lock of wayward hair.

"Yes, no danger of sexual advances from Davey," she stated. "He's all business."

And why did that fact bother her? It's not like she had any actual experience in that particular department.

Sure, she was a shameless flirt, but ever since she could remember (which wasn't all that long actually) Mia hadn't followed through on any of it. She'd get close, like lots of kissing and maybe some over the clothes touching, but no man had ever made her want to go beyond that. So she hadn't.

But then there was Davey... This whole butterfly zinging around in her belly thing was new and directly linked to the brooding blue-eyed soldier. He was... well, she couldn't exactly put a name to what Davey was. But one thing was for certain, he wasn't interested in her the way she was in him.

Drumming her fingers on the white corian countertop, Mia let loose an audible sigh.

"The only other guys I would trust around you without question are Liam and Cole, but they're staying put," Jameson commented, as he continued his chopping. "Hannah is further along in her pregnancy now and they've both agreed to stay close."

"It's fine." Mia waved a hand absently. "Davey's fine. He'll do a good job."

"Damn straight he'll do a good job." Jameson snapped the knife down on the counter and bent to fetch a frying pan from a nearby cupboard. "Or I'll kick his ass."

"I'm sorry..." Cass's voice lifted from the couch. "But didn't the guy try to kill you the last time you saw him?"

"No." Jameson righted himself and popped the pan on the oven before switching on a burner. "Last time he was all good. It was the time before *that* when he tried to kill me."

Glancing over her shoulder now, Mia watched Cass struggle to sit up. Her best friend's brown curls tumbled over her shoulders as Cass's face screwed up in pain. Whenever she moved that damn right leg of hers too quickly, it still hurt.

Frowning, it was all Mia could do not rush over and help, but Cass was proud and pretty damn grumpy about her leg injury. Mia wanted to coddle her and fetch food and pain medication and crutches, but she nibbled on her lower lip instead. Rushing to Cass now would only serve to tick her best friend off and make Jameson even more guilty about leaving. And that's not how any of them wanted to spend these last few days.

Thankfully, Eli swept into the room at just the right moment and hoisted his little sister off the couch with one arm. He was chomping on a bright-green apple, wearing nothing but a white tank top, blue gym shorts and an incredible smile.

"I'll go with you," he volunteered, apparently he'd been listening the entire time. "I can guard Mia's body, no problem."

Shooting Mia that dazzling smile of his, the six-foot three-inch bronze god strolled over to the kitchen counter, leaving his sister to pace slowly behind him.

"No offense bro," Jameson began. "But you don't know your ass from your elbow these days, not to mention that you already *have* a body to guard. Your sister is your priority while I'm gone."

"Oh, so you take the hot one and I'm left with my blood relative? That's bullshit, Garrett and you know it." Eli leaned an elbow on the counter a few feet away from Mia, and took another bite of his apple.

Mia couldn't help but laugh. Eli was beyond charming, with boyish good looks and sparkly hazel eyes. The only problem was... no butterflies. Mia had no butterflies at all when she looked at Eli. Only Davey had the power to do that, apparently.

The sudden realization had Mia's lips pouting and her shoulders slumping. Why was it that the first guy that made her feel something, didn't feel anything for her?

"I know sweet cheeks." Eli reached out with his finger and tapped the end of Mia's nose playfully. "I'm bummed too."

"Enough," Cass announced, coming up behind them. "My friend is off limits. We've had this talk."

Straightening, Eli barked out a laugh.

"Hypocrite much?" He teased. "From what you two told me, Garrett was my friend first."

"Let's not start that again," Jameson intervened and jerked a thumb over his shoulder into the kitchen. "Somebody needs to get in here and help me or I'm going to burn the spaghetti."

"How can you burn spaghetti?" Eli shook his head ruefully, as he made his way into the kitchen.

With a sigh, Cass crept up behind Mia and wrapped her in a tight hug. Smiling, Mia leaned into her friend's embrace. She would miss this. She would miss this so much.

Chuckling now, Cass whispered in Mia's ear.

"You better hope *your* Mr. Hot Stuff can cook," she commented. "Because if you have to eat Jameson's food for the next three months, then you just might starve."

"Davey is not my Mr. Hot Stuff," Mia hissed, but she didn't push her friend away. "So you can just drop it."

"Oh really?" Cass pulled back slightly and angled her head in an attempt to peer into Mia's face. "You sure about that? You were awfully sad after he left the last time."

"I was not," Mia frowned. *Was she?*

"Oh shit!" Eli called out.

All eyes shot to him as he the large pot of water he'd been carrying slipped from his grasp.

Holding her breath, Mia watched as the pot impacted the tile floor and water sprayed everywhere.

"Oops." Eli stared down at the mess he'd created. "At least it wasn't boiling water."

Groaning, Cass immediately released Mia from their hug.

"Are you serious right now?" Jameson's eyebrows hit his hairline.

Grabbing a bunch of hand towels off the kitchen counter, he threw them hard at Eli.

Instead of catching them, Eli ducked.

"It's like nothing has even changed," Cass grumbled, before making her way around the kitchen counter and entering the fray.

The guys were laughing now, and shouting at each other. A few dish rags were launched back and forth. Jameson slipped in the water and almost went down. Eli cackled. The mood was friendly, but it was also loud. Very loud.

Sucking in a sharp breath, Mia froze.

Another memory was coming.

She could feel it swirling in the back of her mind. Voices. So loud.

Standing abruptly from her stool, Mia turned quickly and fled the room. She pushed her way through the living room and entered a narrow hall. Ducking into the guest bathroom, she sucked in a breath and shut the door.

She didn't even have time to flip the lock.

The memory was on her already, causing her eyes to roll

into the back of her head and her body to collapse down to the cold tile floor.

"Just be very careful, okay Marie?" Her mother's blue eyes were pleading. "We can't have an accident."

"Yes, Mama." Nodding her head, Marie kept stirring the bowl slowly.

Usually, the cook and her staff were the only people allowed in their kitchen, but today was special. It was Marie's sixth birthday and she'd always wanted to bake her own cake. Mama said it would be okay as long as they made it while Daddy was still at work.

Blinking down at the pristine marble countertop, Marie gripped the porcelain bowl in one hand and the wooden spoon in the other. She looked forward to putting on the sprinkles the most, but she knew that step came last.

"Alright my love, the eggs are next," her mother commented and reached for the carton.

"May I crack them?" Marie's face burst with hopefulness. What fun it would be to do that part.

Pursing her lips, Mama brushed her perfectly manicured hands down the front of her pale-green dress. It had taken hours in the store to pick just the right one because it matched Marie's own dress. They were going to have a garden party later, with all of Marie's friends from school and their parents too.

There would be a white pony to ride and a catered dinner. That was a special kind of dinner where food was brought from somewhere else instead of made from the kitchen.

Marie's gaze followed her mother's hands as they left her body to clasp together tightly in front of her. Mama's high heels were on and her hair was brushed just right, so blonde and pretty and cut just beneath her jawline. Marie thought Mama was the most beautiful woman in the whole world, even Daddy said so.

When Marie grew up, she wanted to be just like her mama.

"Oh okay." Mama blew out a short breath and then smiled. "Just make sure to hold them over the bowl and not spill any of the yolk."

"I know how," Marie lied.

She didn't. She'd never done it, but she'd seen it done before... on television.

Plucking one egg from Mama's hand, Marie brought it to the edge of the bowl and tapped gently. Nothing happened.

"A little harder," Mama coaxed. "But not too..."

Nodding, Marie slammed the egg down on the edge of the bowl, harder this time. Sure enough, the egg split. But the impact to the bowl was too much, causing it to tip over. Suddenly there was egg yolk and yellow cake batter spilling everywhere.

"Oh no!" Marie cried and jumped back.

The bowl tumbled forward and rolled off the kitchen counter where it landed with a loud crack on the marble flooring. The porcelain bowl shattered into what seemed like a million pieces as Mama let out a cry of her own.

Tears pooled in Marie's eyes. She'd ruined everything. She'd made such a mess.

"It's okay." Mama lunged for a kitchen towel on the countertop. "We'll get this cleaned up quick as anything."

"Hello!" A voice rang out from the foyer as the front door slammed shut. "Rachel?! Marie?! I'm home early."

Marie's heart plummeted to her toes as she looked at her mother.

Daddy was home.

"Hello! Rachel?!" Daddy's voice rose again, this time with an impatient edge to it.

Mama's eyes flew wide as she glanced between Marie and the kitchen doorway. He was coming. She better answer him quick. You didn't make Daddy wait. Ever.

"Go," Mama hissed and pointed to the rear entrance to the kitchen. "Go now, Marie."

It was the servant's entrance. It led past a small bathroom and through a narrow hallway before dumping you outside.

"But. But." Marie's lip quivered as her Daddy shouted again. Closer.

"Go!" Mama hissed before raising her voice to answer Daddy. "I'm in the kitchen, darling! I've been a bit clumsy!"

"Clumsy?!" Daddy's voice gritted in Marie's ears. She could hear his footsteps now, hurrying, stomping. "What did you break this time?"

Sucking in a breath, Marie turned on her heels and ran. She darted through the massive kitchen with its shiny clean refrigerator and spotless cupboards before pushing through the rear door. Stopping just on the other side, she was careful to shut it slowly behind her, so as not to make a sound.

That's when her father entered the kitchen.

"What in the hell?" His voice lowered. "We have company coming in less than two hours and you've already made a mess of everything! You're the reason I have to pay so much for a kitchen staff in the first place. I thought I told you to stay out of here."

"You did," Mama pleaded. "I'm sorry Ed. I don't know what I was thinking. I wanted to bake a cake for Marie..."

Crack.

That's when the first hit happened.

The sound of her father hitting her mother made Marie jump in place. Her tummy twisted and her whole body clenched. Mama cried out, but not too loudly, she knew better.

"Don't backtalk me," her father seethed. "I can't believe this. I

work too hard to be burdened with such a clumsy, useless wife. I'm a United States Senator, for God's sake. I deserve better than you Rachel, and so does Marie."

Another hit.

A whimper from Mama.

Squeezing her eyes shut, Marie winced. Her little hands flew to her cheeks and then up to cover her ears. This would go on for longer, she knew... and it was all her fault.

"I'm sorry, Mama," she whispered. "I'm so sorry. I'm sorry."

CHAPTER NINE_

DAVEY

DAVEY'S KNEE BOUNCED BENEATH HIS PALM. BLOWING OUT A breath, he tried to relax. He'd been perched on the edge of the blue couch for forty-five minutes already. It was nearing dawn on departure day and like always, he was early. Early and ready.

Glancing around the small living room of the one-bedroom apartment, Davey took stock. Everything was clean and in its place. There was no kitchen to contend with so that made things easy, plus he'd only been staying here for a few days.

Down the narrow hall, his single bathroom had been scrubbed clean. Across from it, the bedroom had been emptied. His bed was made with the blankets it had come with, and his closet was empty, save for a few vacant hangers left on the short rod. Everything Davey owned was either tucked neatly in his rucksack at his feet, or strapped to his person.

Rolling his shoulders, Davey's eyes danced from the rifle lying on the coffee table in front of him to the clock on the wall. It was analog, not digital and it was almost time to go. The convoy was scheduled to leave at 0600.

Screw it, Davey thought suddenly, it was better to be early than on time. Pushing up to standing, he retrieved his rucksack and put it on. Next came his rifle. His 1911 was already in its holster on his thigh and the three knives Liam had crafted for him were concealed in various other places.

Striding to the door, Davey hesitated a moment with his hand on the silver knob. This was Jameson's old apartment and directly across from him was where Mia lived. He knew this because he'd watched her come and go over the past three days.

He'd seen her come home extra late last night and he'd noted that she hadn't returned home at all the night before. When she *did* stumble home around nine in the morning, she'd been wearing the same tight jeans and tiny tank top that she'd had on in the warehouse.

Her hair had been neatly brushed and her face had looked fresh though. Davey figured that meant she'd showered at the guy's place where she'd spent the night, although he couldn't be certain. And because of that uncertainty he'd spent all of yesterday holding himself back from making inquiries as to exactly which guy she'd been sleeping with.

Because it wasn't his business… yet. And knowing that information would lead him nowhere that he needed to go.

But in about five minutes, that was all going to change.

There was no way in hell that Davey was going to spend the next three months of his life watching Mia hook up with random guys. His babysitting duties did not extend to listening in during that shit and he couldn't leave her alone for a single second, so they'd have to compromise and do things Davey's way. He'd been celibate himself for the past six freaking years, he figured she could handle a couple of months.

With a shake of his head, Davey twisted the handle on the front door and eased out into the hallway. A quick look around showed him an empty corridor with a long line of closed doors and impenetrable silence.

All clear.

Davey exhaled.

Crossing to door 401, Davey held up a balled fist and rapped two of his knuckles against the white painted wood. There was no response. No shuffling of feet, no murmuring, no nothing.

Firming his lips, Davey knocked again. Harder.

This time, after the count of five, a female voice could be heard from a distance. He couldn't make out the words she was saying, but before long the door swung open.

Mia stood on the threshold and gave him one of her brilliant smiles. Davey's mouth dropped as his eyes did the same, cruising over her pink lace blouse and the shortest pair of jean shorts that maybe he'd ever seen.

"You're going to wear that?" He asked, ignoring the instant spike in his blood pressure.

Mia's brown eyes narrowed as she angled her face up to take him in.

She kept one hand on the door and slowly, silently, tilted her head to the side. Her manicured fingernails tapped her displeasure against the wood of the door. The sound sent a strange tickle running up Davey's spine.

"That came out wrong," Davey blurted, but he was too late.

The door swung shut in his face with a slam. She was pissed.

Biting back a groan, Davey rolled his shoulders and tried again.

Knock. Knock. His fist rapped against the door.

"That came out wrong!" He lifted his voice so she could hear him.

Without a word, Mia opened the door again. This time, Davey kept his eyes locked on her face. Even so, his pulse quickened, thrumming uncomfortably in his neck.

"Are you ready?" He asked.

"Yes, I am," Mia answered sweetly and gestured to five bags strewn on the floor behind her. "It's going to be a long hot drive and Jameson told me there isn't air conditioning in the car. That's why I'm wearing shorts. I did pack pants."

Nodding slowly, Davey firmed his lips and tried like hell not to say what was running through his head.

Mia frowned at him. He lost the battle against himself.

"It would be a lot easier to guard you if you didn't look so..." Davey trailed off.

"So....?" Mia prompted, cocking her hip the way most women do when they're getting ready to tell you what an asshole you are.

Sexy. Attractive. Good enough to eat.

"So feminine." Davey's brain finally settled on an acceptable word. "I was hoping you'd dress like a soldier. You know... try to blend in."

"I don't have a uniform," Mia supplied and crossed her arms over her chest.

Don't look at her chest. Don't look at her chest.

Damn it.

Exhaling, Davey ran a palm over the back of his neck.

They were going to be late. If she'd of just accepted his offer to start shadowing her three days ago, then they would've been able to avoid this entire situation. He would've gotten her a uniform and they could've discussed the strategies he wanted to implement to help keep her safe.

But none of that thad happened and at this rate, he was going to have to rummage through his own rucksack and at least outfit her in a long sleeve shirt. He definitely didn't have pants that would fit her, but if she changed into her own pair of jeans then that would probably suffice. For now.

"Can you help me with my bags?" Mia asked. "I don't want to be late. We can figure out the uniform thing when we get there."

Davey's eyebrows raised. He had a sixty pound ruck on his back and a rifle to manage already. Mia had five bags filled with who knew what... strike that, that were definitely stuffed with clothes, and probably makeup and shoes too.

With a sigh, Davey stepped into her apartment and forced her to retreat. The door swung shut at his back and his eyes darted around the small living room. It was a mirror image to his own apartment, except he knew that it boasted an additional two bedrooms down the hall to his right.

Sitting at a wooden table in the corner, was a pixie-sized redhead that appeared to be just a few years older than Mia. At his entrance, the woman glanced up at him and paused in her note taking. There were open text books strewn all around her, along with a few pencils and a stack of lined paper.

"Soldier *Wells*," Mia emphasized his last name and gestured to her roommate. "This is Shelby. Shelby, this is my escort for the next few months."

"Ah, a male escort." Shelby gave him a once over before huffing a laugh and returning to her writing. "Good luck."

Davey's mouth dropped as Mia rolled her eyes.

"Shelby is a doctor," Mia explained. "Not the kind of doctor that cuts you open, though. She's the kind that does science stuff. Research. She's really smart."

Bobbing her head in agreement, Shelby kept her focus on her writing. She flipped a few pages in one of the text books before brushing a lock of strawberry hair behind one ear.

"I could cut you open," she commented finally. "If the need should arise."

At this, Mia outright laughed.

Jaw snapping shut, Davey fought the flood of unexpected emotion this sassy redhead brought on. She reminded him of Flynn. Fuck.

And of course Flynn reminded him of his brother. Ryder had a little crush on the nurse that had saved him, which meant she'd been off limits to Davey and that had been fine back then. At the time, he'd only been interested in one thing anyway. Ryder's survival. Ryder's recovery.

But now, Ryder was gone. He'd lost his life protecting Flynn in the stone house. They'd died together.

The sharp pang Davey felt stabbing at his chest was replaced by a flash of guilt. He hadn't thought about his brother in twenty-four hours. He was only focused on Mia. She did that to him, he recalled, she took all of his focus.

Firming his lips, Davey inhaled slowly through his nose and dismissed the memories. He needed to get back to the business at hand.

"Unpack a pair of pants and put them on," he instructed Mia. "I'll grab one of my shirts for you, unless you have a long sleeve black one."

"A black shirt?" Mia looked disgusted. "It's going to be a hundred degrees today."

"Fine." Davey snorted as he removed his rifle and leaned it carefully in the corner. His rucksack came next. "What about Army-green? Or brown?"

Groaning, Mia dropped to a crouch and began rummaging through one of her bags. Davey lowered onto his haunches beside her and opened his ruck. He kept his shirts rolled up tight and off to one side, so he was able to grab one quickly.

Pushing up to standing, he tossed the camouflage shirt at her. Mia looked up at him and frowned as it fluttered down to cover her busy hands. She was in the process of ripping out dresses and skirts and shorts and pants. Apparently her organization system wasn't quite as tidy as his.

From his position above her, Davey could see right down her sorry excuse for a shirt. Which was bad. He *knew* that he should be averting his eyes right about now, but he suddenly found that he was unable. His belly clenched and his chest expanded.

He was only a man after all and Mia was... well, exceptionally pretty. And that was all the more reason for her to put on his shirt. If *he* couldn't stop looking, then the two hundred other soldiers they would be traveling with wouldn't be able to stop either.

But before he could say anything, the leggy blonde was snatching at his shirt with one hand and pulling out a pair of her own jeans with the other.

"This is ridiculous," she stated before turning to disappear down the hall. "I'll be hidden in the car the whole time."

Shelby began to hum to herself from just a few feet away.

Davey's jaw ticked. Firstly, they wouldn't be riding in a damn car, they'd be in an armored Humvee packed to the brim with eight bodies (Jameson's oversized ass included). Secondly, they'd be traveling in a convoy containing no less than seven troop transport trucks, a fuel transport vehicle, two supply vehicles, and three armored Jeeps.

The going would be slow. The going would be uncomfortable.

Jameson had estimated that the trip would take two full days of travel, which meant they'd have to camp somewhere overnight at least once. Therefore, there would definitely be times when Mia would need to exit the vehicle. And what happened if they came under attack? What if they had to abandon the vehicle and run?

He couldn't let her stand out like a fucking lingerie model, no matter how annoying she might find that to be. His job was to protect her, to keep her safe and he knew the easiest way to do that was to keep her out of sight.

He didn't want her to get hurt. He didn't want to wake up lying face down in the dirt while some demented fucker tried to rape her just inches away from him. He didn't want to live that experience ever again.

But these were things that Mia didn't think about. They didn't cross her mind. And a part of Davey didn't want them to.

She was naive and silly in ways that reminded him so much of his baby brother. He didn't want to crush that. In fact, he didn't want to *see* it crushed, at least not any further than it already had been by her last trip outside the Wall. Mia deserved to be pretty and flirty and sweet. She deserved to stay that way.

"I'm waiting," Davey called finally. His boot tapped out an impatient beat against the floor.

Dropping his eyes to the mess of clothes at his feet, he fought back a groan. Did any one person need such a variety of clothing? Talk about ridiculous.

You just said you wanted her to stay ridiculous.

Great. Now he was talking to himself.

"Alright!" Mia announced and charged back into the room. "I hope you're happy."

Davey's throat went dry. How was it possible that she looked even better in his oversized cammie shirt and a pair of skinny jeans? He didn't know.

Seeming not to notice, Mia dropped to her bag and began hurriedly stuffing her clothes back inside of it. Davey blinked down at her a moment before giving his head a shake to clear it. He'd have Jameson get a helmet for her, he told himself, covering up her silky blonde hair should help. At least… he hoped like hell that it would help because there was apparently no hiding her body.

Straightening Mia, brushed at her clothes and looped one of her bags over her shoulder.

"Well?" She huffed a breath. "Help me with these. You're making us late."

"*I'm* making us late? Is that what you're going to tell my boss?" Davey asked sarcastically before bending to grab his own rucksack from the ground.

"Oh I don't need to tell her, she already knows," Mia quipped and grabbed a second bag.

"She?" Davey reached for the remaining three bags and looped them over his shoulders. His rifle would come last, so he could get to it first.

"Yeah, me silly." Mia flashed him a teasing smile. "I'm your boss for the next three months or so. Am I right?"

Without waiting for an answer, the blonde shoved past Davey and opened the door to her apartment. She was out in the hallway before Davey even had a chance to swallow.

So not right, he thought, before striding after her.

CHAPTER TEN_

MIA

BLOWING OUT A BREATH, MIA ADJUSTED ONE OF HER HEAVY bags and held back a groan. It was just past six in the morning and it was already hot. The sun's rays were reaching up from the eastern mountains and she swore she could feel the humidity hugging her.

Dropping her eyes to the thick cotton shirt now covering her body, Mia frowned. The long sleeved shirt was going to make this whole close quarters travel thing a heck of a lot more uncomfortable.

Not to mention that it smelled like him. Each time she shifted or inhaled too deeply, Davey's scent crawled all over her body.

Firming her lips, Mia was determined not to be swayed by the butterflies that flitted about in her belly. Davey was striding along just behind her now. She could hear the confident fall of his boots combined with the controlled puff of his breathing.

It was like the three bags she'd left for him had no affect. And that particular fact was a bit maddening to be honest, seeing as how the two bags she was currently packing had her muscles aching.

Up ahead, a long line of military vehicles was strung out along the base of the shining silver perimeter wall. Soldiers (all in uniform, of course) were milling around the vehicles, checking this, carrying that, or just plain standing around in groups, talking.

Mia could hear their male voices like the constant rumble of a motor. Tipping her chin up, she scanned the mass of them, searching for one figure in particular. She was looking for Jameson, and he wasn't that hard to spot, being such a big guy and all.

"Veer to your right," Davey's voice sounded from behind her. "Third vehicle from the front. We need to check in with Officer Jameson and see about getting you some cover."

Throwing a look over her shoulder, Mia lifted an eyebrow. "Cover?"

"Sorry. A helmet," Davey explained, then tipped his head in the direction he wanted her to go.

Returning her gaze forward, Mia adjusted one of the straps on her shoulder again and kept walking. Her ankle high boots created a path through the dewey morning grass, and she noted how rich the soil was here. Would it be like this further south? Down in Utah?

Although she couldn't picture the area in her mind, Mia's brain produced certain feelings for her. Ones she couldn't attach to anything, but nevertheless knew to be true. Utah's climate was very different from here. She'd need to be careful about which crops she chose and when she planted them.

The palms of her hands ached suddenly. If she closed her eyes right now, Mia would be able to feel rich dark dirt running through her fingers. She'd be able to see it collecting beneath her fingernails, smell the fertilizer, hear a tractor buzzing nearby.

With a shake of her head, Mia fought the strangeness of her memories as they circled and creeped all around her. She couldn't afford to have any more fainting spells right now. She'd been lucky enough to shut herself in the bathroom at Cass's place before collapsing the last time.

No one had been the wiser when she'd finally emerged, shaken with the flashback of her childhood, and the remembrance of her real name. Marie.

She'd had dinner with Cass and Jameson and Eli like nothing had happened, and then opted to sleep in their spare bedroom overnight. She'd only felt a twinge of guilt the following morning when Cass had wrapped her in another tight hug and told her she was like the sister she'd never had.

Sisters confided in one another. Sisters didn't keep secrets. And Mia was holding onto a big one.

Holding her breath now, Mia pushed *that* secret away. In all honesty, she preferred being Mia to being Marie. In fact, she wished Marie never existed at all.

Lifting her head now, she focused on the reality in front of her. They were nearing the long line of military trucks and Jameson had spotted them. He was surrounded by a group of soldiers all vying for his attention, but he stood a few inches taller than all of them and picked up a hand to motion Mia closer.

With a relieved smile, Mia tucked an unruly hair behind one ear and then lifted her hand to wave.

Nodding his head at her, Jameson returned his focus to one of the many soldiers standing in front of him. He was running this whole "leave the Wall" operation and so was obviously busy giving orders.

Mia knew from their time together that she would be allowed to address him as Jameson, but that everyone else had to use *Officer* or *Sir*. And despite their familiarity she knew she needed to treat him with the utmost respect.

He couldn't show any weaknesses here and she couldn't reveal any. That's why Cass hadn't come to see him off. Their goodbyes had to be said at home, which was disappointing because that meant Mia didn't get a final send-off hug from her best friend.

Further down the line of vehicles, most of the men continued to talk amongst themselves, but in her periphery Mia could see their faces shifting in her direction. They were noticing her now and that act in itself had a certain energy to it.

In the not so distant past, she wouldn't have thought anything of it. Attention from men (whether she knew them or not) had never bothered her. In fact, she'd *liked* it when they stared. It made her feel good somewhere deep inside her soul, in a place that was always feeling so bad.

But after her last little venture outside the Wall, things for Mia had changed. Now her palms grew clammy and her throat pinched in a little. She couldn't help but think of the soldiers in Hermiston.

No, they hadn't been in camouflage uniforms like these, but she'd overheard Jameson and Cass talking about them later. The men from Hermiston had been soldiers of some kind, with tattooed forearms and an unknown purpose. But to Mia they'd simply appeared from the woods with their guns and their grabby hands, making demands and awakening an old knowledge inside of her.

A knowledge that reminded Mia men could be violent.

Very, very violent.

In many different kinds of ways.

Automatically, her footsteps slowed. Mia's gaze bounced away from Jameson, out over the crowd. Her hands reached up to adjust the straps of her two bags. Sucking her bottom lip between her teeth she bit down.

This was going to be okay, she coached herself. These were not "those" sort of men. Jameson would never have had her come along if that was the case.

From somewhere down the line, an appreciative whistle pierced the air. It was followed by a round of indulgent chuckling. Mia's tummy danced uncertainly and she came to a sudden halt. She'd had men whistle at her before. A whistle wasn't an attack. It was just a sound.

"Who the fuck was that?!" Jameson shouted the question suddenly, making everyone freeze.

Every mouth was silent. Mia's heart pounded in her chest.

"That one," Davey answered from just behind her, and his closeness flooded her with relief.

She'd forgotten he was here. She'd forgotten he'd keep her safe. The sound of her bags dropping to the ground came next. There was the rustling of material and then the solid thump of her luggage.

Turning around, Mia was just in time to see Davey tipping his chin at a group of men standing in front of a large vehicle parked further down the line. He'd already rid himself of everything he'd been hauling, everything but his rifle.

"Soldier Wells, if you could handle that problem." Jameson's eyes tracked to the spot indicated. "I want him out of my division… but not dead."

"Yes Sir," Davey bit out, before slinging his rifle over his shoulder and stomping off.

Mia gaped. Her mouth dropped a fraction and she watched him go. Davey's whole body moved like a predator. He was all sleek lines and shifting muscles and deliberate steps. His hands curled into fists at his sides. Soldiers parted for him before he even got near them.

One in particular shoved off a vehicle where he'd been leaning and held up both hands, palms out.

"Come on, I didn't mean anything by it," the guy was saying.

Davey didn't respond. He just kept right on coming.

"It was supposed to be funny," the guy said again, glancing around in hopes of some agreement. The soldiers on either side of him looked down and away.

Mia pursed her lips, feeling guilty all of a sudden. This whole thing seemed like an overreaction. The guy whistled at a pretty girl… it happened all the time. No harm, no foul. Right? It was unreasonable of her to feel afraid.

Picking up a hand, Davey stopped way too close to the soldier and lifted a finger to point directly in the guy's face.

"Get your shit. You're out," he announced.

"But…"

"Yes." Davey nodded, as his shoulders bunched beneath his shirt. "Just give me an excuse to enforce Officer Jameson's order."

Sucking in a breath, Mia flashed back to Hermiston. She saw Davey's fists covered in blood. She could hear what it sounded like each time he swung down on that stranger's face, until the man's head was flopping side to side and his body had gone limp. The look on Davey's face after it was over, the haunted vacancy in his eyes, was something she didn't want to see ever again.

Frowning, Mia dropped one of her bags to the ground and went to step forward. She would have to intervene. But before she could start marching away, a really big chest moved into her path, blocking not only her view, but the sun itself.

Huffing a breath, Mia looked up into the familiar face. Jameson grinned, a rare sight in front of so many of his soldiers.

"Mia," he said, and reached for the bag still looped over her left shoulder. "I'm so glad you could join us. Is this everything you need? I'll have some of my guys load your things."

"Um..." Mia tried to look around him, but Jameson shifted his weight in front of her.

His intent was clear, let Davey do his job. She gave up her bag.

"We'll be riding together in the vehicle just behind me, but I'll have your things put in one of the supply trucks closer to the rear of the convoy. Is there anything in here that you need to have right now?"

Running a hand back through her hair, Mia thought about his question. The seed canisters that she'd packed were dispersed evenly throughout her bags, cushioned by mounds of clothes. They should make the trip just fine, even while being jostled about in the back of some massive truck.

"I don't think so," she offered finally. "I mean, I didn't pack any snacks or anything. Should I have packed a snack?"

Pursing his lips, Jameson fought back a chuckle. She knew him well enough to recognize the gesture. Without answering her, he lifted his head and glanced at the group of men standing off to his left. Mia followed his gaze.

"Soldier Malik," he called. "Come meet Miss Jones, she's the civilian consultant Commander Linfield has traveling with us."

An athletic man ducked his head before breaking away from the crowd. He was in full uniform, complete with helmet and rifle, but he walked with an easy confidence that made you forget all that.

Mia's eyes fixated on his face where a youthful smile revealed perfectly straight white teeth. His dark eyes matched the smoothness of his skin and the chocolate-brown tint of his hair. He wasn't very tall, maybe five foot nine at the most, but his shoulders were wide and his hips trim. The man was good-looking, no doubt about that, and Mia had seen him before, in passing.

Coming to a stop in front of her, Malik held out a palm to shake. Mia couldn't help but smile and reach out a hand of her own. She could appreciate his beauty, even without the flit of internal butterflies.

"It's a pleasure to meet you, Miss Jones," Malik said, before ending their handshake and reaching down to collect more of her bags. "I believe I've seen you around. You work in the farm unit, is that right?"

Nodding, Mia exhaled a breath as her nerves from earlier began to settle.

"I do," she answered. "I run district thirteen, actually. Or I did before today."

"She still does," Jameson cut in, directing his words towards Malik. "This is a temporary assignment. District thirteen will be waiting for her when we return."

Glancing up at him, Mia's brow furrowed. She wasn't sure if Jameson was saying that to convince her, or himself. All she knew was that Commander Linfield had been very clear. She wasn't to mention her departure to any of her coworkers. He would handle all explanations after she left.

"Wonderful," Malik commented, then straightened. "Where do you want her bags Sir?"

"Second transpo from the rear." Jameson handed off the bag he'd taken from her earlier, before gesturing the soldier away.

Mia watched Malik go just as Davey materialized back at her side. Startled by his sudden appearance, Mia peered around him. The soldier he'd been sent to remove was nowhere in sight. With a quick glance down at his knuckles, Mia exhaled. They weren't all bloody and ripped the way they had been after he'd killed the man in Hermiston.

Stooping to grab his backpack, Davey unhooked his helmet from the side and held it out towards Jameson.

"You got one small enough for her?" He asked before coming up to standing and swinging his pack on his back.

"Oh." Jameson cocked his head. "Good point. I'll send a runner while we finish loading. I want to move out asap."

"What about a uniform?" Davey tucked his helmet under one arm. "She sort of sticks out."

"Hey guys, I'm right here," Mia reminded them. Fisting one hand on her hip she pointed at herself with the other. "You don't need to talk about me like I don't have a say, and I don't need a uniform to farm. If you can't protect me out there while wearing jeans, then I don't want to go at all."

Stepping close to Mia, Jameson wrapped a massive hand around her shoulder and gave her a friendly shake.

"You can wear whatever you want," he said reassuringly before glancing at Davey and adding, "within reason. But we can talk all that over more when we get there. For now, let's just get you loaded up in the truck so we can make a start. Sound good?"

Inhaling, Mia's chest expanded and she shot Davey a look. His pale-blue eyes were trained on Jameson, saying unreadable things. For a moment, she was unsure. He looked pissed. Should she back out now? Refuse to go altogether?

No. Mia blinked.

Commander Linfield had given her this assignment because he said the community really needed her. She couldn't let everyone down. And besides, she trusted Jameson. He was Cass's boyfriend and he'd never put Mia in that much danger. Right? They were close friends now, after all.

"Sounds good," Mia answered and plastered another fake smile on her face.

CHAPTER ELEVEN_

DAVEY

So not good. Davey's eyes widened as Jameson spewed some bullshit at Mia and walked her calmly towards the convoy. No, she could absolutely *not* wear whatever she wanted out there.

In fact, Jameson himself had lectured on this very subject not so many months ago; back when he was busy training a class of civilians on how to survive in the world on the other side of the wall.

Don't wear anything bright. Don't wear anything revealing. If you're a woman, try your best to look like a man. Baggy clothes. Dark colors. Short hair stuffed into a cap, or better yet, shave your hair the fuck off.

Blowing out a hot breath, Davey pursed his lips and scowled.

Clearly, Jameson was giving Mia some serious lip service in order to get her to comply. And for some reason, that pissed Davey off. His throat burned suddenly and the skin all over his body heated.

But it's not like he could call out his commanding officer,

especially in front of said officer's troops. That being said, Davey sure as shit wanted to. The guy was definitely not being honest with Mia about the risk she was taking in agreeing to this mission.

Rolling his shoulders, Davey slapped his helmet on his head and stalked after them. His job just got a whole hell of a lot harder.

The sun was getting higher in the sky now as morning kicked into full gear. Davey could smell the warmth with its first touch of humidity as he inhaled. Mia was just ahead of him, her skin-tight jeans attracting all kinds of attention.

Glaring at the soldiers standing all around him, Davey took stock. They were young, like him, ranging in their mid-twenties to early-thirties with a variety of backgrounds. The one thing that united them (Davey knew this from his previous discussion with Linfield) was experience in war. They'd all been in it, in one way or another, on one side or another, and were loyal to Linfield.

Davey's lip curled. Experienced or not, the idiots were all still staring at Mia. They were a pack of hungry lions and she was the gazelle. Sleek and tantalizing and completely oblivious.

Thankfully after the whistling incident, none of them dared voice their appreciation. When they were done with their gawking and noticed Davey trailing along behind her, most of them tucked tail like good little boys and got busy doing something else.

Grumbling unhappily, Davey came to a stop a few feet from the Humvee that they'd be riding in and watched Mia climb inside. She was all long legs and round ass for several seconds and it had Davey's gut churning uncomfortably, but then Jameson positioned his big body to block her from view and Davey exhaled.

"Not by a window," he called suddenly. "She's gotta sit in the middle."

Mia's sassy voice sounded from inside the cab, but Davey couldn't make out what exactly she was saying. Whatever it was, it had Jameson chuckling out loud, which was a rare slip for him.

Davey's brow furrowed then. He kept forgetting the two of them were friends.

At his back, activity was resuming. Men were returning to their assignments now that the spectacle had been removed from view. Davey shrugged his rifle off of his shoulder and sighed. This was going to be a long three months. He didn't like feeling so on edge… he didn't like *feeling* at all.

Stepping back from the vehicle, Jameson turned to Davey and closed the distance between them. With a sigh, the guy folded his arms over his broad chest and stared down at Davey. For a few silent moments they regarded one another.

Jameson's gaze was speculative. His head slowly tilted to one side in quiet appraisal before he lowered his voice and spoke.

"Let's just get her there in one piece, shall we?" Jameson said. "You can argue over clothing later."

"With all due respect," Davey whispered back. "Your lack of support undermines my mission."

Jameson's eyebrows hit his hairline and the little muscle in his jaw ticked. That last comment might have been a bit… insubordinate.

Clenching his own jaw, Davey refused to blink. He found he just didn't give a shit about respect at this point, although probably he should. If he truly wanted to lead a strike team, then he needed to impress Jameson with his ability to comply even when he disagreed. That used to be something he was really freaking good at. Now... not so much.

"Alright." Jameson's lips pressed into a firm line as he exhaled a moment through his nostrils. "I'm gonna let that last one slide, but only because I know you have Mia's best interest in mind. Understood?"

Suppressing his need to double down and say something stupid, Davey managed a nod and muttered, "Yes Sir."

"For the record, I do support you." Jameson gestured vaguely off to his right. "I've sent a runner for the helmet and a few extra-small uniforms, *which* we will explain to Mia that she *has* to wear *after* we get where we're going.

You forget that I live with her best friend and therefore I practically live with Mia, too. I know a few things about her personality and trust me, this isn't an argument we can afford to have right now."

"Yes Sir." Davey dipped his head more easily as the tightness that had cinched around his chest loosened.

"Not that it's any of your business, but I've been just a little bit busy the past few days," Jameson went on. "I haven't had the chance to get with you and go over our game plan for Mia's protection detail, but that doesn't mean it's not on my to-do list."

"Yes Sir." Davey nodded again as a few of the truck engines began to fire up.

"Now, load your ruck in the back and get in," Jameson instructed, jerking a thumb over his shoulder. "We've got a long ride ahead of us."

"Yes Sir." Davey gave the obligatory response for the millionth time and went to walk off.

Holding out a hand, Jameson stopped him.

The guy was freakishly tall, like Liam was, so even though Davey was six foot one, he had to tip his head up to look the guy in the face. Especially when Jameson took a step closer and leaned in.

"And Davey," Jameson hissed. "I'm fucking watching you. If you disrespect me again, you're walking all the way home by yourself. Got it?"

Clearing his throat, Davey stared Jameson dead in the eye.

"Got it," he answered. "Sir."

For the rest of the day, Davey kept his mouth shut and his eyes open. The view from his seat directly behind the driver was familiar. The towering trunks of trees, the rocky slide of mountains, the overgrowth of green plants that covered the shady floor.

Slowly but surely their massive convoy crept away from the Wall and into the wilderness.

For Davey it was a comfortable sort of alertness that overtook him. He'd hiked these woods more than once, and he'd driven through them before too, in his travels between here and the compound further south and east.

Wedged in the seat beside him, Mia spent the hours chattering away to a way too friendly Malik. The guy was sitting on her other side with yet another solider between him and the opposite rear passenger door. Jameson was riding shotgun and a soldier by the name of Patricks was gripping the wheel with white knuckles because this shit was real and serious.

Yes, they were heavily armed. Yes, there were a lot of them. But still, they were exposed and vulnerable.

The convoy was loud, clunky and slow. The woods were thick, the mountains high. A few well placed snipers could light them up like a Christmas tree, and before the first shot was fired, none of them would be the wiser.

But to look at good ole' Malik you'd think they were on a ride at some amusement park. He was all flashing white teeth and conversation. The constant rumble of the engine and the intermittent squawking from Jameson's radio did nothing to deter him, and it had Davey rolling his eyes on more than one occasion.

Mia, of course, was her usual flirtatious self, even though Malik had this annoying habit of referring to things that she more than likely couldn't remember.

It was back when the Patriots won the Super Bowl. What a game, right? Do you like football? So where are you from? How'd you learn so much about farming? I bet you were popular in high school. Were you a cheerleader? You look like a cheerleader.

Most of the time Mia would nod and smile, playing along even as Davey's gut churned and his jaw ticked with tension. He wanted to tell the guy to shut it, but he'd already been called out by Jameson once today so he needed to demonstrate some self-control. Of course that didn't stop his internal dialogue from making snarky answers.

Easy dumbass, she probably doesn't even know what the word cheerleader means. You can put your tongue back in your mouth now, you're drooling everywhere.

About a quarter of the way through their all-day excursion, Davey caught Jameson's eye in the rearview mirror.

"Bathroom break?" He asked.

It'd been four hours and Mia hadn't asked to stop once so Davey figured he better do it for her. The rest of them were used to holding it until they were authorized to go, but Mia wasn't a soldier.

For a split second, Davey wondered why she hadn't complained about hunger and thirst and using the bathroom the minute they started driving. He'd expected some prima donna pampering, but there had been none.

In the rearview mirror, Jameson's eyes darted from Davey over to Mia before he gave up a small nod. Reaching for the on-dash radio, Jameson held the mic up to his mouth and gave the order to stop.

"Short break," he barked. "Five minutes. Stay within two yards of your vehicles."

Beside him, Davey felt Mia let loose a long sigh. The sound had his chest expanding. He'd made the right call. She needed this. Plus with Jameson's order, Malik had finally shut his trap, so the ringing in Davey's ears began to subside.

Lifting his rifle from its position resting between his legs, Davey pointed it out his open window and swept the nearby hillside with the scope. He saw no movement, no reflective light that might be the sun dancing off the barrel of an enemy's weapon. When the truck lurched to a stop and the engine shut off, Davey sucked in a breath and listened.

Within a few seconds, bird song greeted him. It was faint, but there. His eyes tracked a hawk circling overhead, low and without concern. The past few years spent living in the middle of all this nature had Davey's inner voice tuned just right. He could almost feel the woods speaking to him, telling him when things were normal or when they were off.

And now (other than the convoy's own glaring presence) all seemed right with the world, relatively speaking.

"We're good," Davey announced and threw a look up to the front seat. "Permission to take her further than six feet?" He asked, figuring Mia could use a little privacy for her bathroom break.

"Granted," Jameson replied. "But everybody else stays here."

Popping open the heavy metal door, Davey jumped down from the Humvee and swept the tree line with his eyes once more. They'd been traveling along an old two lane highway for the past hour as it wound steadily down towards the valley floor.

On one side of the road was a steep mountain incline, and on the other was a pretty sharp drop off. Davey just so happened to be standing on the incline side of the vehicle now, but the thick trunks of trees were still about ten yards away. If Mia was going to do her business, he didn't want it to be with a hundred pairs of male eyes tracking her.

Before he could turn around and help her down though, Davey heard Mia jump to the asphalt just behind him. Her boots impacted the roadway and she let out a muted grunt. Up and down the line of vehicles, soldiers were doing the same. The engine noise may have died down, but it was quickly being replaced by the chatter of men.

Hurrying around him, Mia headed straight for the trees.

"Thank you," she said as she brushed past. "I was about to wet myself."

Frowning, Davey picked up his feet to follow her. His eyes slid to either side of him first, noting the push of soldiers keeping close to the convoy, then straight ahead. He scrutinized the line of trees and then guessed which of the large trunks Mia would pick. Turns out, he was right.

Darting around one wide trunk, Mia's slim body disappeared from sight. Davey did a quick turn and offered a middle finger salute to a few of the soldiers who couldn't help but stare after her. Like good little boys, they all ducked their heads.

Davey shook his own head slowly back and forth at them before turning and walking further into the woods.

Mia let out a squeak when Davey crept up beside her. Her back was leaned up against the trunk of the tree and her blue jeans were bunched around her ankles. Keeping her in his peripheral vision, he continued to scan the woods.

"Excuse me!" Mia hissed, clearly scandalized with his closeness. "What the hell are you doing?"

"I'm not looking," he huffed. "At least… not directly at you."

"You are too!" She countered.

He could hear her anger bubbling even though he couldn't see the expression on her face. It made him want to smile for whatever reason, but he didn't allow himself that luxury.

"I've got to keep you in my line of sight," he reasoned, maybe he could convince himself he wasn't a creeper? "If it makes you feel better, I'll go too."

Mia let out another scandalized squeak when Davey doubled down and actually unzipped. Out of the corner of his eye, he watched her turn her face decidedly away from him. Even still, she didn't make a move to get up, she had to go that bad.

And for a moment, Davey felt a twinge of guilt. He was invading her privacy no doubt about it. But what he'd said was true, he did need to be able to see her at all times, even when she was peeing.

His mistake from their time before was letting the girls run free, not containing them and directing their every movement. He wouldn't make the same mistake twice. If Mia was somewhere where she was exposed, then Davey would be within an arm's reach of her. Period. Propriety and good manners be damned.

Returning his focus to the woods, Davey relaxed his bladder and began to pee. After a split second, he heard Mia start going too. That's when he knew for sure that he'd made the right call in peeing along with her. She was vulnerable here, trying to use the bathroom with him close by, and so he'd made himself vulnerable to her as well.

Despite that fact, he could still drop his dick and grab his rifle in less than a second. In fact, he'd actually practiced this particular shot before. There wasn't much else for a bunch of former soldiers to do holed up in that compound, aside from invent ridiculous competitions.

Of course, Cookie had won that one. Well… Cookie always won when shooting was involved, but Davey had come in second.

When he was finished relieving himself, Davey zipped up his pants and put his hands back where they were most comfortable, on his weapon. A few seconds later, Mia pulled up her pants and picked her way over a few gnarled roots to get to him.

"Is this how it's going to be?" She demanded, her dark eyes scanning his face. "I can't even pee without you breathing on me? What if I needed to go… you know… *not* pee."

Firming his lips, Davey glanced between Mia's pretty face

and the surrounding woods. They were taking too long now and they needed to head back. He could hear the others starting to load up.

"As long as you're in an area that I feel is exposed," he answered. "Then I'm gonna be stuck to you like glue. I'm your shadow now, in every sense of the word. Even if it's *not* pee."

Crossing her arms over her chest, Mia nibbled on her bottom lip and looked away, off into the trees. Davey let his eyes drop to her mouth for a second and felt his stomach tighten. Fuck, he thought, he must have indigestion.

Shaking it off, Davey passed the heel of his hand over his chest briefly before reaching for her arm.

"Come on," he said quietly, wrapping his fingers around her and urging her to start walking. "We've got to get back."

With a sigh, Mia let him tug on her until she began to walk. Her head dropped in defeat and her shoulders sagged. Her posture had guilt flooding him. His mind flashed back to that time when he'd screwed up, to that time when she'd gotten hurt.

"I'm sorry," he offered. "But after last time, I can't chance it. I've got to stay this close, even if it upsets you."

"It doesn't upset me," Mia replied as they both walked towards the convoy. "I just… if all this is necessary, then maybe I made the wrong choice. If it's really this dangerous out here, then maybe I shouldn't have come."

Davey's hand lingered on her arm, guiding her unnecessarily, but she didn't shrug him off. He should pull away now, he thought. He should unwrap his palm and put it back on his damn rifle. But he didn't.

"No one will touch you," Davey said, then frowned at his own hand as it remained connected to her arm. "I might annoy the shit out of you for the next three months, but I will get you safely back to the Wall. I swear it."

Deliberately this time, Davey removed his hand and slowed his steps. He let Mia shift in front of him so he could block her body from the thick woods now hovering at their backs. In response to his words, the blonde simply nodded, not giving him a verbal reply as she continued to walk.

Their boots stepped back onto asphalt. Engines roared to life. Men were jumping back into their vehicles now, shouting to one another.

Staring at the back of her neck for a moment, Davey studied Mia's soft skin peeking up from the collar of his very own shirt.

"Why didn't you ask to stop earlier?" He asked suddenly. "You're not a soldier, you have to tell us when you're hungry and thirsty and might piss yourself."

Throwing him a puzzled look over her shoulder, Mia gave him a small shrug.

"You never tell the driver to stop," she offered. "You don't want to make him angry."

"Make him angry?" Davey's face scrunched up, trying to process her reply.

They'd traveled together before, on the way to Hermiston. Liam had been driving then and they'd all been packed like sardines in the back of that Jeep, much like they were now in the back of the Humvee. Had she ever asked Liam to stop? Had she ever mentioned having to pee?

Come to think of it, Davey didn't think so. Did Liam ever get angry? He'd been the driver. Was he pissed at the girls at any time?

No, Davey shook his head with certainty, definitely not.

The guy was intimidating for sure, but women were his soft spot. He never raised his voice or spoke a harsh word in their direction. If anything the guy was overly accommodating.

Reaching for her wrist, Davey brought Mia to a halt a foot from the still open door of the Humvee. He could see Malik and the others already inside, waiting and watching. He didn't care. Mia looked back at him, her brows raised in question.

"What happens when the driver gets angry?" He asked. "Why would you say that?"

Blinking, Mia huffed a nervous laugh. Her eyes danced all around, refusing to land on Davey. Something was off here. He could feel it in his gut.

"I don't know why I said that," Mia admitted finally. "Now we better go, right?"

Letting go of her wrist, Davey firmed his lips and nodded.

"Right," he answered, and followed her into the back of the truck.

CHAPTER TWELVE_
MIA

Perspiration beaded on her brow. Blowing out a long breath, Mia reached up for the millionth time and swiped it away. The sun was setting, the land had flattened out, and yet they were still rumbling along the never-ending highway.

Looking to her left, Mia stared past Davey and through his open window. The forest of the mountains, with its towering trees and lush greenery, had given way to a vast prairie. Tall grasses drifted in the slight breeze, all faded greens and golds mixed together.

On her other side, Malik had finally nodded off. His back was pressed firmly against the seat while his chin was tipped forward, almost touching his chest.

He was a nice guy, really he was, and Mia appreciated what he'd been trying to do by talking her ear off the entire drive. He was offering her a distraction, helping her not to focus on the emptiness all around them and the unease that came with it.

But now the inside of their truck was blessedly silent, save for the occasional crackling of Jameson's radio and the spinning of the large tires over pavement. Inhaling, Mia tried to take in as much of the evening breeze as she could, it was slightly cooler but painfully slight. The smell of vehicle exhaust still clouded her senses.

Reaching up to adjust the uncomfortable helmet on her head, Mia held back a whine. Her hair was plastered down with sweat, her tight jeans were stuck to her skin, and Davey's thick cotton shirt was practically suffocating the life out of her.

Frowning, Mia couldn't help but think that her shorts and airy blouse from earlier would've been perfect for this weather.

And right in that moment, she wanted so desperately to complain. She was hungry. She was tired. Her body was sticky from heat and aching from being forced to sit for hours on end. Her bladder was going to burst.

But despite all those things, there was no way that she was going to voice any complaints out loud, even after Davey's little lecture from hours ago.

Her past life (the one that kept coming back to haunt her now) had trained her well for silent suffering. You don't complain. You don't draw negative attention to yourself. Ever.

Sit.

Look pretty.

Smile.

Fake it.

Giggle… occasionally.

Accept whatever comes to you.

And whatever you do…

Don't. Tell.

"I think we're going to be stuck out here in the open," Jameson commented from the front seat.

Lifting her eyes, Mia watched him scrutinize a large paper map. He had unfolded it a few minutes earlier and had been frowning at the little blue and red lines ever since. The soldier beside Jameson continued to drive, offering no opinion.

Nibbling on her lip, Mia wondered if Cass's boyfriend was talking to himself or actually seeking advice.

"It has its good points and bad," Davey offered finally. "We can see someone coming from a mile away, even in the dark... Sir."

"But we have no cover," Jameson countered. "I planned on making it through this valley before nightfall, but with all the extra stops today, things took longer than I expected."

In the rearview mirror, Mia watched his brows draw together in concentration. The breaks were because of her, she realized, even though she hadn't actually asked for a single one. It was Davey. It was always Davey asking to stop.

"It's either that or run on through the night," Davey reasoned. "We could switch out drivers. Of course, that's up to you Sir."

As he spoke, Davey's right shoulder shifted against her left one. Mia's eyes wandered from the rearview mirror back out his side window. Automatically, Davey rearranged the rifle that he'd been balancing between his legs for the past twelve hours. The tip was pointed at the floorboards, but not resting up against them.

In the front seat, Jameson huffed a sigh before grumbling something unintelligible under his breath.

Mia closed her eyes.

Davey's entire body was pressed against hers and it had

been like that the whole day. You think she'd be used to it by now, but every time he moved, it reminded her that he was touching her. Thigh against thigh. Hip to hip. Foot against foot.

His constant proximity caused tingles to spread and curl in places that Mia didn't exactly want to focus on at the moment. Intense Davey. Reserved Davey. Stalker Davey.

He hadn't been joking during that first bathroom break. When he said he would be her literal shadow, he'd meant it. Each subsequent break, to eat lunch, to go pee, Davey had never let her get more than an arm's length away. Where she went, he went.

Sometimes he directed her with his gruff words, and sometimes he remained completely silent, impassive, letting her choose where she walked and who she spoke to.

At this point, Mia had memorized the cadence of his breathing. She knew he had no nervous ticks. He didn't tap his foot, he didn't drum his fingers on his thigh, he didn't talk unnecessarily. And for the first time in a long time, Mia didn't quite know what to do with herself around a man.

She didn't know what to do with this *feeling* Davey brought out in her. Normally, she'd flirt and smile and tease and enjoy watching his reaction to her, without having any of her own. But now…

Exhaling through her nose, Mia waited for the tingling to subside.

"Fair enough," Jameson grumbled before holding the radio up to his mouth and depressing the call button. "Circle up off to our immediate left. Time to make camp."

The first vehicle in line, an armored Jeep with a large gun affixed to the roof, slowed before easing off of the road. Swallowing, Mia watched the next one in line peel off before their own driver took a hard left. Their tires bumped down into the field and kept right on moving.

Bouncing along now, Mia felt Malik jerk awake in the seat beside her. His head tipped up and he sniffed once before smacking his lips together.

"How long have I been out?" He asked absently.

"Not long enough," Davey grumbled and had the driver in front of him snorting.

Malik sucked in a breath as if he were about to say something, but then his eyes darted to Mia. Whatever retort he'd had ready to fire at Davey, dried up on his tongue. Instead, he flashed Mia a sheepish smile.

Reaching out a hand, Mia patted Malik gently on the thigh and returned his grin.

"It was so quiet while you were sleeping," she offered. "I was bored."

At this little comment, Davey stiffened and Malik's smile grew wider.

"Don't encourage him," Jameson admonished from the front, before holding the radio up to his mouth once more. "That should do it. Let's stop here."

Lurching to a stop, their driver jammed his foot on the brake and threw the Humvee into park. Mia rocked forward with the movement, and was forced to brace her hands on the back of the driver seat as the engine switched off.

All around them, other trucks were stopping as well. Doors were flying open and soldiers were stepping out.

The silent grass of the prairie was suddenly filled with noise and boots and equipment. Mia exhaled slowly. It would feel so good to be able to stretch her legs for more than a few minutes, she thought. Davey popped open his door.

"I'm going to need you to stay close," he reminded her, before sliding out of the truck. "We can find a good bathroom spot first, and then go grab your stuff."

Before she could muster a response, Mia felt the tug of Malik's hand on her right arm. Turning to him, she raised her brows in question. Huffing a laugh, Malik released her and cleared his throat.

"Uh, maybe you'd like to come back in a few minutes," he offered. "I'm going to do a drone fly over and thought you might like to watch."

Mia frowned. Drone. That word was... new... maybe. Her brain tickled, and a fuzzy dark image tried to break through. Giving her head a shake, Mia pressed her fingers to her temple.

"Drone?" She asked.

"Oh." Malik chuckled good-naturedly. "Sorry. Yeah, it's a small aircraft. I control it with a remote I hold in my hands, but it has a camera. You can stand by me and see the world from above. It's beautiful. I thought you'd like it."

"Oh," Mia echoed him as her mind processed what he'd said. "Sounds like fun. Sure, I'll come find you."

"Great." Malik flashed another one of his winning smiles.

Outside, Mia heard Davey groan.

Returning her attention forward, Mia scooted along the bench seat and hopped down to the ground. Tall grass flattened beneath her boots, cushioning her landing. A million tiny insects took flight, flitting and lifting from the field as two hundred soldiers stomped through their once peaceful home.

Mia batted a few from her face before removing her helmet and running her fingers through her damp hair.

"What in the..." Davey scowled and grabbed for her helmet. "What's the matter with you? Keep your cover on."

Flipping the helmet in his hands, Davey popped it back on her head. His blue eyes were boring right into her and the flash in them had her cheeks heating. Mia's heart jumped in her chest and her throat got tight. Part of her wanted to shrink back into herself at his scolding; the other part wanted to put her hands on his chest and shove... hard.

Tipping her chin up, she did neither.

"Am I going to be sleeping in it?" She hissed. Her teeth were gritting together even as she forced herself to smile at him.

"Wear it until dark," Davey instructed. "When no one can see you, then you can take it off. When the guys around you take theirs off, then you can take it off."

"Fine," Mia snapped.

Shoving past him, Mia had to pick her feet up high to wade through the grass. The tips of the stalks brushed against her hips. She needed to go to the bathroom, but out here there were no trees. The only thing she could hide behind was a truck, so she headed for one directly across from them.

"Watch for snakes," Davey spoke at her back.

"I'm not an idiot," Mia retorted.

She'd worked in the fields inside the Wall for months and months. She was used to snakes and insects and worms and wildlife. They didn't bother her. They didn't scare her.

"I didn't say you were," Davey protested.

But you implied it. Mia huffed a breath and kept charging

forward. Past soldiers hauling equipment. Past soldiers unloading supplies.

"Hey," Davey called. She could hear him stomping just behind her. "Let me go first, I'll clear a path."

"I can clear my own path," Mia countered, still plowing ahead.

"First guy in line is usually the first to get shot," Davey reasoned. She felt his hand catch lightly against her wrist. "Whatever you've got going on in your head, you need to forget it."

Whirling on him, Mia yanked her hand out of his grip and glared. "What?"

"Whatever's got you so pissed," he said, stepping closer. "If it's some woman power shit or if you're just sick of my face, you need to let it go. The things I say to you are for one reason, and one reason only."

Tipping her face up, Mia stared directly into Davey's pale-blue eyes. They were impossibly glassy and impossibly serious.

"What's that?" She asked, crossing her arms defensively over her chest.

"To keep you safe," he said. "That's my entire purpose for being here and no one, not even you, is going to screw that up."

Pursing her lips, Mia glanced away. Why was she so pissed again? What was it about Davey that got her so heated? She didn't know.

Stomach churning, Mia exhaled slowly through her nostrils. He was right. He was here to do a job and that job was to protect her. And the thing of it was, after their experience last time, she knew she could trust him. She could trust him to do what he said. Davey didn't take liberties. He didn't look too long, or smile too often, or give any sort of praise.

So this whole thing would end up just like the last time. Eventually he would deliver her back to the Wall, and then he would walk away. Simple as that.

"Alright," she relented.

Stepping aside, she dropped her head and gestured for him to go first. Davey squared his shoulders and let loose a long breath. Picking up his boots, he started walking by her, taking his place in the lead.

"And I know you're not an idiot," he grumbled as he passed by. "I would never say that."

CHAPTER THIRTEEN_
DAVEY

WITH HIS SHOULDER PRESSED UP AGAINST THE SIDE OF A transport truck, Davey was just able to fit under the canvas tarp without ducking his head. They'd constructed a lean-to of sorts, with the tarp coming down off the side of the truck at an angle until it reached the ground a few yards away.

A cool breeze drifted by, causing the tarp to lift and flap just a little. It was the first hint of relief from the oppressive heat that had dogged them all day. The weather tonight promised to be bearable, so there was that.

Just off to Davey's left, sat Jameson. He had a mini command center set up beneath the tarp, with a collection of maps and a PRC-511 propped up on a small metal table. The antenna portion of the device had been placed on top of the very truck they were sitting next to. By all calculations, they should be hearing from Commander Linfield within a matter of minutes.

Sundown. That's when they'd agreed to make contact.

Letting his gaze drift to the other occupants squeezed under the tarp, Davey's jaw ticked in annoyance. Malik was still flying that fucking drone around, even though he'd already searched the area and found no signs of people. The light was waning now, and pretty soon he wouldn't be able to see. You'd think it was about time to wrap things up.

But oh no. There he was with his head leaned in close to Mia's head, showing her how pretty the sunset was from two hundred feet in the air.

Involuntarily, Davey rolled his eyes. This guy. He was definitely pushing it.

"Oh," Mia cooed for the millionth time as she watched the video screen in Malik's hands. "It's amazing. I can't believe it."

"I know, right?" Malik answered her, flashing that damn grin of his in the fading light.

Narrowing his eyes, Davey watched as the guy scooted in even closer. Malik let go of one side of the controls with one hand and looped his arm quickly around Mia before grabbing the device again. Now he was standing directly behind her, with his body pressed up against her backside.

Malik's chin ducked down to that soft spot between Mia's neck and shoulder as he offered her the controls.

"Here," he said. "I'll help keep it steady. You want to fly?"

"Oh my gosh," Mia cooed again (enough with the cooing already). "I'd love to."

Davey's whole body went rigid. *Fuck this guy.*

Kicking off the side of the truck, he made to close the distance between them, but Jameson caught him by the arm. Glancing down, Davey frowned.

"She's fine," he said easily and gave Davey a quick tug before releasing him. "Besides, we're only three feet away and we have things to discuss. Have a seat."

Pursing his lips, Davey sucked in a breath and did his best

to dial in his initial reaction. If not for Jameson here, he'd of already yanked Malik off his damn boots and tossed him into the side of the truck.

An overreaction? Maybe.

Taking the small metal chair indicated, Davey adjusted his rifle and let his eyes fall to the PRC-511. The thing was primed and ready for action but thus far had only dispensed static.

"So when you accepted this assignment you got some preliminary info but no details," Jameson began, drawing Davey's gaze up and over to him.

Davey gave a nod of acknowledgement.

"We're returning to the city that Linfield and I occupied before invading the Wall," Jameson explained. "There were a few hundred men living there when Linfield first arrived and that number grew to a few thousand by the time we left. Most of those men left with us as soldiers, but some did stay behind."

"Alright." Davey's jaw ticked as Mia continued to coo and giggle just behind him. "So the city is still occupied."

"More than likely." Jameson frowned. "To be honest, I'm not entirely sure what we'll be walking into."

"Great." Davey's stomach tightened, thinking of dragging Mia into it.

"No matter what's there," Jameson continued. "We'll be the best equipped to handle it. We have the most fire power and well-trained men. I don't expect a big fight, if anything at all."

Sucking in a breath, Davey dipped his head in acknowledgment once more. What more could he do? Nothing.

"When we arrive, I'll have you and Mia stay in a chase vehicle near the rear," Jameson went on. "Once we breach the city, there's an underground bunker that no one else has access to, so that's where we'll set up our initial base of operations. I'll stash you and Mia there for a few days while we clear everything out and then we'll begin to expand."

Brow furrowing, Davey leaned back in his chair and considered. Abandoned city. Unknown occupants. Underground bunker. Pretty blonde. What could go wrong?

"I know what Commander Linfield said," Jameson continued. "About not letting her out of your sight, but this is three months we're talking about and you're only one person. Most of the time you'll both be traveling with other soldiers, but her safety won't be their job, it won't be their priority. Plus, you're the only one I trust to be with her when I'm not looking. Not that any of these guys would try anything, but still, I can't be certain."

"I'm up for the job." Davey leaned forward now, causing his metal chair to squeak slightly. "I can do this."

"I know that." Jameson nodded, his eyes flicking between Davey's face and something over Davey's shoulder, likely Mia herself. "But you'll need a break. You can't do it 24/7 for 90 plus days."

"I can." Davey's brow furrowed.

"Well..." Jameson sucked in a breath. "You won't have to. The bunker that we'll be staying in is a stronghold. I could house fifteen guys there comfortably, but I'm not going to. It's just going to be you, me and Mia living in it. That means when we step inside the bunker, you're off duty. You'll have your own bedroom. There's a kitchen and a game room and all kinds of shit."

Davey arched a brow. "Game room?"

"Yeah, some rich fucker built it." Jameson's mouth

twitched at the corner, hinting at a smile he wouldn't let come through. "I guess the point I'm trying to make is, if she steps foot outside, then you're on her like white on rice. But if she's inside the bunker, then you're free. Got it?"

"Yes Sir," Davey gave the required response before glancing over his shoulder.

Immediately, his eyes narrowed and his pulse increased. Darkness was truly falling now, the sun was almost completely hidden behind a ridge of distant mountains in the west. But Malik still had his body draped over Mia as they flew the drone together. So much so, that Davey could hardly make out the leggy blonde as she stood in the soldier's embrace.

"Soldier Malik," Jameson called out as static began crackling over the nearby radio. "Time to land that thing. You've had your fun."

Stepping back, Malik separated his body from Mia's and gripped the controls in both hands. The grin still spreading out across the guy's face was so fucking wide, his teeth almost glowed in the dusky light. For some reason, Davey wanted to wipe the happiness right off of him, although logically he knew he had no reason.

Mia wasn't afraid. She wasn't angry or hurting or upset by the contact. Davey's gaze drifted to her as he moved to get up from his seat. She was reaching up to mess with her hair that was still stuck beneath her helmet. Her cheeks were rosy with excitement and she had the most lovely expression lighting up her face.

Sucking in a breath, Davey pressed the heel of one hand over his chest.

"Hey," he said, bringing her focus over to him. "You can

take your cover off now. Let's get you something to eat and set up your bedroll."

Behind him, Davey heard the squawk of the PRC-511 as Uriah Linfield's voice came over the air. All eyes turned to Jameson who leaned forward and plucked the phone attachment off the radio and brought it to his ear.

"This is Officer Jameson," he commented. "I've got you."

Contact with the Wall had officially been made, and it was nobody's business but Jameson's what was being said.

Rotating back to Mia, Davey took a step forward and reached out to wrap a palm around her upper arm. He didn't need to touch her. He could direct her well enough without the contact, but for some reason he found himself doing it anyway.

For her part, Mia didn't seem to mind. She didn't resist him, and instead let him usher her out from under the tarp and further into the bustle of camp. Soldiers were moving around in the near darkness, eating, talking, lounging on the ground where they'd laid out their bedrolls.

Side-stepping more than one body, Davey wove towards another of the large troop transport trucks. The vehicle was big and wide, with long bench seats lining either side of the back. The flat center aisle that ran between the seats should be just wide enough for Mia and he to sleep wedged together.

Jameson had already set up a perimeter for the camp itself with guard shifts that would last all night long so Davey didn't need to stay awake in order to protect Mia from an outside enemy.

On top of that, Malik's sweep with the drone came up with the all clear. Not a soul in sight for miles. So that left only one threat that Davey had to concern himself with during the night. Friendly soldiers. Or maybe a better way to put it was "overly friendly soldiers".

The last thing Davey needed was for Mia to get molested or some shit while he was snoring six feet away.

That's where his brilliant solution came in. He figured that if they slept side by side, he would definitely wake up if someone tried something stupid. Davey would feel her move, hear her call out to him if she was in trouble, or more than likely, he would hear the guy's big dumb boots jump up into the rear of the truck before Mia even woke up.

"You hungry?" Davey asked, dipping his head down so Mia could hear him clearly.

They were almost to the truck he'd picked out, he just needed to make sure no one else was sleeping inside of it first. And honestly if they were, then he'd just kick their asses out.

"Starved," Mia admitted with a sigh.

Her hand went to her belly and tapped as they walked along.

"Let me check the back of this truck real quick," Davey said, before coming to a stop at the rear and glancing in. "Then we can grab some chow and track down our bedrolls. Good. No one's in here."

"Bedrolls?" Mia asked.

"Sleeping bags," Davey explained. "You and I are going to sleep in the back of this truck. It'll be a little tight but I think we'll be able to sleep side by side."

"I'm sorry." Mia gave her head a shake before blinking up at him.

She was cradling her helmet under one arm and gesturing to the truck over Davey's shoulder with the other.

"You think we're sleeping in that..." Mia's brows raised. "Together? What about a tent? My *own* tent."

Huffing a quiet laugh, Davey fought the desire to roll his eyes. Of course the princess would expect her own tent. After all, she and Cass had shared one on their way to Hermiston.

But this trip was different. It was summer, the air was clear. There was no need to haul a shit ton of tents and take the time to set them up and take them down. Plus, soldiers slept where they were put.

On the ground. In any condition.

Hell, they were lucky they weren't in the middle of a rain storm covered in fucking mud right now. Davey had slept through more than one night like that in the past five years.

"No tents." Davey gestured around them at the hundreds of bodies already lying in the tall grass. "And I still need to keep tabs on you even while I sleep, which means I need to be touching you. That way if something happens, I'll wake up."

Sucking her bottom lip between her teeth, Mia glanced away. Her brow was furrowing and her arms came up to cross over her chest. This was the blonde's classic defense posture, Davey was coming to recognize it well. She was uncomfortable right here, right now, even though she wasn't saying so out loud.

Guilt soaked him. He didn't like putting this kind of pressure on her, or crossing these boundaries she had set up for him, but in this case he had to.

"I swear to you," Davey lowered his voice and sighed. "I will keep my hands to myself. I..."

"Look, I know it's not like that with you," Mia cut him off, her brown eyes zipping to his face. "Believe me, I know."

Frowning, Davey's mouth snapped shut. So if it wasn't him

she was worried about, then what was it? Her lack of privacy? Was he cramping her style?

"I know you're used to getting a lot of attention," Davey offered. "You've usually got a line of guys following you around a mile long, but for the next few months that's gonna have to stop. I can't take my eyes off you, and I'm not going to spend my time watching you hook up with randoms."

Mia's eyebrows shot to her hairline and her mouth dropped a fraction. The utter shock that washed over her face had Davey reconsidering his words. Maybe that'd been a bit…

"Fine." Mia bit out suddenly.

Her cheeks were bright red now and her lips pressed into a thin line. Before Davey could blink, she turned on her heel and started stalking away. She was pissed at him. Again.

With a groan, Davey let his head tip back for just the briefest moment and he closed his eyes. He'd never been particularly good at talking to women. It was his baby brother who'd been gifted with all of the silly charm.

Ryder was always cracking jokes and getting everyone around him to smile. Maybe half the time they were rolling their eyes at the naive stuff he came up with, but that was part of his charm. Ryder was fun, guileless and full of energy. Young. He'd always seemed so incredibly young.

Suddenly the loss hit Davey like a ton of bricks. Ryder should be standing right here beside him, smacking Davey on the arm and making Mia smile. He'd spent his whole life with that kid glued to his side and only the past year without him.

It hurt.

It still hurt so damn bad. And what was worse? Davey hadn't thought about him until that very moment. Mia consumed him. Thinking about the leggy blonde and how to do his job properly dominated Davey's thoughts. So much so, that his baby brother's memory had been shoved aside.

Inhaling sharply, Davey opened his eyes and stared into the night sky. It was scattered with a million tiny stars. They winked and glittered at him, making him wonder where his brother had gone and if he was up there… somewhere.

The sounds of the camp filled the space. Guys talking and laughing and chewing. MREs being ripped open and consumed. Canteens being refilled from one of the fresh water tanks the convoy had been hauling.

Mia.

Davey straightened himself and looked around. She was several yards away from him now, her blonde hair catching the moonlight. Rubbing a hand over his chest, Davey blew a hot breath through his nostrils, and then gave chase.

Sadness or no, he still had a job to do, and honestly that was all Davey had left… a job.

CHAPTER FOURTEEN_

MIA

BRINGING HER HAND UP TO COVER HER MOUTH, MIA STIFLED A yawn. Her head felt heavy, her muscles ached. She hadn't gotten a lot of sleep last night… for obvious reasons.

Well, correct that, for *one* obvious reason. Davey.

And *that* particular reason was sitting beside her once more. His arm against her arm, his leg against her leg… giving her that same on-edge sort of tingling sensation that had kept her up all night long.

They were wedged together in the back of a small Jeep now, tracking the long line of military vehicles as their convoy approached civilization. Or what remained of it.

Glancing past Davey out the rear window, Mia purposefully widened her eyes. She was finding it a bit hard to focus. She was so tired. She could probably fall asleep right now, if not for the tension that had suddenly entered the vehicle.

They were drawing closer to the abandoned city, and therefore other people… strange men, possibly violent men. They didn't know.

At the thought, Mia's stomach did a slow roll inside of her.

Jameson wasn't riding with them anymore, he was still up front in the Humvee. About an hour ago, Mia and Davey had been shuffled back to an armored Jeep positioned near the rear of the convoy. Jameson had to lead this "mission" as he'd called it and so Mia was now surrounded by soldiers she didn't know (aside from Davey, of course, her constant shadow).

Soldier Malpas with his tan skin and sparkly green eyes, sat just to her right. In front of him, riding shotgun, was Soldier Evans (dark hair, brown eyes) and the driver was Soldier Locklan (red hair, hazel eyes). They'd all been friendly enough when she'd first climbed in, shooting her smiles before looking at Davey a little sideways and straightening in their seats.

But now they were absolutely silent. Hands were on weapons. Eyes were directed out, scanning, searching.

The radio attached to the front dash was all low humming static. No voices crackled. It added to the thickness of the air, making it hotter and heavier somehow.

"You remember how to work one of these?" Davey's voice broke into her reverie, drawing Mia's attention down to her own lap.

Davey had a gun in his hand, holding it out for Mia to take. It was clean and black. She didn't know the correct name for it, but it was familiar enough. She'd shot one once in the gun range at the Wall, but that was several months ago now.

Frowning, Mia shook her head. She didn't remember enough about it not to kill herself, or someone else, she figured. Davey sighed. He was disappointed, and for some reason that caused Mia's chest to tighten.

"Alright," he spoke quietly, but his voice was the only one

inside the cab of the vehicle. "The safety is right here," he gestured as he spoke, drawing her eyes over the weapon. "You rack it like this, you clear it like this. Keep the barrel pointed at the floor or ground and your finger off the trigger until you're ready to kill whatever is in front of you... preferably not one of us."

"I can't." Mia lifted both hands and pushed the weapon gently away. "I'll hurt someone."

"That's the point," Davey countered. "Better someone else than you."

"I just..." Mia nibbled at her lip and eyed the gun. "I'm just not comfortable using it, okay?"

"If you'd of had it last time," Davey insisted. "Then I'd have woken up to a gunshot instead of your screaming. Don't you wish you would've had it?"

Sucking in a breath, Mia squeezed her eyes shut. Her heart thumped at her and her palms grew clammy. Maybe some memories took their time coming back to her, swirling and slinking on the outskirts of her mind, but that one was fresh. It was loud and gripping and sickening. She hated thinking of it, of the man and his hands, of the helplessness and the fear.

"I'm sorry," Davey's words were rushed now, and low. "I'm sorry, I shouldn't have said that."

Fighting against the hot tears that wanted to come, Mia opened her eyes. She wasn't going to be the weak one ever again. And she certainly wasn't going to show Davey that he'd gotten to her.

Glancing down, Mia cleared her throat. The handgun was still hovering above her lap as Davey's apologies fell from his lips, so she brought her hands around it and took hold of the damn thing.

"It's fine," she bit out, focusing her eyes directly out the windshield. "I'm fine."

The tires kept humming along the asphalt road. Static buzzed. Mia watched Soldier Locklan's fingers tighten on the steering wheel as the convoy ahead of them took a turn and began entering a sea of houses... or what used to be houses. They were pretty well burned to the ground now. Nothing but chimneys and chain link fencing and piles of rubble mostly.

Mia's throat went dry and she forced an uncomfortable swallow. This place. It was eerily empty.

"Don't be afraid," Davey whispered. His head ducked down to her ear. She could feel his breath on her skin. "I won't let anything happen to you. Not ever again."

Blinking, Mia forced her lungs to draw in air. Those words... they were *familiar*.

All around her, the world continued at a normal pace. The driver drove. Scenery flashed by.

There were warehouses now, with metal sheeting for roofs, and blown out windows, and doors left open to the breeze. Mia's heart slowed. A memory was approaching.

There was a figure, blurry, like a gray silhouette. It was coming towards her, walking towards her, but at the same time it was sucking her away. Mia was slipping from the reality of that car ride and there was absolutely nothing she could do about it.

Leaning her head back against the seat in the Jeep, Mia prayed it would be a quick one. She prayed the men around her wouldn't notice. She prayed Davey would think she'd fallen asleep.

And then she was gone.

. . .

"Don't be afraid," Mama whispered. Reaching out, she tucked a loose hair behind Marie's ear. "I won't let anything happen to you. Not ever again."

"But... Daddy..." Marie nibbled on her lip, her eyes scanning her mother's bruised face.

She hadn't been able to hide the swelling with makeup. Not this time.

"Shush now." Mama stood tall once more and adjusted her white blouse. "We're going to take a little drive. Okay?"

Nodding, Marie swallowed. Mama was dressed up like a business lady today. She had a navy blue pencil skirt with a soft blouse tucked in. Her black patent leather heels were so shiny, Marie could almost see her own reflection in them.

Stepping back, Mama selected a matching navy jacket from her massive closet and shrugged it on. Marie watched from her position sitting on the thick carpeted flooring. She wished Mama had dressed her up in a pretty skirt today too. But she hadn't.

Frowning, Marie studied the drab wool dress that she now wore. It was gray and somber, with long sleeves reaching to her wrists and a skirt that dropped all the way to the floor. She'd never worn anything like it, never seen anything like it either.

It wasn't beautiful or soft, the fabric didn't fall like it should.

"Mama?" Marie asked. "Can I change my clothes?"

"No Baby." Mama cleared her throat before stepping in front of a full length mirror and smoothing at her own hair. "We're going to a special church today, and that's what you'll need to wear. All the girls wear them there."

"We're not going to our church?" Marie questioned.

She knew the building well. It was big and beautiful, made of white stone and stained glass. They went every Sunday and sat in the front pew that was made of carved wood. At the end of the the service she always had an ache in her back from sitting.

But today wasn't Sunday. And they always went there with Daddy... with Daddy and his bodyguard and sometimes a photographer who snapped photos as Daddy talked to people and shook hands.

Voters, he always said. They were all voters to him, so he was nice and friendly and charming. It was the only time Marie saw him laugh.

"No." Mama shook her head. "Remember what I told you this morning? About my sister?"

Pushing up to standing, Marie nodded her head yes once more. She hadn't known her mother had a sister until today. But apparently her name was Aunt Jean and she looked the opposite of Mama. Dark hair and dark eyes where Mama's were both light.

"Well your auntie joined this special church when she married your uncle," Mama explained. "She gave up her last name and all of her money. For a long time I didn't know where she was or how to find her."

"But you got a letter," Marie prompted, remembering what she'd been told earlier in the day.

"Yes." Mama pursed her lips. "She wants to meet you, but she lives far away now. I'll bring you to a member of her church and that nice lady will take you to see Jean."

"But why can't you come with me?" Marie tried to keep the whine from her voice... and failed.

Closing the distance between them, Mama pulled Marie in for a tight hug. Her soothing hand ran down Marie's back and then stroked through Marie's hair. Sighing, Marie buried her face against her Mama and fought the tickle of fear that was working through her body. She didn't want to go visit this aunt all alone.

"I will come too... eventually," Mama assured her. "The church just needs you to be a good girl first. Follow all the rules and use your new name. If you behave, then I'll be able to come too. Sound good?"

Sniffing, Marie fought the hot flood of tears that wanted to burst and flow down her cheeks. She didn't want to leave Mama and give up her name and live in this new church with her aunt. Not without Mama.

"Marie." Mama held her at arm's length and stared down into her face. "You be good. Use the name they give you and then I'll come."

"Okay." Marie pressed her hands to her face and began to cry. Her chest hurt all of a sudden. It was hard to breathe.

Giving her a little shake, Mama frowned. Her eyes were all glassy now too, but no teardrops fell across her thick application of makeup.

"Remember how I said no one would ever hurt you again?" Mama squeezed Marie's shoulders in her hands. "This is how I keep that promise. This is how I keep you safe."

"Yes Mama," Marie firmed her trembling lips and forced a smile. "I'll behave. I promise."

CHAPTER FIFTEEN_
DAVEY

SHE WAS GIVING HIM THE SILENT TREATMENT, THAT MUCH WAS clear.

Exhaling through his nostrils, Davey tried not to let it get to him. Sure, he'd said the wrong thing to her... again. He shouldn't have brought up her attack. After all, it was his own damn fault she'd suffered in the first place.

But she *needed* to have a weapon right now. Yes, he'd lay down his life to protect her, to complete his mission, to do his job. Hell, that's what he'd been trained to do, that's what he was truly good at. But what happened if that wasn't enough? What happened if he was taken out for good this time?

She needed a way to end things. She needed to have that power even if it made her... what was the word she'd used? Oh yeah, *uncomfortable*.

Focusing his gaze out the Jeep's rear passenger window, Davey kept his hands light on his rifle even as his jaw clenched down tight. The warehouse district (or whatever was left of it) was giving way to high-rises now. Impossibly tall buildings were stretching up just before them, half of them with pristine glass faces and the other half marred by apparent air strikes and burn marks.

This city had been attacked during the war five years ago. It was amazing this much was left over.

"Potential combatants, right side, hold your fire," Officer Jameson's voice crackled over the radio.

Davey's eyes swiveled to the opposite side of the Jeep.

Evans, who was riding shotgun, dipped his head and looked down the sight of his rifle. He had it pointed out the window, but kept his finger off the trigger. Behind him, Soldier Malpas did the same.

With a nod to himself, Davey refocused his attention outside his own window. He didn't want to be caught off guard when everyone's attention was shifted to the right. He still had to cover the left, and trust that his team was handling their business appropriately.

"Better get down Mia," Davey spoke out. "Just crouch on the floor for a sec. It's probably nothing, but just in case."

Sucking in a steadying breath, Davey listened to the crackle of the radio as Jameson ordered his soldiers to toss packets of food out to whoever the "potential combatants" were. The convoy wasn't slowing down, and no shots were being fired so that was a good sign.

Of course, this was all part of the master plan. The best way to assume control over an area is to get the people already living there on your side. Give them food. Invite them to join your cause. Yada yada, lip service. Back in the day, they called it "goodwill".

"Mia." Davey glanced quickly to his right. "Just bend down for a second, seriously."

She didn't move. Davey did a double take.

Mia's chin was tipped down towards her chest, her body was slumped back slightly against the seat. Davey's eyes darted down to her lap. The gun was cradled there in a pair of limp hands. Palms up and slightly open.

"Shit," Davey spat out the word and brought his rifle quickly back inside the vehicle. His breath caught in his throat and his hands fumbled to find a good spot for it.

"Mia," he called out to her again.

No response.

Suddenly the vehicle took a hard right, causing Mia's body to slide into his. Her head lolled to the side, her mouth dropped open, the gun tumbled to the floor. She hadn't been wearing a seatbelt. None of them were. You needed to be able to jump out and go at a moment's notice.

"Fuck." Davey grabbed her hard with both hands and yanked her up onto his lap. "Mia! What the fuck. Come on now."

His hands were trembling as he brought them to her face. Peeling up an eyelid, he noted her eyeball was rolled up in the back of her head. Letting go, he moved his index and middle finger to that delicate spot on her throat and held his own breath.

Thump. Thump. Thump. Thump.

She had a pulse. It was steady and strong.

All of the oxygen left Davey's lungs in a whoosh. She was unconscious but alive… why? What in the hell was going on?

"Radio Officer Jameson," Davey bit out the words, refusing to take his eyes off Mia's face. "Tell him Mia's passed out. Tell him I can't get her to come around."

As the radio crackled and the Jeep took another sharp

turn, Davey tapped his palm gently against Mia's cheek. Blood was rushing in his ears now, so much so that he couldn't hear what was being said over the radio. He just knew that words were being exchanged.

"Come on Blondie," Davey coaxed, tapping his hand just a bit harder. "Wake up. Come on."

A million thoughts rushed through his head. How long had she been out? Why wasn't she coming to? Was she allergic to anything? When's the last time she ate?

"Soldier Wells." The Jeep's driver spoke his name before punching the brakes, causing them all to rock forward. "Soldier Wells! Is she breathing?"

"Huh?" Glancing up to the rearview mirror, Davey realized they'd probably been asking him that question for a while. "Yeah. I mean, yes. She's breathing. She has a pulse. But I can't get her to wake up."

The radio crackled again. Words were exchanged and Davey's focus slipped back to the woman he cradled on his lap.

This wasn't the first time he'd held her like this. After the attack in Hermiston, when they were racing to get Cass back to the Wall, Mia had curled up on his lap for hours. She'd cried and whimpered and sniffed and sucked his heart right out of his chest.

And now she was wrecking him all over again, but in a completely silent sort of way. It was like watching his mother when he was a child, slip into hours of unwakeable sleep after her chemo treatments. He hated it.

"Hey…" Soldier Malpas was reaching across the bench seat and shaking his shoulder. "We're here."

Looking up, Davey glanced around. "Where's here?" He asked.

"An underground garage," Malpas answered. "Officer Jameson gave Soldier Malik the keys to the bunker. They both lived here before and Malik knows where it's at, so he'll guide you in. Officer Jameson still has to set up a perimeter but he'll send a medic and come himself as soon as he can. That's what he said."

"Okay." Davey ducked his head and pulled Mia closer to his chest. "I'll carry her."

The door to his left popped open then and Malik stood there with his hand gripping the doorframe, panting as if he'd run a mile.

Scowling, Davey's arms tightened around Mia as he began to scoot and shift the both of them out of the vehicle. Her head dropped back, all loose and hanging. The helmet that he'd insisted she always wear, rolled off onto the seat. She didn't like the chin strap, he recalled, it chafed her perfect skin.

"What the hell happened?" Malik demanded and had Davey biting down hard on the inside of his cheek.

"I don't know," he admitted, before managing to place both of his boots squarely on the ground.

Shifting awkwardly around, Davey worked to stand upright.

Darting in close, Malik made to grab Mia, but Davey scooped her up quickly and pivoted away.

"Just show me where to go," he barked.

She still wasn't coming around. It had his stomach twisting angrily inside of him.

Without a word, Malik ducked his head and was off,

weaving his way through a sea of dusty parked cars in the dim underground lot. The place smelled of stale gasoline and rat shit.

In Davey's arms, Mia let loose a tiny groan.

"Blondie," Davey gritted out the nickname he had for her, fighting the rush of adrenaline that was now pushing through his body. "Where you been, huh? Time to come back to us Mia."

He kept his arms around her as he jogged to keep up. Mia's legs swayed with the movement. One of her arms bounced lifelessly up and down, but then she managed to bring her head up and rest it heavily against Davey's chest.

He almost sighed in relief right then, but he held himself back. Her eyes were still shut, and her body was mostly limp. They weren't out of the woods yet.

Davey's heart was tapping at him as his eyes did a quick scan of their surroundings. Empty, abandoned cars. No people. No animals. No nothing.

Arriving at a door wedged in the corner of the garage, Malik slid to a stop and began fumbling around for a key. Coming up short behind him, Davey planted his feet and stared down at Mia, trying to take stock. Her eyes remained closed but her lips were moving. She was murmuring something.

"She left me," Mia said quietly. "She just left me there."

Before Davey could lean in closer, Malik was stepping back and pulling the heavy metal door wide. It creaked on hinges that hadn't been used in a while and the space beyond the threshold was completely dark. Black. Cool air. Silent.

Taking an instinctive step back, Davey realized that he was

without a gun. He'd given her his sidearm and he'd left his rifle in the Jeep. *Fuck.*

Fishing around in his pocket, Malik drew out a flashlight and flicked it on.

"This place has lights," he commented, as he stepped into the space and began jogging lightly down a flight of stairs. "But we need to get the generators working again."

"Generators?" Davey frowned as he followed suit.

Together their steps pounded in the empty space. Malik threw him a brief look over his shoulder, but kept his flashlight facing forward. It was impossible to see the expression on the guy's face.

"Yeah," he answered. "The doors are usually controlled by an electronic keypad. We'll get it all up and running in no time."

At the bottom of the stairwell, they came to a stop at yet another metal door. This one, like the other, was painted a muted sort of blue color, and now that Davey was paying attention, he noticed that there was indeed a black electronic keypad off to one side. It was like back in the time before the war, when you'd beep your way into an office building with a plastic security badge.

In his arms, Mia began to stir. He could feel her waking up, could feel the change in her posture, the weight of her body and the position of her arms and legs. She was shifting and coming closer to consciousness.

And that fact was a relief. A fucking flood of relief. But it was followed quickly by a flash of anger. He was upset suddenly that she could scare him like this, that she could do this to him.

"I behaved," Mia mumbled as her eyelashes fluttered against her cheeks. "I know I did."

"Hey," Davey coaxed, as Malik held the second door wide and they both shifted through it. "Come on Mia. Wakey, wakey. Time to get up."

"She coming to?" Malik asked, picking up to a jog once more.

The flashlight beam bounced off the hallway. More concrete floors and walls and dank underground darkness. This place was like a coffin. This place was like a grave.

Nodding his answer, it took Davey a few beats to realize that Malik couldn't see him, so he cleared his throat.

"Yeah," he offered in response, raising his voice to be heard. "How far are we?"

"Not far," Malik called.

Again their boots pounded against concrete. More darkness. The air smelled of dust and dampness. In his arms, Mia shivered.

"What about that medic?" Davey called.

Coming to another stop, Malik changed the flashlight to his left hand and fished for a necklace from around his neck. Dangling on the end of it was another set of keys. They clinked against one another as Davey and Malik's labored breathing puffed out into the space.

"This is it," Malik commented finally. "I'll show you where the bedrooms are and get some lights going, then I'll go back for the medic."

Nodding, Davey sucked in breath and tried to pace his breathing. It'd been a long time since he'd had to carry a person for any sort of distance. His lungs were burning and his muscles were screaming at him, but he shoved all that aside as Malik opened the extra thick steel door and entered the bunker.

Even with the small circle of visibility that the flashlight allowed, Davey was shocked by what he saw on the other side. Expensive hardwood flooring, a wide hallway, intricately carved crown molding and paintings. Massive oil paintings lining the walls.

When you think *underground bunker* you don't think mini-mansion, and yet with the brief glimpses that Davey was getting that's exactly the impression he got. Money. Wealth. Power. That's what built this place.

Swallowing, Davey followed Malik at a fast walk. The door swung shut behind them. The snap of it latching at their backs was almost palpable.

At the noise, Mia twisted in his arms, sucking in a breath before letting loose a groan.

"Davey?" She asked suddenly, her hands fisting the material of his shirt.

"Right here," he answered. "You're safe. It's just me."

"But what?" Mia's body tensed and she pulled herself in even tighter against him. "What happened?"

"You passed out," he offered, trying hard not to focus on the tap of his heart beneath her hand. "But you're safe now. Just give me a sec."

They passed closed doors and walls lined with paintings until finally Malik came to a stop in the hall and glanced around. His flashlight bobbed from one door to another. He ran his hand up to his helmet and scratched at his forehead.

"There a problem?" Davey came to a stop behind him.

"Well, this is the start of the bedrooms, but I'm not sure where Officer Jameson wants to put her," Malik admitted and gestured to one door. "That one belonged to Hannah Linfield when she lived here. All of her things are still inside."

"Then give us the room across the hall," Davey bit out.

Nodding, Malik twisted the knob and pulled the door wide. Davey blinked a moment as the flashlight bobbled around before the beam steadied on a perfectly made queen-sized bed. Crossing to it, Davey leaned forward and laid Mia on the puffy down comforter. It took more than a second before she uncurled her fists from his shirt and let him go.

The flashlight left her then to sweep the room and Davey's eyes darted along with it. More paintings, this time of flowers and fields. A long wooden dresser, painted white. Twin night-stands with sleek silver lamps. A flat screen television affixed to one wall. A powder-blue area rug beneath their feet, protecting the wood flooring.

No lurking figures. No other men. They were decidedly alone.

"Well then…" Malik sucked in a breath. "I'll go get the generator fired up and then we'll have lights."

"And the medic?" Davey asked again. Priorities man. Priorities.

"Yeah," Malik answered as he swung the flashlight back to hover on Mia. "Then I'll get the medic. How're you feeling? You okay?"

Lifting her hand to block the beam of light, Mia bit down on her lower lip and nodded. Davey frowned and removed his helmet.

"I'll stay with her," he said, like there was any other option.

"Alright," Malik agreed and then left, taking his flashlight with him.

Almost immediately the room plunged into pitch darkness. There were no windows here. No light of any kind leaked in. It reminded Davey just how far underground they actually were. The pristine surroundings made him forget.

Tucking his helmet beneath one arm, Davey shifted on his feet. It was cold in here. The place felt a little like a tomb. His fingers itched for his weapon. Patting at his pockets with one hand, Davey reassured himself he still had all of his knives in place.

Beside him, Mia shifted her body along the mattress. He could hear the shuffling of the comforter, and imagined she was drawing her legs up to her chest… or perhaps she was lying down… and passing back out.

"Mia?" Davey stepped in her direction and dropped his helmet to the floor. Sticking his hands out to feel for the edge of the bed, he asked, "You still with me?"

"Yeah." Mia's voice cracked a little and the pitiful sound caused Davey's chest to crack along with it. "I feel dizzy, but I think it's because it's so dark in here. I can't tell where I am."

"You're not going to faint on me again are you?" Davey's fingertips brushed Mia's body and he froze in place. Was this an arm or a leg or a…?

"I don't think so," Mia sighed.

Then Davey felt the warmth of her hand sliding over his own. Her fingertips trailed up to his wrist and then she was pulling on him. It was a gentle sort of tug, willing him to come closer.

Even though he should be taking a giant step back right about now, Davey did the opposite. Mia was drawing him down to the bed with her, and despite the completely inappropriate clenching in his lower belly, he let her.

"What happened?" He asked, as he took a seat beside her

and snaked an arm around her shoulders. "I thought you were just pissed at me, but then you were out. I couldn't get you to come back." *You scared the living shit out of me... and not for the first time.*

"How long was I unconscious?" Mia's head eased back to rest against Davey's chest. Her soft hair tickled the skin of his neck and chin.

"You're not answering the question," he pointed out.

"Neither are you," she countered, and almost had him snorting a laugh. This freaking woman. She wasn't going to make things easy on him. Not in any way, shape or form.

"Minutes," he admitted finally. "I'm not exactly sure, but you were out for over five minutes, probably closer to ten."

"I'm sorry," she sighed again.

Her chest deflated and she let loose a whoosh of air. Davey's chest was doing the opposite, his was cinching tighter. He didn't like it. He didn't like the power she had over him. The power to make him afraid.

"What. Happened. Blondie." Davey gritted out.

Focus on being mad at her. Focus on her evasion, and how that's interfering with your job, instead of how perfect she fits beneath your damn arm.

"I... Well, I..." Mia began to nibble on her lip, he could *feel* her doing it.

"I can't keep you safe if you don't trust me." Davey let his hand come up and stroke down the side of her head. How did she get him to cave so quickly? How did she evaporate his anger and turn it into a need to comfort, to touch? He didn't know.

All he knew was that he shouldn't be doing this. He

shouldn't be running his fingers over her hair and breathing in her scent. It was too much.

No, scratch that. It was too much *and* it was completely unprofessional. She was a job, an assignment, a way to get what he truly wanted, which was a strike team of his own.

"I had a memory," Mia admitted. "And I don't want to talk about it."

Davey's brows drew together and he exhaled slowly through his nose. Memory recurrence. That made sense. He'd seen Hannah pass out much the same way when she was getting everything back. It was upsetting to watch, but in the end had been harmless, which he guessed was a good thing. That meant they probably didn't have a bigger health issue to worry about with Mia.

Still, he looked forward to the medic's assessment. If the guy ever got here. And the lights ever turned on. What the fuck was Malik doing anyway?

"You were talking a little," Davey said finally. "When you were coming around you said something like… she left me. Who left you, Blondie? Who was she?"

Stiffening in his arms, Mia brought both hands up to cover her face. Davey could feel her exhale and drag her palms back down.

Sitting up straighter, he lifted his arm from her shoulders, wanting to give her space if she needed it.

"My mom," she whispered. "In my memory my mother gave me to someone else. She was supposed to meet us later, but I don't remember that part. I don't know if maybe… maybe that was the last time I saw her, you know? I mean, she's not here with me now, so I obviously know how it all ends, but…"

Squeezing his eyes shut, Davey fought the lump in his throat and the lurch in his chest. Moms were a sore spot for him, that's for sure. And Mia wasn't scooting away from him, so eventually he lowered his arm back down to drape over her shoulders. She was crying now… quietly, but still. He'd heard enough of her sadness in their brief past together that he was able to recognize it.

Clearing his throat, Davey pushed his own emotions down and away. He pushed and shoved and swallowed until they were a comfortable black ball filling his belly.

"Moms are tough," he said. "I lost mine when I was ten. How old were you in your memory?"

"Oh." Mia sniffed and wiped at her face. He could feel her arms moving as she shifted around. "I didn't know about your mom. I'm so sorry. What happened?"

"Breast cancer," Davey bit out the words and glanced away, even though there was nothing to look at.

"Cancer," Mia repeated the last word before giving her head a little shake. "I'm sorry, I don't remember what that word means."

"It's a sickness," Davey offered.

A torturous, agonizingly slow disease. One that steals from you a little bit every single day until there's nothing left but a shell of the person you loved.

"What was her name?" Mia asked, and had Davey's heart softening in his chest.

"Angela," he said. "Like an angel. She was my angel."

"I'm sure she still is," Mia offered quietly.

Her fingertips came up to touch his arm before tracing their way lightly down to his hand. Shifting around, Mia brought her body further up against his, leaning her back into his chest until he was supporting almost all of her weight. Her hair tickled his nose and lips, but he didn't move.

"What was your mom's name?" He asked after a beat.

"Um..." Mia inhaled deeply before answering. "Rachel. Her name was Rachel, and when she left I was nine."

Firming his lips, Davey glanced to his left.

A light flickered on in the distance, illuminating the hallway just enough so that he could see the outline of the open doorway. Malik must've got that generator running, or maybe he was heading their way with the flashlight again.

Untangling himself from Mia, Davey stood up from the bed and walked away. He needed to make space between them. He couldn't think straight when she was curled up against him like that.

Crossing to the threshold, he peeked into the hall just in time to see Malik flip on another overhead light. The guy had a triumphant grin on his face as he jogged closer. Davey suppressed his immediate impulse to smile back. Instead, he ducked back into the bedroom and ran his palm along the wall until he found a switch.

Flipping it on, he rotated around to face Mia. The beautiful blonde was still sitting on the bed, a wrinkled cream-colored comforter beneath her and a million fluffy pillows at her back. There was luxury in every aspect of this room the likes of which Davey had never seen. Crown molding, ornate furniture, intricate area rugs.

And she belonged there, he realized, surrounded by expensive finishes and massive oil paintings. Even dressed in loose-fitting soldier fatigues, she looked like a queen. A woman like this deserved nice things in life and what's more, she deserved a man who could give them to her.

Tipping her face to look up at him, Mia let those chocolate-brown eyes of hers lock onto his for a solid five seconds.

Davey's heart leapt in his chest and his entire body stilled under her gaze, but then her eyes were rolling up in the back of her head again, and she passed clean out.

"Fuck!" Davey shouted as he lunged forward. "Get me that damn medic!"

CHAPTER SIXTEEN_

MIA

LYING FLAT ON THE BED, MIA EXHALED SLOWLY AND CLOSED her eyes. The blankets beneath her were so incredibly soft, the mattress too. If it was silent, she might just be able to drift off to sleep.

But it wasn't silent and she wasn't alone. Nope. The medic was seated beside her now, having just completed his evaluation. His name was Soldier Anthony Bisset, and as he continued packing up his bag of instruments, he cleared his throat.

Mia's eyes popped open then, and landed on him. He was short, with sandy-brown hair and intelligent hazel eyes. He wasn't a medical doctor, not technically anyway. But before the war he'd been pre-med, and during the war he'd had a crash course in emergency medicine, so his qualifications were better than most.

"I'd like you to sit up now," he said quietly. "Let's see if you get dizzy or have another episode."

Nodding, Mia reached out and grasped the hands he

offered her. His palms were warm and dry and as soon as he pulled her upright, he let go.

"How's that feel?" He asked, his eyes darting over her face before he tilted his head to one side, analyzing.

Mia managed a weak smile. She wasn't dizzy anymore and she didn't feel another memory coming on, but she was tired. She was bone weary all of a sudden, overwhelmed by the awful memories from her childhood that were still dominating her mind.

Opening her mouth, she was about to respond when another burst of angry voices sounded from the hallway. Mia recognized the speakers, even with the door to her bedroom pulled halfway shut. Just because she couldn't see the two men responsible for the argument, didn't mean she couldn't hear them. Everyone could hear them.

"We're going to wait for the medic's assessment," Jameson's voice was steady and calm. "If it really is just memory recurrence, then there's nothing we can do about it."

"We should take her back to the Wall," Davey growled. "She needs a full evaluation from a real doctor."

"That *is* a real doctor," Jameson countered. "Or as close to one as we can get anymore. There's no more med school, remember?"

Davey's reply to that was low and unintelligible, but Mia got the impression it involved foul language.

Beside her, Soldier Bisset raised on eyebrow.

"I'm going to ask you just one more time," he said. "Is there any possibility you could be pregnant? I don't have a test with me or else I'd insist on giving you one."

Frowning, Mia felt her cheeks heat. She'd already answered this.

"That's not necessary." Mia folded her arms over her chest. "There's no way I could be pregnant." *You have to have sex for that.*

Glancing over his shoulder, the medic studied the half-open door. Davey crossed in front of the opening, pacing like a tiger in a cage before the argument resumed.

"You hired me to do a job," Davey hissed. "But you aren't letting me do it."

"You're over-reacting," Jameson again, still calm. "And your job involves keeping her safe while she's here, *not* back at the Wall."

"But…"

"*And* you're bordering on insubordination again, Soldier Wells," Jameson went on. "I shouldn't have to remind you that this is *my* op, and I have the final word. *Over everything*. Including, and almost especially, over that woman inside that room. Got it?"

Sucking in a breath, Mia's heart began to beat harder in her chest. The medic turned back towards her then, and leveled her with those intelligent hazel eyes of his.

"You sure about that?" He asked. "It's important that I know the truth. I can help you with whatever you need. I can be discreet, my loyalty still lies with my patient first."

"I'm sure." Mia blew out a breath and looked away.

She hadn't had sex at least since she'd lost her memory, and something inside of her told her she'd never done it before then either. And the memories she kept getting slammed with seemed to confirm that fact. No sex. No baby.

"Alright." Soldier Bisset pushed back from the bed and stepped away. "Then my assessment is that you're suffering from a combination of memory recurrence, dehydration and possibly low blood sugar. You've got to tell these guys when you're thirsty and when you're hungry. Okay? Will you do that for me?"

With a sigh, Mia returned her attention to the medic. He was only trying to do his job, like all of the men currently surrounding her were trying to do. And maybe she hadn't realized it at the time, but when Commander Linfield had recruited her for this assignment, she'd become a critical part of Jameson's mission.

"Yes," she answered and plastered a fake smile on her face. "I can do that for you."

"Good," he said. "Now rest."

Mia fought the annoyed curl that wanted to lift her lip and replaced it with some more of her brilliant smiling. She just wanted him to leave now. She just needed some time alone. That last memory had been a rough one, and a part of her simply wanted to cry.

She wanted to weep for her mother and for herself as a small child. She wanted to sob for how violent and demeaning the man whose blood ran through her veins actually was. And she wanted to shudder at how afraid she still was of him, of his memory, even now.

Giving a small nod, Soldier Bisset plucked his bag from the end of the bed and stood. Mia watched him cross to the bedroom door. When he pushed it all the way open, the hushed debate that was still waging out in the hallway fell away. There was a beat of silence, wherein Mia held her breath.

Giving her a parting glance over his shoulder, Soldier Bisset reached back for the door and pulled it firmly closed behind him. The latch caught and clicked before muted voices could be heard. Soldier Bisset's murmuring was first, followed by Jameson's low responses. Nothing from Davey this time. Apparently he was keeping his mouth shut.

Mia exhaled and tipped her face up to the ceiling. Blinking, she did her best to stave off the flood of tears. She didn't want to be weak. She didn't want to cower or give in to the memory of her father or to any other man for that matter.

I hate you so much. Were you ever caught? Did you pay? What happened to Mama?

Flopping back on the mattress, Mia rolled to her side and tugged the covers down. Slipping beneath them, she curled herself into a tiny ball. She hugged her knees to her chest and squeezed her eyes shut and she fought.

She didn't want to become like the woman in her memories. She didn't want to be like her mother, even though they looked almost exactly alike, save for the eyes. Mia's were dark… like her father's.

A sudden knock at the door had Mia swiping at her cheeks and sucking in a breath. Clearing her throat, she raised her voice.

"Come in!" She called.

The man who entered her room was not who she expected. The pinch of disappointment she felt at the sight of him had her frowning. Lifting up onto one elbow, Mia tucked a lock of hair behind one ear and worked to ease the tension from her face.

"Jameson," she said, unable to stop herself from glancing past him to the still open door.

Raising an eyebrow, Jameson looked over his own shoulder quickly before pulling the door shut once more.

When he returned his eyes to Mia, he rubbed his hands together and sighed.

"You okay?" He asked.

"I'm fine," Mia assured him.

Crossing to the far corner of the room, Jameson grabbed an overstuffed chair and dragged it slowly over to her side of the bed. Mia's eyes followed his movements as Jameson eased his bulky body down and somehow managed to dwarf the large chair. Her best friend's man was all wide shoulders and broad chest and thick arms. Although on the inside, she knew he was as soft as they come.

It made Mia want to laugh. It made Mia want to cry.

She missed Cass. She missed having someone to talk to that understood her, someone that she could trust with the truth now drifting inside her head. She should have told Cass everything when she had the chance.

"No." Jameson gave his head a little shake. "You're not fine and if Cass were sitting here right now, then she'd call you out on it too."

Pursing her lips, Mia glanced away. So, she wasn't the only one thinking about their missing link.

"What's going on with you, Mia?" Jameson began again. "Is it just memories? Soldier Bisset seems to think I'm neglecting you, that I'm not feeding you properly. Is it Davey? Is he making you uncomfortable? Afraid?"

Mia's eyes shot back over to Jameson's face and she huffed indignantly.

"You're passing out on me," Jameson pointed out. "Bisset tells me that *I'm* too intimidating. That you're afraid to tell me when you need something. Now you and I both know that's not true because you've spent more nights in my guest bedroom than in your own apartment this past month."

"I'm not intimidated by you or Davey," Mia offered. "It's just memories coming back. You remember what happened with Cass. You know how it is, I can't control it."

Nodding, Jameson tapped one palm against his thigh.

"What are you remembering?" He asked. "When you black out, what do you see?"

"Davey didn't tell you?" Mia narrowed her eyes.

"Nope." Jameson's mouth popped on the p sound and he flashed her a knowing smile. "He said you didn't want to talk about it and so he wouldn't either."

"He said that?" Mia sucked on her bottom lip and considered. "I mean it's true, but…"

"But… you figured when I threatened to pull my recommendation after this mission that he'd give in and tell me?" Jameson offered, leaning forward.

"Well… yeah." Mia's heart tapped at her and she willed it to quiet down. "Why does he want your recommendation? What did you promise him when this is all over?"

"Ah." Jameson eased back into his chair and blew out a breath. "He wants back on a strike team. Completing this mission will earn him that right, and he might even get a promotion to Team Lead, depending. But that's all up to Uriah, of course."

You're a means to an end, nothing more. There are no feelings here, at least not on his side.

Closing her eyes, Mia laid back down in the bed and pulled the comforter up to her shoulders. Why did that upset her? She didn't need Davey to like her. She was fine just how she was.

Sighing, she let her body relax. The mattress beneath her was soft and thick. The sheets were like silk. The pillow under her head was heaven.

"What am I doing here?" Mia asked suddenly.

"You're here to do what you do best," Jameson answered. "Grow food."

"Why?" Mia persisted. There was something more going on. "Why here?"

"Why anywhere?" Jameson countered.

"Jameson..." Mia warned.

"Mia..." he echoed her tone.

Flicking her eyes open, Mia angled her face so she could peek at him over her covers. "I'm having flashbacks of my childhood. It wasn't what I thought it was and I don't want to talk about it. There I answered your question. Your turn."

Frowning, Jameson ducked his head.

"I'm sorry," he offered, before pushing up to standing. "About the flashbacks. We need to do whatever we can to prevent the fainting, doctor's orders."

"I can sort of feel them coming on," she admitted. "I'll warn Davey next time."

"Yeah..." Jameson clicked his tongue. "That's good, but I don't think it's going to be enough. I've authorized your body-guard/babysitter to start force feeding you every three hours. He'll monitor your fluid intake as well."

"What?" Mia blanched and sat upright in bed. "Are you kidding me? I do *not* want that. I do *not* need that."

"Yeah well..." Jameson rubbed at the scruff on his chin. "We can't always get what we want."

Turning away from her, Jameson dragged the heavy chair back to the corner he'd found it in. Mia's hands twisted in the blankets and her chest burned. There was no way she was going to be pushed around by Jameson… or Davey for that matter. She was *not* her mother.

"Jameson," Mia called and flipped back the covers. "You didn't answer my question."

Stopping at the door, Jameson threw her a quizzical look. "What question?"

"Why here?" Mia swung her legs over the edge of the bed. "What are we really doing here with two hundred soldiers in this abandoned city?"

Letting loose a low whistle, Jameson returned his focus to the door and pulled it open. The knob twisted and the door swung wide on silent hinges. The hallway behind him was vacant, from what she could see.

"Don't worry about that," he answered, before breezing through the threshold. "I've got it handled. You just do your part."

Mia glared at his back as he continued talking.

"You just grow the food, Mia. Leave everything else to me."

CHAPTER SEVENTEEN_
DAVEY

SLIPPING A PAIR OF BLUE CHECKED OVEN MITTS OVER HIS HANDS, Davey bent forward and opened the oven. Hot air blasted over his face, forcing him to shut his eyes a moment and let it pass. He'd forgotten what it was like to work one of these things. After all, it'd been at least six years since he'd baked anything.

Blinking his eyes open, Davey reached in and grabbed the baking sheet with both hands. The biscuits were a perfect golden color now, and the smell... it made his mouth water.

Stepping back, he flipped the oven door closed with a well-placed knee and plopped the sheet down on the granite counter in the massive kitchen. He had vegetable beef soup bubbling on the stove top and it needed some stirring.

Smacking his lips together, Davey shed the mitts and plucked a wooden stirring spoon out of the fancy utensil container that was sitting nearby. Only rich people used such things, he told himself, instead of putting it all in a drawer. Although, his mother had one when he was little, he thought, and they hadn't been rich.

Pursing his lips, Davey dismissed the memories and focused on the task at hand. The soup was from a can (or three), and the biscuits were from a box mix. He'd found them both in the kitchen pantry, which was the size of a walk-in closet.

Before leaving, Jameson told him he could go anywhere he wanted (that wasn't locked) and use whatever he found.

Apparently there was deep freezer storage somewhere, but Jameson needed to confirm there'd been no power interruption before giving the go ahead to use the food that was stored there. If it was good to go, then that meant they'd have milk, cheese, meat, vegetables, eggs, butter.

But Jameson didn't have time to check tonight, he had a perimeter to set up and troops to oversee. Which was fine by Davey, who was skeptical about what type of system would have to be used to keep such a room running for over a year without human intervention.

So he'd made due with the food in dry storage, and it was coming along pretty nicely if he did say so himself.

Lifting his head now, Davey eyed the open threshold of the kitchen. It led to the long hallway that ran from the front door all the way to the rear of the bunker. Mia's bedroom was connected to that corridor and even though Jameson had instructed him to give her space, Davey's senses had a mind of their own. He'd been listening for her for the past two hours.

At first, he'd stood outside her door and listened to her cry. He wanted to make sure she wasn't going to pass out again or have a seizure or something. Not that she'd had a seizure before, but still, what if she did?

But then eventually she'd stopped crying and Davey's pulse had risen. He'd started pacing the hall. Did she just fall asleep, or was she in trouble? He'd wanted to bust open her door right then and check, but he figured he needed an excuse for that sort of thing.

An excuse other than admitting he was officially a creeper now with a serious self-control issue.

So he'd stomped to the pantry instead, retrieved a granola bar, fetched a glass of water and then returned to her bedroom. Rapping lightly on the door for the sake of manners, he hadn't waited for her to answer before pushing it open. What he'd found inside made him all that much more guilty.

Mia was asleep, her body curled in on itself, her hair splayed out over her pillow. Her cheeks were flushed. The skin around her eyes was puffy from all the sadness.

Crossing to her, Davey's heart had pumped hard in his chest and he held his breath. What would be his excuse if she opened her eyes right then and caught him looming over her?

Giving his head a shake, he'd set the water and granola bar down on her nightstand and backed away.

What the hell was he doing?

She was fine. She was his job and nothing more. He was acting crazy. And what's worse, he had to force himself to leave without checking her damn pulse.

Ever since then, Davey had kept himself busy.

He explored the bunker, which was impossibly huge, with more rooms and stuff than he could've imagined. There was a library (complete with a grand piano), a gym (state of the art equipment galore), a game room (did somebody say pinball?), a tanning bed (come on people), and so much more.

Of course, the entire time his ears were still trained on that door. Anytime he passed by it, he paused. He didn't linger too long, a few seconds at the most. And at least he hadn't opened it again, so there was that.

Returning his attention to dinner now, Davey began to open cupboards in search of bowls. This place was equipped to serve an army, he realized, with fine china.

Muttering under his breath, he selected three large soup bowls and three matching plates. Jameson wasn't here right now, but Davey didn't want his "boss" to stroll back in mid-meal and wonder why he hadn't been included. The guy did hold Davey's future in his hands, so to speak, and so it would behoove him to remember that.

It wasn't like Davey to lose sight of his goals. Strike team. Lead Position. Mission to Valhalla. His soul yearned to be a warrior again, yearned for those brushes with death, maybe for death itself.

But something about Mia just set Davey off. He had trouble focusing. He had trouble keeping himself in check, which was weird and would absolutely *not* happen anymore. Nope.

Freezing in place then, Davey's senses spiked. Even with all the banging of cupboards and rattling of dishes, he heard it. Or rather, he heard her.

She was opening her door and stepping out onto the hardwood flooring. He didn't need to see her to know it was true.

Giving his head a determined shake, Davey resumed his work. Bowls on plates. Spoons from a nearby drawer. A spatula to remove the biscuits from the metal cooking sheet. The sounds and smells would bring her to him, he knew. She would find the kitchen soon enough.

When her figure finally filled the threshold, Davey refused to look over. He was ladling hot soup into a bowl and trying hard not to let any drip down the side. Mia's eyes were on him, making his blood heat and his lower belly clench just a little.

Blowing out a breath, Davey dismissed his reaction as hunger. Hot food was soooo much better than an MRE. He couldn't wait to sit and eat.

"Thank you," Mia's soft voice entered the space, drawing Davey's eyes over to her. "For the granola bar."

Waving the half eaten bar in the air, she offered him a smile. It was all pearly white teeth and no actual happiness. He was beginning to recognize that particular smile of hers as faker than fuck.

Nodding, Davey clenched his jaw tight and glanced back to the soup. One bowl down. One to go.

"But I don't need you to feed me," she continued. "I can manage that on my own."

Her feet were padding along the floor now, bringing her closer to him as he worked.

Again, Davey ignored her. He finished filling the second bowl and set it in the center of one of the large plates. Reaching for the spatula, he fished a biscuit off the sheet and set it down on the plate beside the bowl.

"One biscuit, or two?" He asked.

"What?"

"Do you want one biscuit with your soup," he spoke slowly now as he threw her a glance over his shoulder. "Or two?"

"Oh." Mia stopped short and considered.

Davey watched her. Maybe for a few beats longer than strictly necessary.

"I mean I just don't need you to make me eat," she amended. Her hand cruised up to smooth at her hair before her shoulders straightened. "Jameson mentioned force-feeding, and I want you to know that I won't allow that."

Raising an eyebrow, Davey held back a smirk. What the guy had actually said to him was that Mia needed to eat and drink every few hours from now on in case the fainting was triggered by low blood sugar. What Jameson said to Mia was apparently different though, and probably full of sarcasm.

"No holding you down and shoving food in your mouth." Davey returned his gaze to the plates on the counter. "Got it. So, do you want one biscuit or two?"

"Um..." Mia hesitated and Davey could practically feel her nibbling on that bottom lip of hers. "Two. I'd like two please."

Shifting around, Davey fetched another biscuit and plopped it onto her plate before scooping both plates up and carrying them out to the long dining room table. The thing could comfortably sit like fourteen people at one time, but he chose two seats directly across from each other, unloaded the plates, and then sat down.

Not bothering to wait for Mia to join him, Davey adjusted his chair before shoving half a biscuit into his mouth.

If he let himself glance over his shoulder right now, he'd be able to see Mia still lingering in the kitchen. The whole room was open-concept style, with expansive granite counters that wrapped around to create a bar area complete with six stools. *Six* stools. It was almost obnoxious.

He didn't know who in the hell built this underground mansion, but it was obviously somebody who'd had way too much money and time in their past life.

Setting the remains of his biscuit down, Davey took up a spoonful of soup and sighed. As it was, he had a perfect view of the massive living room with its numerous leather couches and even more expensive furnishings. End tables. Coffee tables. Ornate glass lamps.

On the far wall was perhaps the largest flat screen television he'd ever seen. Incredible. He hadn't watched tv in years and years.

"Are you going to eat or what?" Davey asked finally.

He didn't understand what her deal was right now, but the soup he'd poured her was getting cold.

Clearing her throat, Mia took her time walking around to her side of the table and settling down in the seat across from him. Davey couldn't help but track her with his eyes the entire way. After this latest memory, Mia was acting funny. He didn't recognize the girl now sipping politely at her soup on the other side of the table.

What had happened to the confident super model who crushed men's hearts in her bare hand? Where was that woman? The siren?

"Wow." Mia clinked her spoon against her plate and took a delicate bite of her biscuit. "This is actually really good. Where did you learn to cook?"

Davey halted his spoon halfway to his mouth. She was kidding right?

"I wouldn't really call this cooking," he said finally. "More like heating. The soup is from a can and the biscuits are a mix from a box. Just add water. You know, the usual stuff. I had a single dad for most of my life, remember?"

Nodding, Mia let her eyes drop to her plate once more.

Silence resumed for several minutes as they continued to eat. It was almost surreal. Sitting here in a formal dining room, eating dinner with a beautiful woman, off of fine china plates… with absolutely no idea what to say to her.

"I forgot drinks," Davey spoke suddenly. "I'll get us some. You want soda or water? It's not cold but it's wet."

"Soda?" Mia's face screwed up in question and it had Davey quirking a smile.

"You don't remember that one?" He asked.

With a flush to her cheeks, Mia nodded.

"Soda," she spoke the word like she was trying to taste it. "I don't know what to do with that one."

"Well you drink it," he teased.

"Yeah I got that part figured out," Mia scoffed, but her chocolate-brown eyes were twinkling now so he knew he was on the right track.

"How about I open a can so you can try some," Davey suggested. "And then if you don't like it, I'll finish it. We won't waste anything."

Pursing her lips together, Mia fought the grin that wanted to take over her pretty face. After a beat, she gave up and sat back in her chair. Drumming her fingers on the mahogany table top, she eyed him.

There she was, he thought, the flirty siren coming back out to play.

"Alright," she agreed. "Bring it on."

CHAPTER EIGHTEEN_
MIA

SODA WAS... DARK AND BUBBLY AND SYRUPY SWEET. MIA discovered that when you drank it too fast, the liquid burned a path all the way down to your belly. It wasn't unpleasant, but even while drinking it, she couldn't bring a memory of it forward.

She was sitting beside Davey now, sharing a red and white colored can, and Mia had to admit that the stuff was pretty good. The best part about it though, wasn't the taste. It was the look on Davey's face. He was happy.

His pale-blue eyes sparkled as he traded the can back and forth between them. They were angled in, facing each other. Davey had one arm braced on the tabletop and she had one leg tucked up beneath her. The can of soda was almost empty now, but still, they passed it back and forth, each taking a tiny sip while talking.

Mostly they talked about Davey's childhood. He was surprisingly open about his mother, his father and even Ryder, his baby brother. Only once had a flicker of darkness passed over his face when he'd first said his brother's name, but as Mia kept asking him questions, he relaxed, loosened, let his guard drop.

At one point, Davey even chuckled. Not a full on laugh, she noted, but the sound that he did make was full of pent up humor. It was deep and a little rumbly and the way he'd rolled his eyes had her own smile growing wider.

She'd known he was handsome before, in a mournful, edgy sort of way. With haunted eyes, smooth skin, a square jaw and thick blonde hair… but this?

Davey with a smile on his face was absolutely devastating to the entire female population.

As it was, Mia's whole body was warm.

"So this hockey game," Mia prompted. "It has to be cold to play it?"

Rotating the can in one hand, Davey huffed and gave her another smile.

"Yeah," he answered. "But you play it inside on ice so they have to keep the entire building freezing cold. My dad coached us for like five years."

"You really liked it." Mia reached for the can and almost jumped when her fingers brushed against Davey's.

"Yeah." Davey's eyes darted down as his tongue snuck out to wet his lips.

Clearing his throat, he removed his hand from hers and looked away. After a beat, Mia gripped the can and brought it up to her lips, letting the last few drops roll onto her tongue. It was truly empty, but she didn't care.

If Davey could pretend he was still drinking it, then so could she.

Besides, she didn't want to break the spell. She didn't want this *thing* that was happening between them, whatever it was, to end. He was making her forget about her horrid flashbacks, leaving her entire body feeling easy and light. Her smiles came naturally, just as his seemed to, and when it came to Davey, she'd take whatever she could get.

Davey's pale-blue eyes popped over to lock on hers then, making her heart flutter in her chest.

"Mia..." he began, but his words were cut short.

Down the hallway, a familiar sound rattled and twisted and shoved its way into their world. A key in the heavy front door. The swing of it opening. A pair of male voices entering the space.

Pushing up to standing, Davey stepped away from the table. The men didn't need to announce themselves for Mia to know it was Jameson and Malik. The two of them were in no way quiet.

"Soldier Wells!" Jameson's voice called as he approached. "I think we've got all your stuff here, and Mia's too."

"It's a lot of bags!" Malik chimed in. "And they're heavy. What does one woman need with so much stuff?"

Throwing Mia a sardonic look, Davey rounded the edge of the table and moved towards the kitchen.

"You get my rifle?" Davey called.

"Yes, we got your freaking weapon," Jameson answered with a sigh as his body filled the entrance to the kitchen. Jerking a finger over his shoulder, he continued, "It's leaning up against the wall by the front door."

"Great." Davey dipped his head and pushed his way out of the space just as Jameson and Malik were walking in.

Standing up from the table, Mia collected her empty plate and bowl. She eyed the can of soda for a second as well, before deciding to leave it where it was. She'd come back for it after clearing Davey's plate, she figured.

"Mia," Jameson said. "You're up. Great. How are you feeling?"

Lifting her face, Mia gave him a deliberate frown before piling all of the dishes in her hands. She hadn't forgotten about his "order" to force feed her. But Jameson didn't seem to catch her mood, he was already snooping by the stove.

"I'm feeling better," she answered finally and made her way to the sink.

Stopping in the center of the kitchen, Malik set down her bags with a groan.

"This soup still good?" Jameson asked.

"Should be," Mia replied, and reached for the soap.

Water on. Dishes clanking. Sponge swishing. She distracted herself with work.

Walking up to the counter, Malik grabbed a biscuit off the baking sheet, and took a massive bite.

"You make these?" He asked.

She could feel Malik coming closer now, running his fingertips along the granite countertop as he walked.

"Davey did," she answered, and threw Malik a sideways glance.

The soldier looked downright shocked for a second. His brows shot up and he gulped down the bite he'd been working on.

"That so?" He said, and gave his head a slight shake. "They're pretty good. I figured maybe you made them."

"It's a box mix," Davey announced, drawing all of their attention over to him. "It's not that hard."

He was standing on the threshold of the kitchen, his rifle

slung over his shoulder, his arms folded across his chest. Those pale-blue eyes of his were narrowed now as he watched the other man eating his food. All of that former sparkle was officially gone.

"Soldier Wells," Jameson drawled as his focus returned to the stove. "So modest."

Hot water was running over Mia's hands now, causing them to redden and burn. Sucking her hands back to her body, she tried not to jump. She should be more careful, she admonished herself, only an idiot would burn themselves while doing dishes.

Mia's stomach twisted suddenly as she realized that voice in her head was her father talking. She hated that he was in her head now. She wished she could go back to before, to not remembering.

"How are things topside?" Davey asked, unmoving.

"We're settled for now," Jameson answered. "We've been approached by a few of the men living here and I've set up a meet with the guy who is running things."

"You checking for tattoos?" Davey leaned to one side, resting his upper arm against the door frame.

Mia tried to stop glancing at him. Tried and failed. The water ran into the sink, her hands stopped scrubbing the dishes, but no one seemed to notice.

"Don't try to do my job," Jameson admonished, but then he answered anyway. "No code tattoos. Nothing like what Eli and those other men had."

"Well, we should ask around," Davey said, before belatedly adding, "Sir."

Turning to look at him fully, Jameson frowned.

"Keep your fucking eyes on your own lane," he spat, before

glancing at Mia. "Speaking of which, you're officially off shift. Go take a break. I've got her."

Mia's stomach dipped and her brows drew together.

You're just a job, remember?

"I thought you said we were the only ones staying here." Davey gestured to Malik, who answered with a wink. A wink!

"We are." Jameson flipped the burner off, took two steps sideways and snatched the remaining biscuit out of Malik's hand.

"What the...?" Malik's mouth dropped but Jameson cut him off.

"There ain't enough soup leftover for the both of us," he quipped before shoving the biscuit in his own mouth and talking around it. "You're out. See you at 0500."

"Oh come on!" Malik shot Mia a playful smile. "Can't I just stick around for one movie?"

Mia's eyes jumped from Malik's shining face to Davey's cloudy one. Her heart fluttered uncertainly and she fought the heat wanting to take over her cheeks. Turning back to the sink, Mia adjusted the water temperature and resumed her chore.

"No movie," Jameson countered. "You're out."

"Ah well..." Malik's hand reached out to give Mia's shoulder a few friendly taps. "Another time? There's some awesome choices in here, I've got nothing against chick flicks."

Giving him a small smile, Mia nodded her head before sucking her bottom lip into her mouth. A movie was something you watched on a... on a... She couldn't quite remember the last word, but she could picture it in her mind. A large box... a screen.

"It's a date then," Malik supplied before retracting his hand and sauntering away. "Maybe we'll get some time when things settle down in a few weeks. Okay with you boss?"

In her peripheral vision, Mia watched Jameson nod a few times and wave his soldier away.

Finishing up the dishes, Mia switched off the faucet and began her search for a towel to dry with. The silence around her was intense. She could hear Jameson spooning out his soup and clanking his bowl. She could hear Malik's boots retreating down the hallway and out the front door.

When the heavy thing swung decidedly shut, Mia chanced a glance at where Davey had been standing. He was gone.

Disappointment exploded in her belly. He was off shift, she realized, and that was that.

"Don't wash the pot," Jameson instructed. "I'll get it later."

Passing by her, he swung around and plopped down on one of the stools positioned just off the long granite counter. Mia looked past him, her eyes fixating on the soda can still on the table. She wanted it. For some reason, her hands itched to grab it and take it with her. Silly. But still…

"You sure you're okay?" Jameson slurped at his soup and glanced up at her. "I've got another day to canvas the area, but as soon as possible, I want to take you to the growing fields. Are you going to be able to handle that?"

"Absolutely." Mia brightened instantly at the prospect of seeing the land.

Something about growing things made her feel calm, made her feel the most like herself. It was something she could hold onto, something to focus on.

"Good." Jameson ducked his head and continued his meal. "Did Davey give you a tour of the place?"

"No," Mia sighed. "He didn't."

"Well, unless you're too worn out, I'll show you around in a few," he offered.

Glancing over her shoulder, Mia eyed her array of bags still set neatly on the kitchen floor. Seeming to follow her gaze, Jameson cleared his throat.

"I can carry your bags to your room too," he said. "If you want."

"No." Mia shook her head and returned her gaze to the bulky man sitting at the counter. He was hunched over, shoving a biscuit into his mouth like he was just a little boy. Crumbs fell everywhere, making her heart soften towards him.

"I can do it myself," she assured him. "I don't need you to help me. I don't need anyone's help."

"That so?" Jameson's eyes twinkled and he gave her a smirk.

"Yeah." Mia tipped her chin up and folded her arms across her chest. "That's so."

With a laugh, Jameson ducked his head and kept eating.

Firming her lips, Mia exhaled through her nose, and watched.

CHAPTER NINETEEN_
DAVEY

He avoided her.

They spent another thirty-six hours trapped together in the mini-mansion and yet Davey was somehow successful at giving her space. Mia was a job, he told himself. That's it. His concern for her was based purely off of his need to excel at his work, to reach his goals.

And anyway, like Jameson had said, when they were both down here alone, then Davey was officially off the clock.

So he hit the gym (twice), played ski-ball (until the high score was his, thank you very much), watched Terminator 1 *and* 2, and avoided the library.

Why?

Because that's where Mia spent the majority of her time. Reading. Sighing. Murmuring to herself.

How did Davey know this? Because apparently his new super power was a hypersensitivity to everything tall, blonde and pretty. His Mia tracking senses were working on overdrive. He knew when she took a shower. He knew when she went to sleep. He knew when she woke up.

The whole thing was ridiculous actually, and it left him feeling slightly desperate to get outside again. He needed to see the sun, inhale the fresh air, have the possibility of getting shot at, or better yet, the possibility of shooting at someone else. Yeah. At this point, either option was acceptable.

"Morning." Jameson sauntered into the kitchen already dressed in full uniform and stopped beside Davey at the stove.

Stifling a yawn, Davey's "boss" stretched like an overgrown bear before snatching a slice of bacon that was cooling on a plate beside the griddle. The deep freezer storage room had been deemed safe by the illustrious Malik and so now all bets were off when it came to food.

Scowling, Davey's hand snaked out and drilled Jameson's forearm with his spatula.

"Ow!" Jameson yelped and jumped back. "Fucker."

"Sir." Davey replied calmly as he continued to flip pancakes.

Scrambled eggs, bacon, strawberries. *Coffee*. The smells alone were enough to make a grown man salivate.

"She up yet?" Jameson asked, still chomping on the bacon.

Brow furrowing, Davey continued to cook as Jameson rounded the long granite counter and plopped down on one of the stools.

Yeah. She was up.

Davey slept with his door open, so the moment Mia started walking around in the morning, he knew. It helped that he didn't sleep well. It helped that he was constantly restless. It also helped that their bedrooms were right next door to each other and neither one of them had an ensuite bath.

When Mia left her room to walk down the hall to take a shower, Davey watched.

"That's good," Jameson commented. "I'd like to be up top and assembled by dawn."

Glancing at the old style clock on the far wall, Davey dipped his head. That shouldn't be a problem, he figured. He was already dressed and his weapon was waiting for him by the door. All they had to do now was eat breakfast and walk out.

"Something smells amazing," Mia's voice floated to them from somewhere down the hall.

Refusing to look over and watch her enter the kitchen, Davey busied himself removing the last of the pancakes from the griddle. Mia's boots thumped against the hardwood flooring as she walked up beside him and let out one of her contented little sighs. Damn it if the sound didn't have his belly clenching.

"I'll do the dishes," she volunteered, as one of her slender hands reached out to pluck up a piece of bacon.

Swallowing, Davey nodded his agreement and retrieved some plates from one of the cupboards.

"You let her steal bacon," Jameson pointed out from his position on the barstool. "And she doesn't hold your future in the palm of her hand."

Actually she does, Davey thought suddenly, and then pursed his lips. Did she?

Giving his head a brisk shake, he plopped the plates on the sink and stepped back. If Mia got hurt or worse, killed on his watch then yeah, he was fucked. So technically she did hold his future in her hands that way. It made sense if you really thought about it. Yup. It made perfect job-related sense.

When Mia slid over to step in front of him and grab one of the plates, Davey blanched. He hadn't really got a good look at her until that moment. His heart thumped at him and his jaw dropped.

"You're wearing *that?*" He spat.

Skin tight jeans, ankle boots, practically see-through white tank top (she was wearing a hot-pink bra, by the way) and a ridiculous sun hat. It was everything mouth-watering and feminine and completely ridiculous, given the circumstances.

Rounding on him, Mia firmed her lips and fisted her free hand on one hip.

"*Lipstick?*" Davey's eyebrows raised. "You're wearing hot-pink lipstick?"

"It's a gloss," Mia countered, continuing to stare him down. "And there's nothing wrong with my outfit. It's going to be hot out there and I don't want to sweat to death in long sleeves and camo pants. We aren't traveling through dangerous territory anymore and you secured the perimeter or whatever. That means we're safe now… right?"

Davey's jaw snapped shut as a million things flooded his mind. Safe?

There was no such thing as "safe" out here beyond the Wall. There were things you could do to lessen the threat, yes. Perimeters and soldiers and escorts and guns. All those things gave you some measure of security, but it wasn't full proof.

Especially when you stuck a siren with lips the color of bubble gum and a body that begged to be touched in the middle of a sea of men that hadn't seen a woman in years.

"Ah… Mia?" Jameson piped up. "I'm with Davey on this one. We're touring the farming fields today and although I told the guy running things that you were a woman, it's still probably going to come as a bit of shock. Especially since… you know…"

Waving his hand vaguely in Mia's direction, Jameson scrunched his nose and cleared his throat. Davey watched as Mia's eyes narrowed.

"No, I don't know," she said, waving at herself the same way Jameson had. "It's not like I'm wearing my mini-skirt and crop top."

"Well, you're... ah..." Jameson chuckled nervously. "You know, you're not Cass, but... but..."

"But. What." Mia arched an eyebrow.

"You're hot," Davey blurted the words before he could stop himself.

Where the hell had that come from? Wait... she brought a mini-skirt?

"You think I'm hot?" Mia whirled on him, her chocolate-brown eyes zeroing in on his.

Looking away, Davey shrugged. Describing Mia as hot was an understatement, and the idea that she wasn't 100% aware of that fact was beyond his comprehension. Mini-skirt or no.

"You're making my job harder," he offered finally, before stepping around her and grabbing a plate for himself. "Lose the lipstick and change into a uniform. Please."

Reaching for the spatula, Davey plopped two pancakes onto his plate. All the while he could feel Mia's eyes burning a hole in the side of his face. It made his stomach churn and his jaw clench even tighter, but he kept his eyes on the food in front of him. Strawberries, syrup, scrambled eggs, bacon.

Seconds passed.

She still didn't say anything. She was obviously mad at him. Again.

Avoiding her gaze, Davey turned and strolled out of the

kitchen. Play it cool. Let the storm roll past. He wasn't going to back down.

Taking a seat on the stool beside Jameson, Davey focused all of his attention on his meal. Normally, he would've gone to the table, but damn it if he didn't feel like he needed a buffer between him and Mia's silent treatment. Shit. Why did she twist him up like this? He. Shouldn't. Care.

"Fine," Mia spat the word, causing Davey to glance up at her. "Let it be known that I am making the *choice* to change based on your *request,* but unless we are going out to work, then I never want to hear your opinion of my clothing ever again. Got that?"

Swallowing, Davey nodded. His eyes dropped to his plate and he made himself stab a forkful of pancake and shove it into his mouth. He was sweating all of a sudden. Why the hell was he sweating?

"Thank you Mia," Jameson chimed in. "It's not that you don't always look nice, it's just that maybe you look too nice for out here. Okay? It's nothing against your style. You have great style."

"Now you're just saying things you've heard Cass say to me," Mia countered. "You can just stop right there Mr. Faker."

Chuckling, Jameson pushed back from the counter and went to fill his own breakfast plate. Davey continued shoving food into his mouth. He needed the fuel for a day spent topside, even if he was suddenly no longer hungry.

"So, do you think we can be out the door in twenty minutes?" Jameson asked.

"I'll do my best," Mia answered sweetly. Too sweetly?

A tense sort of silence filled the kitchen while Mia and

Jameson piled food on their plates. Silverware clinked against dishes. Boots shuffled across the floor. It didn't go beyond Davey's notice that Mia stalked right past him and took a seat at the long mahogany dining table at his back.

It was like he could feel her staring daggers at him, even though he knew logically she wasn't. He could hear her fork scraping against her plate and her glass of water tapping against the table top. But still, this tension that filled the air all around him was now taking over his body and it was new. He couldn't quite shake it, although he tried.

Grinding his teeth, Davey fought back against the nagging sensation to apologize. Why did he care if Mia was upset? He was just doing his job. He was just trying to keep her safe.

"I'm sorry," Davey blurted suddenly. He was? Shit. "I didn't mean to insult your outfit. I'm just trying to do my job. What I said came out wrong."

Beside him, Jameson choked on a bite of egg. Thumping a closed fist against his chest, the guy hacked for a solid three seconds before gulping down a cup of disgustingly sugary coffee. When he was done, Davey's boss gave him a bit of side eye before swiveling to look at Mia over his shoulder.

"At this rate, we're going to be late," he said.

"We wouldn't be late if I didn't have to change," she countered.

"Mia." Jameson sighed, running a hand down his face.

"I'll scrub the dishes," Davey volunteered. "And wait by the door."

Beside him, Jameson's mouth dropped. Mia didn't say a word.

. . .

Ten minutes later, Davey found himself weaving along a collection of dim corridors on their way to the surface. Mia strode confidently in front of him with Jameson in the lead before her. That silky blonde hair of hers bounced against her shoulders as she clutched her helmet in one hand at her hip.

Thankfully she'd changed into a loose fitting uniform, and yet somehow he still had to talk himself out of staring at her ass.

Frowning, Davey shifted the rifle in his hands, taking comfort in the heavy feel of it. He could do this job and be done with this job and these feelings would go away.

As they moved through the passageways and beeped through heavy doors, Davey could sense the surface approaching. A humidity took over the air. It was almost like you could inhale summer. Perspiration began to bead down his spine and for once, he welcomed it.

Fresh air. Sunshine. *Freedom*. They were only a short walk away.

When they finally shoved out into the parking garage, the noise that greeted them felt almost deafening. Sure, they'd only been isolated together for less than three days, but it had been a quiet three days.

The sound of fifty soldiers milling around was like the rumble of thunder. It was an assault on your senses. The energy built in your bones, pushing adrenaline out into your fingertips.

This was home, Davey thought suddenly. Soldiers. Work. Purpose. Violence. *This* was his comfort zone.

Throwing Davey a quick look over his shoulder, Jameson's eyes sparked and a smile ticked at the corner of his mouth.

Excitement. Jameson *knew*. He understood what this noise was, and he felt the exact same way about it that Davey did.

For maybe the first time ever, Davey saw his new boss as a soldier too. He saw him as a guy just like him, making choices because he's had to do so in order to survive.

Forgiveness was too strong a word for what Davey was feeling, but there was a loosening. That knot of hatred, that knot of anger that he'd carried with him for so long, relaxed inside of him in that moment.

"Alright." Jameson gestured to a Humvee. "We're going to be riding together. Malik, Evans, Malpas, and Locklan will be joining. We have to meet this guy DeKalb down in the fields where Mia's going to work."

"How long will your crew be accompanying us?" Davey asked.

His eyes swept the space, taking in the number of guys milling around, the vehicles present, the mood, the everything. In front of him, Mia shifted her helmet under her arm and tucked a stray hair behind one ear.

"Put your cover on," he instructed, and reached up to tap her shoulder.

With a growl, Mia brushed his hand away and slammed the helmet on her head. Ahead of her, Jameson suppressed a grin before returning his focus forward.

"As long as it takes," he supplied, continuing to walk towards the collection of vehicles. "Weeks or maybe longer, if you feel it's necessary."

Bobbing his head, Davey exhaled. That's the answer he wanted.

"Sir!" Malik's voice rose above the din, causing Davey's eyes to narrow.

The soldier was standing beside the Humvee with a radio in his hand. The front passenger door was hanging open and he gestured to the black mic he was holding.

"You should hear this," Malik continued. "It's the call we've been looking for."

Picking up to a jog, Jameson hustled the last fifty yards to the vehicle. Eyebrows raised, Mia shot Davey a look.

Davey tipped his chin in Jameson's direction, as if to say, keep walking, let's see what this is about.

As they neared the vehicle, the soldiers all around them fell to silence. Jameson slid into the shotgun seat and adjusted the radio. Volume Up. Way up. Malik handed him the mic and pursed his lips.

Coming to a stop beside Mia, Davey adjusted his rifle and glanced around. Still all clear. Only friendlies down here. Then the radio started squawking and the words that came across were painfully clear.

If anyone's out there. I'm calling for help. We have women and children in need of food and…

Static.

Our location is just south of Provo, Utah. If you can hear this message, please bring food and any medical supplies you may have.

Static.

If anyone's out there. I'm calling for help. We have women and children in need of food and…

As the call began to repeat itself, Jameson's eyes rose to meet Davey's. Disbelief. A touch of fear. Davey's heart pounded in his chest suddenly. Hard.

"Is that Eli's voice?" Davey whispered. "Do you recognize it?"

Clearing his throat, Jameson glanced away. "Yeah," he murmured finally. "Yeah, it is."

CHAPTER TWENTY_

ELIJAH ROE

PERSPIRATION BEADED BETWEEN HIS SHOULDER BLADES. THE muscles in his upper back and arms tensed and flexed. Blowing out a slow breath, Eli twisted the bat in his hands. It felt smooth, the weight of it sitting perfectly in his grip.

Overhead, the sun shone down from a perfectly cloudless blue sky. If there was a breeze blowing somewhere in the world, it certainly wasn't felt here.

"You stand like a chicken taking a shit," Liam murmured.

Firming his lips, Eli took his eyes off the pitcher on the mound and glanced down at the oversized catcher squatting just beside him.

"Don't listen to him Eli!" Cass called from a few yards away. "Your stance is spot on!"

Before he could muster a reply, a baseball zipped past him, thumping solidly into Liam's waiting mitt.

"Strike 2!" Hannah shouted and had Liam grinning behind his wire face mask.

"That's total crap!" Cass complained. "It was obviously high and wide. Ball 1!"

Relaxing his shoulders, Eli lowered the bat and stepped back. Liam tossed the ball to Cole who was serving as pitcher and resumed his position as catcher.

Swinging the bat loosely through the air, Eli forced his muscles to relax and his mind to focus. He had no memory of ever playing this game before, and yet… his body seemed to know just how to move.

Lifting his face, Eli's eyes swept over the small crowd of spectators. There were a few dozen people sitting in the grass off to one side. They'd spread out blankets and were eating snacks and drinking. A baby cried. A man laughed.

"Come on princess," Liam commented. "We don't have all day."

With a smirk, Eli continued to swing the bat lazily and survey the crowd. When his eyes finally landed on their intended target, he outright grinned.

The redhead. She was sitting there watching him, just as she always was.

And yes, it was Doctor Shelby's job to study him, he was her project, her assignment. He had no memories past about two months ago and she was trying to figure out how to tap into that darkened part of his brain. In fact, he was playing this very game based on her suggestion… but still, he liked to think that she was enjoying the view all the same.

Tipping his chin at her, Eli let a megawatt smile take over his whole face. Shelby's blue eyes narrowed at him then before she glanced down. That delicate pixie hand of hers started scribbling furiously over her ever present pad of paper, and her tumble of red hair fell forward to frame her face. Eli's fingers itched to touch it, and his chest filled suddenly with air.

"Easy lover boy." Liam made a tisk tisk sound. "The good doc is all business, and you're all play."

Frowning, Eli shot Liam a dubious look before taking his place back at the mound.

"You're too tall for a catcher," Eli commented. "You look like a damn grasshopper."

Liam gave up a non-committal huff and shifted on his feet. The ball came in fast then, and just like Cass had said before, it was a bit high and outside. That didn't matter to Eli though. Before he could blink, his muscles were contracting and his bat was connecting with the ball.

Crack.

The sound of it alone had Eli's insides zinging. He dropped the bat and took off running. The ball soared.

In the background, he heard shouting. Cole was screaming his head off from the pitcher's mound and Cass was screeching at Eli to run.

Not a problem. First base was already his.

Then second.

Then third.

When he rounded the plate and headed for home, Liam was standing there waiting for him. His glove was outstretched, his eyes focused on the outfield. Eli ducked his head and tore the ground up beneath his shoes. Running. Sprinting. Arms pumping and legs jamming.

He slipped a little in the loose dirt and something in his brain registered that wasn't usual. He was wearing the wrong shoes. But the correct type of shoes refused to pop into his head. He couldn't get a word or an image to come forward.

All of these things happened in seconds as the ball whizzed past Eli's head and straight into Liam's glove. Instinct took over. Eli charged hard at Liam and at the last possible moment, he laid down in the dirt and slid, his toe pointing to home plate.

Dust rose up all around him and the feel of the ground burning against his thigh and his side and his forearm came hot and fast. Then the weight of Liam tagging him with his glove registered, but not before his foot hit the plate.

"Safe!" Cass was screaming at the top of her lungs now. "He's safe! He's safe!"

People were cheering. Eli could hear their shouts mixing with applause and hoots of laughter. When the dust cleared, Eli blinked up at Liam who was standing over him, frowning behind his catcher's mask.

"I thought you said he had a football scholarship," Liam stated.

Reaching up, he pulled the mask from his face and stared. His dark eyes were zeroed in on Eli's laughing ones as Cass jogged out to the plate.

"He played both until high school," Cass explained. "But the private school that recruited him needed a quarterback, not a short stop who could run. So he had to choose."

"Is that so?" Liam cocked his head to one side and continued to stare down at Eli. "Fancy rich school, huh?"

Shrugging, Eli dusted himself off and pushed up to standing. He could care less about this conversation. About fancy schools and baseball and quarter-whatever.

His eyes swept the crowd and landed on Shelby once more. She was watching him again, and this time when their eyes locked, a faint blush rose on her cheeks. Glancing down quickly, Shelby shuffled through the pages of her notebook.

The pen she clutched in her tiny hand came up to her mouth and she bit down on the end.

Damn it, Eli thought. She has no idea how sexy that is.

"You're bleeding," Cass said, causing Eli to look down at himself.

The dirt at his feet had a few spots of blood soaking in as the red stuff dripped down his fingertips.

Frowning, Eli rotated his right arm around and examined his forearm. It was hard to tell where exactly the scrape was because of all the black geometric tattoos covering him. The design simply took over his skin from his wrists all the way to his elbows. Circles, dots, squares and lines.

"I hope you didn't just fuck up the pattern," Liam commented.

With another shrug, Eli brushed his left palm down his right arm and winced slightly when he located the scrape. He didn't think it would screw with the tattoo, but the only reason he cared was because Shelby was so obsessed with it. She spent hours tracing it, touching it, studying it.

And Eli absorbed every single second under the redhead's examination. Even if she truly only looked at him in the name of science. Even if she didn't feel the pull between them like Eli did.

"Lucky for me..." Eli shot Liam a cocky grin. "I know a good doctor. One that can patch me right up."

Liam's lips pressed together in a firm line and the two men eyed one another. They were almost the same height actually and that was saying something, as Liam was freakishly tall. In fact, they had a similar look all the way around. Broad shoulders, trim waist, olive skin, dark hair.

The only difference really, was in the eyes. Liam's were obsidian dark while Eli's were a sparkly hazel. Liam was the ice to Eli's fire. Other than that, they could almost be brothers.

"I wonder what that's all about," Cass's voice broke their staring contest as she gestured to the crowd.

Following her line of sight, all the laughter in Eli's body left him. There were soldiers in full uniform pushing through the crowd, and they were clearing a path straight to Shelby. Mouths were moving, but Eli couldn't hear what they were saying to her from this distance.

She was shaking her head no, and spreading her palms out wide. Eli's stomach coiled. She was upset over whatever they were saying to her, and it had his fists balling.

"Huh." Liam gave one of his non-committal grunts, but before the guy could say anything, Eli was off.

Stepping out at a light jog, Eli cleared the baseball field with long strides. His vision was focused on Shelby the entire time. He watched her stand abruptly and run a hand back through that lovely red hair of hers. One of the soldiers stepped closer, into her space, and that's when she looked to Eli. Their gazes locked and he *knew*.

He knew in that moment that whatever was going down, it was about him. Her blue eyes widened a touch and her lips kept moving. She was still talking to the solider, who was just now following her gaze.

Eli didn't stop charging towards them. He didn't stop when the soldier turned to meet him. He didn't stop when Shelby's delicate hand reached out to grab uselessly at the soldier's arm. He didn't stop when the guy shrugged her off.

"Are you Elijah Roe?" The soldier asked, as Eli came up to them.

"I am," Eli answered and expertly slipped his body between the soldier and Shelby.

He used his body to bump her back and it didn't go beyond his notice that her palms planted firmly against the small of his back. All the while, her beautiful voice was running a line of protests a mile long.

"This is premature," she argued. "Any further intervention now could harm my progress. You need to tell your boss that he has to speak with me first."

The soldier ignored her and instead let his right hand drift down to the holster at his hip.

"Elijah Roe," he said. "I need you to come with us."

Before Eli could muster a response, Liam was growling just off to his left side. Eli thought he'd left Liam on the filed. He hadn't even sensed the guy coming after him. Nothing other than getting to Shelby had even registered.

"Where the hell do you think you're taking him?" Liam demanded.

"Officer Byrne," the soldier addressed his superior. "I'm going to need you to come too. Commander Linfield's orders."

CHAPTER TWENTY-ONE_

MIA

All hell broke loose. That's the only way Mia could describe it.

Jameson was barking into the radio with one hand and then barking at Davey standing just beside him. The two men were arguing, going around and around while the soldiers who were once standing still in the parking garage were now scattering.

Some of them were making ready to depart. Others were racing off to locate more equipment. And in the middle of it all, Mia stood silently beside Malik, and watched.

"You *know* there is no better man for this job than me," Davey was saying.

He had one arm braced on the still open door frame of the Humvee and the other jamming a finger at his own chest. Jameson sat shotgun, staring out the front windshield. His long legs were bent in front of him, one boot tapping at the floorboards.

Static burst from the radio then, and had Jameson huffing an indignant breath.

"You already have a fucking job, Soldier Wells," Jameson spat, clutching the radio's mouth piece in his oversized hand. "Are you telling me you're abandoning your post?"

Without glancing back at her, Davey swung a heavy arm in Mia's direction and pointed. She knew the words he was about to say before they even escaped his mouth... because he'd said them already. Twice.

"Secure her in the bunker," Davey argued. "It's a damn fortress. Let me go down south with you and get these guys. You and I are the only two men here who've fought this particular enemy. It's a fucking waste to leave me behind."

"I have a team on site here and they're solid," Jameson countered. "*Not* that it's any of your business because this simply is not your call Soldier. Now I'm warning you to shut your fucking mouth before you make me do something I regret."

The radio squawked once again, drawing Jameson's gaze down to it.

Words were exchanged, although they were garbled and hard to make out. Mia heard the name *Eli* clearly followed by the word *interrogation.*

Jameson swallowed visibly and began to argue with the voice on the other end of the radio. It was a man named Cookie who was apparently the intermediary between them and the Wall. They were too far away to get a direct radio connection.

At Mia's back, boots pounded the ground. Old dust lifted into the dim light as one of the many armored Jeeps roared to life. Mia's heart pounded in her chest then, and her stomach sank.

Why did this hurt? She didn't know why listening to Davey trying to ditch her hurt so bad, but it did.

Swallowing, Mia grabbed her right arm with her left hand and rubbed at her sleeve. She shouldn't have come here. She should never have left the Wall. She missed Cass, and she missed her familiar plot of land in the greenhouse. She missed the buzz of bees and the smell of orange blossoms at dawn.

Birds didn't sing here. Nothing sang here. She shouldn't have agreed to come.

"Hey," Malik's voice sounded against her ear. "You okay?"

Nodding, Mia attempted to clear her throat. For some reason she couldn't rip her eyes from the display in front of her. The broody blonde soldier still arguing like hell to march into danger somewhere south of here had her full attention. She couldn't stop watching Davey, who was either going on this mission to possibly get killed or was about to get knocked out by his boss for insubordination. One option or the other was a surety at this point.

"You're safe here," Malik went on. "And he wouldn't actually leave you, even if he had the chance to go."

Blowing out a breath, Mia felt her pulse skitter and bounce. *Yes. Yes, he most definitely would.*

"Look, I'll show you." Malik wrapped an arm around her shoulders and drew her in close against his body. Then, giving her a squeeze, he called, "I'll stay with her guys, problem solved."

Stiffening, Davey glanced over his shoulder. His pale-blue eyes zipped to Malik's face before narrowing.

For three silent seconds, Davey's gaze traced along the arm Malik had wrapped tightly around Mia's shoulders. His jaw clenched and his nostrils flared.

Storm clouds. That was the only way to describe the look that took over Davey's face. His body was twisting away from the Humvee and he was stomping towards them in less than a breath.

"Keep your fucking hands to yourself!" Davey exploded. "I swear, didn't your mama teach you anything? I can't turn my back for one fucking minute without you touching everything that doesn't belong to you! You're just like a little kid in a damn candy store. What the hell is wrong with you, Malik?"

Before Malik could reply, Davey's hands were wedging between them and shoving the soldier away. Mia was swept to one side as Davey cut between them and angled his body towards Malik. Sucking in a giant breath, he then proceeded to chew Malik's ass. There were just no other words for it.

Holding up both hands in defense, Malik kept a giant grin on his face the entire time. At one point, he even tipped his chin at Mia and winked. Winked! He was notorious for it at this point, but the flash of flirtation had Davey snarling. He stepped further into Malik's space until their chests were a breath away from bumping.

Malik, of course, refused to step back.

Closing her eyes, Mia drew in a ragged breath. A memory. It was swirling around on the outskirts of her mind. She could sense the figures standing just in front of her, like Malik and Davey, but not. It was one man facing down other men. Her uncle? He was shouting… shoving.

Had Mia's father found her?

Clamping her jaw shut, Mia pushed back against the darkness. She couldn't pass out right now. This was not the time. Forcing her eyes open wide, Mia's hands slammed down to her sides where her fingers curled tightly in the fabric of her pants. She refused to let her mind put her under in this moment.

"Alright Soldier Wells." Jameson was suddenly standing beside the two men. His heavy hand landed on Davey's shoulder. "Looks like you've got a choice. Either you join the team that I'm sending out right now and leave Mia in Soldier Malik's care, or you can stay at your post and watch others go in your place.

It's your lucky day that I'm even giving you a choice. I *should* just shit-can you. To be honest, I don't know why I'm not."

Blinking, Davey turned his face to the side and gave Jameson a long look.

"You know why," he said quietly, before stepping away.

Jameson's hand slid off Davey's shoulder and down to his side. Malik's eyebrows rose in question, but neither man elaborated.

Giving her head a brisk shake, Mia pressed trembling fingers to her temples. She could only guess as to the actual reason why Jameson didn't fire Davey, but her history with both men gave her a pretty good idea. It was all about a certain man named Ryder Arthur Wells. It was all about a botched execution that had happened in a thick forest about a thousand miles from here.

Without glancing at Mia, Davey's jaw ticked and he swallowed once. Mia watched his throat bob and the muscles in his shoulders tense.

"I'll stay," he said finally.

"Then it's all settled," Jameson announced. "Malik, you're up. Take your team and run the surveillance op we discussed."

"Yes Sir," Malik snapped the words out as his teasing face turned serious.

"Radio silence. Check-in beeps at 0600 and 1800," Jameson instructed.

"Unless shit goes south and then flip to Operation Burn," Malik finished. "I got this."

"Yeah." Jameson's jaw firmed and he gave a curt nod. "You do. Don't mess up. Come back to annoy me."

With another smile, Malik flashed those perfect white teeth of his. His dark eyes darted from his boss, and landed on Mia. That's when they turned twinkly again and had her swallowing. He was something else, she thought, Malik had personality to spare.

"Maybe I'll get that movie one night soon?" He asked and outright laughed when Davey growled. *Growled.* "But without the babysitter," Malik added.

"Fuck. Off." Davey spat, but before he could step up, Malik was jogging away.

Inhaling, Mia choked on the fumes from half a dozen idling vehicles. She'd been holding her breath for too long, fighting back the memory, fighting her feelings for Davey.

Suddenly the air in the underground parking garage felt hot and thick. Sweat slicked down her spine and she felt dizzy.

Without another word, Jameson stalked back to his Humvee and yanked on the radio. Barking into it, he sent another set of soldiers scrambling. More engines fired up and some of them began to drive away.

Closing her eyes, Mia reached up to twine her fingers in her hair. It was itchy beneath her helmet. She wanted so badly to rip the heavy thing off and she hadn't even been wearing it for that long.

As another fit of coughing threatened to overtake her, Mia's chest rose and fell. The memories were gone now, but the glimpse she'd gotten made her heart squeeze and her mind race. Her uncle had been there, standing between her and other men. She hadn't let herself see him, but somehow she still knew who it was, and she knew they'd been in danger. There was an achey tension in every inch of her skin now because of it.

"Hey," Davey's voice was so close that Mia jumped.

Before she even opened her eyes, she could feel Davey's wide hands landing on her upper arms. He meant to steady her, and to him that's all it was... a necessary touch, a normal touch. But to her it was a jolt of sparks racing through her blood. And although a part of her wanted to yank away from him, another part wanted to come closer, to feel more.

"You okay?" He asked, peering into her face as she blinked her eyes open. "You good? You gonna pass out on me?"

"I'm fine," Mia managed, but she couldn't keep the shake from her voice.

Her uncle. The fear. Davey. It was all too much.

Davey's eyes darted across her face before he frowned. "You have a memory? A flashback?"

"No," Mia lied and gave her head a fierce shake. "It's just hot out."

"You're a bad liar Blondie," Davey commented. His fingers pulsed along her arms and made her thighs clench.

"Let go of me," Mia gasped, hating her reaction and needing more of it all at the same time. Why did she have to want this man? Why couldn't she want the one that had just jogged away? The one who actually wanted her?

Davey's eyes widened in surprise before he straightened and stepped back. His arms fell to his sides where Mia watched as his hands curled and uncurled themselves.

"You ready?!" Jameson called from beside the Humvee.

Davey scowled before glancing at the guy over his shoulder. Mia followed his gaze.

"Ready for what?" Davey asked.

"Our meet with DeKalb." Jameson jerked a thumb at the empty vehicle. "We're already late and we have a limited window of time to spend here before winter. Can't afford to waste a day."

Turning fully, Davey gave Mia his back and crossed his arms over his chest. She could imagine the look currently transforming his face. She'd seen it enough times in their time together.

"You still want to tour the farming setup today," Davey stated. "Even after the call from Provo. Even while you're running an op and all the shit going on with Eli."

"You saying I can't handle it?" Jameson lifted a brow. "Or maybe it's you that can't handle it. You want me to have someone else do your job? Seriously Wells, I'm beginning to wonder about Liam and Cole recommending you. They said you were the best. That you could focus like no other. It's go time Soldier."

"I am the fucking best." Davey's shoulders rolled even as he kept his arms crossed. "I just don't keep my opinions inside my head like a good little boy anymore… call it a newly developed character flaw."

Jameson arched an eyebrow. Davey continued to talk.

"And we can't go today," he said. "Mia had a memory. I need to get her back to the bunker to rest."

"No I didn't," Mia protested.

Picking up her feet, she shoved past Davey and headed straight for the Humvee. "I'm good to go. Let's see the farm."

"What the..." Davey's voice chased after her, but Mia refused to turn around.

"I'm solid." Mia nodded briskly to Jameson before yanking open the rear passenger door and climbing inside. "We're burning daylight."

"You heard the lady," Jameson barked. "Get in."

CHAPTER TWENTY-TWO_
DAVEY

BOUNCING ALONG IN THE HUMVEE, DAVEY KEPT HIS RIFLE HELD loosely in his lap. Hot air blasted in from the open rear window as the radio mounted on the front console continued to squawk. The voice that snapped and sassed from the speaker was a familiar one, and something about hearing Cookie bite at Jameson like the cranky old man he was, helped to keep Davey from losing his shit.

"Well that's all they're willin' to give me over the damn radio son," Cookie's voice crackled. "What the hell you want me to do? Huh? You want me to jog a few hundred miles and break down the damn interrogation door?"

"I want to know why there's an interrogation door at all." Jameson's jaw ticked as he gritted out the words. "Are you speaking to Commander Linfield? Tell him Officer Jameson is the one who needs to know."

Letting his eyes travel over the changing landscape as they drove, Davey took note of everything. Buildings turned to apartments. Apartments to houses. Houses to farms.

All the while, he listened to Jameson's desperate demands and he tried not to care.

But the not caring part was hard all of a sudden. Davey had met Eli on that last mission. He'd seen for himself when the guy gunned down his own men in order to save Cass and Mia. He'd watched as Liam removed that source microchip from the guy's hand and his brain went dead on him. He'd been there when Eli had woken up like a baby, fresh and unknowing just like Hannah and Mia and Cass had once been.

Now the poor sap was being dragged into some little fucking room inside the Wall with the best interrogator the world had left to offer.

Liam Bryne. *The Cutter.*

Liam was a well-known member of the The Hangmen Crew (of which Davey had also been a part… or was still a part of, technically speaking). Although Cole despised that nickname, it had stuck just the same. It was an awful reminder of what they all had become during the war, or after it. It was a reminder of what they still were. Bad. Evil. Brutal. Alive.

Firming his lips now, Davey tried like hell to brush that touch of pity for Eli away. He'd seen his fair share of Liam's work. Hell, he'd *listened* to more of it than he'd wanted to. Some things you can never un-see. Some sounds you can never un-hear.

Beside him now, Mia twisted her fingers together. She was sitting just beside him, sharing the middle seat with Soldier Malpas. Her dark eyes remained straight forward, as if the key to existence lay somewhere directly outside that front windshield.

Davey blew a slow breath through his nostrils as he struggled not to stare at the side of her face. The cold shoulder from her was upon him now, and he would be lying to himself if he said he didn't feel the icicles freezing him right down to his bones.

He didn't know when he'd started to care about Mia, but the truth was hitting him hard right between the eyes. He did. He simply *cared* about her. A lot.

It mattered to him that she'd had a memory and lied about it. It mattered to him that she was putting herself in danger when she could be safe inside that bunker. It mattered to him that she was angry at him. And it mattered to him that maybe she liked Malik.

Because who wouldn't like that guy? He was smart and good at everything and fucking smiley as hell. Girls loved that crap.

Damn it. Did Mia love that crap?

In the seat in front of Davey, Soldier Locklan was gripping the steering wheel tightly. His knuckles were white, but his movements steady as he followed the armored Jeep in front of them. There were five vehicles total all traveling together towards the outskirts of the abandoned city.

That's where the growing fields were.

That's where their meeting with destiny was scheduled for today.

Sitting on the far side of Malpas, Soldier Evans was wedged uncomfortably behind Jameson and up against the rear passenger door. His rifle was at the ready though, and his eyes were sharp on the horizon. Davey pursed his lips as his gaze slipped unbidden to sneak another peek at Mia's face.

She was blindingly beautiful to him, even when she was ignoring his existence.

Returning his focus out his own window, Davey's fingers itched and moved over his rifle. In the distance, large plots of farmland began to appear. There were men in the far-off fields, quite a few of them actually. Davey could make out their darkened silhouettes.

"This is a long way out of town," Davey commented, trying to gather information and ease his own nerves all at the same time. "You guys used to walk the food from here to the city?"

Ducking his head, Soldier Malpas glanced his way. "Nah, Commander Linfield would use a transport truck to get the crops moved when they were ready."

"And during growing season?" Davey's eyebrows raised. "You all walked to work every day?"

"Most of us lived out here during growing season," Malpas supplied. "We only lived in the city during winter."

Nodding, Davey let his gaze skip to the side of Mia's face once more. Her brow was furrowed now as she concentrated on the approaching farmland. Her fingers curled in the fabric of her pants, drawing his eyes quickly down her body.

Swallowing, Davey forced his attention back out his window. The rifle in his hands grew slick with the sweat of his palms. Worry worked and twisted itself in his gut.

They were about to meet with this guy DeKalb, and who knew how many other men. If things went sideways, what could Davey really do for Mia? A thousand scenarios ran through his head. He would do what he had to do, and be unapologetic for it, as always.

The Humvee rumbled along in the convoy as the radio

dropped to silence. Jameson set down the mic and picked up his own weapon. Gesturing to a row of barbed wire fencing, he spoke without looking over his shoulder.

"This is Soldier Wells' show now," Jameson stated. "What he says goes, no exceptions. If he says its time to bug out, then that's what we do. Got it?"

"Yes Sir." Three quiet responses resonated in the cab as the soldiers nodded their heads.

"Mia?" Jameson raised his voice slightly as his eyes darted to her in the rearview mirror.

"Yeah?" Mia's voice was a little shaky, making Davey's heart pound all that much harder.

"We've got you," he assured her. "You just go where you need to, and we'll work around you. Okay?"

"Okay." Mia swallowed and huffed a nervous breath. "I need to see the ground and any equipment their working with. I'd like to see their water source and what crops they've already got growing."

"This guy DeKalb will show us all that," Jameson confirmed. "He's the one in the red ball cap. Right over there."

Davey's eyes zipped to the man in question as their convoy of vehicles pulled to a stop. This DeKalb guy was the most nondescript man Davey'd ever seen. Not too tall, not too short. Not too wide, not too skinny. He had a bland face partially hidden beneath a hat and a light-brown beard.

He was the type of man that you'd see, and then forget you'd seen in the next second. Not bad-looking, but not good-looking either.

Ranged around DeKalb were about thirty other men. They were all on the dirty side, with sweat stained clothes and dusty boots. The vast majority wore hats and more than a few carried weapons. Davey's eyes popped amongst them quickly as Soldier Evans and Jameson opened their doors and stepped out into the sun.

Locklan was next as Soldier Malpas slid away from Mia and exited the vehicle. Before Mia could move, Davey's hand reached out to wrap around her forearm.

Hesitating, Mia's brown eyes locked onto his face.

"We need a code word," he said, unable to remove his palm from her arm. "If you feel a fainting spell coming on, or a memory, or even if you're uncomfortable in any way, then we need a code word so you can signal me."

Nodding, Mia nibbled on that lower lip of hers. Her eyes flitted over his face and in them he no longer saw ice or anger. He saw worry, and a touch of fear. It made him want to yank her to his chest and hold on, but he didn't. He had to respect this choice she was making. He had to let her do her thing, and simply follow her around cleaning up any consequences.

"I don't know what to pick," she said finally. "For the code word. I don't know what to say."

"Alright." Davey considered a moment. "How about you ask me for some tea?"

"Tea?" Mia's brow furrowed.

"It's a kind of drink," he offered, figuring maybe she didn't recognize the word. "Whenever my mom wasn't feeling well after chemo treatments and she wanted to signal my dad that she needed to rest, that's what she asked him for. He'd clear us boys out of the room so she could throw up without us seeing."

"Oh." Mia's face fell and suddenly she was clutching

Davey's arm back. Giving him a squeeze, she nodded her head. "I'm so sorry."

"Don't be sorry." Davey let his fingers pulse along her arm. "Just agree to use the word. Ask me for some tea."

"Okay." Mia sucked in a deep breath. "We have a code word, so now let's go get this over with."

CHAPTER TWENTY-THREE_
DAVEY

STEPPING OUT OF THE TRUCK, DAVEY ROLLED HIS SHOULDERS and glanced around. Jameson was already walking over to the man in the red hat with about a dozen soldiers from the other trucks joining him. Many of the others hung back though, some in their trucks and some standing just outside. Their eyes were all on a swivel, each of them covering a different area.

Thankfully, Locklan, Malpas and Evans all stuck with Davey. They were waiting on his cue and would act under his command. Slinging his rifle over his shoulder, Davey patted at his sidearm to reassure himself this was the right move. They were in close quarters here and he'd need his hands free to grab onto Mia, if necessary.

Speaking of which, the blonde was adjusting her helmet and sliding towards him across the bench seat. When her boots thumped down into the dirt, she swiped her palms along her thighs and exhaled a quick breath.

"You ready to meet him?" Davey asked quietly, causing her to tip her face up and look at him.

"Yeah," she replied after a beat.

Squaring her shoulders, Mia transformed her features from hesitant to self-assured in the blink of an eye. The worry that had been moments ago etched into her skin, was now gone. In its place was confidence and an easy-going charm. And in that moment, Davey realized that Mia did that all the damn time. She hid her true self and her true feelings and replaced them with the sassy princess he'd gotten used to that first time around.

It upset him, though he couldn't say exactly why.

"I want you at my right side, but just behind me," Davey told her, gesturing to the position. "Malpas, you're tracking her and Evans you're on her right. Locklan, you're up and to my left. We good?"

"Good," three sets of male voices echoed while Mia simply flipped her hair and walked to the spot designated.

Swallowing his burning desire to flip her over his shoulder and shove her back into the vehicle, Davey proceeded forward. The dirt beneath their feet was hard packed. They were at the end of one of the fields, on a narrow road that ran along the fence line. Something green was sprouting just to his left, all in neat little rows, but Davey didn't give the crops his full attention.

His eyes were for the man in the red hat. His eyes were for DeKalb and then the men within an arms length of DeKalb, and then the other men standing idly by about fifty yards further back. Jameson's soldiers outnumbered them, outgunned them too, but still, it didn't mean things couldn't go south. They often did.

Keeping his hands relaxed at his sides, Davey's fingers itched to grab the handgun tucked into its holster. That wasn't the right move in this situation, he knew, considering everyone else was behaving, but the need to hold it in his palm was there just the same.

It didn't take more than twenty paces before their small group joined the larger one. Davey's face was hard, his muscles harder as he stared into the boring brown eyes of the man in the red hat. Mr. DeKalb didn't even notice though, because like everyone else, he was busy gaping at Mia.

Like… open mouth, eyes wide, loss for words… gaping.

Davey wanted to slap the look off the guy's face, but then again he couldn't really blame him. He couldn't blame any of them. The first time he'd seen a woman in years, he'd had the same reaction, only it had been a starving Hannah cradled in Cole's arms, not a leggy blonde wearing men's fatigues and a megawatt smile.

Beside him, Jameson cleared his throat loudly and gestured to Mia before making the necessary introductions.

"This is Mia Jones. As discussed previously, she is in fact a woman. Mia is one of our agricultural experts and will be taking a look at the fields like we've already agreed to. This is her bodyguard, David Wells. What he says, goes."

Yada, yada, yada.

All the while, Davey's eyes darted and calculated and brought him information. Third guy back has a knife at his ankle. Redhead on the right has a handgun strapped to his hip. DeKalb has a gun as well, secured in a holster under his left armpit, and so on and so forth.

Davey's brain worked out a strategic response to all of these items, while his body filled with a priming sensation. Some might call it instinct, others might classify it as a conditioned response, learned behavior after years of training and violent interactions.

But Davey called it gut. And he would go with his gut feeling regardless of anything else.

By the time Jameson stopped talking, DeKalb had managed to close his mouth, although the look of shock remained. The guy swallowed once and huffed an incredulous laugh before taking a step forward. His right hand was outstretched towards Mia, offering her a shake.

"No." Davey shook his head and batted the guy's hand away. Everyone tensed. "No touching. A wave is fine."

"Alright." DeKalb chuckled nervously and took a step back. "I didn't mean anything by it."

Davey didn't respond. He just stared, and stared, and stared some more.

DeKalb blinked first.

Sucking in a breath, the guy glanced quickly to Jameson who didn't say anything. Davey could look to his boss as well, but he didn't need to, and frankly he didn't want to give away that kind of power. In this scenario, Davey looked for approval from no one.

"Okay…" DeKalb looked back to Mia and offered a wave. "Mia, can I call you Mia?"

"Sure." Mia's voice floated over the late-summer air, causing the tense vibe to dissipate with her relaxed response.

A few of the men in the background smiled, shifted on their feet, murmured to one another. No doubt their muttered conversations were about her.

"What do you need?" DeKalb asked, his eyes moved from Davey's scowling face to Mia's pretty one. "What do you want to see first?"

"I'll need to…"

"Before all that," Davey interrupted. "*I'm* going to need you to roll up your sleeves."

"Excuse me?" DeKalb frowned.

"Roll. Up. Your. Sleeves." Davey repeated, gesturing to DeKalb's shirt.

"Seriously?" DeKalb turned to Jameson. "We all already did this."

Shrugging, Jameson gave no verbal response.

"And I'll need to see your spine too," Davey added. "And I want to inspect both your hands. Plus, as long as Mia is working here, then everyone with a weapon is going to need to leave them at the edge of the field while they're working."

"That's unnecessary," DeKalb scoffed, his face screwing up at the idea.

"That's how it's going to be," Davey corrected. "Your men can belly crawl to your weapons if need be, but I'm not turning my back on any of you while she's here."

"So your guys will keep your guns?" DeKalb gestured to the soldiers. "And we have to give up ours."

"Consider yourselves under our protection," Davey offered.

DeKalb's mouth snapped shut and he looked down. His hands came to his sides were he gripped his hips and exhaled slowly through his nostrils.

The conversation died.

Men murmured to one another. Boots scuffed in the dirt.

More than one set of eyes swiveled from Mia to Davey. They were still shocked to see a woman alive, but now Davey was drawing their attention. That was good. He preferred it that way. They needed to focus on him, not her. They needed to be concerned with where he was, not where she was, because he was the threat.

Without a word, DeKalb's hands came off of his waist and he began jerking at his sleeves, working to roll them up to his elbows. He was wearing a blue plaid button down shirt and in this heat it protected his skin from the sun, but it was also suspicious to Davey. Long sleeves in late summer raised a red flag.

But as Davey watched, he checked one thing off his list. No code tattoos on this guy. No tattoos on this guy at all. Jameson had already confirmed this fact for him, but Davey wanted proof. He couldn't do his job without seeing it for himself.

With a quick glance to Mia over his shoulder, Davey's brain hunted for a million different things. Was she upset? Was she afraid? Were Evans and Malpas still in their designated positions, protecting her? Was anyone approaching from far off?

The answers came zinging to him in less than a breath. No threat.

And so, without consciously thinking about any of it, he knew he was free to step away. She was fine. Everyone was fine.

Returning his attention to DeKalb, Davey closed the distance between them. After only a moment's hesitation, the guy offered Davey his hands. Davey took the right one and felt along the skin between the guy's thumb and pointer finger.

He couldn't detect any lumps that would indicate a source microchip, but the damn things were so tiny, it was possible one was hidden there that he just couldn't feel. The only way to find out for certain would be to cut the guy open and Davey knew that line wasn't about to be crossed here and now, so he'd have to be satisfied with a quick check.

Dropping the guy's right hand, he checked the left. Same thing. No lumps, no scars, nothing to indicate a chip.

Giving him a glare now, DeKalb sucked his arms back before rotating around and yanking up on the back of his shirt. Davey kept his hands to himself this time, but gave a cursory look at DeKalb's exposed spine. Again, he found nothing. There were no code marks, no laser inscriptions, no tattoos.

"Alright." Davey nodded his head once.

Backing away, Davey kept his eyes on DeKalb and the others until he was standing just behind Mia, instead of in front of her. Lowering his voice, he whispered in her ear.

"It's all you," he said. "I'm your shadow."

Sucking in a steadying breath, Mia plastered a brilliant smile on her face and took charge.

"Okay," she announced, and everyone fell silent. "I'd love to see what you've already got planted first."

CHAPTER TWENTY-FOUR_
MIA

LEANING BACK AGAINST THE PLUSH SOFA CUSHIONS, MIA balanced the hardbound book on her up-drawn knees. Her eyes skimmed the inky black words as they ran in perfect rows across the thick paper.

Licking her thumb, Mia turned another page. The papers slipped and shuffled together. They were the only sound coming from inside the beautiful library.

With a sigh, Mia closed her eyes.

The music, on the other hand, she could hear drifting slowly from far off down the hallway. She hadn't known Davey could play the guitar. He hadn't told her and she'd never asked, but a few days ago he'd found an acoustic one somewhere in the underground bunker and now every single night, he played.

She had yet to hear him sing, although she always listened for his voice. Creeping quietly along the halls, she would pause and linger outside his bedroom door. It was never closed, but for some reason she never stepped up to the open threshold.

There was something so melancholy and beautiful about his playing, she was afraid to interrupt it. She was afraid that his seeing her listening would make it stop. She didn't want him to stop.

So even now, halfway through reading this old farmer's almanac from the 1950s, she closed her eyes and just breathed. She could research more about early fall crops and the shift in weather later. At this moment all she needed was the strum of the strings and the slow rhythm of his songs. He tugged at her heart with each ballad, making it pump just that much harder for him.

"Does it help you?" Jameson's voice coming from the open doorway had Mia jumping.

"Hmmm?" She asked, pursing her lips and opening her eyes to blink over at him.

"The music." Jameson waved a hand over his shoulder. "Sometimes it helps with the memories. At least, that's what helped Hannah."

"Oh." Sucking in a breath, Mia closed the almanac and set it on the wooden coffee table in front of her. She was still dusty and dirty from her day in the fields and Jameson had only been home an hour himself.

"No." Mia shook her head as she thought about his question. "It doesn't make me remember. Is that why he plays? Did you ask him to?"

Taking a step further into the room, Jameson sighed.

"No," he answered. "I didn't know he could play at all. Does it bother you? You want me to ask him to stop?"

"No, no." Mia brushed at her thighs and went to stand up. "I like it, actually. It's sad, but it's nice. You know?"

"Yeah." Jameson quirked a smile. "When Hannah lived here

she used to play that piano in the corner all the time. I swear every song she played made your heart want to crack in half. It used to drive her brother crazy, but I loved it."

Arching an eyebrow, Mia rested a hand on her hip. "Made you think of someone in particular?"

Ducking his head, Jameson chuckled. "Something like that. Speaking of which, I sort of have a favor to ask of you."

Shoving his hands into the front pockets of his pants, Jameson rocked slightly on his heels. His hair was matted down with a days worth of sweat and he'd been letting the scruff on his face and neck get away from him.

Mia knew he was busy, with so many moving parts to his job here, not to mention the past several days of helping Davey to babysit her in the fields. On top of that, Malik and his team still hadn't returned from their mission to Provo. It had everyone on edge.

"Is everything okay?" Mia asked, nibbling on her bottom lip. "Did Malik check in?"

Arching an eyebrow, Jameson gave her a knowing look. "You care?"

Rolling her eyes, Mia tapped one bare foot impatiently against the expensive area rug beneath her feet. She cared because Malik was a great person and she didn't want him to get hurt. Of course Jameson would tease her about it though, as if she wanted more. He could be fun like that, bantering and laughing when his soldiers weren't around to see.

"It's still radio silence, but I got my check-in beeps so they're in one piece," Jameson acknowledged.

"And Eli?"

"Guess Liam pulled the plug on the interrogation." Jameson rocked forward, his head tipping down to the ground. "That's what Cookie said at least. But that's not what I came here for. What I need from you is more... advice related."

"Advice?" Mia frowned.

"Cass advice," Jameson supplied. "Follow me."

Turning on his heel, Jameson slipped through the doorway without looking back. He was so sure of himself, Mia thought. He was so certain she'd follow without question.

After a beat of hesitation (wherein Mia wanted to call him out on his vague demand) her curiosity got the better of her and she hurried her steps after him. Out in the hall, Jameson's broad shoulders shifted as he walked.

Pursing her lips, Mia trailed him past massive oil paintings, closed bedroom doors and the open threshold to the kitchen.

Davey's music grew louder as they approached his doorway. There was the strumming of chords, the movement of fingers over strings.

She couldn't actually see him, but it was like she could *feel* him playing. Her brain knew that there were words that should be sung as well, but as always, Davey kept his mouth shut. He didn't even hum.

Throwing her a quick glance, Jameson's eyes lit when he confirmed what he'd suspected. Mia was following him like a puppy intent on a treat.

There was nothing so tantalizing to a woman as a request for advice and the mention of her best friend. Mia couldn't decide if she was worried or excited, and so she settled on the word nervous to describe the flipping in her belly.

As they passed the doorway to Davey's room, the strumming stopped. Jameson's body moved by first and then next came Mia. Unable to stop herself, she looked inside.

Davey was sitting on the edge of his bed, the acoustic guitar braced on his lap. One of his hands paused on the neck of the guitar and the other, the one that had been doing the strumming, was draped casually over the body of the guitar. His pale-blue eyes were a bit glassy as they stared at her, into her, piercing her soul.

He hadn't been crying, she knew. They weren't red-rimmed or bloodshot, but they were shiny and tragic and for some reason it made her stop dead in her tracks.

Mia's feet simply stopped moving and her neck stayed twisted as her eyes refused to leave the man on the bed.

For several seconds, they simply stared at one another. Davey made no move to continue playing, and Mia couldn't find the words to speak. Her lips were slightly parted and her pulse was skittering but she was frozen in time.

Maybe she'd still be there, regarding him, if not for Jameson's impatience. It was his voice that finally broke the spell. He'd realized that Mia was no longer trailing him, and so she could hear him grumbling as his heavy boots backtracked their way down the hall.

"Mia." Waving a large palm in front of her face, Jameson drew her attention back over to him.

When she blinked and turned her head, Jameson frowned. "You all there? You're not gonna faint on me are you?"

"Huh?" Mia huffed a breath and cleared her throat.

Then of course Davey was up off the bed and striding over to her in less than a second. She could see him in her periphery, still clutching the guitar in one hand as his brow furrowed.

"She needs to sit," Davey said, he was hovering at her shoulder now. The feel of his body so close was overwhelming.

"I'm fine," Mia managed. *Dial it back sister. Do not embarrass yourself anymore than you already have.*

"Are you sure..." Jameson began, but Mia cut him off.

Slicing a hand through the air, she fought the flood of heat wanting to creep into her cheeks. "No fainting. No memories. I'm all good. Let's just go wherever it is you're taking me already."

"Where are you taking her?" Davey's blue eyes shot to Jameson.

"Well I just..." Jameson turned his attention to Davey, and in a rare moment, he seemed flustered. "I guess I just need..."

Davey's brows rose as he waited for an explanation. Mia folded her arms over her chest and smirked. Jameson was embarrassed about whatever this was... and that little fact had Mia settling. Her statue impersonation under Davey's stare was all but forgotten now.

"It'd be easier to show you," Jameson said finally, throwing his hands up in the air. "Follow me... and don't make me regret it."

Shooting her a questioning look, Davey set the guitar down carefully at the door beside his rifle. They were both propped up side by side, the black weapon and the shiny light wood of the instrument. They were like the two sides of Davey, Mia realized. There was the soldier, and then there was the man from before. In that instant, she yearned to know both.

With a low groan, Jameson turned his back on Mia once

more and stalked away. His shoulders were bunched with a light tension now, and after several feet, she heard him sigh.

Gesturing for her to go first, Davey's chest brushed lightly against her shoulder. Avoiding his gaze, Mia tipped her chin up and swallowed. She was determined not to lose her cool around him again.

As they walked further into the underground bunker, Mia focused on her surroundings. The hall was wide and well lit, but even so you knew you were underground. There were no windows here and it gave you a heavy feeling.

As if to make up for it, the walls were adorned with painting after painting. They all depicted life above ground.

Seascapes, vineyards, flower fields, lily covered ponds, sunsets. It made you want to inhale the salt air, hear the call of birds and feel the warmth of the sun kissing your skin.

Behind her, Davey's body moved on silent feet. She could sense his energy at her back. His eyes were no doubt on her, and she'd be lying to herself if that fact didn't make her hips sway just a bit more than necessary.

A heat collected and tingled in her lower belly, making her glance at him over her shoulder.

Yep. He was definitely staring. Blue eyes, unblinking, handsome as ever jawline with a touch of scruff coming in.

Swallowing, Mia returned her focus forward, but didn't manage to suppress her smile. Ahead of her, Jameson came to a stop at a locked door. Instead of reaching for his key ring, his fingers moved deftly over a keypad affixed to the wall.

After a series of beeps, the sound of metal sliding against metal signaled the release of the lock. Jameson rubbed a hand over his mouth and cleared his throat before turning to Mia.

She came to a stop beside him and peered curiously at the

still closed door. It was made of metal, thick dark-colored metal. Steel maybe? She couldn't quite place the name of the material in her head.

Davey walked up beside her and folded his arms over his chest, but remained silent.

"You know how I feel about Cass," Jameson began, his eyes zeroing in on Mia. "You know I'm all in. Right?"

Brow furrowing, Mia wondered where this was going, but nodded her head. "Yes, you love my best friend. I get that."

"Well..." Jameson sucked in a quick breath. "I want to ask her to marry me."

Davey's mouth dropped then, and he let out a little grunt. Beside him, Mia's heart soared. Clapping her hands together she held back performing a little happy dance.

"Yay!" Mia cooed, her eyes darting to the door once more. "That's so exciting."

"You think she's up for it?" Jameson asked.

"Well, I can't answer for her or anything..." Mia nibbled on her lower lip as her chest fluttered.

Cass loved Jameson, no doubt. *But* there was always that chance that she would say no. What if Cass wasn't ready? What if she never wanted the word marriage assigned to their relationship? If it were Mia, then she'd for sure say yes, but this was Cass and Jameson they were talking about. Not that Mia had a special someone who would even think about asking her, but still.

Slanting her eyes to Davey, Mia noted with surprise that he was quietly watching her. His blue eyes were searching, scanning her face. Heat cruised to her neck but she battled back and cleared her throat.

"So, are you going to show us what's behind the locked door or what?" She asked Jameson.

Sucking in a breath, Jameson twisted the handle and stepped back. The interior of the small room was pitch black, but Mia took a tentative step forward. Her hand slipped along the wall until she found a switch and flipped it on.

"Wow." Mia's mouth was the one to drop this time.

Hundreds of glittering jewels winked at her. Every wall was lined with tall wooden cabinets and each cabinet had a glass door. Inside those cabinets, every sort of rich bauble was displayed. Sapphire necklaces, diamond bracelets, ruby earrings, tanzanite rings.

"Uriah needs the yellow diamond ring," Jameson spoke from just behind her. "But he said I can choose from any of the other rings for Cass. Will you help me? I've gotta get something that'll make her say yes."

Closing her mouth, Mia inhaled a deep breath and simply smiled. Jameson was engagement ring shopping for her best friend, and Mia got to help. Bringing her hands together in front of her, Mia glanced over her shoulder at Jameson.

"I'd love to help," she confirmed and couldn't stop her giggle when Jameson's stressed expression melted in relief.

"You really thought I'd turn this down?" She quirked an eyebrow.

"Honestly?" He hedged. "I'm all over the place with this one. I've never been more nervous in my life."

Returning her focus to the cabinets in front of her, Mia nodded her head and walked further into the space. The overhead lights made everything sparkle in the most enticing way. Running a hand in the air just an inch from the glass doors, Mia wiggled her fingers as her eyes cruised over each item.

She didn't want to mar the pristine glass with her fingerprints. At least, not yet.

"Who in the hell built this place?" Davey's voice was quiet. He was still lingering in the open threshold of the door.

Mia's eyes kept darting to him, then back to the jewelry. Him, then necklaces. Him, then bracelets.

"Some rich fucker," Jameson supplied, before chuckling. He was well into the room now. One hand came up to rub at the back of his neck. "You could help too… if you want."

"I don't know." Davey pursed his lips and glanced around. "I don't know anything about women."

"Nothing?" Jameson countered.

Davey shot him a glare as Mia's tummy fluttered.

"Nothing about getting them to marry you," he corrected. "Which has gotta be an uphill battle seeing as you're a… well, you know what you are."

"No, I don't know Soldier Wells," Jameson spat. "Enlighten me."

With a groan, Davey folded his arms over his chest and leaned against the doorframe.

"Let's just say you're going to need something really big and expensive. Maybe a heart-shaped something or other. Women like that, right?" Davey's blue eyes zipped to Mia and held.

He was asking her what women liked. Jameson's focus followed until both men were standing there, waiting for her answer.

Humming to herself, Mia looked away from them and gave her full attention to a large selection of rings. She wasn't going to answer that question because there was no singular answer to that question. And maybe part of why men were so intrigued by women was that they enjoyed the mystery.

"Can I see these?" Mia asked, refusing to look away from the glass case.

"Yeah, they aren't locked." Jameson's heavy footsteps approached her from behind. "Which one do you like? The diamonds, right?"

Resuming her humming, Mia opened the large glass door and bent her face low to inspect the rows and rows of glittering gems. Without knowing why, the names of each jewel popped quickly into her head.

Emeralds. Opals. Garnets. They were threaded with yellow gold, rose gold, silver, platinum, and white gold. There were large solitaire settings and then many intricately mixed designs, with well over a dozen small gems arranged on one ring.

"This must be the one Uriah needs." Mia gestured to an enormous round-cut yellow diamond ring. The band was peppered more than 15 smaller blue diamonds.

"Yup, that's the one," Jameson confirmed, but he left it where it was. "I'll pack it up before we go. This is the safest place for them."

"I'll bet," Davey muttered, his voice still coming from the doorway.

"Have you talked to her at all about this?" Mia's face tipped to Jameson's briefly and then back to the display.

Her hands reached out and she began picking up various rings, bringing them up to her face to get a better look, slipping them onto her fingers to get a better feel.

"Not exactly." Jameson reached out then too, and began picking up different rings. "I can't decide if she'd want a traditional diamond or maybe something green, you know, to bring out her eyes. She's got the most amazing eyes."

Nodding, Mia wiggled her fingers, now weighed down with eight different choices and considered his question. Cass was an artist, but not in the traditional sense. She worked with fabric and had an obsession with color. Lots and lots of color.

"It's your ring that you'll be putting on her finger." Mia turned to face Jameson fully. "So it has to be a part of you too. It has to make her happy, but it has to make you proud as well. When you think of her wearing it, what do you see?"

"I see her eyes sparkling," Jameson answered quicker than anything. "I see glittering green."

With a Cheshire Cat grin taking over her face, Mia nodded.

"Emeralds it is then," she gestured to the case. "Emeralds and diamonds."

CHAPTER TWENTY-FIVE_

DAVEY

Standing in the dirt, Davey gripped his rifle loosely in front of him and held back a sigh. The sun was finally setting, and the heat of another day spent in the fields promised to fade away.

His eyes scanned the horizon, noting the far off line of trees, the familiar bodies slogging their way to the end of their rows, the soldiers positioned every so often.

Directly in front of him, Mia balanced one closed fist on her hip and watched as DeKalb continued to tinker with a large yellow tractor. The guy had the hood on the side engine compartment open and was currently elbow deep in grease and cooling hoses.

"Do you think you can get it running again?" Mia nibbled on her lip as she asked the same question for the millionth time. "Because it would be amazing if we could use it."

DeKalb grunted and muttered under his breath and yanked at some more parts he clearly had little experience with.

Davey's gaze shot over to Soldier Locklan whose hazel

eyes twinkled in response. This idiot is never going to get this thing running, he seemed to say.

With an answering smirk, Davey raised a finger and circled it in the air. In silence, Locklan nodded and turned away.

Time to wrap it up. Davey refused to have Mia out after dark. No way. No how.

"It's time," Davey announced.

Crossing the few steps to Mia, he positioned his body between her and DeKalb. The guy paused in his pointless work and glanced up into Davey's face.

"Same time tomorrow?" He asked.

"Dawn," Davey confirmed, before taking a few seconds to observe the engine carnage for himself.

He could fix it.

Well… it would take some doing and maybe some part poaching from a few of the abandoned vehicles in the city, but yeah, he could get it running. Probably. His dad used to do some mechanic work on the side for extra money, and after their mom passed, Davey and Ryder had always come along.

Davey's brain seemed to have been built for puzzling and so he'd taken to helping his dad straight away. Handing him tools, learning parts and how they connected, how it all fit together. Sorting through a broken vehicle was a puzzle that begged to be solved and Davey had loved it.

But Ryder's brain didn't work like Davey's, and so he used to bring an old guitar along and sing to help pass the hours. Davey could almost hear him now. His brother playing, his dad humming along.

He's got real talent, his father had said. *His voice is just like his mama's. You should play backup for him Davey. He's going somewhere someday, and you could go with him.*

So Davey did what his daddy said. He learned guitar for his brother, and whenever they were at home together, he played for Ryder while his brother sang.

Swallowing, Davey's heart beat harder in his chest then and he turned away from the tractor. He'd never hear his brother's voice again, nor his daddy's for that matter. Maybe they were together somewhere, he thought. Singing.

Reaching for Mia's hand, Davey guided the blonde to their Jeep. Their boots thudded against the dusty ground. Their breaths puffed out into the air. Davey's throat had grown tight on him, and his nostrils burned, but the feel of Mia's palm against his palm centered him somehow.

She brought him back to earth, back to the present day. And the fact that she let him hold onto her like this, to guide her, even when it clearly wasn't necessary, helped to make his pain go away.

"I want to bring my seeds," Mia said, causing Davey to glance back at her. "For tomorrow, I'm ready to plant a test crop."

"Alright," Davey agreed without thinking.

His eyes were darting beyond her, to where some of the men who worked the fields were standing. They were watching her, as they always were. And although it wasn't menacing exactly, he knew what it meant, what their eyes wanted from her, and that bothered him.

Stepping aside, Davey ushered her in front of him and then walked close behind. In doing so, he was forced to let go of her hand, but it was worth it to shield her from view with his broad back.

Involuntarily, his left hand jumped up to the small of her back. He placed the tips of his fingers against her spine and held them there. The contact. He found he needed it.

"It's my turn to cook dinner," Mia continued, as they neared the vehicle. "So I get the first shower."

"I thought you cooked last night," he countered, recalling some of the best spaghetti he'd ever eaten.

"No." Mia shook her head slightly. "It's my turn. And if Jameson isn't there on time, then I'm overriding that stupid water control he has on the bunker and I'm taking fifteen minutes in the shower."

Barking out a quick laugh, Davey's eyes glittered as they zeroed in on the back of Mia's neck.

They'd had this routine for over two weeks now, and it was all blurring together on him. They woke before the sun, ate breakfast, packed lunch, and then drove to the growing fields with a team of ten soldiers, all under Davey's command. He shadowed Mia all day long, ran his team of guys, and then packed it home before the sun disappeared in the west.

"He never should've shown you the override for the water," Davey teased and had her turning back to poke an accusing finger against his chest.

"If it were up to you, then we'd be showering every third day!" She exclaimed, her nose wrinkling in disgust.

"More like once a week," he corrected with a shrug, and was rewarded with another one of her shocked gasps. He liked those… maybe too much.

Arriving at the Jeep, Davey did another cursory sweep as Mia climbed into the backseat. Locklan was already sitting driver, and turned over the engine. Evans and Malpas loaded up as well.

With a nod, Davey looked to the rest of his unit. The six remaining guys loaded into their Humvee and that driver turned over the ignition. With two engines purring at his back now, Davey gave a last long look to the collection of farm workers lingering in the fields. They were watching him, or rather, watching *them* depart.

Davey's gut tightened on him, but he couldn't come up with a specific reason as to why. None of the guys working here were threatening. In fact, they never did anything out of line, ever. But the feeling that something was off swirled within him anyway.

Frowning, Davey cataloged his reaction and turned back to the Jeep. He was the last one to load up. That was always the way they played it. Locklan was the first in, and made ready to drive, then Mia went next, then the rest of his soldiers. Davey's boots were the last ones to leave the soil each day.

As his heavy body hit the backseat, Davey adjusted his rifle and jerked the metal door closed with a final slam. Without a word, Locklan shifted into gear and drove them straight back into the city.

"Any word from Officer Jameson?" Davey asked. The big bastard had more important matters to attend to these days, he didn't have time to hang around the farm.

"None Sir," Soldier Evans answered. He was riding shotgun, his rifle aiming out the open window, his finger extending straight, just above the trigger.

"Any radio chatter from the other units?" Davey again, watching the buildings in the distance get bigger.

"Nothing out of the ordinary," Evans responded. "Same shit, different day."

"Good." Davey nodded, then slanted his eyes at Mia. "How about you? Need some tea to cool down?"

Smiling, Mia closed her eyes and rested her head against the backrest. Her helmet sat crooked on her head. Straggles from her short pony tail fell forward to frame her flushed cheeks.

"No tea," she commented. "Just tired. And I wish we could get that tractor running. It would make a huge difference."

"Diesel fuel is in limited supply," Davey reminded her, unable to stop staring at her lips. He needed to stop staring.

"I know." Mia's eyes opened on a sigh and she caught him looking.

Davey jerked his head away. Why did he suddenly have to force himself to do his damn job? Frowning, he gazed out his open window and cataloged potential threats. Just like the day before, there were none. At least, none that he could see.

Vehicle tires hummed. The radio crackled with indistinct static. The engine rumbled.

"Officer Jameson brought along a mechanic team," he admitted finally, still giving her his back. "You might be able to convince him to use them."

"Davey," Mia's scandalized voice grew closer, until he swore he could feel her breath exhaling over the back of his neck. "You've been holding out on me."

Yes Ma'am. It's better than holding you under me, which is going to happen unless you back the hell up and save yourself.

Clearing his throat, Davey rolled his right shoulder and eased back into his seat. It didn't pass his notice that his arm bumped against Mia's chest in the process. Shit. And just like that, he was wired.

"What's our ETA?" Davey raised his eyes to the rearview mirror and caught Locklan's quick glance.

"We're five minutes out," Locklan replied, his brow quirking. "Same as always… Sir."

Pursing his lips, Davey nodded. The Jeep was slowing now as they entered the outskirts of the city. Burned out suburbs gave way to dilapidated apartments and then the high-rises from downtown were popping up all around them.

Dirty men walked the sidewalks beside soldiers clad in fatigues. They were talking in groups, sharing information, sharing food, sharing work.

The locals weren't staring wide-eyed at the roar of an engine anymore. Jameson was doing his job well, they'd taken the city back without firing a single shot.

"What do you want for dinner?" Mia asked, as the Jeep entered the underground parking garage. "I was thinking chicken pot pie."

"That sounds like a lot of work for you," Davey countered.

His eyes tracked their headlights as they wound down, down, down. His shoulder pressed into the side door panel as Mia's weight leaned against him. On her other side, Soldier Evans groaned.

"That sounds delicious, Miss Mia," Evans commented, his dark eyes slanted over to her, then further still to twinkle at Davey in the dim light. "My mom made the best chicken pot pie."

"She did?" Mia's face brightened as Davey's frown turned to an outright scowl. "Maybe I can make you…"

"No," Davey cut her off as Locklan pulled into a parking space with a jerk. In the front seat, Malpas failed to suppress his snickering. "Not happening Evans. She does enough work as it is."

"What?" Evans spread his palms out innocently as Locklan cut the engine and Malpas popped open his door. "She really did make the best pot pie."

"I'll bet," Davey spat and shoved open his own door. "Besides, it's my turn to cook and there's a frozen pizza calling my name."

With a groan, Mia threw her head back and stared at the ceiling of the Jeep. Davey planted his boots on the ground as the others slammed their doors shut and the Humvee that had been trailing them parked and began unloading as well.

"What's with you and frozen food?" Mia narrowed her eyes at him then as she began scooting to the still open door.

Davey watched her come towards him. She had dirt beneath her fingernails and smudges on one of her cheeks. The pink lipstick she applied religiously each morning had been long since chewed away. Even like this, or maybe especially like this, she stole his breath.

"Single dad remember?" He stepped back as she climbed all the way out.

Pursing her lips, Mia nodded before glancing away.

"I still get first shower," she teased finally, and it had him melting. She was always doing that, always trying to find a way to ease his tension.

"Save me some water," he commented and was rewarded with one of her genuine smiles.

She was actually pleased, actually happy. He could tell by the way her eyes danced and how she huffed a little under her breath, like she was flustered by the feeling. It was a million times better than her fake smile. He hated that one. He hated that she felt the need to use it.

"Are you guys coming or what?" Evans called.

The others were all heading towards the corner stairwell. It would lead them down to the underground bowling alley, which is where all of Jameson's soldiers lived when they weren't above ground on duty.

Ducking his head, Davey stepped back and gave Mia enough space to scoot by him. His arm dropped from the place it was braced against the roof of the car. He'd been boxing her in and hadn't even realized it.

Frowning, Davey slammed his door shut and stalked after her. He shouldn't have done that. He'd have to be more careful with his body position from now on.

CHAPTER TWENTY-SIX_
MIA

IMMEDIATELY UPON ENTERING THE DIM STAIRWELL, THE incessant heat of the day dissipated. It was replaced by a cool dampness and the thunder of about a dozen sets of boots descending. Not to mention the smell. It was a mix of earth and concrete and male sweat.

Mia's nose wrinkled involuntarily, but then she couldn't help but smile to herself.

She liked it here. The ground was good for planting and she couldn't wait to start experimenting with her own seeds. The report she was writing out for Commander Linfield was a positive one so far.

Reaching up, Mia pulled the helmet off of her head and ran a hand back through her mess of hair. It was long enough now that she could tie it in a low pony tail at the base of her neck. But even so, strands of blonde silk escaped and tickled around her face.

At the landing just below her, a single beep sounded before a heavy door swung wide. Bodies crowded the space as, one by one, the soldiers slipped through.

Behind her, Davey reached for her elbow and pulled her to a stop on the stairs. He didn't have to say anything for her to understand his intention. He didn't want her bunched in with all the guys. He didn't want their bodies bumping up against her body.

Slanting a look up at him, Mia blew out a slow breath. The tingles that his grip on her caused should have gone away by now, shouldn't they? Now that his touch was familiar, a daily occurrence even, the excitement should have worn off.

Truth was though… it hadn't. Nope. If anything, the tension building within her was increasing.

"Okay." Davey nodded and just like that they both started walking again.

His hand dropped from her arm and she tipped her chin up. Once through the door, they navigated a series of hallways before being deposited in the underground bowling alley. The place was well lit, with voices echoing and the smell of food drifting in the air. All of the soldiers slept and ate here. All of them save for Davey, Jameson and of course, Mia.

Pausing at a wide balcony that overlooked it all, Mia sighed. There was a staircase a few yards to her right that led down to the first level. That's where the rest of their team was currently disappearing, jogging down the steps and out of sight.

Directly below her, a few of the bowling lanes were up and running. Men laughed and pins tumbled and balls thumped down with a smacking sort of pop on the wooden floor before rolling, rolling, rolling.

The sights, the sounds, the press of people. She couldn't deny her curiosity.

She'd never been invited to play a game here, nor had she

been allowed to linger and mix with the men. Of course, she'd never outright asked either. Davey had always just ushered her through to the bunker. It seemed like until they were both locked inside, he was forever holding his breath.

Pursing her lips now, Mia took several seconds to watch. Somehow she knew that she'd never played this game before even though she still didn't have all of her memories back.

Clearing his throat, Davey stepped up beside her. One of his hands spread out over the black metal railing and the other ran a single finger down her arm before retreating back to rest at his side.

"You good?" He asked, his eyes following her line of sight. "You want to go down there? You want to hang out with them?"

"You would let me?" She asked, her heart thumping in her chest suddenly.

"It's not a matter of let," he answered, frowning. "I know you were, ah… very *social* before. Maybe you miss it. I'll try not to get in the way but I'm warning you that I can't let you out of my sight, not even down here."

Shifting her helmet beneath her arm, Mia turned so that she could better scrutinize Davey's face. He was still staring down at the men below them, refusing to make eye contact, letting her look at him, but not looking back.

"You think I want to go flirt with them," Mia supplied, nodding her head at the chaos below.

"I don't know, maybe." Davey's hand tightened on the railing. "Why else would you want to go down there?"

Maybe because I'd be hanging out with you? Ever thought of that?

Huffing an incredulous laugh, Mia nibbled on her lower

lip and stepped further into Davey's space. She had to tip her head back to keep her eyes on him, and the explosion of butterflies in her chest made it a bit hard to inhale, but she couldn't help herself. She had to be closer to him.

"I think I'll pass," Mia responded. "There's no one down there that I want to spend time with. Plus, you owe me dinner. A deal's a deal, right?"

Unable to hide his surprise, Davey's pale-blue eyes sought her own, brows raised in question. When Mia simply stood still and stared back at him, his cheeks flushed just a touch. Then, as quick as the color had come, it was gone, replaced by a ducking head and a departing body.

"Right," Davey answered and grabbed for her hand. "A deal's a deal."

Tugging her along, Davey led the way further into darkness. The balcony had a metal door that opened onto yet another narrow hallway, and then all the way at the end of that, there was the entrance to the bunker.

Mia couldn't help but notice how he kept hold of her until the very last minute, only dropping her hand to fish the key out from a chain he wore around his neck. It was completely unnecessary. They weren't in the fields surrounded by potential threats. They weren't being jostled and shoved together with a group of soldiers. There was absolutely no reason for him to touch her like that, to continue touching her like that... unless...

Mia's head jerked on her shoulders as a single thought took root. It was at that exact moment, when it hit her.

Davey might actually like her... as in, he might actually be interested in her as more than just a job, as more than an acquaintance who'd turned into a sort of friend.

Up until this point, she'd been so focused on her own reaction to him, that she'd never stopped to notice his reaction to her. Was there something here? Could it be that this feeling wasn't just one-sided?

"Davey…" Mia began, blinking at his back.

"Home sweet home," Davey announced, throwing the door wide. "And looks like you're in luck. No Jameson yet, better grab that shower while you can."

Walking into the space, he stepped aside and held the door. They always left the hall light on, so it wouldn't be dark when they returned. Mia's mouth snapped shut then, and she forced an easy smile.

"Shower's all mine," she intoned, brushing by him.

"Don't take all the water," Davey called, as the heavy door slammed shut. "I'll get that pizza going."

Striding off down the hall, Mia's belly flipped and a warmth crept into her body. Her hips swayed and she kept her shoulders back. All of a sudden a days worth of dirt and sweat didn't seem to matter. All that mattered to her in that moment was one thing. Was he looking?

Nibbling on her lip, Mia steadied herself and decided it was time to find out. With a quick glance over her shoulder, she beamed.

Gotcha.

Davey's eyes widened before he turned his back on her and began busily shrugging out of his gear. But Mia knew that he hadn't propped his rifle up by the front door in a very long time, and it seemed an unusual thing to start again now.

Returning her focus forward, Mia couldn't wipe the triumphant smile off of her face. *I may have no idea what to do after we kiss, but tonight… I am definitely going to find out.*

CHAPTER TWENTY-SEVEN_
DAVEY

IT TOOK TWENTY MINUTES OF WAITING (DURING WHICH TIME HE burned his finger removing the pizza from the oven) but Davey finally got that cold shower. And by the time it was his turn in the bathroom, the icy water was much needed.

Why? Because Mia had sauntered into the kitchen smelling like lilacs and showing off so much leg that it made Davey's breath catch in his throat.

Tiny little pajama shorts, tiny matching tank top, both of which had a white background covered with red cherries. Red. Cherries.

When she'd walked up beside him at the counter and hummed happily over the freshly cooling pizza, Davey had literally swallowed his tongue. Like, he blinked and choked and straight up had to slam his own fist into his chest a few times.

Mia, for her part, had ignored him. She poked at the toasty crust of the pizza and inhaled deeply.

"This is going to be so good," she commented. "I'll get us

set up while you wash off. Are you thirsty? You want to share another soda?"

Davey couldn't remember what he'd said, if anything at all, before scurrying from the kitchen like a man on fire. Blowing out a breath now, he leaned his forehead against the pristine white tiles of the shower stall and closed his eyes.

Frigid water poured over his head and down his back. It bit into his skin and yet he needed the sting. Between that and his hand, he'd managed to eliminate the little problem that Mia had caused for him back in the kitchen. It was a problem he was having more often lately, blood flowing where he didn't necessarily want it to go.

Insistent. Demanding.

And after a year of complete disuse, it was like Davey had suddenly turned into a sixteen-year-old boy again. He'd officially woken up from his depression, and he had yet to decide if it was a blessing or a curse. He wanted things. He felt things. He remembered what it was like to laugh, to smile, to burn on the inside.

The numbness was gone but with its absence came a vulnerability. He cared about someone again, like really cared. Which meant if something happened to her…

Shoving back from the wall, Davey let loose a low groan. The water timer on the wall (which he didn't override, thank you very much) was two seconds from clicking off. Thankfully, Davey was already scrubbed and rinsed and ready to step out.

"You've got this," he muttered to himself before reaching for a plush towel. "You're hungry. She's hungry. You'll eat and go to bed, same as always. Just keep your eyes to yourself and your dick should behave."

Looking down at said dick, Davey arched an eyebrow. He better wear a pair of briefs under his sweat pants, just for an added layer of security.

Tossing the towel over the sink, he ran his hands back through his hair before reminding himself he needed a shave. Not that there was a reason to keep cleaned up… and besides, it was only a little stubble around his mouth and chin.

"Stop," he commanded the guy in the mirror. "Just go eat the damn pizza. You'll have a table width between you anyways."

Exhaling, Davey did as instructed. He got dressed in his sweats, pulled a grey shirt over his head and shoved out of the bathroom. The smell of dinner was still heavy in the air and he followed its scent as his stomach rumbled in anticipation. But as he entered the kitchen and looked through to the mahogany dining table, he frowned. It was empty.

"Mia?" Davey's voice rose and with it a spike of panic. He'd just seen her five minutes ago. Literally.

"In here!" She called from somewhere further in. "I thought this would be more comfy."

Davey's stomach dipped then as his feet ate up the distance. He cruised through the kitchen, past the open concept dining room with the table where they normally ate, and rounded the corner. There, he stopped.

"Hey!" Mia exclaimed from her position on one wide couch. "I thought dinner and a movie would be fun. You up for it?"

"Um…" Davey was at a loss for words as his eyes soaked up the scene.

Mia was sitting on a leather couch, one arm slung over the back, her head turned to watch him. The flat screen television that hung on the wall was turned on and already had a movie running previews. On the coffee table directly in front of her was the pizza, a pair of plates, napkins, silverware (isn't pizza a finger food?), two glasses of water, and one can of soda.

"It's not a chick flick is it?" He commented, trying to suppress a smile.

"What's a chick flick?" Mia's face scrunched up as she tried to think.

Circling around the couch, Davey flopped down next to her and picked up the remote. The couch dipped beneath his weight, causing her body to bump lightly into his. Pressing pause, Davey read the stats on the movie and almost groaned aloud.

"This is definitely a chick flick," he teased, knowing full well he would watch whatever she wanted.

"Ah, but it looked so good!" Mia's pretty face fell as her eyes darted back to the screen. "We can change it if you…"

"Nah." Davey wrapped his arm around her shoulders and gave her a little squeeze. "I'm just joking. This is the best movie ever. Can't wait to watch it."

"Wait…" Mia nibbled on her lower lip and drove his blood pressure up a few notches. "You've seen it?"

"Nope," Davey lied and pressed play. "I'm just guessing."

"Davey…" Mia warned, but he was already setting the remote down and reaching for his pizza.

"Do you remember eating pizza?" He asked before taking a giant bite.

"Well, yeah, it's your go-to meal when it's your turn to cook," she replied, rolling her eyes and reaching for her silverware.

"You know you're supposed to eat it with your hands

right?" He raised his brows as she delicately sliced off a bite with her silver knife. "And no... I mean *real* pizza, not the frozen from a box kind, but the kind that comes hot and fresh from the delivery guy. *That* pizza."

Still chewing, Mia covered her mouth with one hand and shrugged her shoulders. Davey figured that meant no.

"What do you remember?" He asked. "I know you didn't want to talk about it before but..."

"Still don't," she cut him off, but with a smile instead of a frown.

Nodding, Davey couldn't help the dip in his gut. He wanted to know everything about her. Badly.

And maybe he hadn't realized just how badly until right now when she refused to tell him. What was Mia hiding? Didn't she trust him by now?

She knew all about him. About Ryder and his mom and his dad and all about his past.

Except, he hadn't given her many details about his strike team work... or the war. But that was ugly and dark and in the past. Because that's the stuff you don't tell people. The bad stuff.

Setting his half eaten slice of pizza down, Davey wiped his palms together and shifted to look fully into Mia's face. She was ignoring him, eating her pizza one carefully carved bite at a time. The movie was playing, flashing colors against her skin.

"You know you can trust me, right?" He began, his eyes darting over her cheeks and her eyes, her lips and her way too stubborn chin. "I will always protect you, no matter what. I won't judge you."

Swallowing, Mia set down her silverware and gave him her full attention. Davey's heartbeat slowed.

"I trust you," she said. "But do you trust me? When I say no to something… will you just keep pushing anyway?"

"No." Davey frowned and reached for her hand. "I don't want to push you. I just want you to know I'm on your side no matter what. That's all. No more asking, I swear."

"Alright." That fake smile crept across Mia's face as she reached for the soda and handed him the can. "Ready to share this and enjoy the movie?"

Pursing his lips, Davey regarded her for a few seconds. His hand left her warm skin as he accepted the soda.

"I'm ready as long as you give me the real smile," he commented and popped the tab on the metal lid. "No more fake smiles for me. Either you frown at me, or you give me the real deal."

Huffing a laugh, Mia's fake smile automatically transformed into the real one, making him answer with one of his own.

"What?" He arched a brow. "You think you're fooling me with that nonsense? No, Ma'am."

Handing her the now open can, he tipped his head at her. "First sip is all yours."

"But after that it's every man for himself?" She teased.

"You got the idea," he agreed and somehow kept from drooling when she put the drink to her lips.

Forcing himself to look away, Davey ate three slices of pizza, downed his glass of water and watched as the poor maid was swept off her feet by the handsome billionaire. It didn't escape his notice when Mia snuggled up against his side and let loose a sigh.

Automatically, he reached around to wrap her shoulders with his arm, his palm landed on her bare skin. Without his permission, his thumb stroked lazy circles. He needed to stop.

"That was good," Mia commented. "But I'm full, you can have the rest."

Patting at his stomach with his left hand, Davey puffed out his cheeks.

"No way," he groaned. "I can't fit another bite."

Chuckling, Mia reached for the can of soda on the coffee table and brought it to her lips. Davey's gaze tracked to her mouth and time stopped for him. Like literally, his thumb stopped stroking her skin and his body tensed. He needed to break the spell. He needed to stop watching her like a total creeper.

"Hey, hey," he teased. "Save some for the rest of us."

"I thought you said you were full," Mia countered, and waved the can side to side in the air. "I don't think I should let you have anymore."

"Is that right?" Davey shifted to grab the can but Mia sat up straighter and moved it away, laughing.

"I'm saving you from yourself," she giggled, twisting to face him, but keeping the can at her back. "You should be thanking me."

"Should I?" Davey's voice was incredulous as he doubled down on the game and made a grab for the can.

His arms were way longer and her body was still close to him, so she really had no chance. But Mia wasn't backing down. Not one inch. So when Davey leaned forward, arm outstretched, his chest bumped up against hers.

Mia let out a playful yelp, her breath catching as laughter bubbled up her throat. The can of soda dipped perilously close to the couch cushions then, and their faces were suddenly an inch apart.

Davey's throat went completely dry.

His eyes locked on her eyes, darting back and forth as his tongue snuck out to wet his lips.

Mia was no longer laughing. She sucked in a heady breath and then her lips were parting. Davey tensed. His body was all bunched muscle and straining while his heart pounded crazily against his ribcage.

Mia hesitated then, but only for a second. Before Davey even knew what was happening, her eyes flipped down to his mouth and she closed the distance between them. When her lips hit his, Davey's brain blitzed. It was just that simple. He lost control.

His eyes slammed shut, his mouth opened and his whole body leapt forward. She was on her back on the couch before the soda can even hit the floor. And Davey? Well, he was on top of her, kissing her, groaning into her mouth.

His hands threaded themselves in her hair, as she gasped. His hips pinned her in place.

His awareness came in bursts.

Mia wrapping her arms around his neck. Her tongue licking at his lips, then venturing further to lick at his tongue.

The sound of her tiny cries as he ground himself against her. The feel of her body beneath him. A low groan emanating from somewhere deep inside his chest.

The thinness of her pajama shorts.

The fact he was hard for her.

Again. Even after the shower.

Then their kisses were turning frantic. She was arching

her back and rubbing her body against his. Her chest against his.

He swore.

Pulling back, he opened his eyes and watched her. She was out of breath and so was he. But he couldn't stop, and then she was leaning up to kiss him again. His heart exploded as he dove back in and kissed her deeper, longer, more.

Slow down. Slow the fuck down.

Davey's left hand cruised down her side. He felt the cotton of her pajama shirt, then the silk of her bare skin. He wanted so much more, to touch so much more, but it had been a really long time for him and he didn't want to screw this up.

Mia was gorgeous and smart and funny and she'd obviously had a million boyfriends. She was way the hell out of his league and Davey wanted to impress her, to make her remember him, even after this was all over and she found someone worthy of her.

But at the rate he was going right now, he might just go off dry humping her like a fucking teenage virgin.

"Mia," Davey murmured her name against her lips and tried to pull back.

"Hmmm," she hummed the sound, her cheeks flushed and her eyes closed.

Her body wriggled beneath his, pushing against his, and it had him melting back into her.

Cue more kissing. More moaning… on both sides. Davey's chest expanded and his head was rushing. He wanted this, wanted *her*, so damn bad.

But all it took was one single sound to stop all that.

One single noise and Davey was shoving away from her,

off of her. His feet were planting on the ground and he was blowing out a controlled breath.

The lock. It was flipping. Jameson was home, or someone who had Jameson's key.

Fuck. Why had he left his rifle by the front door? What in the hell kind of sloppy…

What if it wasn't Jameson? What if someone had killed the guy and took his fucking key? Davey's gaze shot to Mia who was propped up on one elbow on the couch, looking entirely sex mussed and beyond beautiful.

"Get to your room," he spat.

"What?" Mia frowned.

"Someone's at the door," Davey hissed and took off at a jog.

Maybe she hadn't heard the snick of the lock, but he could sense that shit from a mile away. On the outside, it was the difference between life and death. And here he was, once again failing to do his job properly. When he was around Mia, his brain simply lost full blood supply, that was the only explanation.

"Davey!" Mia called his name, but he was already in the kitchen. "It's only Jameson!"

Well… Davey thought, as the sound of the front door opening filled his ears, we're about to find out.

CHAPTER TWENTY-EIGHT_

MIA

SITTING UP ON THE COUCH, MIA'S HEART POUNDED.

"Davey!" She called. "It's only Jameson!"

Putting a hand to her chest, she pursed her lips. His bare feet slapped against the kitchen flooring and then turned silent.

He didn't give her a verbal response. He was already gone.

As the sound of the front door swinging wide filled the bunker, Mia rolled her eyes. Sure enough, Jameson's voice broke the air, then Davey's answering grunts.

That man.

Mia flopped momentarily back onto the couch and ran her hands through her hair. He had her all twisted up. Pulse skittering, lips tingling, thighs clenching. He left her wanting more, like he always did.

"Why?" Mia groaned the word and looked to the ceiling.

Then a few more voices sounded and they had her sitting up straight. Her hands hit her thighs and she frowned. It was Malik, and then more men, ones she couldn't pick out from just listening. He was back. The guys were back from their mission.

Jumping up from the couch, Mia yelped. Her bare foot landed on something metal.

Stumbling a little, she looked down to discover the forgotten soda can. It was crumpled now with dark syrupy liquid sinking into the expensive area rug.

"Oh no," Mia whispered. "No, no."

Crouching down, she worked her hands feverishly over the stain. How could she be so stupid? How could she be so clumsy? Her pulse spiked and her breathing turned hot.

She had to clean this mess up. She couldn't let anyone see it.

Swallowing, Mia grabbed for some napkins she'd left on the coffee table. There weren't nearly enough of them to satisfy the pool of soda, not to mention that they would do nothing to combat the stain. She needed cleaning products, and time.

But the voices were getting louder now, approaching the kitchen. Mia squeezed her eyes shut as a million memories assaulted her. They were violent and quick, making her choke on her own saliva.

All of a sudden she couldn't breathe.

"If your father finds this..." Mama trailed off, her eyes wide. The nail polish was everywhere.

"I know Mama, I know." Marie licked her lips. "I'm sorry."

"Me too, baby." Mama flinched. "Me too."

"Where are my beautiful girls?!" Daddy's voice echoed through the large house.

Marie's stomach contracted as her eyes popped up to watch Mama.

"I don't feel very good," Marie whispered. "My tummy hurts."

Nodding, Mama sucked in a ragged breath. Her hands were flying over the carpet, and the bright-red nail polish that was sticking everywhere.

But then Daddy's steps were coming closer and the door to the bedroom was swinging open and...

"Mia," Davey's voice was low and close and clear as day. "Mia, stop."

"What?" Mia gave her head a shake as her vision blurred in and out on her.

The carpet. It was dirty. The stain. Nail polish. No... soda?

He's gonna hit you.

"Mia," Davey spoke again.

His hand landed on top of her hand and it was like an angry electric shock.

Sucking her hand away, Mia rocked back onto her butt and gasped. Her eyes flew wide and she swallowed.

"Whoa," Davey held up his palms in defense. "You okay? Mia..."

"I'm fine." Mia's breath left her in a rush.

Her heart was wild, painful. Why? She couldn't catch her breath.

Davey watched her. His brow was furrowed and his head tilted to one side. He was crouching down between the sofa and the coffee table, one knee pressed into the ornate area rug. And the voices, the male voices, were everywhere. Echoing.

"I'm so sorry," she whispered.

"For what?" Davey glanced from her to the carpet.

"For the mess. I'll clean it. You won't even know it was here." Mia's words rushed out as she shoved forward.

Her hands sought the napkins, only to find they were rubbed and torn and shredded into a million tiny white pieces. Had she done that? When?

"It was an accident," Davey supplied. "No big deal. More my fault than yours actually."

Reaching out, Davey's hand sought the side of her face. *He's gonna hit you.*

Biting hard on her lower lip, Mia flinched. Her face scrunched up and her shoulders folded in and she braced for the impact.

"Whoa." Davey's hand stopped just inches from touching her. "You think… you're scared of me?"

"No." Mia forced a huff and scooted backwards, avoiding his eyes. *Get it together. Don't pass out.* "Of course not."

"But you just…" Davey paused, exhaled through his nostrils. "Someone hit you. For making a mess. Am I right?"

Closing her eyes, Mia pressed her fingers to her eyelids and fought against the hot tears that were collecting there. She didn't want to do this. She didn't want to live like this. But she felt absolutely ill and had zero control. Zero.

"Davey," Jameson's booming voice traveled from the kitchen. "I need to debrief and the medic's on his way for Malik. I'll need most of this space tonight. What's your plan?"

"Mia's tired," Davey raised his voice. "I'm going to take her to her room."

"Sounds good," Jameson called.

Cupboards were banging open and chairs were scraping

against the floor. Men were talking all at once. There were a few groans and a lot of cursing. Mia forced her eyes open and stared at Davey. He hadn't moved, not one inch. Her heart was so sad all of a sudden.

"Can I carry you?" He asked quietly. "I'll take you around the back way, through the game room and into the hall. We can avoid most of them. It'll be quick."

"Yeah," Mia exhaled the word and nodded. "Yeah, let's do that."

Clearing his throat, Davey eased forward. His eyes stayed on hers as his hand reached out, brushing lightly down her arm. When she didn't shy from him, he crept closer, wrapping one arm behind her back and easing the other beneath her knees. Rocking quickly onto his feet, he hoisted her to his chest and was off.

After a moment's hesitation, Mia circled her arms around his neck and buried her face against his chest. Inhaling, she took in the scent of bar soap, aftershave and clean cotton. It was soothing. His smell, his presence, made her feel okay, made her feel calm.

Her feet dangled with each step and Davey's breath came quicker as he walked. He pushed through doors, walking sideways. The rooms were darkened, the halls dimly lit. The voices of the men grew quiet, faded.

"Here we are," Davey commented.

His body dipped, but he didn't put her down. Bracing her with a well placed thigh, he balanced and snuck out a hand and twisted the door knob. Her bedroom door swung open and Davey muscled their way inside. He didn't stop until he got to her bed.

Bending forward he placed her down carefully before

stepping back. The blankets were cool against her hot skin. Mia's head sank into the pillow.

Opening her eyes, she watched him move through the dark, the light from the hall illuminated his body.

"Are you going to lock me in?" She asked.

"I've gotta get my bedroll." He paused at the threshold. "With all the guys staying here, I'm going to sleep on the floor, just to make sure."

Nodding her head, Mia blew out a ragged breath. She was calm enough now to feel incredibly embarrassed. She just wanted it to go away. She wanted the flashbacks and the images in her head to stay gone. Nibbling on her lip, she turned her head to the side.

Davey disappeared from the doorway then, but was back in seconds. He stepped inside, tossed his rolled up sleeping bag on the floor and shut the door behind him. The room fell to immediate blackness. Mia inhaled.

"I'm going to flip on the light," Davey said, and flicked the switch on the wall.

On either side of the queen sized bed, a pair of matching silver lamps illuminated. It was enough light to have Mia bringing her hands up to shade her eyes. Which happened to also be a great excuse to cover her face.

"Sorry," Davey commented. "Let me turn one off for you."

His body traveled closer. She could feel his energy, see him moving through the cracks in her fingers. Approaching her side of the bed, he leaned down and clicked the lamp off. She didn't lower her hands as he knelt down to the floor and waited.

"I don't want to pressure you," he said finally. "But I wish you would tell me."

"I know," Mia whispered, her heart squeezing tight in her chest.

"Is he someone I know?" Davey asked, his voice measured. "Or someone I could track down?"

Shaking her head, Mia sniffed. "I'm pretty sure he's dead," she answered.

"But you're not sure?" Davey again, leaning in closer.

Reaching out, he lightly traced his fingers along her arm and up to her hands where they still covered her face. After a few seconds, he tugged gently on one wrist, willing her to reveal herself.

Giving him her hand, Mia turned to face him and stared into those pale-blue eyes of his. Davey was quiet, patient, his lips pursed, his face almost unreadable.

"He was my father," she admitted. "But I don't remember what happened to him."

CHAPTER TWENTY-NINE_

DAVEY

HIS BACK WAS ACHING FROM BEING PROPPED UP AGAINST HER headboard, but she'd finally fallen asleep on his chest, so it was worth the pain.

Looking down, Davey stroked a palm along Mia's hair, like he had been doing for the past half an hour. Her face was turned to the side, lying over his heart. Her body ran the length of his body, her arms circling his stomach.

When she'd told him what had happened, or at least the parts she could remember, Davey's heart had broken right along with hers. He'd climbed into bed, pulled her against him and listened to her sobs.

All the while his chest had constricted and he'd found it difficult to stay calm. His instinct was to get angry. Really fucking angry at the man who'd beaten the shit out of a little girl and her mother.

But it wasn't the first time he'd cradled Mia while she cried herself out. And in the end the effect on him was the same as before.

Exhaling through his nostrils, Davey tipped his head back

against the headboard and blinked at the ceiling. There was one bedside lamp still on and he needed to turn it off. On the other side of the closed bedroom door, voices murmured. Malik had returned with his team a bit banged up, but with stories to tell, information to share.

Davey's gut lurched and his jaw clenched just a bit. He needed to know more about the men with the code tattoos. Maybe Mia's piece of shit father was out of reach for justice, but Davey could probably track down more of the tattooed men and make them pay instead... like he had before.

"Stay sleeping," Davey whispered, and began the slow process of inching his way out from under her.

Easing out of bed, he was careful to lay her head on a pillow and pull the covers up over her body. Thankfully, she didn't stir. Between the day at the farm and their little escapade on the couch and then the flashback from hell, she was well and truly spent.

Running his hands roughly through his own hair, Davey held back a groan. He didn't know where this was going, or what the hell he was doing with Mia, but he found one thing was for certain. He would protect her until she didn't need it anymore, or until she told him to get lost, and even then he'd probably find it hard to stop.

When he got to the door, he flicked off the light, throwing the room into utter blackness. The key was still on its chain around his neck, so he stepped over his bedroll, pulled the door open and walked into the hall. The voices became clearer now, but were coming from multiple sources.

Pulling the door shut behind him, Davey locked Mia safely inside. It's not that he thought any of these guys would try anything, but without the door being secure he wouldn't be able to focus. The possibility would nag at him, and he couldn't function like that.

Glancing down the hall, Davey figured a few of the op team members had been given beds in the bunk room at the far end. The rest of the voices, including Jameson's, were coming from the kitchen.

Choosing that direction, Davey slung the chain back around his neck and tucked the key beneath his cotton shirt. Within seconds, he was at the threshold of the kitchen, silent, observing.

"Ah! That fucking hurts!" Malik's face scrunched up as he sucked in a sharp breath. He was spread out on the kitchen floor as the medic, Bisset, worked sutures into his exposed thigh.

Blood was everywhere. Soaked gauze, bandages, the rubber gloves of the medic. Malik's stained pants had been cut off of him and tossed in an ugly heap in one corner. A solider paced in the dining room, another knelt beside Malik, bracing his legs.

"Quit being such a puss," Jameson commented. "It's your own damn fault."

The hulking officer was crouching on the other side of Malik, holding his shoulders flat to the floor. Frowning, Davey folded his arms over his chest.

"You weren't supposed to be the bait," Jameson continued. "We knew that was a risk. They kill who they capture."

"Yeah well..." Malik's eyes were glassy as they blinked up at the ceiling. "How could I send anyone else in? Knowing that. Ah! Fuck!"

"You're okay." Jameson glanced to the medic who

continued working steadily. "It'll all be done soon. Only a flesh wound."

"More like the luckiest stab wound I've ever seen," Bisset grumbled, but didn't look up.

"Any more morphine?" Jameson ventured.

"No." Bisset shook his head.

"You can cry you know." Jameson stared down at Malik. "I won't tell anyone."

"Fuck. Off." Malik gritted his teeth but then huffed a pitiful laugh. The joke got its desired effect, Malik's mind escaped the pain, if only for the moment.

"How many did you let go?" Jameson again. "You're sure they understood? You're sure they got the intel?"

Brow furrowing deeper, Davey held his breath. Let go? Intel? What the....

"Three," Malik hissed. "Fuck, can you just knock me out?"

Jameson clucked and shook his head. "I had no idea you were such a little bitch."

"If this doesn't put him over the edge," Bisset commented, lifting a bottle of liquid to pour over the wound. "Nothing will. It's deep."

Malik's scream echoed in the kitchen, pinging off the expensive cabinets and floor. Davey sucked in a breath and it was like every set of shoulders in the place hunched reflexively. But then the sound was cut short. Malik's eyes rolled up in the back of his head, and he was out.

"I'll try to be quick," Bisset said, his hands flying.

"Risk of infection?" Jameson rocked back on his heels and released Malik's now limp body.

"High," Bisset acknowledged.

Glancing over his shoulder then, Jameson caught Davey

staring. The two locked eyes and Davey's gut churned. There was something here, something more.

Pushing up to standing Jameson dusted at his pants and sighed. His hands had a bit of dry blood on them, but not much.

"She alright?" Jameson asked, crossing to where Davey was standing. "You lock her in?"

"Yeah." Davey dipped his head, swallowed the lump in his throat. "Mission go sideways?"

"A bit." Jameson frowned, then gestured to the hall. He wanted to take this conversation somewhere more private.

Stepping aside, Davey let Jameson pass through the threshold first. The bulky guy veered left and headed for the front of the bunker. They didn't stop walking until they reached the library and Jameson shoved inside.

"Care to clue me in?" Davey asked finally, as the door swung shut behind them. "What's going on?"

Turning on him, Jameson shoved both hands into his front pockets and puffed out his chest. "You have your assignment. It's best you just focus on that."

"Seriously?" Davey's eyes widened. "You offered me the damn operation three weeks ago, now you're holding back?"

"I made the offer knowing you'd never take it," Jameson countered.

"Well it's a damn good thing." Davey jerked a thumb over his shoulder. "Because there's obviously a shit more going on here than meets the eye."

"Just keep your eyes on your lane, Soldier Wells." Jameson stepped closer. "And everything will work out fine. You just give 110% to your assignment and we'll all walk out of here in a few months happy. Got it?"

"The fuck?" Davey huffed an incredulous laugh. "If you're running bigger shit through here, then I need to know. It effects my ability to do my job. I need the full picture."

"You need what I tell you to need." Jameson's brows raised. "Do your fucking job and let me do mine. Got it?"

"And that's all there is to it?" Davey pressed. "That's it. I'm out."

"Do your damn job," Jameson's voice lowered. "That's it."

CHAPTER THIRTY_

MIA

KNEELING ON THE HARDWOOD FLOOR, MIA REACHED OUT TO clasp his warm hand in hers. They'd put Malik on the bottom bed in one of the bunks sometime in the night. When he squeezed her palm and smiled, she smiled back.

"I think you scared everyone," Mia commented. "Now Davey doesn't want us to go out."

"Nah." Malik's face scrunched up and he rolled his beautiful dark eyes. "Guy's just getting lazy. That's all."

Shaking her head, Mia glanced from Malik's face out the open threshold of the bunk room doorway. Davey was standing just a few feet down the hall, having yet another heated discussion with Jameson. The former was doing most of the talking, while the later had his massive arms folded across his chest and a sour expression on his face.

There was something going on, but as usual whenever she approached, the discussion between the two men cut off. All she knew was that when she'd gotten ready to go to the farm this morning, Davey had pulled the plug. He was refusing to let her go out, and Jameson was losing his patience.

"Hey." Malik cleared his throat and drew her attention back over to him. "So how about that movie night? You up for some popcorn? I'll let you pick the show."

"Oh, you'll *let* me?" Mia arched a brow.

"That's right." Malik chuckled. "Ladies choice."

"Hmmm." Mia pursed her lips.

Malik was awesome. He was handsome and easy to talk to. But if she had a choice about who to watch a movie with… it wouldn't be him.

"I'll even sneak us a soda." Malik's eyes sparkled as Mia's heart gave a little kick.

She could still taste the syrupy liquid that she'd licked off of Davey's lips. Soda and Davey. She'd probably never be able to drink one again in her life without tasting him along with it. Instantly her cheeks heated and then certain other places too. He'd left her wanting. There was no denying that.

Before she could voice an answer, a shadow darkened the doorway. Looking up, Mia blinked into Davey's face. He was standing with his brow furrowed and his jaw tight.

"Looks like we're going topside after all," he offered. "You ready?"

"Um…" Mia nibbled her lip and glanced down to Malik. He released her hand.

"Yeah," she said finally and stood up. "See you later, Malik."

"See you later," he replied.

The journey down the hall was a tense one. Davey's broad shoulders stalked in front of her. Tilting her head to one side, she watched him move. He had purpose and a bit of an edge to each step. This something that was wrong, seemed worse.

When they passed his bedroom, he paused to collect his

rifle from its spot by the door. Mia blew out a slow breath when he refused to make eye contact.

"Is everything alright?" She asked, tentative.

He nodded and resumed their walk to the front. Mia frowned, but followed. Before they got to the heavy metal door, Mia caught Davey by the wrist and spun him to face her. His pale-blue eyes landed on her face before darting away once more.

"Did something happen?" She asked, searching him for answers. "Is it not safe up there?"

Jaw ticking, Davey stared at one of the massive oil paintings on the wall for several seconds. It was all crashing waves and violent storms. Blues, blacks, whites. Heavy and light all at once.

"There's no direct threat," he said finally, his gaze swinging back over to lock with hers. "All this stuff with Malik and his team, it's got me on edge. That's all."

"You're sure?" She stepped closer, transferred her hand from his wrist to his chest.

After a beat, he reached up and grabbed it. Squeezing gently, Davey ran the pad of his thumb along the side of her hand. Mia's breath caught in her throat and her thighs clenched.

"Just stay extra close today," he said. "Don't do anything crazy."

Nodding, Mia exhaled.

"I won't," she promised.

A few hours later and she pretty well blew that promise all to hell. They'd been in the fields for half a day and she'd tried to be good, really she had. But some things were better shown than explained.

So while Mia and DeKalb motored off together in the tractor, Davey was left swearing on the ground.

"He's pissed," DeKalb commented, peeking at a scowling Davey over his shoulder. "Does he ever leave you alone?"

"No." Mia shook her head but kept her hands on the steering wheel. "But this is only for a few minutes to show you how to I want this done. There isn't room for three up here anyway, there's barely room for two."

"Right." Returning his focus forward, DeKalb sighed. "He even watches you use the bathroom. Doesn't that bother you?"

"It used to," Mia admitted with a shrug. "But he doesn't look directly at me, he looks around at everything else while I go."

"Are you okay?" DeKalb asked, his brows raised. "Do you ever wish you could escape him? Or them? This is the first time we've been alone."

"Oh." Mia spared him a quick look. "I'm fine. He's fine."

Nodding, DeKalb gestured to the field stretching out before him.

"You wanted to start here," he reminded her.

"That's right." Mia smiled, swiped at the dust collecting on her upper lip and turned the wheel. "Now here's what I want you to do."

CHAPTER THIRTY-ONE_

DAVEY

"If you ever do that again..." Davey pressed his forehead to the closed door of the bathroom and shut his eyes. "I don't think I'll survive it."

It was safe to say something like that out loud. No one else was left in the underground bunker except him and Mia, and she couldn't hear him anyway.

On the other side of the closed door, the shower was running full blast and Mia was inside of it, naked. He tried really hard not to focus on that last part.

Blowing out a breath, Davey pressed his dirty palms flat against the wooden surface. It was cool to the touch, calming. A complete 180 from the heat outside and the fire in his body when she'd climbed up on that tractor and drove off like a badass.

And sure, she'd been in the wide open where he and his entire team could see her. And yes, nothing had happened to her and there was no direct threat against her.

But still, she was out of his reach. She was out of his immediate control, his sphere of influence if you will. And the full ten minutes it took her to show DeKalb what an inept driver he was, were enough to give Davey a fucking ulcer.

When she'd finally swung back around and parked the damn thing it was all he could do to keep from jumping up there, throwing her ass over his shoulder and storming away.

Of course, she was all megawatt smile and sparkly eyes, which had him completely fucking melting for her. He couldn't even get angry at her then, so the sick fear just settled in his gut and he counted the seconds until sundown when he could take her home.

He wanted to punish her and kiss her and do all sorts of things to her to make her his. Rocking back a step, he tipped his face up and stared at the ceiling.

Dial it in buddy. Dial. It. In.

Abruptly the water switched off. He listened as she sighed, then stepped out of the shower. The stall door clicked. A towel slid off a rod. More sighing. She was killing him with the sighing.

Rubbing a hand roughly over his face, Davey held back a groan. Then the door was popping open and he practically yelped.

"Did I scare you?" Mia asked.

She was wrapped in nothing but a fluffy white towel. Her hair was darkened just a touch by the water with the ends dripping fat droplets along the skin of her shoulders and chest.

Yes.

"No." Davey shook his head, more to rid himself of lust than to confirm his answer.

"Well, the shower is all yours," Mia said cheerfully, then pushed past him and headed to her room down the hall.

Davey watched her go. He couldn't help himself.

When she disappeared from view, he quickly shoved inside the bathroom. It was filled with her leftover steam. The huge mirror was foggy, the space was hot like a sauna.

Snapping the door closed behind him, Davey shed his clothes and stepped into the stall. There was an electronic display affixed to one wall that controlled the temperature of the water and length of the shower. Mia had overridden the damn thing once again, but Davey found he didn't need to. He wanted this thing ice cold and three minutes long. Rinse. Scrub. Rinse. Done.

Maybe then he'd get some relief.

Closing his eyes, he let loose a long sigh of his own. Only, it didn't give him any satisfaction. He was wound tighter than a... well... something that was wound really fucking tight.

"You don't even know what's wound tight," Davey grumbled, jabbing an impatient finger on the control pad until said water poured onto his chest. "A spring? Yeah, wound tighter than a spring."

The shock of cold was painful at first, but he didn't jump. Nope, Davey held steady under the punishing spray and got to work. His movements were a bit jerky, but that was okay. He tried not to let his mind go there. He tried not to let his thoughts scare the living shit out of him.

Mia taken from him. Mia in pain. Mia's father, whoever the bastard was, terrorizing her as a child.

"Stop," Davey spoke the word into the air as the water shut itself off.

Stepping out, he grabbed his own fluffy white towel from the long silver bar and pressed it to his face. He exhaled, then dried his hair for like five seconds, dabbed at his chest and wrapped the thing around his waist.

His dirty clothes were lying in a heap on the bathroom floor so he picked them up and tossed them into the laundry hamper he shared with Mia. They alternated that chore as well. Dinner. Dishes. House duties. He didn't exactly mind it.

"She's not your wife," he reminded himself. *You can't afford her.*

He was losing his mind now too. Great.

Shoving out of the bathroom, Davey kept his head down and plowed straight into his bedroom where he was brought up short. His head whipped up at the figure seated on his bed and his mouth dropped just a fraction.

"Hey." Mia gave a little bounce and smiled.

She was sitting crosslegged on his bed wearing some sort of pajama night dress thing that showed way too much skin. Was she wearing shorts under that thing? Or maybe just underwear? Or maybe nothing at all?

Lowering his arms, Davey crossed his fists in front of his waist and stared. What the hell was she doing?

"I looked for Malik but he's gone," she commented. Davey scowled.

"Yeah he was well enough to be moved to the bowling alley. Jameson wanted to clear all the guys out of here and it's easier to take care of him there," Davey offered, as a quick flash of jealousy took care of his initial shock.

"Oh good." Mia glanced around the room, continued to fidget on his bed. "I was worried."

"You like him," Davey gritted out the words. "Don't you."

"Well, yeah he's great," Mia offered.

Locking eyes with him then, she tilted her head to one side and frowned slightly. "You're upset all of a sudden."

"No," Davey denied the obvious.

"Hmmm," Mia hummed and continued to scrutinize him before sucking in a sharp breath. "Well, I'm going to go out on a limb here and just say that I like Malik only as a friend, it's not the same way that I feel about you."

"Uh…" Davey's heart pounded. "What?"

"So, I wasn't sleepy yet…" Mia ignored him and flashed a mischievous smile. "And I thought maybe you could play for me."

"Play?" Davey's brain had lost blood flow. He wasn't following.

"Your guitar." Mia gestured to the corner where the instrument was propped up. "Unless you're too tired. I can go if you want."

Following her line of sight, Davey pursed his lips.

"You want me to play for you," he repeated, not failing to notice he was still wearing nothing but a damp towel. "Right now."

"If you want," she echoed. "Or I could go."

"No." Davey gave his head a quick shake and crossed to the guitar. He didn't want her to go. "What would you like to hear? Any requests?"

Picking the instrument up, he strummed lightly before stopping to adjust the tune. When he glanced back to Mia, she was watching him intently. Her brown eyes seemed darker in that moment and it had his body humming along with the guitar.

"No requests," she spoke softly and leaned back against his

headboard. Her bare legs curled up beneath her. "I don't remember the names of songs. Something pretty."

"Something pretty," he repeated, as he continued to adjust the tune. *Like you.*

Walking to the bed, he sat at her feet and braced the guitar across his lap. The towel that was draped over his legs shifted as he spread them, revealing more skin, but somehow kept all the important parts covered.

He prayed for focus and in that moment, he got it. He ignored the thumping of his heart, the tightness in his body, the spiking of his pulse.

Choosing a soft song, Davey began to play.

It was pretty, like she wanted, and slow. In his mind, he could hear the words and his brother's voice signing them. And for the first time in a really, really long time, it made him happy instead of sad… and inside his head, Davey sang along. He sang the song for *her*, to her, even though she couldn't hear it because he kept his lips closed.

When the song was over, he looked at Mia. She was still reclining against his headboard, her hair a wild mess, her dark eyes watching him. She was so unbelievably beautiful. He couldn't help what happened next.

Setting the guitar aside, Davey closed the small space between them and kissed her. His hands braced on either side of her body, his chest hovered above her chest. He didn't touch her with anything other than his lips, but those were enough.

Sparks left her body and entered his. There was just no other way to describe it. When her lips parted for his, pressed against his, he groaned. Out. Loud.

Sinking down against her, Davey clutched at her body and

deepened their kiss. He dipped his tongue in, tasted her. Candy and strawberries and everything sweet and seductive filled his senses.

His hips jerked forward and her legs spread for him. Her body shifted beneath his, her chest arched against his.

The stupid towel he had tucked around his waist wasn't doing him any favors. The material loosened until he could feel the thin cotton of her night dress against his skin. She was so hot.

His hand leapt down to her thigh where he stroked and then squeezed.

Mia gasped.

Davey's eyes opened then and he stared into her face. Her cheeks were flushed, her lips plump from where he'd been nibbling on them.

"You okay?" He asked quietly, unable to stop his body from rubbing itself against hers. He was shameless, unable to silence the roar in his blood, the demand for contact, for more.

"It feels good," Mia whispered, her eyes wide as if she were surprised.

Chuckling, Davey dropped his mouth to her neck and sucked at her sensitive skin. *You ain't seen nothing yet.*

A low moan worked its way from Mia's throat. Arching her back, Mia's breasts rubbed teasingly against his bare chest. Her night dress was so thin, he could feel the peaks of her nipples.

Enough with this fabric, he thought.

Sliding his hand up, Davey's fingers traced along her thigh, under her dress, to her hip. His thumb worked over the barely-there panties before continuing higher. Soft belly, softer breasts.

Mia's breath hitched, causing Davey's entire body to clench. He wanted her so unbelievably bad in that moment.

Biting at his own lip, he forced his hips to separate from hers for just a few moments. He had to slow this whole thing down somehow, or he'd never last. Taking his time, Davey worked her dress off over her head. Mia's eyes were hooded, watching him.

Bracing himself on one elbow, he used his other hand to trace down her body. His fingers danced over her lips, down her slender neck, spent a whole lot of time on each breast. Bending forward, his tongue followed the path of his fingers, causing goosebumps to ripple over her flesh.

By the time his mouth got down to her panties, Mia was panting. Davey couldn't help but feel just a touch smug at her reaction. Whatever her past had been with a million boyfriends behind the Wall, he intended on erasing it in the next several minutes.

"Davey?" Mia exhaled his name, causing him to look up at her as he crouched between her legs. "I um…. I…"

Arching a brow, Davey looped his fingers in the straps of her panties and started to slide them down. Mia's eyes widened. Her tongue snaked out to wet her bottom lip.

"You want this?" Davey asked, and pressed a single kiss to that particular spot, the one that made girls come completely undone.

Mia's mouth dropped open and she gasped. Davey smiled against her flesh. She smelled so incredibly good, like sex and heat and everything he wanted to devour. His tongue darted out and he tasted her.

"Oh my God," Mia cried out, her head dropping back and her body coming alive.

Davey's chest expanded. Yep. She definitely wanted this.

Looping both hands around her thighs, he pulled her closer up against him. Mia's fingers came to thread and tug at his hair. He listened to her little sounds, the ones that told him what he was doing was just right.

For the next few minutes, he worshipped her. He buried his face in his work and licked and sucked and kissed and lapped until her hips were rolling against him and her cries came out strangled. When she was finally limp and breathless, he pulled away.

Running a finger down her, he felt how wet she was, how hot. He wanted her still. His body was humming, like electricity was running through it. Glancing up at her face, he watched her work to get air into those lungs of hers.

"Do you want more?" He asked, drawing her eyes over to him.

"I want..." she panted, "you."

Nodding, Davey crawled up her body and braced his elbows on either side of her head. She was still trying to catch her breath, so maybe he should just wait for a bit. But then her legs were spreading for him and his hard length came up against her slick core.

No waiting.

Davey's mouth crashed down to hers. His heart hammered at him and his body went taut as nature did what nature did. His hips rolled and then he was pushing inside of her, slowly, well... as slowly as he could manage. She was tight and hot and his brain was exploding with the sensation.

But then he came up against this barrier and he couldn't

quite figure out what was happening until it was too late. He pushed through it, until he was all the way flush inside of her. She cried out, her body tensing beneath his.

Davey's heart fractured. Closing his eyes, he buried his face in her neck and used every strength reserve he'd ever had to freeze.

"Why didn't you tell me?" Davey whispered against the skin of her neck, it was slick with sweat.

Mia's chest was straining against his, her breath coming out in puffs. His body was screaming at him to continue, to move, to do anything except what he was doing. But he held back.

"You're a virgin," he continued. "Why didn't you tell me?"

"Would it have changed anything?" Mia panted, the strain in her voice was clear and it broke him, he'd hurt her. "Would you not have been with me?"

"I would have done this a little differently," he admitted. *Like slower, if possible.* "Do you want me to stop?"

Mia's arms came up to wrap his neck and she held him in place. He shifted his forehead against her chest, placed a slow kiss to the valley between her breasts.

"Don't stop," she whispered. "I'm in love with you."

I'm in love with you too.

Squeezing his eyes shut, Davey held his breath. He couldn't love this woman. He couldn't love anyone anymore. That just wasn't in his cards.

"I'm not worthy of you," he spoke finally and felt her cinch tighter. "Tell me if it hurts too much."

Exhaling, Davey let the weight of his body press Mia further into the mattress. His hips began to move, slowly. He pulled out, felt her brace herself, then he pushed back in.

Lifting his head, he covered her mouth with his, swamped her in distracting kisses while his body did all the work.

Sneaking a hand down, he used his thumb to tease and rub as he slid in and out of her. Before too long, Mia was relaxing, pushing against him, sighing. But those cues set off a timer in him.

All of her sounds, all of her movements, encouraging him, telling him she was liking what he was doing… they made him rush towards his own end. He could feel the tingling, the demanding, the pulsing throb that roared within him. He wouldn't be able to make her come like this, not before he did.

"I'm gonna come," he hissed the words against her mouth.

When those luscious lips of hers curved into a smile… he lost it.

Groaning, Davey's body jerked and pulsed and he found his release. Now it was his turn to cry out. Now it was his turn to moan and bury his face in her hair.

And the awful fucking truth kept ringing like a bell inside his head.

You are so into this girl. You're just as much in love as she is... possibly more. You're just too much of a pussy to say it.

"Mia," Davey spoke quietly as he worked to get air. "I am truly not worthy of you."

CHAPTER THIRTY-TWO_
MIA

Opening her eyes, Mia blinked up at the ceiling. Davey's heavy arm was draped across her stomach. His sleeping face pressed into her chest. With a smile, Mia angled her head down, trying to look at him.

His naked torso ran the length of hers, partially twisted in the cream-colored sheets. Biting at her lower lip, Mia suppressed a smile. She could feel his even breathing against her skin, and the weight of his left leg as it tangled up with hers.

Had she really just done that? With him? A hundred tiny butterflies took flight in her belly and she sighed.

She finally understood what all the fuss was about. She got why all those guys were so frustrated when she stopped them at kissing. She got why Cass watched Jameson stalk around their apartment like a predator in the evenings right before bed. She got it.

Taking a deep breath, Mia shifted her body a little. The area between her legs was definitely sore, but not entirely in a bad way. If not for the pressing need to use the bathroom, she'd probably just stay happily right where she was... maybe forever.

But the need was definitely pressing and she was finding it a bit hard to breathe with Davey hanging all over her. So as much as she warmed at the contact, Mia wriggled and scooted and inched her way off the bed.

She hadn't made it two feet when Davey's sexy gruff voice chased after her.

"Where you going?" He grumbled. She could hear him sighing and the sheets slipping together as he rolled over.

"It's morning." Mia threw him a quick look over her shoulder before doing a cursory search for her nightie. "We'd better get up."

"There's no way it's morning," Davey protested, still groggy. "We just went to bed."

Shaking her head, Mia huffed a laugh. Where the heck were her clothes? She couldn't even remember getting out of them.

But one thing's for certain, her uncle had raised her to be a farm girl, and so her body rose with the dawn. There was no need for a window to show her what time it was outside. She just knew.

"It's definitely morning," Mia countered before giving up on clothes altogether and crossing to the bedroom door. It was still open, they hadn't even bothered to shut it the night before. "Time to start another day."

"Wait." Davey shoved up in bed and frowned. "Where the hell are you going naked?"

Laughing now, Mia blew him a kiss before slipping over the threshold and out into the hall. At her back, Davey released a string of curses as the bed frame groaned under his weight. He was clearly pushing out of bed, but she didn't dare turn to watch.

All was silent in the bunker and something told her they were alone. Jameson sometimes spent the night in the bowling alley, or taking care of business on the outside. It wasn't so unusual for him to miss a day or maybe two down here, so she shrugged and darted to the bathroom first thing.

When she was finished in there, she stepped back into the hall to find Davey waiting for her. He was leaning up against the wall, his arms folded across his chest.

He'd put on a pair of his camouflage pants and tucked in a brown t-shirt, but his feet were bare. He looked beyond sexy and tempting in his uniform.

Mia tipped her chin up and attempted to stroll past him.

"Not so fast," Davey grunted out the words as he made a grab around her waist.

Lifting her up, Davey wrapped her against him and silenced her giggles with his mouth.

"You can't."

Kiss.

"Walk around."

Deeper kiss.

"Naked."

More kissing.

Pulling back, Mia tried to catch her breath. Davey stared at her, those pale-blue eyes of his searching her face like they so often did.

"You okay?" He murmured finally.

"I'm good." Mia's heart swelled. "Really good. You?"

"Well… I think you might be the death of me," Davey responded seriously and had her cracking up all over again.

"You can release me," she commented. "I need to get dressed. We've got work to do."

"Work." Davey's face twisted momentarily, but then he loosened his hold and let her go. "You can't do that again."

"What?" Mia ran a hand through her hair and headed towards her room. "Walk around naked?"

"No." Davey chased after her. "I mean yes, that too, but taking off on the tractor. You can't do that again. You've got to stay close to me."

"Alright," Mia conceded and threw him a look. "I promise."

A half a day later and this time, she'd made good on her word. Mia's hands were wrist deep in rich earth while Davey's shadow loomed over her. It was comforting, being able to yank out weeds and watch Davey's silhouette shift on the ground.

On the next row over, DeKalb was hunched over a pile of his own weeds. The guy was quiet, his red hat pulled low, his hands always busy. She didn't know much about him, despite the fact they'd worked side by side for weeks now.

"DeKalb," she called, not looking up. "What's your first name?"

"Hmmm?" DeKalb paused in his pulling and dusted his hands on his dirty jeans. "What?"

"What's your first name?" She repeated and glanced over at him. "Where are you from, originally?"

Not that the information would be beneficial to her, it might ping off the blurry part of her brain and fall useless. But still, seemed like she should try.

"Oh, the name's Randal," he answered. "Randy for short."

"Randy," Mia repeated, nodding. "Where did you grow up Randy?"

"Houston." He smacked his lips together. "But that feels like forever ago."

"'Cause it was," Davey interjected. "So that makes you a South-Westie Soldier."

Pausing, DeKalb tipped the brim of his hat up and sniffed. "Does it really matter?"

"No," Davey acknowledged, his eyes leaving the pair of them and traveling to the far side of the field. "No, I guess it doesn't."

Following his gaze, Mia brought her hand up to shade her eyes. The sun was bright today and it was well past noon. The giant yellow orb was already retreating in the west. A wind had picked up, making things cooler.

On the edge of the field, an argument was brewing.

"Looks like a pair of yours," Davey commented. "I recognize the one, but..."

DeKalb pushed up to standing and stared off at the men facing each other. Their voices were raising on the wind, mixing and hard to make out, save for the intent. They were upset with one another.

Grabbing at the radio on his hip, Davey brought it up to his mouth and depressed the call button. Static sounded and he began to speak into it.

But the words he said faded as an old memory charged towards Mia. It was one she'd fought off before, one that she'd been denying and could no longer prevent.

"Davey," Mia gasped and reached back for him. "I need tea."

But his response, whatever it was, never came. Because the

figures on the field morphed from two men to three. The voices were sharper, closer, clear as day.

And the fear… it rocketed straight down her spine.

"I don't know what to say." Uncle Everett spread out his palms wide. "I've got no idea what you're talking about."

"That's bull and you know it," the man in the suit responded, as his partner took a step closer, hand on his hip.

The three men were standing on the train platform, while the rest of them were already loaded onto one of the cars. Aunt Jean and the boys, Mia and the rest of their church. They'd packed their bags, and loaded onto one of a hundred cattle cars filled to the brim with men, women and children.

That's when the two men in suits had come along, and yanked Uncle Everett out the door.

Now the three of them were faced off on the nearly empty platform. The roar from the train's engine sounded. Soldiers stalked along the tracks. One in particular took an interest in the dispute. Stepping towards the men, he didn't say anything, just stood there and observed.

"Get back," hissed Aunt Jean.

They were all standing at the open doorway, watching. She pulled on Mia's arm, but Mia was frozen to the spot. This was about her.

They'd found her. Daddy's men had found her. He'd killed her Mama, because she'd never come for Marie. But now Daddy had… or at least, he'd sent his men.

"We know you have her," the man in the suit continued. "And it's time to hand her over. If you do that, then you get to walk away. You and your wife and your boys can all just walk away."

"You've got the wrong man," Uncle insisted. He didn't turn around.

"No, we've got the right one," the man again. "Now where is she? Which one is Marie?"

At that, the soldier turned and appraised the train car. They'd all come with the church, so they were all dressed the same. Long hair. Long sleeve woolen dresses. No makeup. Plain shoes. There were maybe a dozen teenage girls altogether, and most of them had the same coloring.

"What does she look like?" The soldier asked.

Uncle Everett's shoulders tensed and everyone on the train car held their breath. One of the men in suits, the one that did all the talking, spoke up.

"Blonde, brown eyes, about 18 years old." He gestured to the car. "She's in there. Her name is Marie."

Nodding, the soldier strode over to the car and jumped inside. Everyone sucked back, as if he were on fire.

Mia's eyes slammed to the wooden floor, her heart was hammering in her chest. If he came any closer, she was going to vomit all over his boots.

He took his time, looking into each girl's face, not saying anything. From somewhere further up the tracks, the train whistle blew. It had everyone jumping, and Mia's face tipped up. The soldier's dark eyes locked with hers and he pursed his lips.

"This one," he called. "The only blonde with brown eyes. Are you Marie?"

"No... no..." she shook her head and looked down. "I'm not."

"Bring her down!" The man in the suit called. "There's money in it for you."

Grabbing onto Mia's wrist, the soldier brought her to his side and jumped out of the car. She had no choice but to jump along with him, or risk falling and breaking her neck.

"I don't know that girl!" Uncle Everett's face drained of color as his voice raised. "She's just a church girl. Set her back on the train. I don't know these men."

"That's gotta be her." The man in the suit nodded and pulled his phone from his pocket, swiping across it before bringing up a photo. He slid the screen in front of the soldier's face.

"That's a little girl," the soldier commented, and frowned.

In the background, the roar of the train's engine increased. There was the groan of metal, the clank and tack of wheels as they began to grip along the track.

The train.

It was leaving.

Glancing over her shoulder, Mia's mouth dropped open as Aunt Jean began to cry. The soldier held tight to her wrist, but even so she began to jerk and yank her arm.

"Please," she begged. "Please let me get on the train."

"Give her over boy," the man in the suit said. "Kids grow up. That's her."

People on the train began to call out. They were yelling and jostling each other at the still open door. The car began to roll slowly along the track. Aunt Jean was sobbing now. Mia's cousins were screaming, fighting to jump out, while members of the church held them back.

"Let her go!" Uncle Everett yelled and lunged for the soldier, but he was too slow.

Pop.

The second man in the suit pulled a gun, and Uncle Everett dropped like a stone to the ground.

Mia's mouth went slack and her eyes widened. She stared at her uncle's unblinking eyes as blood poured from beneath his body. The only thing she could hear then, were her aunt's sobs turn to screeching as the train picked up speed and carried them all away.

"Well, that's that then," the first man in the suit commented dryly. "Thanks for your help son. We've got cash for you."

But the soldier didn't respond. He just continued to frown and hold tight to Mia's wrist. She could feel his grip intensify, instead of loosen.

As the man in the suit removed a wallet and began counting out crisp hundred dollar bills, the soldier glanced back at her. Mia's eyes pooled with tears and she shook her head no.

He blinked once, returned his focus to the two men in suits, pulled his own weapon and shot them both in the head.

Boom.

Boom.

Mia staggered back and fell to her butt on the platform as the last of the train cars whizzed by. The soldier remained unaffected. Calmly, he replaced his weapon at his side, crouched down and took everyone's pulse. After a full minute, he stood up and walked over to her.

Looking down at Mia, he heaved a big sigh.

"You shouldn't be on that train anyway," he said matter of factly. "The next one should be safe, I'll send you on it instead."

CHAPTER THIRTY-THREE_

MIA

"MIA." DAVEY'S VOICE SOUNDED, THEN THE SNAP OF HIS fingers. "Mia, open your eyes. Come on."

Mia's face scrunched up as her stomach rolled. Her eyes were slammed shut, her heart rattling around in her chest. A part of her was still at the train station, lying on that platform with her dead uncle a few feet away.

The young soldier who ended up saving her life, was walking away like nothing had happened. Tears poured down her cheeks, her hands were shaking.

But Davey's voice was sucking her back to reality.

He kept calling out her name, willing her to come to him, and something inside of her relented. Her mind was jumbled, her memories coming back to her all at once.

Opening her eyes suddenly, Mia blinked into the light, turned onto her side and threw up.

"Oh shit." Someone said, but she couldn't place the voice.

"Mia." Davey's hand landed on her shoulder, steadied her. "Hey, come here Mia. You're alright. You're okay."

Choking a little, Mia opened her eyes.

DeKalb was crouching in front of her, his eyes wide and questioning. She was lying in the dirt between two rows of broccoli sprouts. Davey was at her back, his palm steady on her body.

Glancing at him over her shoulder, Mia's blurry eyes met his sharp ones.

"That's not my name," she said.

"What?" Davey's face screwed up.

"That's not my name," Mia repeated. "Not my real name. Not Mia."

"Okay, stop." Davey looped his rifle strap over his shoulder. Reaching out he began to collect her body in his arms.

"My real name is Marie VanPell," she told him. "I remember that part now."

Freezing in place, Davey's eyes widened. His gaze jumped from her face to DeKalb's, then the men standing all around them.

"Get back!" He shouted. "You're crowding her, she needs air."

"Davey…" Mia started.

"No," Davey cut her off and gathered her in his arms. "You need a medic. You're confused."

"I'm not confused." Mia shook her head, but wrapped her arms around his neck as he hoisted her off the ground. "I've finally remembered. She never came for me, Davey. Mama never came to get me, so he killed her. He must have killed her."

"Stop," Davey shushed her again as his boots stomped along the earth. Throwing a quick look over his shoulder, he called, "Locklan! We're out. Get everyone moving."

"Yes Sir!" Locklan's answer came, then radio static and men talking.

Exhaling, Mia rested her face against Davey's chest and shut her eyes. The world was spinning all of sudden. She could feel her legs jostling with each step Davey took, but she tried to focus on the sound of his heartbeat against her ear. It was pumping quick. Tap. Tap. Tap. But it was steady.

When they got to the Jeep someone else opened the door and Davey crawled inside with her still in his arms. Cradling her on his lap, he held the back of his hand to her forehead, then pressed two fingers to the side of her neck.

Other doors opened and slammed shut. The vehicle shook with the weight of bodies. There were a few grunts. The engine fired up. Mia opened her mouth to speak but Davey frowned.

"Just rest," he said. "We're going to call the medic. He'll meet us at the bunker. Right Evans?"

"On it." Evans snapped a reply.

He was sitting shotgun. The Jeep began bumping over the uneven dirt of the farm. Mia felt tears pool in her eyes, then a lick of fear. Daddy had found her. His men had found her in the end and they'd killed Uncle Everett. It was all her fault.

"It's my fault he's dead," Mia whispered. "It's my fault they're all dead."

Pursing his lips, Davey brushed away the tears that trickled over her cheeks.

"You're confused," he tried. "You must've hit your head when you fell."

"I didn't hit my head." Mia reached for her hair, felt the dirt threaded in it. "I just remembered."

"You think your name is Marie VanPell," Davey began. "But that's just a name you heard when you were little. Your brain is substituting it in. Whatever you remembered, it's not right."

"Wait." Mia's brow furrowed. "You recognize the name?"

"Well, yeah." Davey shrugged. "Everyone does. It was awful what happened, it was all over the news for years."

"Wait… what happened?" Mia's voice lowered, her heart slowed.

"Vice President VanPell's daughter was kidnapped," Davey supplied. "Taken from their home when she was nine years old. They never found her."

Mia blinked. Slowly. She felt the world shrinking around her, wrapping its arms tightly around her chest. It was sort of hard to breathe.

"My father was a Senator," she hissed. "So maybe you're right. Maybe I got the name wrong. My name."

The color drained from Davey's face and he glanced up to the front of the Jeep. Whoever he locked eyes with, whether it was Locklan or Evans, she couldn't see. But his gaze raced back to hers and he swallowed.

"What did he look like?" Davey whispered. "Your father, the one in your memories, the one that…"

Beat me. She finished his sentence for him, because he left it floating there in the air.

Mia closed her eyes and fought the twist in her belly. She watched the image swim up to her. The empty brown eyes that were so like her own. The short crop of black hair. The sound of his voice, how it sent coils of adrenaline to her fingers and toes. How it made her want to hide.

"She called him Darling…" Mia took a breath and opened her eyes wide. "Mama did. She called him that when he was happy, and Ed when he was not. He was tall, and strong. He… he had eyes like mine, but his hair was black, he kept it short."

"Fuck." Davey's face fell and his eyes closed briefly.

"Vice President VanPell was originally a Senator," Malpas offered, he was seated beside them, his fingers drumming nervously on the interior door panel. "When his daughter was taken, he was a Senator. He didn't become VP until just before the start of the war."

"What?" Mia's face screwed up as she tried to process the information.

Her father… he reported her missing?

Davey grabbed for her hand and held on. His lips pressed together and his eyes locked with hers. Mia searched his face as her throat began to close.

"VanPell's wife… Marie VanPell's mother…" Davey swallowed. "Rachel VanPell. She was still alive when the war started."

Mia's eyes flew wide. Her other hand came to slap over the one Davey was already holding. He squeezed her tighter. *Mama?*

"She's alive?" She asked, tears flowing freely once more. "Mama didn't come for me?"

Davey ducked his head then and drew in a breath while Mia's world crumbled all around her. Mama didn't come. She stayed with him? She sent Mia away and she went back. How? Why?

"No one breathes a word of this," Davey gritted out the words then, his head tipping up to survey the men in the vehicle. "Not one word. To anyone."

CHAPTER THIRTY-FOUR_
DAVEY

"IT'S BEEN FIVE DAYS," JAMESON POINTED OUT. "BISSET CLEARED her. No fever, no vomiting. Just more memory recurrence."

"Yeah but..." Davey ducked his head and kept working over the stove. "She's tired. She still needs to rest."

Pacing away, Jameson huffed an impatient breath. He'd been accepting at first of Mia's absence from the fields. He'd sent the medic when Davey had requested him, and had her checked out.

After that initial visit everyone had left well enough alone, which is what Davey had wanted. Space for her to cry. Space for her to work through what had happened in her life.

Her fucking father being in power. Her mother hiding her, but going back. The kidnapping allegations. All the lies. So. Many. Lies.

And Davey had been there to pick up the pieces. He filled in the blanks as best he could remember them. At the time, it had been an international sensation, a missing girl case that never really went away. They'd never found a body. There was never a ransom note or a demand for money.

But he'd been young then too, when it had first happened, and his knowledge was spotty. Even so, when Mia cried, he held her to his chest. He rocked her, kissed her, did things to make her forget. Maybe he didn't have the guts to tell her how he felt about her, but he could show her, and he did.

But now Jameson's need to get the job moving again was threatening to explode all of that.

Coming up beside Davey, the guy leaned a hip against the granite counter and folded his arms in front of him. His stare pierced the side of Davey's head, but Davey said nothing. He just kept stirring the soup, a rich broth filled with steak, green beans, potatoes and carrots. It smelled amazing. It would taste even better.

The truth was, he couldn't wait for Jameson to leave. He couldn't wait to bring this dinner back to Mia in bed and then climb in beside her.

"This is about the Provo Op," Jameson commented finally. "Isn't it."

Pursing his lips, Davey exhaled through his nostrils. It actually wasn't about the Provo Op, but now that Jameson mentioned it… yeah it'd be nice to be clued in to the bigger picture around here. Something larger was happening than exploratory farming of a new colony.

But he knew better than to dignify that with an answer. So he stayed silent and just kept stirring, stirring, stirring.

"This isn't going to work," Jameson again, his body shifting, his muscled arms flexing. "You tried to leverage her before, by not letting her go up top, and now you're doing it again. It's not going to work."

Turning to look at his boss, Davey arched an eyebrow. They'd had this argument before, when Malik had first returned. Davey had tried to keep Mia in the bunker until Jameson gave in and told him what the hell was really going on. And for a few precious hours it looked like that plan might actually work, but then Jameson's assurances had got the better of him and he caved.

"It's your job to make her safe up there," Jameson continued. "I've got the big picture handled and you've got the small one. Keep her with you, by you, and it will all work out. But the farm is falling to shit already and she's got to get back to it."

"No," Davey replied and returned his focus to the stew. It was pretty well done.

"No?" Jameson leaned forward.

"She needs more rest." Davey fell back on a tired line. "The farm can wait."

"She doesn't need more rest." Jameson jerked a thumb over his shoulder. "I just checked in on her. She seems perfectly fine, a bit homesick maybe, but aren't we all. And you know what's going to fix that? You know what will help her?"

Davey heaved a sigh and flipped off the burner on the stove.

"Completing our mission, then *actually* getting to go home," Jameson supplied. "And to do that, she's got to get back up top. Period."

Opening his mouth, Davey started to protest, but Jameson cut him off.

"End of discussion," the guy said, swiping a hand through the air. "We go first thing in the morning tomorrow."

Davey struggled to answer, and Jameson ran right over him.

"I'm gonna need to take a bowl of that soup to go," he said suddenly, gesturing to Davey's stew.

"You what?" Davey frowned, thrown by the flip in conversation.

"I'm sorry I haven't been around to help the past week down here, but with Malik and everything, I'm needed elsewhere," Jameson went on. "That'll change. Okay? We go up top tomorrow, we start our routine again, I help down here. We good?"

"You're going to the farm tomorrow?" Davey squinted.

"Yeah." Jameson nodded. "I'll help cover detail tomorrow. I need to get a better progress check on it anyway."

Considering, Davey turned away. He took three steps to the side, grabbed a large Tupperware from one of the bottom cabinets and set it on the counter. Tupperware. They actually had the plastic stuff down here. It never ceased to amaze him.

Sliding the thing along the counter, he tapped on the lid and eyed Jameson.

"Alright," Davey relented. "Tomorrow morning."

Nodding quickly, Jameson reached for the container. "Tomorrow morning."

CHAPTER THIRTY-FIVE_

MIA

"MMMM, THAT WAS GOOD." MIA SET THE EMPTY BOWL ON HER nightstand and sighed.

Davey was propped up beside her on her bed, thumbing through a book. He'd long since finished his stew. He was such a fast eater, it amazed her he didn't get indigestion.

Looking over at him, Mia nibbled on her bottom lip. He'd shaved recently, the skin on his cheeks and chin were smooth. Reaching over, she traced the tips of her fingers along his face, feeling the softness and causing him to smile. She loved it when he smiled. Loved. It.

"What are you doing?" He asked, and flipped another page in his book.

The paper shuffled and slipped and made the most delicious sound. Davey frowned down at the words on the page.

Inching closer, Mia let her hand drop from his face and cuddled up to his side. Reflexively, Davey wrapped one arm around her body and drew her in closer. Mia closed her eyes and absorbed the contact.

They'd been like this for days now. Holed up together.

Eating, talking. He let her cry herself hoarse over her mom and then he kissed her. That act in and of itself seemed to relieve much of the hurt binding up her heart.

"Jameson said we're going to the farm tomorrow," Mia murmured.

Shifting slightly, Davey closed his book and set it aside. Mia opened her eyes and stared at the skin of his chest as it peeked up from the collar of his cotton shirt. She wanted to put her lips there. The thought warmed her from the inside.

"Are you okay to go up top?" Davey asked, rubbing his hand down her arm. "We don't have to."

"Yeah." Mia considered a moment. "I think I am. It'd be good to get back to work, a distraction, you know? And I heard DeKalb is struggling already."

Huffing a breath, Davey shifted again, making the mattress bounce with his weight.

"You think he'd be able to handle a week by himself," Davey pointed out. "It's not rocket science."

Chuckling, Mia pushed back a little so she could watch Davey's face. He was grumpy, frowning a little and pursing those lips of his.

"He's never worked with these particular crops before," Mia explained. "It can be a learning curve."

"Pfft." Davey made a motion with his hand as if swatting at a fly.

Mia's brows raised. Crawling up to her knees, she reached out and took Davey's chin in her palm.

"You don't like him?" She asked.

"I don't anything him," Davey retorted. "The guy's a nonissue. A non-anything. He's blank."

"He's not blank, you're so mean," Mia teased.

Sliding onto Davey's lap, Mia tilted her head to one side and braced both of her hands on his chest. She felt the quick expansion of his lungs as he sucked in a breath, watched as his tongue darted out to wet his lips.

"Mia," Davey warned, but his hands went to her waist where they pulsed lightly.

Rocking her hips, Mia brought her face within an inch of Davey's. His lips parted. Her eyes fluttered shut.

She didn't need to close the space between them, because he did. He always did.

Davey's mouth sought hers, his lips working against hers, his tongue teasing against hers. The moan that crawled out of her throat was involuntary. It came from that place between her legs, the one that was throbbing now against his hard length.

She was hot and wet and she wanted him. And after that first time, she wasn't so sore anymore.

"You're killing me here," Davey groaned into her mouth.

Mia smiled and kept working her hips, dragging herself over him, making his hands cinch down tighter on her.

Her breasts were aching too, so she rubbed her chest against his. Davey swore.

"Too much clothes," he murmured, peppering her neck with kisses.

Then his hands were everywhere, tugging and tearing and yanking until her shirt was over her head and his was gone as well. Lifting up with his hips, Davey worked to slide his pants down, causing Mia to rock to one side and almost fall off of him.

She laughed out loud and he smiled at her then, the tips of

his ears turning pink, along with the skin of his neck and chest.

"Are you blushing?" Mia held onto his shoulders as Davey scooted them further down the bed, until he was lying on his back with her seated on top of him.

"Nope." Davey reached up and began fondling her nipples, his eyes were focused, following everywhere his fingers teased. "Men don't blush."

Gasping at the contact, Mia forgot the retort she had swimming in her brain. All of sudden, she couldn't think clearly. All she could do was feel.

His hands stroking her body. His hips rolling beneath hers. His mouth coming up to close around one breast.

"Davey," she panted his name and heard a rumbling growl come from his chest.

Then those panties of hers were being yanked to one side and he was sliding in. No testing finger first, like he usually did, just him, all of him, at once. Crying out, Mia squeezed her eyes shut and felt a tremor of pleasure rocket through her.

"Couldn't wait," Davey gasped the words. "Can't wait."

Nodding, Mia bit down on her lower lip and pushed back against him, grinding down, seeking more, further, deeper. Whimpering, she felt herself building. The pressure was increasing with each roll of her hips.

Opening her eyes wide, she looked down at Davey. He was staring up at her, his mouth parted slightly, his breath coming out in short bursts.

His pace quickened. His right hand came around to play with that spot between her legs, rubbing and teasing, bringing her closer and closer to the edge.

More. Again. She couldn't stop. She couldn't resist.

Crying out, Mia's eyes slammed shut as her release shot through her. Her fingers dug into the skin of his chest, but Davey kept moving. Faster. Harder. Until he was coming too. Until he was moaning out loud and jerking against her and pulling her down to him.

"Why do you do that to me?" He asked, breathless. His hand coming up to trace through her tangle of hair.

Still tingling, Mia's forehead pressed against his. "Do what?" She asked.

"Make me feel like that," Davey answered, before he kissed her, slowly then spoke more words against her lips. "You make me feel everything."

CHAPTER THIRTY-SIX_
DAVEY

"HEY, WAKE UP," MIA COAXED.

Davey felt her hands tap on his chest, before moving along his arm. She shook him just a little and he sucked in a breath.

"We overslept," she continued. "I'm sorry, I never oversleep."

"Huh?" Davey's eyes blinked open and he groaned.

Throwing his arms wide, he arched his back and glanced around. He was still in Mia's bed, tangled up in her blankets. One of the lamps was switched on and she was already half dressed.

"Oh." Davey's face fell. "You've got a bra on."

Rolling her eyes, Mia shrugged a loose-fitting cotton shirt over her head before tucking it into the pants of her uniform. Even dressed in men's clothing, she looked fucking edible. Licking his lips at the thought, Davey's eyes crept slowly along her legs, as his own body did that thing men's bodies do in the morning.

"I'm serious," Mia hissed and ran her hands back through her hair. "We're late. I'll grab us a quick bite to eat."

Turning from him, she fled the room on bare feet. He heard the pop of cupboard doors in the kitchen and the sound of running water. How had she turned him from a relentless work machine into a lazy ass in the span of a week? He didn't know.

No wait. Scratch that. He definitely had an idea of how she'd made him a slave to her bed. But then the front door was swinging open and it had Davey shooting to his feet.

Oh shit.

"Rise and shine ladies!" Jameson's voice echoed down the hall. "We had an agreement!"

Fuck. Fuck. Shit. Fuck.

Davey tore through the covers on the bed, his hands raking over the fabric, his eyes searching, but he was unable to find his pants. His shirt? Yup, got that. But his pants? No. They were nowhere.

A pair of heavy boots slapped steadily closer, and an instinctual sort of panic rose in Davey's throat. No underwear. No pants. Boss coming. Not good.

His eyes landed on the twisted top sheet. Better than nothing, he figured. Yanking the entire sheet off in one go, he wrapped it around his waist and darted from the bedroom.

"What the...?" Jameson's voice sounded close as Davey scooted out of Mia's room and into his own.

"Morning Jameson!" Mia called from the kitchen as Davey quickly shut his own bedroom door.

Whatever conversation the two of them were having, it bought Davey enough time to get dressed. Boxers, pants, socks, shirt, boots, belt. He was just blowing out a long breath and willing his heart rate to decrease when the knock at his door came.

A closed fist against hard wood. Boom. Boom. Boom.

This wasn't the gentle rapping of knuckles. This was a big man wanting answers and Davey knew there was nothing to be done but face the music. He hadn't hidden his new relationship with Mia, but he hadn't exactly come out with the information either, and with Jameson absent this whole past week, well...

"Open up Soldier," Jameson growled. "That's an order."

Squaring his shoulders, Davey ran a hand over his sex-mussed hair and did as he was told. He opened the door.

Jameson's electric-blue eyes locked on Davey's pale ones and the level of heat he saw there was somewhat surprising. He'd been caught with his pants down (or off, technically speaking), and yes, that was embarrassing. But Mia was an adult and so was he. What they'd done... what they'd become to one another... that wasn't illegal (not that anything was exactly illegal anymore, but still).

Frowning, Davey glanced over the big guy's shoulder, but he couldn't see into the kitchen so Mia was nowhere in sight.

"Tell me you did not," Jameson began and jerked a thumb behind him. "Take advantage of that girl in there."

"What? No." Davey's face screwed up.

"Oh thank God." Jameson gritted his teeth. "Because I could have sworn I just saw you running naked from her fucking bedroom. Must have been my mistake."

"Well, I mean," Davey backpedalled. "It wasn't like *that*. I would never..."

"Have sex with a woman who is completely under your control *and* doesn't have all of her memories *and* is more than likely a damn virgin?" Jameson hissed the words and stepped into Davey's space. "Because that is exactly what I hired you to prevent!"

"Whoa." Davey held up his hands as his own anger started to build. "How did you know that?"

Jameson's brows raised. "Know what? That she's never slept with anyone before? Oh I don't know... maybe because Cass is her very best friend and they tell each other everything. Loudly. In my living room. After a few glasses of wine.

I've got all kinds of information that I don't want to know. And you know what that makes me?"

Jameson shoved Davey backwards and stepped fully into the room. Slamming the door behind him, he swiped a hand through the air.

"That makes me like a brother to her," he growled. "And I think I might have to kill you now."

Another man might have taken a step back in that moment. After all, Davey had to look decidedly up to maintain eye contact with his boss. Jameson's jaw was ticking and his fists were clenching and to be sure his hit would be powerful when it came.

But Davey was not just any man and he did not back down from a fight. Nope. His chest filled with air, his chin tipped up and he stepped toe to toe with Jameson.

"You want to take a shot?" He asked. "Then take it. You think I could do anything to hurt that girl in there? Then I fucking deserve it. But know this, I'm not going down without a fight and when it's all over, I'm going to get up and leave this room and take what's mine. I'm not going anywhere."

"Is that so?" Jameson's brow raised and he folded his

substantial arms across his chest. "Take what's yours? What's yours, Davey? Hmm? Something out there belong to you?"

"Yeah." Davey nodded and let Jameson's forearms bump his chest. "Mia belongs to me. I'm not leaving without her, no matter what. Nothing can change what I did, and to be honest I wouldn't take it back. Not one thing. She's got all of her memories back now, she knows what she wants and what she doesn't."

"And you think she wants you?" Jameson stared hard into Davey's face.

Davey didn't blink.

"I hope to God she does," he said finally.

Ducking his head, Jameson let out a whoosh of air and stepped back. His arms were still folded over his chest as he bobbed his head quickly.

"You in love with her?" He asked, suddenly going still.

"I am." The words leapt out of Davey's mouth, they were automatic.

"Is that why she passed out in the fields the other day?" Jameson tilted his head to one side. "You were distracted from doing your job?"

"What?" Davey's face screwed up. His pulse spiked.

"You're in love with her." Jameson poked a fat finger in Davey's direction. "You're distracted. You let her pass out. You weren't doing your job how you should be doing it because feelings cloud judgment. You know this."

"No." Davey shook his head. "No. That's not what happened."

"It is." Jameson nodded vigorously. "There's a reason they don't have doctors work on their own family members. There's a reason they don't have bodyguards watching their own wives. It doesn't work. Emotion is a distraction. Distraction equals death. You. Know. This."

"No, Jameson..." Davey's lungs began to cinch in on him. He swiped a hand through the air. "I've been on point this entire time. I'm the best man for this job. The only one for this job."

"No you're not." Jameson sucked in a breath. "Not anymore. Now you're just her lovesick boyfriend. And you know what that means right? I've got to find a new bodyguard."

"That's not the right move," Davey protested, unable to keep the strain from creeping into his voice. The panic. It was coursing through his veins now. "I'm the only one that can take care of her how she needs. I'm the only one that can keep her safe. Do not pull me from this job. I swear to you..."

"Davey?" Jameson sighed. "You're fired."

CHAPTER THIRTY-SEVEN_

MIA

"Don't you think you're overreacting just a little?" Mia asked.

Leaning up from the back seat, Mia tilted her head towards Jameson and gave him a long look. The Jeep continued to rumble down the road. Locklan was driving, Evans and Malpas were wedged on either side of her, and Jameson was riding shotgun.

They were all heading towards the farm, same as always, except for one huge missing piece. Davey had been left behind in the bunker.

"No, I don't think I am," Jameson retorted, but he refused to meet her gaze.

"Look, Davey is still the best man for this job," Mia argued.

"Davey is actually *not* the best man for this job." Jameson shifted his broad shoulders and stared out the front windshield. "Because now you're no longer a job to him Mia. He's not thinking with a sharp mind when it comes to you. He's thinking with... well..."

"His heart?" Mia offered with a smile.

Beside her, Soldier Malpas cleared his throat and Evans choked just a little. Turning around abruptly in his seat, Jameson glared.

"Yeah," he answered her, staring hard at the two men in the back. "He's thinking with his *heart,* which is when people usually start dying. So no, he's out of a job."

"You're sure this isn't more like a punishment for going behind your back?" Mia ventured.

Returning his focus forward, Jameson reached for his radio and let loose a long sigh. Locklan kept his hands steady on the wheel. The boys in the back fell silent.

It wasn't until Jameson brought the radio to his lips and started demanding status updates that she realized the discussion was over.

Flopping back against the seat, Mia adjusted her helmet and frowned. The sun was well and truly up by this point. Between her oversleeping and Jameson and Davey's hour long argument, they were definitely late getting out to the fields.

Thankfully, the morning wasn't terribly hot. Summer was fading, bringing with it fall winds and the promise of change. The farmer in her thought of rain, and how it would affect the ground. She didn't plan on being here for the first frost, but she wanted to prepare DeKalb for it nonetheless. She wanted him to succeed, even when she returned to the safety of the Wall.

Would Davey be going back with her? She wasn't sure. She wanted him to, of course. She wanted him to come back to the Wall and stay. But they hadn't talked about it and she was afraid to bring it up.

Her heart clenched just a little and she pursed her lips.

The vehicle slowed and bumped onto the dirt road that

would take them out to the farm. Mia's body rocked with the movement as Evans braced a hand on the side door panel and adjusted his rifle. It should be Davey sitting there, she thought, and sighed.

She was so crazy about him, so intensely swallowed up by being with him, and she didn't even know if he felt the same way. He hadn't told her that he loved her, even though she'd blurted it out in the middle of... well. And although it had hurt not to hear him say it back, she'd taken it in stride. It didn't change how she felt about him. The fact that he may not feel the same way about her didn't change her desperation to be his.

"Alright, everything's clear, we haven't had any chatter," Jameson commented and set the radio back in its holder. "I'd like a tour of what you've been doing, Mia. Tell me everything you're thinking about with the farm, don't hold back."

Throwing her a look over his shoulder, Jameson waited for confirmation.

"You got it." She nodded and forced a smile. "Boss."

Four hours later and the promise that cool breeze had made earlier was well and truly forgotten. Removing her helmet, Mia swiped at the sweat beading in the line of her hair. She was hot and sticky, frustrated and dirty. And she had to pee. Did she mention she had to pee? Yeah, there was that.

"How badly do you need it to work?" Jameson was frowning at the yellow tractor. Its engine compartment was all torn apart and his team of mechanics were busy grumbling beneath it.

"It would save us weeks." Mia made a wide gesture with

her arms. "Increase productivity, cut down waste. There's a good reason people used these things. They work."

"Well this one fucking doesn't," Jameson spat, folding his giant arms across his chest. "What's the progress on this thing?"

"Wiring is shot," one of the mechanics grumbled.

"Can you fix it?" Jameson again, tapping his boot impatiently.

"You can slap lipstick on a pig Sir," the soldier replied, still working. "But it don't make it less ugly."

"Yeah, but a beer might," another one piped up and had all the men chuckling.

Slanting a look at Mia, Jameson rolled his eyes. In response, she shrugged.

"I'm just thankful you were willing to call them out here," Mia said. "I know you've got more important things for them to do."

"It's fine," Jameson assured her. "You say you need it and DeKalb agrees, so… what's a little more time and diesel fuel."

A few feet away, DeKalb ran a hand over the brim of his red hat and nodded. He'd been quietly watching while his men continued to work further out in the fields. By Mia's judgment, he'd done an alright job while she was gone. She wasn't sure why he'd told Jameson everything was falling apart. It wasn't.

Crossing her legs, Mia propped a hand on her hip. Lunch had come and gone, but there were quite a few more hours of daylight left. Without Davey beside her, she felt the need to get home. She wondered what he'd done with his forced day off. Was he working out? Playing that guitar? For sure it was his turn to cook dinner. No doubt about that.

With a smile playing along her lips, Mia uncrossed her legs and stretched her back.

"I've got to go to the bathroom," she admitted finally, and gestured to the far row of trees that bordered one of the fields.

It's always where Davey would walk her, but with him, she never had to announce it. He always suggested going before she realized it was even time.

"Evans." Jameson nodded. "You're up."

"Sir?" Evans blanched and looked from his boss to Mia.

"Miss Jones needs to use the bathroom," Jameson spoke slowly. "Go walk her there and back. It's not like you haven't seen Wells do it a million times. You're. Up."

"Yes Sir." Evans swallowed and gripped his rifle harder.

"I gotta take a quick break too," DeKalb put in. "But I'll go to the next field over."

"Alright." Jameson sighed and rocked back on his feet. "Nothing's happening here anyway."

Flipping her helmet back on her head, Mia strode off along one of the rows. She could hear the thump of Evans boots trailing her.

Glancing at her surroundings, Mia took quick stock of everything she saw. Soil could use more water here. It was a bit more crumbly than she'd like. Instinct would have her crouching down and taking a pinch of it in her hand but, giving her head a shake, she resisted the urge. First thing's first. Gotta go.

When they made it to the shade of the trees, Mia let out a little groan. Behind her, Evans stopped short.

"Can I just wait here?" He asked and had her laughing.

"Of course," she said and scooted around the trunk of a wide tree before shimmying her pants down her legs.

Sweet. Relief.

"This is awkward," Evans announced. "I can hear you."

"So talk about something else!" Mia exclaimed.

"Like what?"

"I don't know, what do you see?"

Grumbling, Evans shifted around. His boots scuffed the brush growing beneath the trees. Mia heard the slip of his rifle strap and the click of metal.

"Huh," he murmured. "That's not good."

"What?" Mia finished and hoisted herself up to standing. "What's not good?"

"Looks like something went wrong at the tractor," Evans supplied.

"Wrong?" Mia reached for her pants and yanked them up. "Like what?"

"I don't know," Evans continued. "Someone's hurt. Shit. One of the mechanic crew is on the ground. Crap. Everyone's standing over him."

Rushing around the edge of the tree, Mia came up to Evans' side. He was standing with his rifle held up to his shoulder, peering down the scope, watching the spot they'd left not a few minutes ago.

"Oh no." Mia worried her bottom lip. "What do you see?"

"Blood." Evans sighed. "Shit. A lot of blood. It's his hand or his arm or something."

"That's awful." Mia's heart sank and she fumbled to close the button on her pants.

At Evans' hip, the radio crackled. Jameson's voice came through, calling for a medic, calling for everyone to move out.

"Time to go," Evans commented, and lowered his rifle.

Blowing out a breath, Mia nodded and started walking. The vehicles they'd all caravanned in were on the opposite side of the farm, with the tractor positioned somewhere in between. As she and Evans hiked towards the melee, they could see the injured soldier being hoisted up and carried away.

Evans picked up his pace then, and grabbed the radio from his hip. Mia followed him, worry working in her gut.

Static burst and then Jameson's garbled voice came through. *Evans... you got her?*

"Yeah Boss," Evans responded. "We'll catch the second vehicle out."

Static came again. More voices criss-crossing and muddying up the sound. Evans looked back at Mia and made a motion with his hand for her to hurry up.

Nodding, the two of them began to jog. They weren't even to the tractor yet.

Engines were rumbling. Men were shouting. Doors were slamming. One Humvee began to roll away. It was followed quickly by the Jeep.

Evans brought the radio up to his mouth again, but when he called into it, the thing burst with other voices. There was confusion. A rush. No one could hear what anyone else was saying.

"Fuck," Evans spat, and he started to run.

Mia struggled to keep up. Her helmet was shifting on her head and her boots landed awkwardly between the rows of vegetables. Before they made it another hundred yards, the last vehicle pulled away.

Slowing to a stop, Evans looked skyward a moment. His

breath was coming in gasps and his rifle was slung over one shoulder. Mia pulled up beside him and placed her hands on the top of her head. She was panting and sweating.

"Well…" Evans' shoulders slumped and he looked over at her. "Guess this means I'm in trouble."

"Oh, it's not your fault," Mia managed, and imagined the look on Davey's face when he found out they'd been left behind.

"Hey guys," DeKalb called and had them both turning to watch him approach. "What's up?"

"Oh, hey man." Evans ducked his head. "There was an accident of some kind. Everyone had to move out."

"Hmm." DeKalb came to a stop on the other side of Evans and followed his line of sight. "They coming back for you anytime soon?"

"Nah." Evans shook his head. "They don't know we aren't with them yet."

"Oh." DeKalb pressed his lips into a thin line and placed his hands on his hips. "You didn't radio them?"

Holding the radio up in the air, Evans twisted it side to side and shook his head.

"Couldn't get it to go through," he explained. "I'll try again in a bit."

Blowing out a breath, Mia removed her helmet and ran a hand back through her hair. They could walk, she figured, or they could wait. She was just about to voice that opinion when Evans' shoulder knocked into hers.

He was bigger than her by a lot, so the hit caught her off guard. Staggering to one side, she dropped her helmet in the dirt but managed to keep on her feet.

"Evans what the…" Mia's voice trailed off.

Evans' body was landing on the ground next to her helmet. A red ribbon was snaking across his throat. Blood. Mia's eyes widened. So much blood.

Her gaze shot up to DeKalb and a scream tore from her throat. He was standing there calmly, wiping a large silver knife on the side of his blue jeans. Blood dripped from his hand and smeared across his pants.

When he looked up at her, he blinked.

"Time to go," he said.

CHAPTER THIRTY-EIGHT_
DAVEY

RESTLESS. HE COULDN'T REMEMBER THE LAST TIME HE'D BEEN this... restless.

Leaning one shoulder against the concrete wall of the underground parking garage, Davey narrowed his eyes. It had been dim in here at first, after all he was a layer or so underground, but after the first hour of waiting, his eyes had adjusted somewhat.

Light filtered in from the far corner, where the Jeep carrying Mia had left from just this morning. He wasn't ashamed to say that he'd watched them go.

And at the time he'd stood there like the angry, frustrated little bitch that he was. His shoulders had heaved, his boots had paced along the dusty ground. He'd wanted to scream and yell and jump in the vehicle with her and tell Jameson to go fuck himself.

But... his pride, and about a dozen soldiers watching him, had held him back. It was his team mostly. The men he'd led on protection detail for the past month. They were still with her, looking after her along with Jameson himself, and that gave him pause.

He could work his way back in. Between Mia and himself convincing Jameson, he knew that given time, he could work his way back onto her detail and everything would be fine. He'd keep her safe, she'd do her job, then they'd go home. Done.

Home?

Davey's face scrunched up at the thought. Before this past week with Mia that place had been clear as day to him. His home was at the compound in the mountains with Ace and Cookie. Her home was behind the Wall. But now?

Blowing out a solid breath, Davey tipped off the wall and shoved both hands in his pockets. Now he didn't know where he belonged. All he knew was that the *place* no longer mattered. It was her. Davey's home was now a person. His home was wherever Mia was.

"You've really done it now," Davey murmured to himself and kicked the toe of his boot along the ground.

The radio at his hip crackled. Static. Indistinct voices.

Removing a hand from his pocket, Davey adjusted the volume and waited.

A voice came through. A call for a medic. It wasn't Jameson's voice, it was a relay request. He was on his way though.

Adrenaline spiked in Davey's system. He felt the hit immediately. His heart pumped harder, his arms and legs tingled, his chest expanded.

Jameson was on his way. He needed a medic.

Davey's boots paced across the ground. His eyes squeezed shut and he tried to shake the dizziness from his mind. Control. He needed control.

Forcing himself to stop, Davey exhaled. He wouldn't be worth a shit to anyone if he lost it right now. Dialing back, Davey measured his breathing and dismissed the fear. In the distance he heard the strain of engines, the spin of tires, the squeal of brakes.

They were coming.

Jumping up and down on his toes, Davey clapped his hands together and then settled on his feet. A Humvee came roaring into the garage first and headed straight for Davey. Just behind him was the door that led down to the bunker.

Doors were popping open and guys were jumping out even before the vehicle came to a complete stop. Voices were calling out. Jameson was growling.

Rushing forward, Davey peered inside. Mendez, one of the mechanics, was lying on his back with one arm folded up onto his chest. His hand was a bloody mess. The white tips of bones were peeking up where they shouldn't be.

Stepping back, Davey spat excess saliva onto the ground.

"Fuck," he said. "What the hell happened?"

"Got it caught in the tractor," someone answered. "It started running all of a sudden."

"Shit." Davey sniffed and took another step back just as the Jeep and another Humvee came roaring into the space.

For a solid minute, it was complete chaos. Doors were slamming and boots were thumping. When they lifted Mendez up and slid him out of the vehicle, he screamed. It was the kind of thing you felt right down to your bones.

"Where's that medic?!" Jameson called.

"Waiting in the bowling alley!" A soldier answered him, and then they were off.

Watching them go, Davey removed his helmet and ran a

hand back through his hair. His heart was settling now that he knew it wasn't Mia. Glancing around, he frowned. Where was she anyway?

Most of the soldiers were standing around now, talking. They were trying to come down off the rush, trying to make sense of what had happened to their buddy. A few of them were taking a knee and praying. An injury like that out here meant death was a distinct possibility. Certainly, his hand would never work the same again.

Walking over to the Jeep, Davey pulled open the rear door and frowned. No one was inside. His heart kicked at him, but he pushed the feeling away.

"Hey Locklan!" Davey called to the driver who was sitting on the hood of the vehicle, his head in his hands.

"Yeah Boss?" Locklan lifted his face and ran a hand beneath his nose.

"Where's Mia?"

"Evans has her," Locklan replied. "They took the second vehicle out."

Bobbing his head, Davey pursed his lips and kept moving. He stalked to the other Humvee and peered inside. No Mia.

"Who rode in this one?!" He lifted his voice and gestured to the vehicle.

A few sets of eyes popped up and one hand raised in the air. Davey approached the men and tilted his head to one side.

"Where's Mia?" He asked. These guys had been working with him for a while now, they knew the drill.

"Evans has her," one of them replied. "They jumped in the second car."

Davey's brow furrowed. His chest cinched down tight.

"She didn't ride in this one?" He gestured to the Humvee again.

"No Sir," the guy confirmed.

"What about Evans?" Davey fought the heaving breath that wanted to burst from his lungs. "Have you seen him?"

Frowning, the guy looked for confirmation from his buddies. They all shook their heads. The guy looked slowly back to Davey and shrugged.

"Haven't seen him," he confirmed.

Dread. It's this black sort of ink that pours over you. Davey could feel it slipping along his spine, covering his shoulders, weighing him down. It was cold and it sunk into every single inch of him.

Turning from the men, he ran back to the Jeep. Locklan was still sitting on the hood, but Davey reached up and yanked him to the ground.

"Where's Evans?!" Davey practically screamed it. "When's the last time you saw him?"

Locklan's eyes were wide with shock. He held out his hands, palms up in defense.

"I... I don't know," he admitted. "He didn't ride with me. He's got to be here somewhere."

"He didn't ride with you," Davey spat, then gestured to the second Humvee. "He didn't ride with them. I watched Mendez get unloaded with Jameson, and Evans wasn't in that vehicle either. Where. The. Fuck. Is. He."

"I... I... I..."

"You! You! You!" Davey shook the guy hard before releasing him to fall back on the ground.

Stepping away, Davey turned a full circle. His eyes darted

over every face. Took in every sound. All male. No Evans. No Mia.

They were gone.

They'd been left out there. Alone.

Exposed.

"Give me the fucking keys!" Davey shouted suddenly. "You left her! You left them behind."

Scrambling up, Locklan searched in his pockets. Other soldiers were gathering around now, drawn in by the panic Davey was no longer able to hide.

"I'm sure they're fine," Locklan said. "I'm sure they're still at the farm."

"Well they damn sure better be," Davey hissed. "Or someone's about to die."

CHAPTER THIRTY-NINE_

MIA

HER HEAD HURT.

Groaning, Mia brought her hands up to her left temple and winced. Her quick intake of breath wasn't the only sound filling her ears. There was the whir of an engine. The click and tap of metal against plastic. Over and over.

Opening her eyes, Mia gasped. She'd forgotten. How had she forgotten?

"You're awake," DeKalb commented.

He was sitting behind the wheel of a car. His red hat pulled low, his blood stained hands easy on the wheel. They were driving down a narrow road, with trees all around them. It was nearing dark.

"I'm sorry I had to do that," he continued, tipping his chin at her. "But you wouldn't stop screaming."

Mia's mouth opened and closed like that of a fish. She swallowed air. She was unable to utter a word.

Looking down, she noted that her hands were bound tightly together with what appeared to be her own belt. Her pants were still on, but the button was popped open. Her stomach twisted and her lungs closed in on her. Had he? While she was unconscious?

Closing her eyes, Mia fought the swimming dizziness that wanted to force her under. Blood drained from her face and she felt the strong urge to pass out. But she couldn't let that happen. She couldn't faint.

Fighting against it, Mia took careful stock in her body. Her brain itself throbbed, the entire thing pulsed inside her head, not just the sore spot on her temple. But the area between her legs? It was free of pain. She had no sensation at all, which meant that she probably hadn't been violated there. Probably.

Exhaling in a whoosh, Mia opened her eyes. The world around her continued to whizz by. How was she in a car? How had any of this even happened? Evans. Mia's mind supplied the image for her. He was dead. DeKalb had killed him.

"Why?" The word tore from Mia's throat, she could feel the burn it left behind.

"Why what?" DeKalb was calm.

He checked the rearview mirror briefly, then slanted a look at her. Mia started to cry.

"Hey now," he said. "Everything's going to be alright. I promise."

He's crazy, Mia thought, as tears continued to pour over her cheeks. They dripped freely, streaking her skin, dribbling to the end of her nose and chin.

"I just finally got lucky," he went on. "I had to bide my time, be really patient. But it finally paid off. Here you are. I still can't believe it. My boss is going to be really happy."

Sniffing, Mia worked to take a breath.

"Boss?" She asked, her vice quaking.

"Yeah." DeKalb nodded. "I mean what are the chances? Blonde. Brown eyes. Age looked to be about right. You fit the description."

"I don't..." Mia's face scrunched up. "I don't understand. Please. Please, let me go. Take me back."

"Hey, hey." DeKalb reached over as if to pat at her arm, but Mia recoiled.

She threw her whole body against the door panel and brought her hands up between them. DeKalb's eyes widened and his hand stopped short. After a beat, he returned to driving.

"I know this is confusing," he commented finally. "God, if it really is you, then your whole life has had to be so damn confusing. But that's over now. I'm going to take you home."

"Home?" Mia demanded. *He's. Insane. He's completely insane and you're as good as dead.*

"Yes, to your parents." He nodded. "To your mom and dad."

"My parents are dead," Mia pleaded. "Please. Just take me back, or just let me out here. I'll walk. You can keep driving."

"Well... you said your name is Marie, right?" DeKalb glanced over at her. "Marie VanPell. If that's so, then your parents, your real parents, are not dead. Far from it."

Mia's mouth dropped and her heart slowed to a stop in her chest.

DeKalb kept driving, and talking.

"Your father is the President of the United States now," he said. "Or what's left of it. We've been living in a bunker in California, and all this time he's been searching for you. See? What a great father, right? He knew you were alive somewhere."

"My. Father." Mia puffed out the words. *Mama? Alive?*

Mia's lungs shrunk completely. Pitching forward, she opened her mouth and gasped for air. None came in.

"Hey," DeKalb said. "You okay?"

Bringing her bound hands up, Mia clawed at her throat. She couldn't breathe. She couldn't. Breathe.

"Ah shit," DeKalb again, tapping a foot heavily on the brakes. "What's this now? Just my luck."

Sliding to a stop, Mia's body rocked up and impacted with the front dash. Hard.

Her face smushed and slid against plastic. Her hands folded into her chest as she slammed against the hard surface. But then suddenly her lungs were working again. Air flooded in and she started to cry. Great big sobs. They just bubbled up out of her body without her consent.

"Just hold on," DeKalb grumbled. "I'll go clear this out of the road and be right back."

The driver side door popped open and the vehicle rocked with movement. DeKalb climbed out and strode away. Mia could hear the thump of his boots along asphalt and then the incessant dinging from the interior of the car.

Ding. Ding. Ding.

He'd left the key in the ignition, and the door hanging wide open.

Blinking, Mia's eyes zeroed in on the keys. He'd left them. Oh shit. He'd left the keys and her alone.

Scrambling, Mia tried like hell to hoist herself up from where she was wedged on the floor. Her hands were still bound in front of her and her legs were crumpled awkwardly beneath her but her body demanded she leap forward.

Grunting and clawing, Mia managed to pull herself upright and peek over the dash. There was a tree down across the road and DeKalb was tugging at some of the branches. Lifting his red hat, he swiped at his brow before glancing back at the car.

Mia locked eyes with him and he opened his mouth to speak.

But she never would get to hear what he had to say. Because right at that moment his head simply exploded. Blood and chunks of flesh. They were everywhere, covering the windshield like the most grotesque snow.

Then there was the screaming.

Screaming.

Who was that person that kept on screaming? Mia couldn't say, but the sound, it just kept coming. The woman, whoever she was, sounded hysterical.

Then the door beside her was being ripped open. Hands were on her, and she fought them. Scratching and clawing and kicking out with her legs. Then Mia was screaming, her voice joined the woman's voice and that's when she realized one true thing.

It had been her screaming all along.

There was no other woman. Their voices were the same.

It was her.

The next thing she knew her wrists were being cut free. Arms were wrapping her up and dragging her from the car. She tumbled against a hard chest, her knees hit the asphalt. A shaking palm pressed to the side of her face.

"Mia," Davey shushed her, squeezed her body tight to his. "It's okay. I'm sorry you saw that. I'm so sorry."

Dragging in a ragged breath, Mia stopped screaming. Her heart pounded and pounded, knocking against her ribcage, trying to get out.

"You're okay," he repeated, his lips brushing the top of her head over and over. "You're okay. I've got you. I've got you. He's dead now. No one can hurt you. I've got you."

Closing her eyes, Mia focused on the sound of Davey's words and tried to banish the picture of DeKalb's death that kept playing on repeat in her mind.

"Mama," Mia whispered. "My mama is alive."

CHAPTER FORTY_

DAVEY

"You don't have to stand directly in the doorway," Jameson pointed out. "She's safe in her own bedroom. Let's give Bisset some room to work."

Folding his arms over his chest, Davey tipped his chin up and stared hard into Jameson's face.

Two choice words came to mind, but in this moment he clamped his jaw shut and held back. Truth was, he didn't trust himself to speak. His pulse hadn't leveled off since he'd figured out she was gone, which meant he'd been close to a heart attack for over six hours now.

Behind him, Mia murmured answers to the medic's questions. Davey was poised in the open threshold to her bedroom and it was all he could do to give her his back. If he'd of had his way, he'd be literally lying next to her on the mattress right now, facing down Bisset and the truth of whatever the hell DeKalb did to her while she wasn't under Davey's protection.

Swallowing, Davey let another wave of nausea flow through him.

He'd failed.

He'd sworn to her, given her his *word*, that no one would lay a finger on her. And still, DeKalb had managed to slit Evans' throat and snatch her up quick as anything. It didn't matter that Davey wasn't there. It didn't matter that he'd been sidelined, forcibly, and therefore not directly responsible. It. Didn't. Fucking. Matter.

When he'd found her helmet lying there in the field beside Evans' body…

"Hey." Jameson reached out a hand and braced it against Davey's shoulder. "Stay with me, okay? This isn't on you. I should never have fired you. You were right."

The words were true but they didn't make a difference. Excuses, each and every one of them. They pinged off Davey's brain and fell back to earth. He didn't absorb them. How could he?

Glancing over his shoulder, Davey's eyes drank her in. Mia was sitting up on her bed, her knees drawn to her chest, the blankets tucked all around her. Bisset was nodding and talking. Her eyes were downcast, her finger tracing a circle on the quilt.

"You did good." Jameson shook him a little, drawing Davey's eyes forward once more. "You are the only reason that we have her back right now. If not for you then…"

He trailed off and Davey let him.

The sickening pitch in Davey's chest was automatic and all consuming. He couldn't shake the terror, couldn't shake the worry, the sensation that she actually wasn't here at all, that Mia was gone forever and this rescue part was just a dream.

Closing his eyes, Davey sucked in a steadying breath. He played through what happened again, just to remind himself it was real, or to convince himself maybe. He thought back to when his world had changed, he thought back to the moment he'd realized they'd left Mia behind.

He'd jumped in the Jeep, quick as anything. Locklan and Malpas had slid in as well.

The engine turned over and then they were tearing out of the garage and into the late afternoon sun. No one spoke a word during the drive to the farm. Not one word.

It took longer than Davey wanted, but he knew now that it couldn't have been more than ten minutes. He'd driven like a bat out of hell the entire time.

When they got there, a few of the farm workers were standing around the yellow tractor. Davey hadn't slowed, nor had he done the usual thing and parked the Jeep along the dirt road that bordered the crops.

Nope. He'd floored it straight for the group of people, sending the men scattering like cockroaches in the light.

That's when they'd found Evans. And the helmet.

Blood was everywhere, soaking the dirt, spraying the crops. That's all Davey was able to see. It was like a curtain of red death fell over his eyes, like a red sash he had to peer through.

Locklan began questioning the workers. They pointed towards the tree line. That's when Davey saw the tracks. There were drag marks for about twenty yards before DeKalb had apparently hoisted Mia over his shoulder and began to carry her away. After that only a single pair of heavy boot prints marred the earth.

Davey followed them, his breath catching in his throat. The tracks led them deep into the trees. It was shady and too quiet. Locklan and Malpas crept behind him.

There was a spot fairly far in, Davey didn't know how far, that had hidden a vehicle. A small car most likely. Branches pulled down, dirt pushed aside. It smelled of fresh gasoline. There was an empty plastic canister lying on its side, then tire tracks weaving away, heading for the old highway nearby.

The next part wasn't hard. He didn't really have to think about what to do at all. Training kicked in. Hunt. Capture. Kill. The words hummed in his veins, they were an old story to him, they were an old song to sing.

The asphalt highway was the only place for a car with that tire size to drive easily. If DeKalb wanted to get any type of distance, then he would have to use it. And they all knew where it led. Thanks to Malik's little flying drone, they knew every road in this area, by heart.

So Davey had looked at Locklan, and Locklan had nodded. No words, just blind acceptance. They were realistically only about half an hour behind DeKalb. The only way out of this area using a car was the nearby two lane highway and if that's what he was on then they could head DeKalb off using the Jeep and an old dirt road.

They'd have to be fast and reckless and lucky as hell, but if they could sweep around and cut him off then they could block the highway with maybe a tree or something. Then all they'd have to do was wait. Davey could pick the guy off with a rifle.

And unlike every other moment in Davey's Godforsaken life, that particular plan had gone off without a hitch. DeKalb was driving a small car. He had decided to drive south. The Jeep tore down the old dirt road without issue. The dead tree fell across the road after ramming it with the Jeep four times.

It was all so smooth and heart pounding and in the end, beautiful.

Watching DeKalb's brain burst like a fucking watermelon thrown to the ground was the most satisfying kill Davey had ever made. It was pure. Soul-cleansing, if you will.

But then there was Mia. Her fucking screaming. It had gutted him, crumpled him, stolen the words from his mouth.

So here he stood, a sentinel in her doorway. Unable to give her space, unable to think, unable to put two words together, unable to eat. He wanted to die and to live all at the same time.

"Look." Jameson sighed and dropped his hand from Davey's shoulder. "I'm calling this mission. We're packing up and heading out as soon as she's able. Okay? You hear me? We're done. We're taking her back to the Wall."

Dropping his head, Davey felt a tiny curl of relief. He was going to take her back regardless, but now he'd have a full escort. That was a good thing.

"Davey," Mia's voice calling to him had him whirling around.

She was still on the bed, the covers pulled up, but her hand was outstretched. She was reaching for him, her dark eyes blinking. Bisset was in the same spot, sitting on the edge of the mattress.

Stalking towards her, Davey closed the distance and took her hand in his own. His eyes danced across her face briefly before he turned his attention to the medic and tried to figure out if he should be pissed at the guy or grateful.

"The strike to her temple is significant," Bisset began. "She lost consciousness for a long period of time, and she definitely shows signs of a concussion. I don't have the equipment here to assess any further, but you need to keep her awake tonight."

"I can do that." Davey's stomach twisted. Mia squeezed his hand.

"Watch for signs of fever, disorientation, vomiting," Bisset went on. "If you see any of those changes, then come get me. I'll be staying in the bunk room at the end of the hall."

"Okay." Davey heaved a sigh.

Looking at Mia, Bisset tapped an open palm on his knee a moment before returning his focus to Davey. He sucked in a breath.

"Miss Jones is uncomfortable with me performing a pelvic exam at this time," he said. "I am unable to ascertain if there was any trauma there without looking…"

"Then you don't look," Davey cut him off. "Are we done here? Is there anything else?"

Pressing his lips into a thin line, Bisset blinked back at Mia for a few more moments before nodding his head. Pushing up to standing he packed his bag of medical equipment and cleared his throat.

"If there's anything else I can do," he said seriously. "I'm just down the hall."

"Thank you," Mia whispered and looked away.

Letting go of her hand, Davey walked the medic to the door. Jameson was still lingering in the hallway.

"Should take me a day or two to get everything packed up," Jameson offered. "Maybe three at the very most. Let me know when she's ready."

"I will," Davey confirmed, before stepping back inside and shutting the door.

Keeping his back to her, he breathed quietly for several

seconds. His eyes zeroed in on the heavy lock and he debated flipping it.

Normally he wouldn't think twice, but it was only Jameson and Bisset staying down in the bunker, and Davey would be in Mia's room the entire time, keeping her awake, making sure she was okay. What if something happened and he couldn't leave her side to unlock the door? It would be better left unlocked, so Bisset could get in if needed.

God. He hoped Bisset wasn't needed.

"He didn't rape me," Mia said.

Hunching his shoulders, Davey closed his eyes and blew out a steadying breath. He felt fucking sick just hearing the word.

"That's not what he wanted from me," she went on.

Sucking in a breath, Davey turned away from the door and stared at Mia. She sniffed and fidgeted with the ends of her hair. She was nervous. It made him nervous.

Crossing to her, Davey climbed onto the bed and wrapped her in his arms. He buried his face in her neck, and cried. *Cried.*

Tears leaked from his eyes as he squeezed them shut and tried to be as silent as humanly possible. Mia accepted him. She clung to his back and pulled him in closer, if that was possible, until he was basically lying on top of her.

Bracing his weight as much as he could, Davey told her he was sorry. Over and over, he apologized. DeKalb had taken her. He'd hurt her, and even though the guy was dead in the middle of an abandoned roadway, it still had Davey feeling helpless and weak.

Mia ran her palms along his back and pressed kisses to the side of his face. He understood very well the irony here. He was supposed to be comforting her, but here she was taking care of him.

When he finally calmed down, Davey rolled to the side, but kept Mia close. His body ran the length of hers, with her under the covers and him on top.

"We should sit up more," Davey commented. "I can't let you fall asleep."

Shifting onto her side, Mia took his hands in her own and ran her thumbs along his knuckles. Davey brought her fingers to his lips and kissed them. She sighed.

"DeKalb he..." Mia began.

Davey's whole body tensed. He couldn't help it. His spine stiffened, his fingers gripped hers harder.

"He told me things," Mia went on.

"Things?" Davey's brow furrowed. He was going to have to kill this motherfucker all over again.

"I don't..." Mia nibbled on her lip, her eyes seeking his. "I don't know how to say it."

"Say it," Davey prompted. "Whatever it is, just say it."

"He said my father... my real father... is alive." Mia tried to hide the fear that passed over her face, but she was unable. "He's been looking for me."

"What?" Davey's face twisted in confusion. DeKalb was clearly a nut job.

"He said there's a bunker or something, it's in California," she offered. "And my father, he's there with more people. He's... he's..."

"Mia." Davey reached up and ran a thumb down her cheek.

"He's the President now," Mia blurted. "That's what DeKalb said, and..."

Davey's brows raised as his gut began to churn. "And..."

"And my mother is there too." Choking a little, Mia's eyes began to brim. "He said my Mama is alive too. I've got to find her Davey. I've got to. I've got to go to California..."

"Whoa, whoa, slow down." Davey pressed his forehead to Mia's and shut his eyes.

His heart was thumping a million miles an hour. He didn't know what to do with this information. DeKalb was clearly a crackpot. He was clearly crazy.

"I've got to find her," Mia began again. "Please, you have to help me. If she's been with him this whole time, then I've got to save her. He's... he's a monster, Davey. A monster."

"I know," Davey cut her off, shushed her. "I know."

"Please," Mia whispered. "If you care about me at all..."

"Care about you?" Davey opened his eyes, his heart thumping hard against his chest. "Mia, I'm in love with you. I'm sorry it took losing you to say it out loud, but I'll never screw that up again. If you give me another chance, I swear, I'll tell you how much I love you every single day."

Those chocolate-brown eyes of hers sought his then. They darted over his face, seeking, searching. Davey held his breath and prayed. He prayed for her to believe him. He prayed for her to forgive him. He prayed for her to still feel the same.

"If you love me," she said finally. "Then you'll help me find my mother."

Blowing out a breath, Davey swallowed.

"I promise," he replied. "To spend the rest of my life looking for your mother. But first, let's get back to the Wall. We can start from there."

"Okay." Mia's lips trembled. "Okay."

"And my mother is more lost. Oh Katie, little Miss Eve— [illegible]. He said my [illegible] like you. I've got to find [illegible] so we can go to California."

"Oh my, what, slow down." Davey pressed his forehead to Mia's and shut his eyes.

His heart was thumping a mile a minute. He didn't know what to do with this information. [illegible] was clearly [illegible]. He was clearly [illegible].

"I've got to find her," Mia [illegible] again. "Please. You have to help me. If she's been with [illegible] this whole time, then I've got to [illegible]. He's a monster, Davey. A monster."

"I know," Davey cut her off [illegible]. "I know."

"Please, Mia," [illegible]. "If you care about me at all."

"Care about you?" Davey opened his eyes, his heart thumping hard against his chest. "I'm in love with you. I'm sorry [illegible] doing what I did [illegible] but I'll never screw that up again. If you give me another chance, I swear I'll tell you how much I love you every single day."

Those chocolate brown eyes of hers sought his out. They darted over his face, searching. Davey held his breath and prayed she'd [illegible] believe him [illegible] prayed for her to [illegible] still felt the same.

"If you love me," she said finally, "then you'll help me find my mother."

[illegible] Davey swallowed.

"I [illegible]," he [illegible]. "I'll spend the rest of my life looking for your mother. But first, let's get back to the [illegible] start from there."

"Okay," Mia's lips trembled. "Okay."

CHAPTER FORTY-ONE_

MIA

THREADING HER FINGERS THROUGH HIS, MIA BROUGHT DAVEY'S hand to her lap. They were sitting side by side in the back of a Humvee and the Wall was looming in the distance.

"Almost there," Davey whispered, leaning his face close to hers. "Then we tell them."

"Okay," Mia exhaled the word and tipped her head back against the seat.

He'd convinced her not to say anything about her true identity to Jameson. He'd told her to wait. They needed to get to the Wall first. They needed to get back to safety, where there were lots of soldiers and lots of people.

Once they were inside, then Davey would call a meeting. They would get a strategy together and talk about options for traveling to California. There were just so many "ifs" it would be impossible to take on a task like this alone. Regardless of that, Davey had assured her he would still go. If no one believed them, or if Uriah didn't see fit to send a team, then Davey would go by himself to find her mother.

Swallowing, Mia fought the tightness in her chest at the thought. The truth was, she couldn't let Davey leave on a mission like that alone. There was no way she'd be able to stand it, the possibility... no the likelihood... of losing him. It was just too great a risk.

Squeezing his hand, Mia focused her gaze out the front windshield. The shining metal of the Wall was reflecting the setting sun. It was all oranges and pinks. A stiff wind blew in through the windows. Fall had already arrived up here, in the north.

"They should make a cursory stop, but then wave us through," Jameson commented from his seat up front. He'd made contact with Commander Linfield several hours previous using the long range radio.

"Yes Sir." Locklan bobbed his head but kept right on driving.

They were the lead vehicle this time and the soldiers standing at the entrance to the Wall were coming into view. Rifles were in hand, but they weren't pointed in their direction.

Mia looked to Davey. He'd sucked his hand away from hers and placed it on his own weapon. It was habit, or training, she knew, but still, it had her pulse spiking.

"It's all good," Davey murmured to her, his eyes slanting quickly over her face and then away. "It's all good."

Nodding, Mia adjusted the helmet on her head and held her breath. The vehicle rocked and bumped along the vacant ground that stretched between the forest and the Wall. When they got to the entrance, Locklan tapped the brakes and a soldier came to the already open window.

"Officer Jameson Sir." The soldier ducked his head. "They've been waiting for you. Welcome home."

Stepping back, the soldier motioned them through the blown out entrance in the perimeter wall. Mia exhaled. Jameson turned around in his seat and offered her a smile.

"All done," he spoke quietly. "You did good Mia."

"Thank you," she mouthed the words as the Humvee hugged the perimeter wall and made for the military staging area in back.

Apartments shot up to her left, along with gleaming office buildings that all had perfect window glass and potted plants at the front steps. Green grass, winding cement sidewalks, people walking hand in hand. A child laughing.

The sights and sounds flooded in the vehicle, settling around each one of their ears. It was beautiful and peaceful and suddenly it was heartbreaking. Their entire country had been like this once. Their whole world had been filled with places just like this one. Now it was truly a wasteland, filled with violence, uncertainty and death.

Davey's hand left his rifle and came back to curl around hers. His palm was warm and steady and fit just right against her own.

"Stay with me?" He asked, his eyes searching hers. "I've got the apartment across from yours."

"For tonight… or?" Mia nibbled on her lip.

Davey shook his head. "For longer, if you want," he said. "We could just move your stuff over."

Smiling Mia nodded her head. "I'd like that," she murmured.

"Me too." Davey smiled back and squeezed her hand.

As the Humvee lurched to a stop, Mia's gaze was drawn past Davey and out the passenger window. There were a few hundred people standing all around, women mostly, smiling and waving at the long line of vehicles as they arrived.

Doors began popping open and soldiers flooded out. Noise exploded. Names were being called. People were hugging and shouting, squealing and crying as the two groups blended together.

"Are we dismissed Sir?" Locklan kept his hands on the wheel as the radio crackled.

From what Mia could tell they were the only vehicle left frozen in time. With a single nod, Jameson released them. Doors swung wide, the Humvee shifted with the weight of bodies leaving. Malpas and Locklan were gone in a blink. Jameson was outside too.

Opening the door, Davey stepped out and Mia followed him.

"You can take off the helmet," he said. "You won't need it in here."

Mia left the uncomfortable thing on the seat and took Davey's hand. They weaved through the crowd then, sliding past people, making their way home. Home? Together.

When they were just on the other side of the throng of people, a familiar voice called her name. It had Mia turning around and locking eyes with someone she hadn't seen in way too long.

"Mia!" Cass shouted.

She was dragging Jameson along by one hand, walking without a limp and with a purpose.

"Cass!" Mia cried and met her halfway. "Your leg! You're walking so well."

"Oh my gosh I missed you." Cass squeezed her hard, until all those curly brown locks of hers were tickling Mia's face.

"I missed you too." Mia bit at her lip as her heart lurched.

So much had happened in such a short amount of time. Now she was getting all emotional. Rocking a bit, Cass released her and stepped back. Her face fell with concern as her eyes skipped over Mia's face.

"Hey." Cass reached out and tucked an errant hair behind Mia's ear. "What's the matter?"

"I remembered everything," Mia whispered. "I remembered who I am and it's so awful."

Wrapping her back up in a giant hug, Cass rubbed at Mia's back. Mia closed her eyes tight. She could feel Davey shifting behind her and hear Jameson clearing his throat.

"I've been there, Mia and I'm so sorry," Cass soothed.

"That's not even my real name," Mia's voice hitched. "I'm Marie VanPell. People think I was kidnapped but that's not what really happened. That's not it at all."

"Oh wow." Cass sucked in a breath and squeezed tighter. "I remember that name. I'm sorry."

"We were going to tell you," Davey spoke from behind her and had Mia pulling back from Cass. "We just wanted to get here first."

Jameson's face had drained of color, as his eyes darted from Mia, then back up to Davey. Sniffling, Mia swiped beneath her nose as Cass continued to run a comforting hand up and down Mia's arm.

"Why do you look like that?" Davey frowned, he was talking to Jameson. "You don't look surprised, you look... guilty."

Turning to look at her boyfriend over her shoulder, Cass

let go of Mia's arm. All eyes were on Jameson now, and he blew out a long breath before speaking.

"We need to talk," he said finally. "But not here."

CHAPTER FORTY-TWO_

DAVEY

THEY WERE SITTING AROUND A LONG MAHOGANY CONFERENCE table in a room with no windows. Davey held Mia's hand tightly in his own and glanced around.

He had no idea why Uriah Linfield would set up his conferences in a space like this. All gray blank walls, no artwork, black leather office chairs and way too many bodies.

It was like being in a tomb, or underground. Davey was sick to death of feeling trapped underground.

"First off, Officer Jameson has briefed me about what went down in Utah, and I'd like to say that Mia, you did an excellent job. Thank you for your work and I'm sorry we failed to keep our promise and keep you safe." Commander Linfield was seated at the head of the table, his brown eyes focused entirely on Mia.

She was the only female in the room and under normal circumstances that would have Davey feeling a bit stabby. As it was, he wanted to yank her into his lap, wrap her in his arms, and mark the living shit out of her.

This is mine and I will die to protect what is mine, so don't breathe in her direction.

But there were way too many familiar faces in here to do that. And with those familiar faces came one underlying truth. In this room, he had a hell of a lot of back up.

Liam was sitting across from him, and right beside Liam was Cole. The pair of them alone made Davey's breathing just a bit easier. These were his brothers. They'd bleed for him now, as he'd bled for them in the past. There was no escaping *this* family and for the first time in a really, really long time, he was grateful.

"Thank you," Mia murmured before ducking her head and looking to Davey.

She was uncertain, overwhelmed by all of this and frankly, so was he. They'd driven all day for the past two days in a row, it was dark out now, both of them needed food and sleep. But the moment she'd uttered the name Marie Vanpell, a flurry of activity had followed.

So now they were here, in this room, with every officer under Linfield's command and more coffee than either of them cared to drink. Frowning momentarily at his still steaming mug, Davey spread a palm flat on the table and stared at his Commander.

"What's all this about?" He asked. "Why the dog and pony show?"

Uriah lifted an eyebrow and drummed his fingers on the tabletop.

"Sir," Davey added belatedly, and with little regard for tone.

That old pipe dream of leading a strike team was well and

truly over for him now. He had other plans, bigger and better, and they all involved Mia.

Across from him, Liam actually smirked. Liam, of all people. It had Davey's anger slowing, if nothing else.

"Several months ago, and against my better judgment," Uriah stated. "We began turning on and reviewing the computer systems here."

Beside him, Jameson leaned back in his chair slightly and swallowed. His eyes refused to meet Davey's, instead they looked past him, somewhere high and over his head. Davey knew there was nothing back there but an ugly empty wall.

"We did it in phases," Uriah continued. "And we used the best minds available to begin the process of combing through all the data. There were a series of anomalies, and then there were a series of patterns."

"This was after the incident in Hermiston?" Davey questioned. "After the men in Oregon, with the radios and the tattoos. Am I right?"

Uriah nodded. No one made a sound. Davey's jaw clenched and his eyes jumped to Liam. The guy simply stared right back at Davey, into Davey.

Beside him, Cole lifted a single finger and tapped the table once. Pay attention, he seemed to say. His eyes traveled to Mia.

Davey's gut sank.

After several moments, Uriah kept talking. "At first we thought the source was in communication with something else, someone else. Maybe it was another one of the refugee centers, but after a lot of digging we found that was not the case.

The source controlled all of the other refugee centers, and

this thing, its communications were only going one way. It sent inquires to the source, and the source diverted them away."

"I don't understand," Davey admitted.

His palms were growing sweaty. Why were there no windows in this Godforsaken room? There needed to be more air in here. There wasn't enough cool air.

"There was another entity, a computer-based entity," Uriah explained. "And it was trying to gain access to source data."

"What data?" Davey again.

"It wanted population data for this particular refugee center," Uriah gestured around them. "It wanted DNA results. It was looking for something in particular, or rather someone."

Davey's throat went dry. "What did it want?"

"Well at first it wasn't specific, it just wanted access to the source records," Uriah offered. "And the source kept denying access so that was the end of it for several years."

Frowning, Davey's eyes jumped to Jameson, and he caught the guy actually looking at him this time. The two men stared at one another, and in that moment, Davey knew.

Betrayal.

It was fucking right there, plain as day.

"So you let it have access," Davey supplied. "Didn't you? You let that thing, that person, whatever the hell it is, you let it search the DNA database."

"No." Uriah shook his head. "But the source finally did, right before we killed it. The source let it do a cursory search of the population stats, no DNA."

"And what did it find?" Davey leaned forward in his seat, not wanting the answer but needing it all the same.

"It was looking for women, blonde hair, brown eyes, height range 5'5 to 5'9, age range 18 to 27 years approximate." Uriah's eyes drifted to Mia. "And there was a name request too. Marie Vanpell."

"Oh my God," Mia whispered, her hand going limp in his.

Turning to her, Davey pulled her closer and gripped her chin in his hand. His eyes sought hers, held hers, as she visibly paled.

"You're just fine," he hissed. "You're okay. I've got you. You hear that? You're okay."

Licking her lips, Mia nodded and shut her eyes. Davey stood abruptly. He kept one hand on her shoulder as his eyes shot around the room. Liam and Cole were already standing up too. Half the men in the room were murmuring and shifting now.

But when Davey's eyes landed on Jameson, they narrowed.

"You." Davey spat. "You son of a bitch. You *knew*."

Jameson's jaw ticked, but in that moment, he looked away.

"You fucking knew!" Davey escalated, heat exploding in his body. "She was bait! You didn't want her down there to fucking farm! You son of a bitch. She was bait!"

Jameson refused to answer.

Instead, Uriah pushed up from his spot at the head of the table and took on the accusation full force.

"We didn't know she was actually Marie Vanpell," he argued. "She just fit the description. All we needed was for a blonde haired, brown eyed woman to be seen by other men. That's it. She wasn't supposed to get taken. *You* were supposed to keep her safe while we flushed out whoever sent the inquiry."

"Fuck! You!" Davey scrambled across the table as all hell broke loose.

Uriah stepped back. Jameson stood up.

Davey's feet landed on the floor just as Cole wrapped an arm around him from behind. Mia cried out, her voice dim in the background of Davey's mind.

"I've got her!" Liam called, and Davey's vision tunneled.

"You. Fucker." Davey growled and took a swing at Jameson.

And much to everyone's amazement, the big guy actually walked right into the hit. Davey's fist connected with the side of Jameson's head with a satisfying thump.

Despite Cole's grip on him, and the dozen or so men shouting and cursing and shuffling in the room, Davey used all the force in his body to advance.

He was fast. He'd always been fast. And the fact that Jameson maybe knew he deserved this, helped the situation. Davey got in two, maybe three solid cracks before Cole yanked him back. Jameson's lip was bleeding and his left eye was already swelling, but he maintained eye contact the whole time.

"That's enough!" Uriah shouted. "Get him the hell out of here!"

"Now you get to tell Cass," Davey spat. Their eyes never left one another. Jameson and him. "Now you get to tell her what you did to her friend."

A flicker of pain danced over Jameson's face then, and he nodded.

"You're right," he said. "Now I get to tell her. I get to tell her that I had no choice. That I was doing my damn job. That there's a threat out there and it knows about the Wall, and it knows how many people live here, and I couldn't sit back in good conscience and wait for that something to come attack."

"So you used Mia to draw it out," Davey supplied, his chest heaving. "You put an innocent woman at risk and she got hurt!"

"I picked the best man that I could to protect that woman," Jameson countered. "And yes I put one person at risk to benefit tens of thousands of others, including children.

So yeah, I get to tell Cass all that, and I get to tell her how I fucking failed. You happy? You think I wanted to put Mia out there? And now we're right back where we started."

Shaking Cole off of him, Davey rocked on his feet and ran his hands through his hair. Glancing over his shoulder he assured himself of what he already knew. Liam had Mia. She was safe, with her hands covering her mouth and tears pooling in her eyes.

Davey stared at her while his lungs worked to draw in air and the roaring in his head began to subside. She blinked at him then and nodded once. Go ahead. He could almost hear her say it. Tell them.

Turning back to Jameson, Davey let his eyes skip to Uriah and then back.

"You're not back where you started," he said, and sucked in a breath. "The person looking for Mia is hiding in a bunker somewhere in California and he likely has lots of men and supplies at his disposal."

Frowning, Uriah took a step forward. "How do you know this?"

"The man looking for Mia, or Marie," Davey went on. "Is her father, Edward Vanpell, who is now supposedly the President of the United States, or what's left of it. At least, according to the guy who took Mia."

"Vice-President Vanpell is alive," Uriah repeated. "He survived the war."

"President Vanpell is a piece of absolute shit," Davey corrected. "And he's still looking for his daughter… AND you are *never* going to give her to him."

CHAPTER FORTY-THREE_

DAVEY

1 MONTH LATER

DAVEY LEANED UP AGAINST THE SIDE OF HIS APARTMENT building and stared into the darkness. There was a sliver of moon tonight, and it did just enough work for him to make out silhouettes in the distance. Even so, he heard them long before he saw them.

It was the laughter. Mia's laughter mixed with Cass's voice. Those two women made each other so happy, which was the only reason Davey was able to stand her being away from him for a few hours each week.

That, and the fact that he knew there were eyes on them the entire time.

He would walk Mia to Cass's apartment building and wait on the sidewalk until she went inside. She'd stay with Cass for dinner, talking and doing girly stuff. Then on the trip back home, Jameson trailed the pair of them.

Davey knew this because he'd seen the guy doing it. They'd locked eyes a few times, but hadn't said a word to one another.

Out of respect, Jameson always stopped about halfway across this last lawn. It was a silent custody transfer. An unspoken agreement between two men that had been enemies, then almost friends, and then enemies again.

Davey could see Jameson's hulking figure now, arms folded, waiting by the far tree. The sting of betrayal still simmered in Davey's blood. His neck muscles tightened and his jaw ground slowly.

Seemingly oblivious to their stalkers, Mia and Cass kept on coming, their arms linked, their voices anything but quiet.

And it'd been like this for about a month now. Davey followed Mia wherever she went. It was just like it had been in Utah. Mia went to the farm, resumed control over her district, and Davey hovered around her, holding his rifle and scowling like a shadow with indigestion.

Which maybe he was.

Coming to a stop in front of him, the girls embraced, wrapping their arms around one another and rocking a bit to the side with the force of the hug. When they broke apart, Cass stepped back and gave Davey a small wave.

"Hey Davey," she called. "You treat my friend right, okay?"

"Always." Davey ducked his head and made the same promise in his head that he had since the day he'd gotten her back. She'd never get hurt again. Not by him. Not by anyone.

Linking her arm with his, Mia laid her head on his shoulder and watched her friend go.

"Same time next week?" She asked and had Cass turning around and nodding.

"Same time," Cass repeated before giving a final wave and fading back into the night.

Tugging at his arm, Mia walked to the door of the apartment. Davey pulled it open and they went inside. The stairwell was at the far end and they made their way there quietly. No one was in the corridor and you couldn't hear anything going on inside the apartments.

"I don't know how you do it," Davey spoke finally as they began their ascent to the fourth floor. "Eat dinner with that guy once a week."

"Well…" Mia sighed, her hand sliding along the metal railing. "Somebody has to bring our list of demands to the opposing camp."

When she glanced back at Davey, her eyes were twinkling. In response, Davey rolled his.

Mia was so freaking forgiving. Too forgiving. Too understanding. But that's how her uncle and aunt had raised her. It was maddening to him sometimes. He had a much longer memory. There was no way he could let this thing go.

"Anyway, Jameson is so sor-"

"Sorry, I know," Davey cut her off with a huff. "I'm not impressed."

Another sigh had Mia cresting the final landing. Davey jogged in front of her and opened the door.

Pausing on the threshold, she looked into his face and smiled. He would do a million things for that smile. The genuine, soft, happy one. The one that she used more and more now.

"After you," he said and gestured with his hand.

He could almost hear his brother's laugh at his manners, but his mother would have been pleased.

He repeated the gesture at their own front door, making sure to turn and lock it behind them.

Removing his rifle from his shoulder, he propped it against the wall. Mia moved away from him, humming and flicking on light switches. Davey stalked after her, looming and lingering like a great big creep.

If she found him creepy though, she didn't say. Mia just made her way to the bathroom, left the door open, undressed. Davey stood in the doorway and watched. His eyes roamed her entire body as she took a shower, dried off, brushed her teeth, combed through her hair.

She laughed when she had to bump him aside to get to their bedroom.

He smiled at that, shoving his hand deep into the pocket of his pants, where he found the ring he'd been hiding from her.

Spinning it through his fingertips, he reminded himself what it looked like. Liam had made it, upon Davey's request. It wasn't covered in precious gems, like the ones in the vault in Utah, and at first he'd wished to God that it was.

But Liam had assured him that he could make Mia something pretty. And in the end, he had.

It was a silver band etched with a million tiny hearts, and if you held it in the right light, it sparkled. The feel of it beneath his fingers now had his heart pumping and his nerves rattling around in his bloodstream.

Now he just had to ask. Now he just had to pray to God above that she'd say yes.

"So, do you want to know the latest or do you suddenly not care?" Mia slipped into one of his t-shirts and settled on their bed.

Her legs crossed beneath her and she tilted her head to one

side, blinking up at him. Davey's heart slowed in his chest. He. Loved. Her.

"Well?" Mia huffed a laugh. "You're being weird. Everything alright?"

"Yeah." Davey gave his head a little shake and crossed the room to her. "I'm fine. Tell me everything."

"They're considering sending a team to scout California," Mia explained. "They'd use a drone to do flyovers, try to keep it as discreet as possible."

Nodding, Davey frowned. Winter was coming and California was huge. That would be a really long trip with no communications cability. The risks were high.

"Any movement on Eli?" Davey couldn't help himself. He knew that guy's memory was the key. It would make things so much easier. It would give them a place to start looking, maybe more.

Mia's face fell and she glanced to her lap. Her hands came up to twine together. Eli was Cass's brother, and a sensitive subject for everyone involved.

"No." She shrugged. "He still can't remember anything."

Stepping into her space, Davey knelt down to her eye level. Mia avoided his gaze. She didn't want him to see her disappointment, her fear *for* her mother, her fear *of* her father. But he already saw all those things. He felt them *with* her. He suffered *with* her. That's what love was.

Reaching out, he took her chin in his hand and rubbed the pad of his thumb along her jaw. Mia's eyes came up to his.

"Hey." Davey leaned in and kissed her softly, once. "It's okay. Eli will remember eventually, and I made a promise to you. I'll find her, okay? I'll put my attitude aside, and I'll work with whoever I need to. I'll find her."

"I know." Mia nibbled on her lip, then pressed her forehead against his. "It's just… I don't know if I want you to keep that promise anymore."

Davey's gut dropped and his fingers tingled.

"What?" He frowned, his breath catching in his throat. "What are you talking about?"

"I…" Mia licked her lower lip, her hands wringing together in her lap once more. "I…"

Davey gripped her hands in his own, ran his fingers over her wrists, felt her pulse jumping. His eyes danced up to her face.

"Mia…"

"I'm late," she blurted, her dark eyes locking with his. "It's early still… but I'm never late."

"You're…" Davey repeated the words as his brain swirled. "Late."

"I'm sorry," Mia whispered as tears rimmed her eyes. "I'm…"

"Pregnant." Davey's eyes dropped to her flat little belly, then popped back up to her face. "With my baby. You're sure? You're absolutely…"

"Not absolutely." She shook her head and laughed a little. A tear trickled down one cheek. "I haven't taken a test but also… I'm pretty sure. My boobs hurt and I'm a little queasy. I'm late. I know this isn't planned but…"

Exhaling in a whoosh, Davey's hand rushed to her stomach. He placed a tentative palm there as a spark of something big took hold within him. His baby. Their baby. Mia and him.

He'd never felt such instant fear and excitement wrapped up in one package.

"Marry me." He said it more than asked it, his eyes still lingering on her belly.

Mia covered his hand with her own. "Davey… I don't want you to feel obligated."

"I'm sorry," Davey cut her off. "I did that wrong. Give me a do-over."

Keeping one hand on her stomach, Davey fished around in his pocket with the other and brought out the ring. Holding it up to her, he swallowed as nerves exploded in his body.

"I've carried this ring around for two weeks," he began. "Thinking of the perfect time to ask you to be my wife. I guess I was a day late, so that makes two of us that are late."

Mia laughed. Davey's heart beat harder.

"Mia, I'm so crazy in love with you," he confessed. "You are the light that shined into my darkness and now… I can't imagine my life without you in it. I want you to be my wife. I want this baby. Please… will you marry me?"

Sliding off the bed and into his lap, Mia wrapped her arms around his neck and cried. Her shoulders shook and her body hiccuped and Davey clung to her. His eyes shut and his lips kept pressing against the side of her face, her hair, her neck.

Say. Yes.

Let these be happy tears. Let this be happy crying. Pregnant crying.

"I love you too," Mia sniffed finally. "And yes, Davey. Yes. I will marry you."

CHAPTER FORTY-FOUR_

ELIJAH ROE

THE DREAM WAS THE SAME EVERY TIME. THERE WAS THE SOUND of a train. A whistle blowing once, then twice. They were long, deafeningly loud blasts, and they turned his insides sick.

Looking down, Eli could see the wooden platform under his boots. His black rifle was gripped in his slick palms.

It was fucking hot. The sun was beyond intense here.

"Stand back!" Someone yelled. It was another solider, the guy's name escaped him.

Eli took a giant step back as the train came screeching and grinding and crackling to a stop. The cars banged and hit together, as the wheels slowed. Car, after car, after car. They should be filled with cattle, with livestock, with animals. But Eli knew they weren't.

They were filled with people.

"Hey," the soldier spoke again, walking over to stand beside him. "You worked these trains down in Arizona?"

Swallowing, Eli nodded. His stomach twisted and turned. He could taste vomit in the back of his throat, but he forced it to stay down.

"How'd you get here? In Cali?" The soldier again, watching as the cars came to a stop and the people inside started groaning.

My sister, Eli thought, I'm looking for my baby sister. And if I'm the luckiest man alive, then she's going to be riding in one of these awful trains. If I'm fast enough, I just might be able to save her.

"Man of few words." The soldier rocked onto his toes and rolled his eyes.

Eli released a controlled breath. He didn't give a fuck about conversing with this guy. Time was of the essence, and once those doors opened, then the clock of death started ticking.

"Alright!" A voice boomed over a loud speaker. "Face masks on! Remember, they're all sick, there's no saving them! Open the doors!"

Slipping his mask down over his face, Eli breathed in the hot stink of rubber and his own breath.

Bracing himself, he watched as a dozen other soldiers stepped up to the doors of the cattle cars and began working the latches. Inside, people shifted and moved. They called out. They were hungry and thirsty. Some, he knew from experience, had already died.

Gripping his rifle tighter, Eli blew out a quick breath before charging forward. His boots slapped against the wooden floorboards of the platform while his heart turned to stone.

When the door in front of him slid open, he jumped in without hesitation. He was the first one inside, but he was not the first one to fire a shot. But shoot he did.

Shoot. He. Did.

ACKNOWLEDGMENTS_

This book was hard fought.

It survived a pandemic, homeschooling two little kids, isolation, the implosion of my marriage, filing for divorce, moving to a new city, starting my life over. So this book is truly only here because of YOU. My reader. You gave me something to strive for and I thank you so very much for your support. Life is hard. Be true to yourself. And whatever you do… Don't. Give. Up.

Oh and hey… Eli's story is next. We're going to California people, to get us some dang answers. You won't want to miss this one, I promise.

FINDING FOREVER - BOOK 6

A word from the author:

There's a sixth book! FINDING FOREVER (Eli and Shelby's story) will be making its debut February 23, 2021. Order now!!!

Book hangover much?
Might I suggest my completed series…
THE CAPTIVE BORN
It'll be right up your alley… wink, wink.

Join my email list...
LK MAGILL NEWSLETTER

Join my ARC Team!
ARC TEAM - LK MAGILL

Reviews, pretty please...
Each and every positive review makes a huge difference. Be it Amazon, Kobo, iBooks, Barnes and Noble; no matter the retailer, I read and appreciate them all.
Thank you and I hope to see you in the future.

Websites:

www.lkmagill.com

Facebook:
https://fb.me/LKMagill1

Instagram:
https://www.instagram.com/lk.magill.author

Amazon page:
http://amazon.com/author/lkmagill

ALSO BY LK MAGILL_

Standalone novels:

VANISH ME

The Captive Series:

THE CAPTIVE BORN - Book One

THE CAPTIVE MISSING - Book Two

THE CAPTIVE RISING - Book Three

Outlasting Series:

OUTLASTING AFTER - Book One

CHASING TRUTH - Book Two

SURVIVING THE WALL - Book Three

BREAKING BEFORE - Book Four

TAKING TOMORROW - Book Five

FINDING FOREVER - Book Six (Coming February 23, 2021)

www.ingramcontent.com/pod-product-compliance
Lightning Source LLC
Chambersburg PA
CBHW010346170726
48284CB00011B/2810

* 9 7 8 1 9 5 0 9 2 8 1 5 6 *